REALM OF THE BEAST

A Novel

REALM OF THE BEAST

A Novel

Thomas Rath

Copyright © 2015 Thomas Rath
All rights reserved.

ISBN: 1511778415
ISBN 13: 9781511778411

With love and gratitude
to those who have given me so much:
my loving wife Christine,
my children, and my ten grandchildren.

And all my realm reels back into the beast,
       and is no more.

                              (Tennyson)

PROLOGUE

Italy
Rome

The Tiber has flowed for millennia and perpetually purges all debris that enters its waters. It carries to the Tyrrhenian Sea whatever substance floats along its rapids. Some might regard the river as a depository for anything to be discarded much like flotsam and jetsam on the sea. Then again, another views it as a means of escape from a despicable point in his life. If that life is as scornful as he believes, then escape from it he sees as a recommended and preferred choice. Thoughts and deeds shadowed by guilt can be quelled in only one way as he sinks down in despair. All aspects of life and spirit are clouded and then darkened by the swift stream intended to nurture or rejuvenate. Any beams of goodness from the universal light are drowned and die.

▲ ▲ ▲

Lieutenant Giancarlo called Captain Lorenzo from the radio in his cruiser and startled him with some unexpected news. "Captain, a body was just fished out of the Tiber near the Ponte Sant 'Angelo. It's Father Alfredo Legados. It doesn't appear the angels on the bridge were looking over him and offering guidance."

Thumbing through a sheaf of papers on his desk the startled Captain exclaimed in an exasperated voice, "What! Lieutenant, are you positive it's him?" The captain sat in disbelief with a look of absolute consternation on his face.

"Well, I saw him a few times before, and I recognize him from the interrogations we held at the precinct when we brought him and Montoya from Milan. Though there's some facial distortion from bloating, I know it's him."

"My God! I can't believe it. I'll want to see the body and be present when the medical examiners give it the going over. I'll be calling Cardinal Salvacco to come down to make a positive ID for the record. There are a lot of men who wear black with white collars in this part of town. I absolutely want a forensics ID."

Damn it! Just when that bastard was where we wanted him. The skulking coward.

"Yes, Sir. Do you want me to go to the Cardinal's residence and bring him over to the morgue?" asked the lieutenant.

"I'll make sure he's at his quarters first, and available. Hold on for the time being, and I'll get back to you as soon as I reach him. I'll contact the Missionaries at their main residences to see if they know where Alfredo is, or if it appears to them that he went missing. Lieutenant, does it seem that any foul play may have been involved?"

"Hard to tell. I don't think the body has been in the water that long from the looks of it, maybe overnight, but it has taken a couple of good smacks against an abutment in the area where it was discovered. That's quite obvious from the bruises and lacerations."

"Who found the body, and when?" the Captain asked.

"A guy who said he was up to go fishing this morning. He went down river about a mile to a spot he likes, and said he saw something ragged looking stuck against a piling with debris attached to it. Thought at first it was a log, but when he got nearer he saw distinctly that it was a body floating. The guy was quite shaken on seeing the body. He'll be finding a new place to fish."

"Okay, Lieutenant. I'll get back to you in a few minutes about the Cardinal. Meanwhile start going upstream to see what you can find. The body could only have floated a short distance from some point where it entered the water. There must be a spot where some evidence is hiding, just waiting to tell us something."

"I'm on it Captain. If I find anything, I'll stay with it and call you immediately. Do you want me to send one of my officers to take the Cardinal to the morgue to meet you?"

"Ok. No. I'll pick him up at his residence on my way."

An hour later Lieutenant Giancarlo radioed Lorenzo and told him he found something interesting that ties in with Father Alfredo's drowning. On the Ponte Sant 'Angelo a billfold with both euros and Mexican currency was found stuck between some narrow black bars of the railings on the bridge. It had to belong to Father Alfredo, and looked like it was intentionally left there by someone who had no thoughts of retrieving it later. Perhaps intentionally left to be found by the police.

"Captain," said Lieutenant Giancarlo, "I believe we have found Alfredo's wallet. There's no ID in it, but some papers and the mixed currency indicates that it's his."

"Good, Lieutenant, when you finish at the crime scene, bring everything that you have back to the office, and I'll see you there later. Looks to me like the good father took the plunge, rather than wait for us to bring our evidence against him in court. Damn it! I wanted to get him for planning that murder! I know he would have been prosecuted and convicted. Now, we just have Montoya and Vilardo." Lorenzo was thinking of all his effort over the past months to gather enough evidence to arrest and charge Legados. He felt cheated.

"Yeah, but, you know, Captain, this proves his guilt. If he had nothing to worry about, he wouldn't have committed suicide. He knew where his life was headed, and didn't want to face the shame here and back in Mexico."

"I know," said Lorenzo dejectedly in a barely audible whisper.

"Did you and the Cardinal ID the body at the morgue?" asked Giancarlo.

"Yes. The coroner is still working on it. We can rule out any dirty work. It's an obvious suicide. I'm heading back to the station for only a few minutes. Then I'm going to the bridge to see for myself if there's anything I can come up with that connects to this case. See you later."

I'm sure Alfredo had this in mind all along. He knew he wouldn't stand trial and be convicted. His hubris wouldn't allow it. There won't be many lamenting his death.

"Yes, Sir," Giancarlo answered.

Disappointment was obvious in both officers that Father Alfredo had escaped the inevitable fate he truly deserved. Captain Lorenzo had spent weeks in planning the return of Father Alfredo from Mexico and being meticulous in gathering the needed evidence for the prosecutors in Rome. Now, there would be nothing, he worried, except a burial and a few words spoken extolling the man and his virtue by some of his followers who never truly knew the kind of man Father Alfredo was nor the kind of enigmatic life he had lived.

I

Italy
Iles d'Arda

This was a new experience for me. I had only seen the inside of prisons on television when ABC or CBS was doing an expose of some kind. I didn't know what to expect. The doors were unlocked, then locked again. Even those without bars slam with a clang you don't forget long after you leave. I walked in and placed my notebook on the table, and then a guard instructed me to sit down. The gloom of the place gave me the weirdest feeling. Was I going to adjust to this situation?

Marco, a gaunt Hispanic man about six feet tall wearing the customary prison garb stood and greeted me in a grouping of short staccato sentences. "Thanks for coming," he said. "We finally meet face to face. I didn't know if you'd really show up. When I first wrote to you, I did so hoping you would be interested in hearing my story."

"It wasn't every day the postman delivered mail to me from someone in your circumstances and from so far away," I said. "I was surprised at your request after I felt we had gotten to know each other, though superficially, through the exchange of only four letters over a two month period. My editor helped persuade me to take you up on your offer."

I never would have made the trip to Italy on this occasion if I felt insouciant about what this assignment may very well produce.

The guards afforded us cramped space in a room where I felt too confined, but I couldn't be selective in a place like this. I sat across the

5

table just staring for a couple of minutes at the man whom I regarded as a total stranger. He appeared very ordinary, not a very imposing figure, but rather someone aging with prison life. He didn't look like he belonged here, but his sallow complexion is all that shouted to me that he did. He didn't seem like someone you see in a bad movie who's incarcerated for a crime for thirty to forty years. As he appeared composed and staid, I sensed a distance or remoteness in his eyes like one who is present, but not sure he really wants to be, rather that he has to be. I regarded him as a journalist would examining his features and whole physical constitution. His deep-set eyes and prominent nose and wide mouth with pearly white teeth did not present a picture of movie star likeness. But there was a kind of handsomeness to the man in spite of his prison complexion and slouched shoulders. I stared for several seconds and thought that he probably was a fairly good-looking young man when he breathed free air before incarceration.

"I'm grateful you agreed to hear my story because it's one that involves several people attached to the Order and Familia Dei," Marco said. "They will be very pissed off when they read about themselves if you agree to tell my story. With me being here I'm somewhat protected I like to think; I can't be hurt. Unfortunately, others who were close to me are in hiding or are already dead."

Later, when I knew the circumstances with his own family, I felt I knew who he was referring to, and he meant they were dead in a figurative sense. Through his letters I knew about the Order.

"What was it about me that made you make contact in the first place, Marco?" With candor I added, "I'm not your big time journalist like someone on a national paper or the network news; I'm not even a recognized small time journalist like the guy on the local TV station. What's the connection you felt in deciding to call me to do your story? For as long as I've been on the scene as a reporter, I've never broken a big story. I've fought hard just to get an occasional by-line. You're giving me an opportunity. My editor will be more than pleased."

This could be my moment and I'm not going to blow it.

With a casual motion of his left hand, and looking directly into my eyes, Marco said, "I know. I want you to have that opportunity because I feel strongly that I owe it to you for something that happened a long time ago when I knew someone very close to you. Some people in my past got screwed over when I was steeped in the Movement where my position forced me to make decisions that took them to early graves. Of course, I have regrets, now." His eyes lowered to the black tabletop his forearms rested upon.

"Seems there's lots of time for me to listen, Marco. I'll write it all down and record on this Sony to make sure I get it right. And by the way, am I going to find out somewhere through this who I'm connected to that caused you to invite me here. I don't want all of this to be a gross waste of my time in regard to that," I said in as stern a voice I could find.

Grimacing, he said, "You're going to know, but that's not important right now, perhaps right at the end. There's a whole lot of material I'll be working through before we even come close to that. In fact, to me that's only a small part of the story."

The thought in my mind was "What could I do at this point?" I was here. Though I kept wondering if he was continuing to reel me in.

Marco stopped speaking and his expression showed clearly that at some point very recently he had come to an epiphany where he knew it was time to come into the open and reveal his life. I felt more assured than I did a minute ago. I only hoped I was reading him correctly.

"Like I said, let's not deal with that right now. I want to start at the beginning and get rolling; it'll take time, I told you."

Hell! If I told him anything right now, he'd be on the first plane back home to Georgia.

▲ ▲ ▲

His story did take time. And I was anxious to hear a lengthy recount of events that gravely affected the life of a contumacious kid from El Ritero, Colombia as he was going to tell a story as he knew it firsthand, filled in with important details by others who would become involved in certain parts of his very ignoble life. He had been in this prison for a while, and undoubtedly had many hours to think about his life's story. Going into this I wasn't aware of the far reaching implications his life would have. Simply knowing that a guy had been convicted of a crime and was confined to a prison cell in a foreign country did not give me any prior awareness of the number of people his life touched, nor the influence of some of them in the Church. Stirring in my mind were thoughts about my own capability and skill in crafting a writing that would reflect a truthful biography to be believed and not seem to be fiction. I wasn't certain that this man's life story might be seen as "stranger than fiction," so I promised Marco and myself that I would pull it together into a fascinating narrative to provide a valuable lesson, if that's what he intended it to be. I was ready to listen hoping to be able to separate the plausible from what might seem implausible.

I left the prison after that first meeting and got situated on the mainland. I felt that mentally I was prepared to remain for the necessary length of time it would take me to complete a biography of Marco Montoya detailing the bad and ugly that I would hear from his lips, and whatever good the man may have accomplished during the years he was not behind bars. I had no thoughts as to how many prison visits I'd be making, but figured I was destined to remain in Italy for quite a while.

The next day is when the reality of the prison and its surroundings really hit me. I was reminded from a documentary I had seen of Alcatraz off the California coast and mentally took note of some similarities: the long ride from shore, the choppy waters, and the isolation. I got off the commuter boat that transported the working staff of everyone from cooks and maintenance to guards and visitors to d' Arda. In the Warden's office I finalized all the paperwork from him, and then was escorted to meet Marco. He wasted no time and began his narrative as we both settled at a large desk. I came to do my job. I never inquired of him how he engineered all the arrangements with the Italian authorities to make all of this happen. He did have some very good lawyers, so I suspected they were the agents who exerted whatever influence was necessary and more than likely provided whatever money it took.

2

Mexico
Tulavatio del Rio

Tulavatio del Rio, a small town in Mexico comprised of only a couple hundred families, was the locale determined to be the genesis of the events that took place over the next three decades. The town was a picturesque village on a slow moving creek that snaked its way along the open prairie of wild grasses and cacti with lizards of various dimensions living among the rocks and sun-rotted stump remnants. Insects that once lived in the wood had no doubt died long ago as they baked to minute cadavers in the blasting sun. Any other creatures living in this desolate area were only seen and heard at night, as their sounds shrilly penetrated the bleakness and moroseness of the place. The entire environment conveyed to anyone, especially someone who had spent his early life in such a God-forsaken place, the feeling of gloom and discouragement, not a place from which distinguished events would happen to affect lives.

But one such event was a dream of a small boy who used to play in the countryside and think of the day he could bring special attention to his town. He thought of his home as such an extraordinary place that the rest of the world would also think that it was.

This boy, Alfredo Legados, was a gifted individual in a religious sense, as he always knew he had a calling, a vocation. He had no particular fondness for the village priest so he was not a favorable influence on this boy's life, but Alfredo had an idea that one day he would be a priest and bring recognition to his town by creating an Order of priests that would devote themselves to a higher mission. He knew the purpose of the Church and all that it existed to do for the good of the people, but he had it in mind to do something extraordinary with the men who would want to follow him and help fulfill his desires for establishing schools that would form young students in the Christian belief to enter the priesthood and perpetuate his dream. This, Alfredo contemplated as he sat on the hillside overlooking the old town.

Many times during his youth he saw his dream reflected colorfully in the beauty of the land and he prayed that one day long after he had left the seminary, he would return to his village, and while satisfying his priestly obligations, he'd spiritually entice others through his writings to answer their call and join him in his mission. Later, he wrote prolifically about spirituality and specially designed schools and a society of adults very much like Opus Dei, an organization he had read about. His dream was to become reality.

▲ ▲ ▲

Years later long after ordination Father Alfredo Legados had created a strong following in Mexico. Many mothers, faithful adherents of the Church, could envision a son having a vocation and answering the call to enter the ecclesiastical ranks of the Church. Of course, they had the vision because they prayed for it more than the sons did. With the permissions that he needed to be granted him from Rome, Father Alfredo established his Order, Missionaries of the Holy Church, and through its members' vocations and the enticements that the priesthood could offer, Alfredo saw the genesis of his grand plan: a growing army of zealous soldiers.

To complete preparations, Mexican seminarians left and then spent three years in Seville, Spain where they finished their studies before going to Rome to study theology and Canon law before ordination. Several long years it took for the education to be complete, so it was an arduous program before a man was ordained and said his first mass.

Father Alfredo stood out as one of the most resourceful men in Mexico. He knew that it would be possible to have an army of priests to see the fulfillment of his dream: establishment of schools dedicated to the purpose of educating young students to transform society, and establishment of an organization within the Church which he called Familia Dei. This organization would be comprised chiefly of adults who would be ordinary members of society, but would be prayerful zealots who would hope to stand as religious models in their communities.

3

Colombia
El Ritero

Marco Montoya, son of Consuela and Fernando, was from a later time than Alfredo and from a distant country, but very connected in both a familial sense and a religious sense. Though a good thirty years separated the two men in age, a relationship between them would be revealed in the future and only because of a confession that had to be made. Their attachment grew out of what one might call a nefarious occupation or profession, as well as an immoral situation.

▲ ▲ ▲

The cocaine trade had been rampant for years in Colombia. Ramon Munoz, as well as other drug lords before him, had an immense influence upon the poor of the country. When a man needed work where was he to go? He could attempt to scrape out a living for his family by working a meager plot of land, but this was arduous work and the recompense from it was most often not sufficient to feed several hungry mouths. At times, a man could be persuaded to get involved in illegal trafficking and reap a far greater reward for his risks. Periodically, a few prayers and confession would assuage him from any guilt that he had presuming that in the completion of his duties he was not responsible for any bodily harm to any person, which was seldom the case. Of course, in the confessional absolution was given, and the priest was obligated by his Church's rules to swallow and digest what he heard.

Sabastino Alvarez confronted Fernando in a predatory manner with a simple request. "Fernando, I have a job for you. A package must be delivered to a man who is flying to Cuba, and I don't have a choice about getting it to him. It has to get to him without any attention being drawn to me. Come to the Plaza Granada in El Poblado tomorrow evening and take the package from me and then go home. Next day you will take it to the address written on this paper. I'm being watched, but you will not be suspected that you are doing anything for me. When you get the package home you are to change the shape of it by re-wrapping and then placing loaves of bread over it in a basket. You must hide it! Can you do this? I can give you 500 pesos right now if you will say that you will do this. After the job is completed I will give you 500 more pesos." His coercion was somewhat gentle considering the kind of man he was.

You'll do this for me Fernando, or get your farmer's dumb ass blown off.

How could Fernando resist this amount of money? He had never held such a sum like this in his hand at any one time.

Sabastino Alvarez was only a halcone in the organization, but had some authority from his lugarteniente to go beyond just reporting activities of rival cartels. He was taking a real risk in recruiting Fernando to make a delivery as his position was extremely tenuous. If there had been a slight miscalculation the capo would have two bullet ridden bodies displayed in the town plaza.

"Alvarez, I know what you do. How can you ask me to do this? You know that I need money. How can I be sure I will not be suspected by the police?" asked Fernando suffering great anxiety and feeling perspiration on his eyebrows.

"We take every precaution for your safety, Fernando."

Realm of the Beast

▲   ▲   ▲

Fortunately for Fernando the operation was successfully carried out. Fernando felt much more comfortable the next time his assistance was required and before long, he was regularly working for Sabastino and the cartel. At this time many politicians and police officials were involved in illegal activities and turned away from implicating any of those dealing or selling or transporting drugs just as long as their bribes were received when expected. Occasionally, when governmental authorities became aware of trafficking activity and evidence was compiled, a grand jury handed down indictments, but rarely were Colombians imprisoned.

The only time Fernando found himself in a precarious situation was when one minor official in local government on the take for a long time, but a halcone, summoned Fernando to an out of the way location where he spoke quite privately and threateningly to him. The threat was that if his wish for Fernando's daughter Rosita to give herself to him was not fulfilled, he would bring accusations of crimes against Fernando. It was obvious to Fernando that Rivera had designs on his daughter as Rivera had made remarks in the past that Fernando thought best to ignore. But now his anger and hatred were at an incendiary level. Fernando refused to prostitute his daughter and felt he had no choice but to resort to reprisal and this meant in a lawless way for there was no other way. After he killed a man, he reconciled that he had surrendered to Satan.

When he got home he said to his wife, "Consuela, I've killed Diego Rivera! I don't think anyone will find the body. I was very careful to hide it in the swamp where I'm sure it will be feasted on until there is nothing left but bones. But what I'm most worried about is what will happen to me if the lugarteniente finds anything out. Diego was an important man for cartel purposes as a plant and conduit for information."

I don't know how I'm going to get out of this, but I did the right thing. I believe it in my heart.

With a hollow feeling in her stomach and an ache in her heart, Consuela said to her husband, "Holy Mother of God! What have you done? You will have to run. What will happen to the rest of us now? Your sons. What will happen?"

In a vain attempt to sound comforting, and holding her close, Fernando said to her, "I know that no one will harm you. They will only kill me, if they don't understand what I had to do. What Diego did was against the code of the cartel."

▲   ▲   ▲

Dire circumstances led Fernando into a life of criminality that eventually involved another member of the family. Until Marco and his brothers became old enough to clearly see what kind of life as a mural their father had been painting over the last several years of their boyhood, they led an ordinary life in the village. The only event they questioned many times was the reason their father had to leave the town and be gone several days at a time on business. The picture of their father's life was now bleak and distorted. At the beginning of their young lives they knew their father was simply a farmer, and he worked hard with his brothers on the land. Later, however, they knew he had undertaken another manner of employment and were happy along with their mother that there was a great deal more money coming into the house. They were not opposed to that even though they missed their father when he said goodbye to them so often as he was off on cartel business. Did Consuela actually understand how the money was earned? Being an ignorant peasant woman, she remained unknowing of her husband's life away from home. But suspicions often entered her mind.

Marco was older than his two brothers and sister and for some strange oddity he seemed different from them. Perhaps the contrast was in his interpretation of what is, a philosophy of tragic acceptance. Tragic in the sense that he and the others, too, knew the life they were living was not the one intended, but an artificial one that could ultimately lead to tragedy in the form of destitution and complete indifference to life. His siblings accepted this; he would not. Marco was fully aware of what his father and uncle had turned to. He, too, would enter this world of crime and ultimately make his escape from a life of boredom and indolence on a small acreage outside El Ritero.

Agitated, as a distressed father, Fernando spoke, "Why do you question me, my son? I'm saying that it is not right for you to want to be a part of the organization. Do you know what happens to you when you're in?"

Marco stood upright and tall opposite his father and with the strength of his conviction said, "I'm smart. Smart enough to know what to do. I'm big and can handle myself." Words typical of a youth with no life experiences. "Besides I will learn from others and not make any mistake. I can see that this is the quickest way for me to be somebody."

Does he think I'm going to stay here to live and die the life of a poor farmer? I will not be that foolish.

With fire in his eyes and the combination of anger and frustration, Fernando slammed his fist on the table and shouted in a determined voice, "No! It's not going to happen. I won't allow it to happen. I know the consequences that will occur. You can't see that because you are too young and don't know."

Fernando standing there not believing he was even having such a conversation with his son, seemed to stare off into some unknown region. Quietly in his mind he was cursing himself to the devil for ever having become what he was. He was certainly the most pathetic example. How could his own son desire to work for the cartel? It's not anything a father wants to see. It's bad enough that he himself is immersed in crime. No! Not his son, too.

▲ ▲ ▲

Marco was close to his father and from an age when a boy can do most of the chores of a man, Marco was of tremendous help to his parents on the farm. The relationship between father and son was nurtured on sincere paternal and filial love. Every day toiling in the fields together or shoveling dung outside the barn, father and son were side by side. Fernando loved all his children and each in a special way, but somehow there was a type of spiritual bond that bound Fernando and Marco.

So, Fernando took a firm stand against Marco's interest in the cartel. His own situation was different. A severe downturn occurred when the farm suffered a long period of drought and the family was confronted by ruin. This forced Fernando to get help, and he felt the cartel was his only answer. It had served him well for a time, and when he would have desired to escape the cartel, he knew it was an impossibility. When Marco approached his father and indicated his interest in becoming a member of the cartel thinking it was his channel to a prosperous life, thousands of thoughts soared through Fernando's mind. Those thoughts were of the years he and his son labored to be successful ranchers and do things the right way. His thoughts were of the numerous conversations between himself and Marco sharing feelings and dreams. No! Fernando wouldn't hear of his young boy throwing his life away for what might be an abbreviated life regardless of what financial gain would come to him. But in spite of Fernando's pleading, Marco's stubbornness prevailed and he was determined to fulfill his intentions that were the opposite of his father's sage advice. He went the way of the mob. Marco required a sustenance that working the land could not provide. In his mind his decision was the one and only palliative measure he was able to take to have a real life.

▲ ▲ ▲

So many years later sitting in a dark prison, when Marco is telling me of this early ambition and his loathing to remain on the land, I wonder how many times he regretted his choices as he would approach his adult years which naturally brought a much more mature level of reasoning. I knew this is something I'd discover after I heard his complete story and learned all about this man. While not condoning either his or his father's decision, I felt slightly sympathetic toward his father whose advice was completely disregarded by his errant son.

4

Ireland
Tipperary

Across the ocean in southern Ireland families struggled to eke out a living. Many men worked as ocean-going fishermen, some worked in mines, and some in factories. But the pay was little to show for the long hours that men labored. Poverty covered the towns and countryside like the abundance of green grass that made the place the Emerald Isle. And so it was in the lovely seacoast city of Tipperary that a religious family of a mother, widowed and haggard and worn, diligently attempted to raise her two sons. Strife and struggle were all that she knew, but hard work didn't hinder her perseverance in trying to do the best she could. The squalid conditions in which they lived have been often depicted in images presented by books and movies of past and present times. Conditions like crumbling shanties regarded as houses on streets lined with litter where young boys kick a soccer ball kept soaked by puddles of water in the street hindered from flowing by clogged sewer drains. So the sons, Shamus and Edmund Kelley, had quite a rugged beginning, but not one they couldn't cope with. They grew and developed as average type boys hurdling over their years helping their mother, When children and going to school, they did very well, and generally behaved as decent respectable young guys. Mum always told them that education was the path to their successes as so many mothers who have inhabited this planet have said. The fact is the truth, and the boys knew it as well, for they were excellent students amid the nasty surroundings, and they never disappointed their mother with terrible grades or bad reports from the schools.

Shamus was sturdier. He was a six foot muscular lad and older by two years than his brother. He was more the protector of the home and its inhabitants and was actually the better student in that he had a great inquisitive and analytical mind. His excellence was equal to the amount of effort he chose to devote to his academics. And most often his effort was admirable. But he felt satisfied after high school and saw the necessity of getting a job and helping the family, so his formal schooling ended. Edmund had loftier expectations and continued with education. He was completing his second year of a two-year program with a major in psychology and was grateful that his brother had been generous. He was somewhat demure and in form his body would be regarded as delicate, so much smaller and shorter than Shamus. It's not to anyone's amazement that he became interested in the priesthood as a child and this persisted through his adolescence. Studious, prayerful, contemplative he was. He loved the Church and from childhood blissfully attended morning mass every day that some pain or ache or a severe croup didn't have him in its grasp. He was not that attentive to the parish priest as a model or mentor, but something affected his life that no one in his community would ever have suspected. A beacon was about to shine.

5

Ireland
Tipperary

Father Alfredo's resourcefulness showed itself in his recruitment of Irish boys to his seminary in Mexico. Alfredo knew of the conditions in Ireland and felt that this country would be fruitful ground where he could entice those who had, or thought they had, the calling to be a priest. Through his many writings he was certain that if he saturated key poverty areas of Ireland, he would have a plethora of young boys and young men who would be eager to leave their country for a much better life. Certainly, he did the necessary screening to ensure that the ones with a true calling would be selected. There were the interviews and the scholastic credentials, etc. that would be mandatory. He was a good man with noblest of intentions, therefore he needed to be as close to one-hundred percent sure as possible in selecting candidates. There was no intent to simply give Irishmen who appeared pious a free passport to Mexico. After all, Mexico may have looked poorer than the land they left, if they defected and headed away from the seminary. How far could a boy get not speaking Spanish, or attempting to with an Irish brogue?

⋏ ⋏ ⋏

"Your name is Edmund Kelley. How long have you known that you wanted to become a priest in the service of the Lord?

"For many years now, Father. I always loved going to mass in the morning and often spoke to my mother about wanting a life like Monsignor Quinn where I could do God's work in the community and where I could help souls get to Heaven."

"I know that you are here today for this interview with me because your parish priest, the good Monsignor has spoken so well of you, and he assures me that he feels you are ready to enter the seminary. You do know all that studying for the priesthood means, don't you, Edmund?"

"Yes, father, I do, and I feel that it is what I must do with my life. I have prayed for a very long time to be certain, and I feel the Lord has answered my prayers."

"And your mother feels that it is the right decision for you to make?"

"Yes."

"Your mother seems to have had a hard life. I know she must depend upon you and your brother for so much," said Father Alfredo.

With little emotion being shown Edmund responded, "I believe that we have both been very aware of what we have to do to help my mother get along. My brother Shamus is two years older and has it in mind to work in the factory and continue to be of help at home. He says he is done with school. We have talked about my going to the seminary and he feels it is the right thing for me to do. He has prayed, too. I know that my mum has had it difficult trying to raise us and keep the house such as it is. She is not an educated woman and after my father died she was widowed early and could only find small jobs to do. Mum takes in laundry. She works hard and never complains. She does this for me and my brother. She gets no help from anyone."

"Your Mum is an admirable woman who deserves more for all the troubles she has had in life. In fact, I look at the picture of her that you showed me when she was young, and it's not pleasant to see how she has changed as the years have worn on. She is a saint in the eyes of God, I'm sure. The picture reminds me of another woman I knew so long ago whose beauty was as striking. It was far away from here in South America."

The dark hair and obsidian eyes that glistened radiantly. That's where I see the resemblance. Both beautiful women.

Edmund didn't quite know how to react to this. In fact, he was stunned by the priest's remark, perhaps because he never remembered his own mother looking anything but haggard, or because he saw something in the good Father's brief reverie.

Instantly seeing the puzzlement in the youth's eyes, Father Alfredo realized that was a memory best forgotten, and for a time he sat reflectively as if lost in some revered moment of another life.

"Well, I'll be meeting with Monsignor and we'll discuss all that will be involved in your attending the seminary in Mexico. Later today, I expect that your mother and I will be discussing this also." Father Alfredo was rather excited and agitated over the prospect of seeing and speaking to Edmund's mother for various reasons. He had some trouble reconciling the fact that such a beautiful young woman could have degenerated physically to the condition in which she presently found herself. But, he supposed, after all the hardship she has endured over the past several years, it was not that mysterious to understand. Also, by the comparison to the woman he once knew in Colombia, he wondered if she too was in such a state of degeneration. This bothered him.

▲ ▲ ▲

Edmund was ecstatic contemplating his future. He never believed that such an opportunity might be available to him. Just to think that he would study in Mexico and then Madrid and finally be ordained in Rome. This wasn't even a dream that he could have imagined. In his mind he saw all the beauty of the world and how everything would come together to make his life complete and perfect. He thanked God for all that was entering into his life, and beyond the realization that his hope of becoming a priest will come true, he felt that God was allowing him to be able to care for his mother. He had that special kind of love that seems to be characteristic of Irish sons for their Irish mothers when not under the spell of the bottle.

With tremendous excitement still stirring within him, Edmund said, "Mum, I had an interview with Father Alfredo, the founder of the Missionaries of the Holy Church in Mexico. It was brief, but he knows of my sincerity that I have a true vocation. I know he will accept me into his seminary. I know that you don't want me to go to such a distant country to study; you prefer that I stay home in Ireland or go to study on the Continent, but we have to see what this opportunity can mean for me. It is what I want to do."

Characteristic of a mother who believes she is soon to lose a child, Mrs. Kelley didn't have too much to discuss with her son. She'd spend time shedding tears in private as she thought about his long time away, too long away. Mary Kelley appeared morose, and at the same time happy for Edmund. She spoke softly and was terse in the expression of her sentences.

▲ ▲ ▲

This scene was one repeated several times over in households in Ireland as Father Alfredo went about recruiting. His advance work had been done, his reports from the numerous parish priests, Monsignors, and Bishops had been filed. He and his staff simply made the house calls and conducted the final interviews. All was set up to populate his school with moldable minds and dedicated hearts. Father Alfredo would ensure a sanctuary. After years of study he'd turn them out into regions of North America and other parts of the globe to establish academies where young students would flock paying heavy tuitions to be "formed" and indoctrinated with the message that they would deliver to the secular world in hopes of transforming it.

6

Colombia
El Ritero

El Ritero is an old village where large beautiful mountains can be seen in the distance. The magnificent Spanish colonial architecture, the town square with the big church and the open markets give one the feel of so many quaint South American villages. The modest farm houses and the sight of people tending cattle and other domestic animals, as one travels the winding roads through the hills, creates the impression of driving through parts of New Mexico like farm areas such as near Chimayo. The scenic beauty is splendid. Or, perhaps, a traveler would think he was driving Interstate 101 in Northern California passing through verdant valleys while viewing the glorious surrounding mountains devoid of any pine trees. The rustic setting could seem familiar to people whose memories of farm country reminded them of distant and beautiful places.

El Ritero is the village where Fernando and Consuela established their home decades ago and raised their sons and daughter. The Montoyas were the country family who grew crops and attended animals for the length of time until Fernando took that fifteen mile ride into Medellin where he met Sabastino Alvarez. That was a fateful day indeed, as life changed from a beauteous state to an ugly form. The form that emerged with all the new wealth it brought was in reality the ugly head that reared itself. Fernando would assent that the ugliest part was his son joining the forces of the devil, the drug purveyors. It is astonishing how a young child can pass from Christlike innocence to become a man possessed with the intention of becoming prosperous by any means. All that the lessons of the Gospel taught them in the church, and that they adhered to was that the rapacious man will lose his soul to the devil and will suffer eternal damnation. But the ultimate misfortune was that Marco made the wrong choices and took all the wrong avenues to reach that level of prosperity he so yearned for while growing up poor. He felt that the road not taken would bring the traveler to doom.

"Arturo and Ricardo are younger, Father. They can stay here and be with Mother and care for the land. I'm going with you and my uncle to Medellin."

"Fernando, it will be okay. With the two of us working for the cartel we will be able to watch Marco and guide him along," said Benito.

"It's not what I want. You know, Benito, my brother, that our lives are in danger every day. Anything could happen along the road. We're not protected every hour of the day even with the force that Ramon has. It is impossible for his army of men to push the police and the Colombian troops so that we'll never get hit. We take our lives too lightly not to believe that one day tragedy will strike and we'll go to our graves. Though I know we do wrong, I pray to the Virgin Mary that we will be safe and spared when the army or militia one day overruns the city and our compound."

"Don't speak like that, Fernando. Like a damn idiot. If those close to Ramon become aware of your feelings, we will be taken out not by the army, but by his closest halcones. I don't want to think that you are a coward. I, too, pray to Our Lady that we can get enough from the drug trade to one day walk away and leave this life behind." His innocence overshadowed his naivety.

"In the last raid that took place the gun battle was unbelievable. If we didn't have the fire power that Ramon has gotten from Chavez we would have lost more comrades. We had to console Argenio's family after his loss. I hate to think that I will lose another brother, or that you, my brother, will lose me one day. I can't conceive of the thought that my own son, Marco, could be in a position where I could lose him too. I refuse to think that is a possibility, and only because I hope to not see him in the cartel."

The man was sincerely grieved just exchanging these words with his brother, but his words and his grief were to no avail because Marco was determined to carry out his own ambitions in spite of his father's protestations. Marco did go to Medellin and was well received by the drug cartel. New blood with so firm a purpose was always welcome. They would test him, of course, and he would be successful.

7

Mexico
Coalcojana

There are many things about a person and an institution that no one knows about when all they do know is what appears superficially on the surface. This was the case with Alfredo Legados as a young boy, as a seminarian, as creator of a newly formulated segment of the holy church he was responsible for nurturing. Along with the Order he founded with the blessings of Rome, Fr. Alfredo extended his mission to include a wide cross-section of people. He sent his disciples out into the parish communities to recruit believers who would define themselves as special members of a clandestine society within the church. They would see their participation as a follower of Christ with the noblest mission. In some way the prodigious boy from the village of Tulavatio del Rio may have had a premonition that after his education and ordination he was predestined to lead a Christian society in fulfilling the work of Christ. Familia Dei became that special society which to some people would be more of a cult due to a degree of fanaticism that to others would overshadow their mission in the church.

There are many minor secret societies that develop within established religions or faiths, so Father Alfredo's creation and his hopes for its successes were not the incipience of something which had never been done before. Zealots are in abundance waiting for opportunities, so it was not unthinkable, nor a mystery, that Alfredo could appeal to the type of individuals who might think they would enhance or bring some level of importance to their lives by expressing their faith through good deeds and serving the Lord. While most would be sincere, some would be sanctimonious.

Many of his inspirational messages given and lessons taught to his faithful followers were good thoughts and words to promote good deeds, but unfortunately, too many of these writings were not originally conceived by Father Alfredo Lagados. He had read philosophers and many theologians whose ideas he thought worthy of repeating for the indoctrination of his Familia Dei followers. However, exposure of his plagiarized works might have diverted him from shameful paths he followed. There were many examples of plagiarism that literary discoverers made many years later. One would have thought that the Order itself had some scholars who could have related Alfredo's material to written sources decades or even centuries earlier. In the case of Father Alfredo it was later rather than sooner that his fraudulence would be detected. Another disgrace piled high on top of the many others.

8

United States

As time passed and the word spread from Mexico to the United States, the legion of loyal adherents to the tenets of the Movement grew tremendously. Schools were built in several cities throughout the Midwest and the South. The northeast housed the principal seminary which was actually a command post for the clergy where members would come to conference and establish plans to develop a secular curriculum, but more importantly, delineate a superbly defined religious program of formation. The earliest stages of the schools were quite simple: have two female members of the Movement rent space somewhere even in the basement of another denomination's church, or even in an old building which would undergo some renovation. It didn't matter just so long as word got out that a private religious school was open for students of all faiths whose parents could afford to send them. In some of the states regulations were not stringent, so establishing a school that the Missionaries wanted was fine. After all, there were all sorts of charter schools springing up and also home schooling was widely accepted. Realistically, an organized school headed by an order of priests was a welcomed entity.

In essence, the underlying philosophy of the educational and religious plan was that students must be taught to see their lives as a work of art allowing God to create His masterpiece in each one's soul. Exceptional acts of virtue such as perseverance, charity, generosity, punctuality, preparedness, creativity will be rewarded. This is the formation: to become truthful and good, to guide one's life according to the Christian perspective, to worship one's Creator by actively participating in His "Art of Creation." One must habitually extend to others appreciation for truth and goodness.

There would be a vigorous attempt to balance intellectual formation with religious formation. To develop a true sense of giving of oneself for the benefit of community, an element referred to as mission work was another pillar of the students' formation. While a perfect balance was the objective, there was no question that occasions for religious activities or rituals would adumbrate the academic classroom. This was understood and completely accepted by parents many of whom were already members of Familia Dei or soon would become members. As long as a bona fide curriculum with good balance of religious teachings and academics was offered, parents were most satisfied that their students were in the correct environment for nurturing the mind and soul. They were indoctrinated into a system seeing the regimen as the one true process to develop a moral, principled, virtuous person. This plan and process of educating the entire person with emphasis on the spiritual aspects are tantamount to a noble endeavor of great significance. The paucity of spiritual elements is the reason Familia Dei parents reject secular education for their students though completely knowing of the separation of Church and state. They feel that students being educated in secular societies do so at the risk of becoming morally and ethically degenerated, so they are the proponents of a system of education which provides correct and comprehensive answers to basic questions of human beings' purpose in life and the link to the afterlife.

9

Colombia
El Ritero

As long and as hard as Fernando Montoya discussed and argued with his young son, pointing out what might become every possible consequence for his desire and actions if he joined in that most unholy of alliances, Marco remained adamant. He was blinded by what he saw as the only avenue to pursue a life of exuberant living in a metropolis. Why would he be expected to remain in such a small village of exhausted peasants and farms where dreams were nothing more than nightmares? No. He had made his decision and it would not be difficult to realize because any young blood was ideal for recruitment into a cartel. And, his wishes known, he was eagerly grabbed by the most profligate of vicious men, Ramon Munoz.

Munoz was the lord of the jungle. He had come from a notorious stock dating back to the pirates that were most savage along the coast off Venezuela. It was told that all the pillaging and murderous acts conducted by Colombian outcasts were without comparison even when the stories of the nefarious and colorful Caribbean plunderers were related. Ramon came much later, but with that same ruthlessness coursing through his body.

"Marco, I, we, welcome you into our organization. I can only promise you that with much hard work and loyalty cemented with absolute obedience you will not only be one of our honorable band, but also, will be of great importance and value to your family."

When this single sentence was spoken, Marco told me, a shudder of fear as well as an expectation, overcame him to the point where he immediately cursed his foolish decision. He couldn't turn back. The die was cast. What was his new life to be? He had only imagined it before in the most glorious pictures; now reality is front and center and the pictures may not be glorious.

▲ ▲ ▲

At numerous intervals during the telling of his story as we sat facing each other in the prison, I, either in thought or in direct statement, questioned Marco's motivation. Sometimes he responded, sometimes he did not. But each time I sought to figure it out to have a clearly complete picture, I was left with nothing conclusive. I hearkened back to the idea expressed by an author, producer, and director I had previously studied, that the specific circumstances into which a person is born, and in which he is raised, determine the person's goals, obstacles, struggles, adaptations, and actions. Marco was not able to give me a lengthy analysis of circumstances, but would allow me to discover them as he progressed with the narrative of his life. He would come to expose all details that would make his story interesting as he allowed me to participate in it from event to event and beginning to end.

As a writer, I also understand that one needs to explore circumstances that surround people or things that are a direct causation of a person's acts. Marco made it perfectly clear that there were many familiar objects he was surrounded by which had special meaning at a specific moment that had enormous impact on his aggressive, abusive, and downright impetuous and frenzied behavior. These objects all had one common bond: power and greed.

10

Mexico
Coalcojana

Edmund was eager to begin studies in Mexico in a recognized and renowned seminary under the tutelage of the Missionaries. While a naïve boy he had visions of what he might become after intense theological study and becoming an intellectual in the example of the dedicated priests that formed the cadre of the seminary. And his visions increased dramatically as he progressed through a rigorous regimen of study. To transform the world. That was the goal, the purpose. To establish schools that would be solely dedicated to molding the minds of young pupils and sending them on to transform society. To use every influential moment to move pliable and easily guided students in the direction of one day being ordained. Edmund was eager to begin his theological journey with the Missionaries' singular goal in mind.

He had arrived in Mexico with five other boys who were equally gratified to leave the Old Sod, and because of their calling were filled with excitement to begin studies that would take them into the world to do the work of the Lord and fulfill the goals of the Missionaries. Though all were united in culture and purpose, Edmund was only as close as any new students might be in a foreign setting. However, an American, Teddy O'Driscoll, was perhaps the one student whose friendship with Edmund would be the closest and endure through their seminary years and their initial assignment after ordination. Ted was a couple years older than Edmund.

Teddy's background was the opposite of Edmund's. He came from a higher-class of society and a well-educated background. Ted's father was the founder of a Massachusetts firm that was listed on the Fortune 500. He had a strong allegiance to his alma mater and was a heavy donor to the coffers of his University of Pennsylvania. The O'Driscolls smacked of wealth which was quite the contrast to Edmund's poor family back in Ireland.

Ted entered the sem later than most. He had been reared in the lap of luxury and knew society like a debutante. He had already graduated from college and had the usual number of secular experiences that a young collegian was bound to have. Parties, girls, cars, good times, in general. Though he claimed to have remained chaste throughout these years, reality might cast doubt. Ted was a man who fit the proverbial description tall, dark and handsome. He was a perfect choice for any female of similar background and breeding who might also bring a substantial inheritance to a union one day. But, Ted persisted that he was all that he said he was for one very simple reason. From his senior year at St. Mary Margaret High School in Boston Ted felt that he was hearing an inner voice telling him he would be a follower of Christ. He said he knew that if one day he answered that calling, he could not yield to temptations of a sexual nature before he came to enter a seminary and then enter the service of the Lord. His conscience would suffer him enormously even if confession absolved him.

It wasn't a case of poor boy befriends rich boy that tied these seminarians together. There was a plethora of reasons that Edmund and Ted would be compatriots through significant changes in their lives. Besides their environment which included their vocations and their heart-felt purpose at the beginning, there were other interests and desires and dreams that would come into play as they developed into learned and courageous men. And some of these might not be those of dedicated and judicious people, but only time would tell, and for them exoneration is one short step away from the confessional.

II

Mexico
Tulavatio del Rio

Who was that boy who had the dream of becoming a priest and founding an order that would establish schools to educate or indoctrinate boys and girls in transforming the world? Who was that man who would form a cult-like organization within his Order to reach out to thousands of zealous adult Catholics, principally parents of the school boys and girls?

Alfredo Legados was born in Tulavatio del Rio, some miles northwest of Mexico City, the son of peasants, Raphaella and Antonio. He began his life with some frailties and hardships difficult to overcome and work out to his advantage, but his struggles would be rewarded through his efforts and the burdens he placed on himself. His smallness in stature and physical weakness along with meekness was counterbalanced by a sturdy spirit and average intelligence when it was applied to fulfill a purpose. What would see him through to success was perseverance and diligence to completing easy or arduous tasks he saw before him. The periodic illumination of his mind and his eloquent expression of deep thoughts that stated and elucidated his philosophy are the components that drew people to his side. His ability to attract the young men he diligently sought out to enter his Order and the thousands of people he would invite into Familia Dei are the true testament to his innate powers.

His small town in Mexico was a parallel to that of the Montoyas in Colombia. Like El Ritero, Tulavatio del Rio was not a village where a child born into the world with an occasional vibrant mind and a free spirit would be content and joyful to grow and develop into manhood. Alfredo saw the Church in an opportunistic way to render homage to his God through the priesthood while being able to act out his life on a larger stage. All of his characteristics, physical and otherwise, led him in the direction of the Church. No one in the community was stunned by his decision at a young age to enter the Church. His parents much like the mother of Edmund Kelley many years later in a far off country of the world encouraged their son to enter the ranks of clergy who had been influential in prior years, and were exuberant with joy when they felt their prayers had been answered.

The influences Alfredo had were members of the family who had preceded him in the priesthood. He had uncles who had been ordained, and one, Rafael de Valasio, later was canonized. In fact, it was only after private study under two of his uncles that Alfredo was ordained because he had been asked to leave the seminary in Mexico City for reasons that were never disclosed. It would be several years later that many truths about this man would be uncovered.

▲ ▲ ▲

When hearing much of this narrative in the straightforward way that Marco was speaking, it was quite obvious that through the experiences he would reveal that included a large number of people, he knew them all so well. It seemed like he was reading from a biography, for example, when he told me about Father Alfredo and his background. His extensive knowledge of these people, or his involvement with them could not have been founded on such trust. From a psychology standpoint he acknowledged the need to balance the positive and the negative sides of each person he spoke of. This was intriguing to me because much of the negative sprang forth from the positive, and at times this could be confusing or deceitful. For instance, with Father Alfredo we wouldn't want to believe that anything wicked could possibly spring from a holy and devoted man of the cloth. Likewise, could a good man like Fernando Montoya turn from a humble and God loving man to a killer? But Marco revealed both sides mainly in a way that expressed some feeling without being judgmental. To be certain he recognized the rightness and wrongness of actions, but allowed me to voice any intellectual and judgmental statement about what I heard. Whether he commented on my viewpoint depended entirely on the moment in time and what was passing through his mind. Often, no response as he appeared enigmatic and musing looking at me and hearing me, but lost in his mood.

12

Colombia
Medellin

The illegal drug trade was widespread throughout much of South America. Not only were the capos of the cartels living in luxury from the millions of dollars they illegally amassed, but so too were the hired guns. In a relatively short span of years Marco had become wealthy by the standards of the local indigent villagers. He felt he had earned it all for what his responsibilities were. He had been a part of many shoot-outs. He lost count. But he knew that the rival tradesmen who infringed upon his boss's network had to justifiably be eliminated for their transgressions, and he showed no hesitation when the trigger had to be pulled and blood must flow. He admitted to himself at least that he had some recrimination, some pangs of conscience, but when entrenched so deeply in the poison-dealing industry, there are no choices to be made. A poor boy, now becoming a rich man, a killer. All that he was when his faith was important and meaningful was placed in a small compartment in the rear of his brain. Though oftentimes he would sit and ponder his life of crime, he had become hardened and knew he'd never find his way back. He felt this was acceptable for it was what he had chosen, the high price for freedom and a better life. But he knew what he had become.

It's impossible to be involved in this kind of criminal activity without becoming a junky. Marco was far gone and spent many hours living in an empty mind. Of course, he regretted all that he was, but still got the greatest pleasure when he'd become zonked and unfeeling of everything and everyone surrounding him. However, when he had to be cool, he was cool, aware of his job and what it demanded of him. And of course after marriage he'd seriously alter his wicked and destructive habits.

"Marco."

"Yes, Ramon."

"We've got some work to do in Mexico and I want you to go with your father and uncle to clear the way for us to get a whole lot of shit there without anything bad coming down on us. I want this to go clean and easy."

"I know what you're saying, Ramon. It'll get done. Where's the dropoff?"

"A little place near Cotija de la Paz called Coalcojana."

"Who's getting it?"

"That's something you don't need to know. It's a major distributor."

"I guess it's better that way in case something breaks. I'd rather not know anything especially names, if things get tough and there's a fight. Everyone should not have a name. If you kill or get killed, that's just the way it goes," Marco said with the aplomb of a seasoned halcone.

What did he expect? A picnic in the plaza. Any time there's "a delivery" to be made, chances are it's going to be a bad situation. No matter how much secrecy is attached to an enterprise, it almost inevitably always turns out that a rival cartel finds out about it and a battle ensues. But he was perceptive. Better to realize consequences than think there'd be no conflict.

▲   ▲   ▲

It was scary even when he was telling me about his dangerous encounters, and I wasn't even there. I could feel the tenseness through his voice when he told the story, and I could sense the danger that he faced. Again, this was the life he had chosen.

"My father and my uncle and I got the load ready and with sufficient guards we started off for Coalcojana. We thought everything was in place for a smooth run, but our experience tells us to always be ready for the unexpected anywhere along the route. One thing that no one better underplay is the hard fact that you never know if one of your own will turn traitor and that's when you're not in for a surprise, but rather you're usually going to end up dead. Northwest of Medellin in the region of Choco before entering Panama, they hit. The fucking Michoacán cartel opened up on us. Luckily, they underestimated our fire power and we shot the shit out of them leaving a pile of bodies behind. They weren't prepared for the resistance we put up. This would mean payback at a later time, and when Ramon is crossed, it wouldn't just be a gunfight, it would be annihilation. It was a matter of time. So much for Ramon wanting things to go easy.

"We got there with enough kilos to make us rich and a whole bunch of customers very happy; the load would bring us about 15 million. I had no idea at the time why my father and uncle would not confide in me the name of our buyer. I couldn't even be there when the stuff was delivered. Uncle Benito just told me to wander off and ask no questions. I knew enough just to listen. It would be much later, of course, that I'd learn why I was to be kept ignorant of the identity of the buyer. This was a mystery to me because there were many times when the run to Coalcojana was made and each time lots of the specifics were kept hidden. Ours isn't the kind of business where one gets inquisitive because you know it's better not to know too much than to be dead. There was always a degree of apprehension on my uncle's part each time we headed to Coalcojana, and I instinctively felt he concealed something, or was suspicious of something that one day I would have to know as it means something to my life. I wondered, too, why Ramon said that I didn't have to know. He was safeguarding me, I know. It wasn't like this before when I was a part of other operations and was in the know regarding all the details. Naturally, I was pissed off that they had some reason for keeping me at a distance. It was only this run to this location that would be kept secret. There must be a good reason for it; that's all that stayed in my mind. This only disturbed me when various questions would arise in my mind, but soon were dismissed from it."

13

Mexico
Coalcojana

The Missionaries of the Holy Church Order was founded in Mexico City by Father Alfredo along with a local bishop whose name became obscured through the dominance of Alfredo's. A seminary at Coalcojana was established and Alfredo would later be praised by Rome for his incredible ability to attract young men to study for the priesthood. Following studies in Mexico the seminarians were sent to Madrid for a period of three years to continue study at Seminaria del Fontanara Their final destination for completion of all theological studies and ultimate ordination into the priesthood of the Missionaries of the Holy Church was Rome.

For several years Alfredo taught in the seminary and wrote extensively on the formation of priests. Eventually, the Pope instructed that Father Alfredo's congregation of priests be responsible for the creation of a Movement, Familia Dei, consisting of lay people, especially in Latin America, to create leaders of the faith. This extension of his ambitions offered the laity formative and spiritual activities so that families might share in the apostolic ideals of the Missionaries.

Alfredo was pleased with the progress of his enterprise. On a visit to Rome he met with Pope Paul:

"Papa, the seminaries are at capacity in Mexico and Spain, the La Familia Institute has opened our schools in the United States and have been extraordinarily well received, our priests are true missionaries and are promoting the Familia Dei Movement in a magnificent way. We have generated much money to support all of our undertakings, and the foundations we've set up are flourishing. We are embarking on the establishment of the first formation center for consecrated women, one in Ireland and one in Spain. These wondrous institutions are the spiritual arms of the laity that became a natural extension of the recruiting I did in Ireland so long ago." Alfredo spoke with great pride.

"Your work has been blessed, Father. The Order and the greatest Christian laity movement is gaining world recognition. The Church praises all members for their good works and the renewed faith they have brought to many souls. I needn't remind you, Father Alfredo, that the continuance of good that members can bring about, and the excellent spiritual example that they show must always have a strong spiritual leader. Not only is continuous recruitment important, but continuous fund raising is an absolute necessity to maintain any organization. Familia Dei membership through the Missionaries' schools must be promoted as those members bring spontaneity to funding our enterprises. You have shown remarkable ability and zest for encouraging the wealthy society in Mexico to support and sponsor your organizations. You've made them aware of how vital these are to the Church. I respect all your efforts and tremendous work."

I hope the notoriety you have brought to yourself doesn't signal your undoing, my friend. One never knows.

Alfredo gloated with the adulation he received from the Holy Father. He was buoyed by the constant approbation of his accomplishments and never regarded the possibility that his work might ever be put into question. He was a vain man his entire life, and this the Pontiff understood.

14

Mexico
Coalcojana

"Yes, I've heard it too. But it can't be true, just a vicious rumor that someone's spreading. It's impossible. There's no way that such a thing could occur," Ted said shaking his head in complete disbelief.

"There are too many people who'd know about it, and would do something about it," Ted added.

"Maybe you're right. I don't want to think that anything like that could occur, but we both know that everybody in this place isn't straight." It's been obvious since day one," Edmund said in utter disgust.

"Well, I'm not that naïve to think that certain types of men aren't capable of doing things like this, but I know that Father Alfredo would be the first to quietly handle any deviant he might be aware of. He's got too much to be concerned about in making his organization the most successful Order in the history of the Church. He and the staff of professors will squelch any rumor of that kind before it gets too far to do damage."

"I don't know where this will end up, Ted. I haven't been aware of anything of that sort, but I do know that back in high school we had a couple of faculty members that were rumored to be homosexual, and also were suspected of molesting one or two of the students. It didn't go anywhere, of course, when our monsignor and the bishop wouldn't allow it to. Just like today, they hid and denied whatever they knew and threatened any kid that came up with a story that would contradict them. They didn't give a care about anything like evidence."

I don't think I'll go any further with this. I don't want Ted to hear more of this story.

"We know they can be rotten bastards when it means protecting themselves and not caring about whom they hurt. I'm keeping my mouth shut for now. We'll see how this plays out, Edmund," said Father Ted in a rather despondent voice while shaking his head in disbelief that he and his friend were engaged in this conversation.

"You know something, Ted? I just vaguely remember a movie I once saw about a young priest who finally came to grips with his sexuality, and made the decision to leave his Order. He had the strength to do what he knew was right for all concerned. He was wise enough to consult an older priest and friend who had functioned as his counsellor in the past. The man had a sixth sense and all along knew that his young colleague was fighting demons, and advised him to leave."

Damn! You just told yourself to curtail it, and you start running off at the mouth again.

With grave concern written all over his face, Ted responded, "Well, we have to wait and see. Not all situations are the same that they can be handled in like manner. I think we're up against something very big here, and it's going to ultimately force us into action. I hope we have the guts for it."

Letting his friend know he stood stalwart with him, Edmund said, "The last thing I'd want is for this type of anomaly to move sideways from the periphery into our way of life. We'll always stand together, Ted, and face the outcomes as accomplishments or consequences, but we'll know the right thing was the action we took."

15

Colombia
Medellin

Calling Marco into his office at the compound, Ramon offered Marco a rum and coke and asked him to sit. He liked offering the smooth dark Bicardi Select that his men enjoyed drinking. Ramon stood next to his oversized mahogany desk with a Tequila Sunrise in his hand and began, "There's a friend of mine in Mexico who began an Order of priests and opened a seminary a few years ago. And there's a movement of ordinary people called Familia Dei that seems to be flourishing not just in Mexico but in Spain and the United States. I want you to join it, Marco, to make some inroads for us."

"Why me?" Marco asked." I'm not religious like when I was a kid when I always went to church."

Why am I being chosen for some special mission like this? I'm not a freakin' missionary. I'm happy here.

"I need you in this organization. The priest who set this whole thing up and we have been doing business for a while. He'll set everything up for you. It has nothing to do with you being religious. You're going to be acting a role, just like my friend, the priest, and some of his followers. In fact, you will have a dual role where you're going."

"This doesn't have anything to do with the deliveries we've been taking to Coalcojana, does it, Ramon?"

"I told you that you'd find out things when it was necessary for you to know them." But you're right. It does."

"Has some priest been dealing for us?"

Holy Jesus! The cartels have made their way into the Church. I don't believe it!

"You might call it that. I told you before that our biggest distributors are in Mexico."

"Jesus, we've been delivering tons of the shit. His organization must be incredible, and I don't mean the church group or his Order."

"Oh, he's been a friend to a lot of people. The guy was a thieving genius since he was born a poor boy somewhere around Mexico City. Incredible! When the guy wants to get rich he has the perfect cover, the Church and a religious Order that has tremendous contacts all around the world. How perfect it's been for us," Ramon said with a big smile on his face.

"Well, I know I can fit into his network," Marco said. "What could be easier than for pious me to become accepted? It would be hard for some North American guy."

"Don't bet on it, amigo. You have no idea how some members of the Order have organized into one of the biggest cartels crossing borders and oceans. You wouldn't believe the number of North American guys who are our compadres. They don't shy from the work that falls on them either."

▲   ▲   ▲

Attributable to his youth and naiveté, Marco did not realize this to be a crossroads in his life. He dichotomized into two separate selves and would remain thus for the rest of his life to the moment he sought reconciliation and redemption.

16

United States

According to all reports particularly those of the F.B.I. who did most of the investigation of the cartels in South America, Central America and Mexico, the illegal cocaine trade has always been a great source of profit. Within a decade it went far beyond coffee or sugar as the major export of that immense region. It perhaps accounted for as much as one-third of exports coming from Colombia, Bolivia, Peru, and Honduras. With the vast amount of wealth acquired, the purchase of land by the drug lords was phenomenal. Land wealth that added to their coffers of dollars allowed these barons to become politically powerful and that power was used to further their illegal interests. An era of seemingly unstoppable crime ensued as guerrillas attempted to take land away for distribution among the peasant people.

Kidnapping, extortion, murder were widespread. Car bombings and motorcycle drive-by shootings were a rampant form of assassination. It came to a point where several organizations including the cartels, politicians, ranchers, and even a United States corporation met in Puerto Boyacá to form the Muerta a Secuestradores (Death to Kidnappers) to protect dignitaries of one type or another and to defend economic interests.

Colombia had four major cartels during those critical years where the drug trade was the dominant force in the country that dictated the everyday course of life of the citizenry and the government. Cali, Medellin, Norte del Valle Cartels and Los Rastrojos ran the country with the operating groups (producers, suppliers, financiers, and money launderers) until the collaboration of

Colombian government, paramilitary groups and the U.S. government successfully ended the terrorism by extradition and imprisonment and assassination of cartel leaders and members.

▲ ▲ ▲

I had been informed by Marco that his father and uncle had not been fortunate to escape a raid by paramilitary forces that stormed the bastion, a compound, near Medellin and killed many members of the cartel. It was not the last attack that would take place, but it did little to halt the cartel's strong drug activity. His father's and uncle's deaths were critical in Marco's willingness to go to Mexico when Ramon directed him to act as a go-between.

Marco said, "When I got word of the fight and that my father and my uncle were killed, I wanted to know some details of the attack. No one said much to me. Revenge was all that occupied their minds. A family friend confided that my father and uncle were together with others and were shooting from an outer building of the compound. Some incendiary device, a crude grenade of some type, was thrown and the shack exploded. No one walked out of the place. Bodies were blown apart and widely scattered. Nothing was left but a charred piece of ground on the jungle floor that would commemorate nothing or nobody."

17

Mexico
Coalcojana

The cartels' influence extended to the United States, Europe, and Canada and brought in billions of dollars. The Colombian cartels fought off vigorously any semblance of competition, but saw that Mexico was the main entry point for getting the drugs to the U.S. and Canada. This, of course, is where most of the money would be generated. The connection that Ramon Munoz had with the cartel in Mexico was through one man whose influence was global. He had direct influence with the legislature and courts and local police. He had envied contacts in the United States. He had European connections in Madrid and Rome.

The cartel operated where no one would expect an organized ring of racketeers and traffickers to be located. The place was ideal because the capo could run his operation under the cloak of complete secrecy and behind sacred walls with no one, including legal authorities, to observe.

It had long been known that the familiar cartels maintained their areas or regions of crime and terror throughout the country. For example, Tijuana, Juarez, Acapulco, de la Sierra, Barrio Azteca—they all controlled the drug activity in their respective sections of Mexico. Hombres en Negro (or Men in Black) Cartel, secret and silent with an unassuming little man in a cassock and biretta at the head had an incredible sphere of influence that would rock the world, if and when, it became known he and his organization were behind the drug trafficking that crossed the Mexican borders.

▲ ▲ ▲

Marco made it clear to me that after he became an important presence in Coalcojana as an intermediary between the two cartels; he saw the true composition of the Mexican group. He did not want me to mistakenly believe or even assume that all the members of Hombres en Negro were the men in black seminarians or priests of the Order under Alfredo. It was a clandestine operation hiding in plain sight, and only the members of the cartel were cognizant of its presence. I told Marco that in my work I would not misrepresent anything to implicate anyone or any group whom I could be certain was not involved in any criminal or scandalous activity. Behind the walls and gates of the seminary at Coalcojana there were two groups of men: the good and the bad, those aware of cartel activity and those dutiful to God who were completely innocent of any crime surrounding them. There were Father Alfredo's men and then everyone else. Such a dichotomy was the first of its kind, at least in modern history.

18

Colombia
El Ritero

Ireland was not the only country outside of Mexico that Father Alfredo visited to solicit possible candidates for his seminary. He ventured to some South American countries, one of which was Colombia. He was a young man when he reached out to various dioceses to talk to parish pastors who gave him leads from their knowledge of boys who might think they had a calling or who might be persuaded they had a calling. Many of the church altar boys who felt a pious devotion to the church became subjects for consideration of an interview. Alfredo made the rounds and spoke to many young boys who like the Irish boys felt it was an opportunity to become an educated man, and also a man destined for a religious life. Again, like the Irish parents, the peasants of rural communities in Colombia saw the good father's interest in their sons as a blessing.

Long ago on one of his visits to El Ritero Father Alfredo was introduced to a family who had one son that had heard about the priest's interviewing for his seminary in Coalcojana. Father asked how the family might fare if the boy were to leave the farm and go to Mexico which was so distant from their home. The boy's parents humbly assured the priest that they along with their daughter would be quite able to manage their farm. Though responsibilities for their livelihood would be a burden on only three sets of shoulders instead of four, they could endure with the grace of God because He would be caring for their only son.

Father Alfredo stayed on for a few days to give assurance that the boy and his parents were making the correct decision. He acknowledged that their daughter, Consuela, would be carrying a heavy load, but that God would bless and reward her and them one-hundred fold. Something there is that is appealing to simple people who work the earth, about a priest who exudes charm and charisma to get what he wants, when they from whom he takes believe they are the recipients of such goodness. If they could ever know, he took more than they would ever have given. Too often Alfredo's inclement behavior was practiced on the ignorant and unaware. They believed in a man who represented their faith in the meaningfulness of the Church and Christ's guidance in living a good life which leads to salvation.

19

Mexico
Coalcojana

Rumors were rampant that Father Alfredo had a long history of sexually abusing young seminarians. Ted and Edmund were in a continual quandary over the suspicions that they and some fellow students felt. No one was confirming anything. No one really knew anything for sure. So, what was there to be concerned about until someone came forth with viable evidence to prove an accusation? What young boy would dare come forth when he knew the incredible force he was opposing? Nonetheless, with questions on everyone's mind, it was not a wholesome environment for anyone to be in.

Edmund asked Ted if he thought it appropriate for him to write to his mother and brother back in Ireland and mention the notion that something of such an immoral and illegal nature might have taken place. He said, "Who would be believ'n such a thing if I was to say that there's suspicion that a person, and a priest at that, was abusing a seminarian, Ted?"

"No one, Edmund, my friend. I know I can't bring myself to write to my family and broach the subject. My father would go nuts.

Geeze, I can't even imagine how ballistic dad would go about something like this.

"He's the kind of guy to go storming without hesitation to his higher up friends in Congress and demand an immediate inquisition. And if I knew this stuff was true, I'd actually expect my father to do just that, take decisive action. But, not knowing anything as absolute at this point, I'm not mentioning anything to him. Not at this time with nothing to back me up."

"You're right, Ted. We have to find out the truth ourselves. I think we had better talk about this with the others, and also talk to our mentors whom we know we can trust."

"We'd better do it quickly because we are not going to be here for much longer," said Ted. "We depart for Spain in one month, you know. Believe me, I can't wait to leave Mexico and get into more involved studies at Seminaria del Fontanara in Spain. I want to become much more proficient in the language and begin studying Italian for the final phase. My Spanish is a little more than passable; three years of further study in Madrid will make me think I was born there."

"Yeah, I'm traveling home to Tipperary for a week before I fly to Madrid. I'm really looking forward to getting home. It's been a long time. The only visit I had from family was last year when my brother spent ten days in Mexico, and I was allowed to spend only limited time with him. With these questions bothering us, it's going to be tough keeping my mind in the right place and trying to enjoy the number of days I'll have at home," Edmund said.

"I feel the same way, Edmund. My thoughts seem so mired in confusion," Ted uttered in a solemn voice.

I feel I'm going to be obligated to say something to the family, but I don't know how to approach this topic. I guess I'll have to say something though even if a tempest surges. And though he respects me as a future priest, I know Dad will be repeating "that son of a bitch, that son of a bitch."

"Parents are quite perceptive as you know, Edmund. If discussion takes place, I'll hope for some good advice. I'll get in touch with you immediately. You do the same if you speak to your mother or brother. Call me right away so we can prepare a plan to follow when we get back to Mexico."

20

Italy
Iles d'Arda

I asked Marco how he had come to know so well Teddy O'Driscoll and Edmund Kelley. Were they acquaintances in Mexico while he was immersed in the dealings of the cartel and they were still seminarians?

No, he said he did not really get to know them as students at the sem. He had seen them around several times and on occasions when Father Alfredo had the seminarians doing what turned out to be some of his dirty work. He actually got to know the men many years later when the drug interests of the Hombres en Negro Cartel hit the outlets (Missionaries' schools) in North America, and they had already been ordained. Marco got assigned to Crestbrook, a school not far from Atlanta, Georgia, to take a bogus position that offered him cover as a peddler, and the two priests were assigned to the same school by their Order. Ted was a chaplain and Edmund was a counselor. They had been in these assignments for a while, and with Marco a ranking member of Familia Dei, they were close acquaintances. This was all planned out and put in motion by the mastermind behind the cartel and Order in Coalcojana, Father Alfredo.

So what did Marco do at the school? I asked. Aside from being placed there by Alfredo, he had to have a function. After all, it was a school and had an administration and teachers who had no idea what kind of set up Crestbrook really was beneath the surface of the classrooms and rebuilt chapel. Marco was positioned as a quasi-administrator whose job it would be to function as a martinet for the male students and coordinate with the consecrated men and women the Familia Dei programs. The man could not have brought the cartel closer to the community. He could not have placed himself more cleverly to do the work of the devil in Mexico who used the Order and a private school as his means to an evil end.

Marco admitted to the genius of the priest in thinking through the entire process he would develop from a very young age when growing up a destitute boy northwest of Mexico City. Marco thought of his mother Consuela and wondered what she was thinking about the success he had achieved; he thought of Father Alfredo's mother Raphaella long ago taken to Heaven, and wondered what she was thinking of her son's success, and if it were possible for tears to be flowing from her soul. This was an image that he created in his mind and he thought that one day he would try to depict it in a tattoo on his chest.

21

Ireland
Tipperary

Mary Kelley could barely contain her composure upon greeting her son at the airport. Tears of joy flowed from her weary eyes. Seeing his mother after so long a time away from home, he held her and kissed her cheek not noticing any change in her appearance, but just magnificently happy to be with her now as his eyes teared.

"I'm glad you're home, Edmund. Tis been too long for my son to be away from his mother. Lord knows how much I've missed you and prayed for you."

Shamus and Edmund hugged each other and exchanged warm words.

"I'm glad to be home, Mother. It has been a long time. I told Teddy O'Driscoll that I only saw Shamus last year, but I haven't seen you since I went to Mexico three years ago. I can't tell you how much I have missed you and home, even though I did receive a good education, met good friends, and experienced things I would never have seen if I didn't join the Missionaries. There are many things I want to tell you," said Edmund with complete joy in his heart.

"But first, Shamus said, let's head down to Paddy's Pub for a pint. Ma, put on your shawl and let's be gone for a little while to relax and drink and talk."

"Aye, Shamus, like old times except that now Edmund is legal, not that that made any difference before."

My God! How he's grown and the weight he's gained. What has he been eating there? A daily diet of fattening tacos and enchiladas.

"Oh, Ma, how I remember some of those nights when neither of us could barely navigate home and get in the door without falling and cracking our domes." But those were sweet and joyous occasions indeed long to live in me memory."

"Do you remember, my son, the time we hadn't three shillings to spare, but we went down to Paddy's and had a few pints, only to tell him we had no coin. He came roaring at us and booted our arses out the door, saying don't ye ever darken me doorway again."

"Yes, I do. And I turned and called him a buffoon for ever lettin' us darken his doorway in the first place."

"Paddy, another pint of Guinness for each of us over here," shouted Shamus to the rotund bartender officiating over the taps.

▲ ▲ ▲

Only having a week to spend at home with family, Edmund didn't want to waste time. Sitting in the comfort of the house with all familiar surroundings poor as they were, Edmund began talking just about everything he could recall from that first day he arrived at the seminary in Mexico. He told of the Missionaries of the Holy Church and their history; he told stories of his professors and fellow classmates; he told so many things of his limited travels in and around Mexico City; he told his mother and brother all he could think of about his best friend Teddy O'Driscoll. They were intrigued by all he had to say and were delighted beyond belief that they had made the decision three years earlier that he should answer the Lord's call and attend the seminary at Coalcojana.

Then, in a solemn tone he began to tell them the troubling things that reverberated in his mind. He was looking for solace and felt that he might find it in the words and suggestions of his family. They were astounded by the idea that the Director General and founder of a Catholic seminary could be a child molester. Boys attending the minor seminary were middle school age. How horrendous to imagine that a superior would take advantage of their youth and innocence to harm them. Mary Kelley was horrified at what she had heard. Of course, Edmund's mother and brother were united in their response as to what their son and brother must do. They offered that if Teddy had spoken to his family as openly and candidly as Edmund did to them, they knew the O'Driscolls would encourage their son to join Edmund and go to the proper authorities. It made no difference that the perpetrator was the founder and leader of the revered Order. It must be done.

Naturally, Edmund knew what his family's position would be in this matter. Motivated by that reassurance Edmund went to the phone in the ill-lighted hallway of his mother's modest house and dialed Teddy who was with his family vacationing in New Hampshire. The O'Driscolls wanted a week long holiday at their place in the mountains for complete respite before their son had to fly from JFK to Mexico City knowing he would be gone for a very long time.

"Hello! Is Ted O'Driscoll there?"

"Senior or junior?"

Close friends occasionally called Martin by his middle name.

"Junior, please. Tell him it's Edmund Kelley."

"Just a minute, Sir, he's out at the dock," said the unfamiliar voice on the line.

"Thank you!" Edmund answered respectfully, assuming he was speaking to a family housekeeper.

Ted entered the house and picked up the phone. "Edmund, what's happening? Everything alright?"

"Yes fine, Ted. I needed to call you as soon as possible for a very important reason."

"Ok, let's hear what you have to say, Edmund. Although I think I can guess."

Edmund proceeded to tell Ted about his candid conversation with his family regarding the rumored seminarian abuse in Mexico. Ted acknowledged that he had done the smart thing, and said that he, too, had gotten into dialogue with his family over that matter. As he said so long ago about what his father's reaction would definitely be if he had been told previously, he was right. Ted's dad said he'd positively rip any pedophile, priest or no priest, a new asshole if he had been there. The O'Driscolls were unanimous in their thoughts as to the proper course of action for their son to take. They were elated to learn after Ted's and Edmund's phone call that both future priests intended to go to the church authorities in Madrid when they arrived there, and then to the civilian authorities if necessary. Their belief was that if Father Alfredo was guilty in Mexico, then he was guilty in Spain too, as he spent about equal time at both Missionaries' seminaries where it seemed obvious he had done equal damage. They knew that a fierce battle was before them going into this, and striving to convince the powers of the Order, but they were mentally prepared, and counted upon the full support of the seminarians behind them including those who would testify.

22

Mexico
Coalcojana

Marco continued: "The movement of drugs from Colombia through Central America to Mexico was an easy enough journey for the traffickers even when government authorities were not unobservant or were tolerant because of being paid off. With venal men in office and power it was more or less a given that there would be no troubles of any consequence in transporting the drugs a few thousand miles. Moving them from Mexico was a matter of getting them to the coast somewhere near La Placita or Pomaro and boating them up the Gulf of California and then surreptitiously going on shore, or moving them to Juarez and heading east. Naturally, when the Mexican cartels reached full strength there was little agreement as to how, when or why anything they didn't need from South America was going to pass overland into Mexico. An alternate route was to Nicaragua then crossing the river to Costa Rica, but this passage was rarely used.

"At the time the drops were going to Coalcojana for their recipient to move the contraband into the U.S., the passage was made clear, the payoffs were given, and everyone involved made money and was content with the operation. This was the period of time when I was handling things for Ramon Munoz in Colombia and became fully acquainted with Father Alfredo and his part of the drug flow. It was afterward when the Mexican cartels really heated up that I was sent to the schools in the North where Father Alfredo already had his cohorts in position and where the Familia

Dei society was widespread. Its members were solidly embedded in communities with their sons and daughters attending the Missionaries schools. How could any local American police or the DEA have any suspicions regarding drugs when the Familia Dei members were model upstanding citizens in the community? It appeared they all had respectable jobs and most seemed relatively wealthy. At least, one could say most were upper middle class economically to be able to afford the tuition of the schools and reside in upscale subdivisions.

"I knew them all. Becoming a pillar of Crestbrook looking after the boys as disciplinarian, teaching religion, coaching one or two sports, and joining Familia Dei, I was the role model that might never be suspected of any wrongdoing or conduct bordering the criminal. I had gained everyone's respect, and had the reputation of being a firm disciplinarian that kept the boys in line which is something many of the parents couldn't do in their homes. The trust factor was in place for those who thought my dedication was to Crestbrook. I played my role perfectly and pulled it off for many years. For the most part when I met with parents or groups of the parents privately and socially, we conversed in Spanish which made me appear even more convincing in the school setting. Father Alfredo referred to me as protean before I looked the word up in a dictionary to see what the hell he was calling me. When Ramon sent me I never could have known what my life was to be."

I sat quietly and just listened.

How the hell could they all be so unsuspecting? This guy couldn't have been that perfect.

23

United States
Atlanta

The parents of the children attending the Missionaries' schools in North America were a cross-section of society in terms of race and ethnicity, but not of economic status. Simply because of numbers or percentages there were many Caucasians and few Afro-Americans. The vast majority of students were of Hispanic descent. The influence of the Order in Mexico and the Familia Dei membership among the hundreds of thousands of Catholics living and worshipping in the Spanish speaking nations led parents to seek schools that the Order ran in the U.S. and elsewhere. This is not a strange phenomenon, but a significant one. The cultural and language sophistication that these people shared made it reasonable that they would develop a social bond in the regions where they settled and worked in American cities.

The parents of students were well educated and came from the upper classes of their respective societies. The money to be inherited by children was the inherited money of the previous generation. And there was usually lots of it. Businesses that were begun and grown by grandparents, and then passed down to children were the sources of great family wealth and influence. Granted, there were self-starters who over time made it big and entered the ranks of the well-to-do. There were people who apparently amassed their fortunes by having the political connections that allowed them to succeed. In a new environment this was not frowned upon, but sycophants of men in politically high places were not as admired for accomplishment as those people who acquired family wealth or otherwise made it on their own in an enterprising way.

Rather than explain and track the origins of the money of individuals, Marco chose to generalize and inform me of the connections many of these new, but legal, citizens had in the Latino countries, particularly Mexico and Colombia. For his part in the distribution of drugs in the U.S. he only needed a few people of influence in his organization. These were not difficult to secure because, as well off as they were, greed is an incredible motivator even when major risks are likely. But these men were generous too when it came to spending. One story he related to me I especially detailed in my reporting.

"Marco, we need to do something with some of this money," Angel Gomez who was a cartel associate and a Familia Dei member at Crestbrook said. "We have been talking of using two to three million dollars to construct a permanent building for the primary and elementary grades. As it is now the little school classes are held in the temporary building that was put up several years ago which is now quite run-down and requires too much money to renovate. It appears necessary at this time to construct an appropriate school building suitable for our children. I want you to approach the Missionaries' Fathers and offer our proposal to put up a new building. I don't think they will say no. Tell them how it will improve the campus as a whole, and also how it will serve to entice the registration of many more students who attend public school today. They only need to know that the building will be paid for completely, and that they will have no mortgage to worry about. You can say that a group of donors came to you, some being parents of the children. Knowing how the Church operates I do not think there will be a discussion, just permission to go ahead and get started with the project. They won't even ask you the origin of the money."

Being very pleased with the suggestion and offer, Marco responded affirmatively. "Angel, this is a great idea and a noble one. We do need a modern facility for the children. Also, it offers a place, a safe place, to put some of the money that would find itself being laundered. I'll speak to Father Tim here and bounce it off the Executive Director and then Nuestra Padre when I go to Mexico next time."

24

Italy
Iles d'Arda

"With the backing of Alfredo by many Cardinals in Rome even the attempt to bring charges against him appeared ridiculous," Marco said. "It was common knowledge that all but a small number of Cardinals were beholden to Father Alfredo for the gifts he had given to them in the past. Most all had accepted gifts and sums of money many times from Alfredo without knowing it was all manipulation. He was clever enough to bestow gifts with the knowledge that one day he may need their support against charges and claims that he would not be able to avoid. In order to defend himself he must rely on the Cardinals and others of the Vatican family who had eagerly accepted his largess over the years. Many of these men held high positions in the Vatican and were able to offer an impenetrable protective shield for Alfredo. One Secretary of State and another who was Prefect of Consecrated Life were ardent defenders of the man. Father Alfredo had received many donations over the years from Mexico's richest families and much of these were channeled to Rome, according to several priests who had long tenures in Rome. Of course, the sums of money from doing business were laundered and held in off-shore accounts. But there were hundreds of thousands of dollars humbly solicited from affluent Mexicans. Alfredo paid for an extensive renovation of the home of an Argentinian Cardinal. Examples of this type were later documented when Father Alfredo was finally brought to justice in the first trial."

▲ ▲ ▲

Marco did not say that he was aware of any complicity of the Vatican with Alfredo's long career as a criminal in the drug trade. It was known that certain members of the Curia had knowledge of Alfredo's addiction to morphine which they must have felt was not a concern any more than if he had been a long time alcoholic How they knew of his addiction, Marco did not reveal to me at this time.

The contention that two seminarians brought against Father Alfredo was rebuffed by the Director of the Seminaria del Fontanara in Madrid and the two seminarians were chastised for bringing such an absurd and even ludicrous suggestion to the attention of the Director. They brought forth the rumors of Father Alfredo being a pedophile knowing that upon investigation they could be substantiated. It was a completely repulsive thought that anyone could think that the august Father Alfredo with all the accomplishments he had brought to the Church could be suspect of such a heinous violation of any human being. Ted and Edmund were rebuked with such austerity that they reconsidered bringing an official charge against Alfredo to any higher authority in the Church, or even going to the civil authorities. The Director reminded them of a portion of the Order's constitution referred to as "Clandestine Vows." In essence those men ordained in the Order pled never to speak against their founder and their superiors. A corollary to this was the obligation to report anyone who even expressed criticism. This was a major rule instituted by Alfredo to deflect any scrutiny into his conduct as an abuser and pedophile. Internally, it was a well-established fact that fear, rather than faith, was the guide that kept members of the Order in line. Over a long period of time only three examples were noted of men with a conscience taking grave concerns to their superiors in the seminary and then being transferred with immediacy to distant posts not especially desired. They all had been warned about the pejorative nature of the issue.

Edmund and Ted felt that a smarter course of action was to regroup and wait for a more auspicious occasion to file a charge when they could assemble a good number of their colleagues in both the seminaries of Coalcojana and del Fontanara. They knew that their time would come when Father Alfredo sank deeper into a pit he could never pull himself from. They knew they could patiently await that moment.

Marco assured me that that moment definitely came.

25

Italy
Iles d'Arda

"Since the beginning of time when men realized the value of the magic plant that could turn weed into gold, they also knew that they had to have ways to transport and distribute the product," Marco began. "Methods were established and most of them were highly efficient. The roads and highways were the most accessible so they were utilized and provided an exceptionally good avenue for moving drugs from place of origin to distribution point. Cartels moved their merchandise at will sometimes encountering hostility along the way. Oftentimes government authorities or rival cartels would intercept shipments and men would die in the dirt. Planes on airfields hidden in the density of jungle foliage also provided a quick means of transporting drugs and proved reliable. There was always a plethora of unemployed pilots who would take risks of capture and imprisonment to fly cargo. Their services were well compensated. Also, with Colombia having a coastline it was very convenient for drug runners to solicit all sorts of marine apparatus to convey their contraband to places far and wide. Risks were taken to float the drugs, but men and sailors were willing to take chances for the money. It was far more lucrative than trying to sell a boatload of fish at market."

▲ ▲ ▲

Marco informed me that the cartels were now attempting something new because of the increase of crackdowns on moving tons of cocaine and marijuana into Mexico. At approximately $2,000,000 per vessel the cartels had engineered special built submarines to continue their enterprise undetected. Some of the submarines are fitted to hold eight tons of cocaine and can travel to the African shore. For distribution from Mexico a sub takes about eight or nine days. Marco said that the technical know-how behind design and construction of these vessels is remarkable, but he had no idea where they were coming from. Ramon Munoz informed Marco of this latest delivery system because Marco had to help with the preparations near the secret locations on the Mexican coast where the submarines would be off-loaded. Security all the way from the dropoff point back to Coalcojana would be a massive undertaking involving hundreds of cartel personnel heavily armed. How many of the submarines were being employed by the cartels Marco said he did not know.

I found this information amazing. Some submarines in use were 30 to 40 meters long. Doing my conversion of meters to yards I figured some subs were 50 yards long and had to hold several crew members in addition to the tonnage of drugs they contained. Marco did know that Ramon's subs left Buenaventura, a poverty stricken port on the Pacific, and he mentioned to me that even the success of one sub reaching its destination unscathed carrying eight tons of cocaine would put hundreds of millions of dollars or euros into the cartel's coffers.

It was these immense shipments that reached Mexico that Marco was responsible for distributing across the border to the United States as Marco was Father Alfredo's number one trafficker for a long period of time. He felt that one country's efforts to end the transport by sub would never happen, but that eventually all enforcement agencies of both Americas would have to combine forces to detect and destroy the drug cartels' submarines. Until such time the cartel would continue making millions of dollars for Marco, himself, and for Father Alfredo to maintain his life style and his contributions to his beloved Order and the Church.

It was during this conversation that Marco told me about Ramon Munoz's death. Not knowing all that I was going to hear with this man's story of a life steeped in illegal activity and crime, I was stunned with this part of the story concerning Ramon. The reason was that from the beginning when we first sat down and I began to learn who all the players were, I just figured that a man like Ramon Munoz was a survivor. In my mind he was eventually going to surrender to authorities, work out a great deal and ride off to a hacienda in the countryside with millions of U.S. dollars hidden or even buried in various places. Not so.

▲ ▲ ▲

Marco told me that among the many petty squabbles and more severe altercations that resulted from a meeting of cartel capos who disagreed, there were some that left very hard feelings on an individual. An intense dispute arose between Ramon and Carlos de Rigga on one occasion where agreement couldn't be reached and the effects of that would be carried to extreme limits. It was an accepted rule that all cartel members attending a meeting and sitting at table would be unarmed. This did not hold for others who were present, but not at table directly engrossed in the business of the day or night. Meetings normally were held at a remote place which was a compound only known to the capos who would attend. Their bodyguards would escort them to the meeting, but would not have knowledge of the rendezvous beforehand.

 A shipment of cocaine was sent by submarine out of port on the coast, but it never arrived in Mexico as scheduled. Evidently, an alternate sea route was selected by Ramon or one of his top underlings to seclude the cargo. This was the logical thought that Carlos applied to the situation. Ramon with the most urgent remonstrations attempted to persuade Carlos that he was completely unaware of what was now a calamity. His protestations were being ignored. Carlos reminded Ramon of the value of the cargo and without a second's hesitation signaled to a sicarios to assassinate. Instantaneous gunfire found several targets on both sides of the room. Carnage! Carlos emerged unscathed, and was in total command.

▲ ▲ ▲

"By this time I was a major player at Coalcojana with Father Alfredo and, therefore, was not back in Colombia at Medellin," said Marco. "I hadn't even been to El Ritera in the past year, and I hadn't heard about Ramon's death for several weeks, but knew it would be inadvisable to ask any questions. My heart told me that Ramon was honorable and would do nothing to deceive or cheat. At this time I had no direct connection with the Colombian cartel and was solely interested in my position in Mexico and the United States. I surmised that it would be up to Alfredo alone to deal with Colombia for future shipments. Any future dealings were out of my control; I was satisfied that the good Father would be negotiating with de Rigga's cartel, which was a tremendous sense of relief for me to know that I was not answerable to the capos in Medellin. Besides, Alfredo and Carlos had a history together. Carlos was a carryover from the Cali Cartel who regarded the system that Alfredo set up as ingenious. Alfredo had seen the dissension in the way things were run, so he set up smaller controllable groups. One's responsibility was to smuggle the drugs from Colombia to Mexico. Another's was to control the jungle labs. Another's was to transport the coca base to the labs from the fields. He brought some harmony to the whole operation where previously greed for complete control created a messy situation. De Rigga was a damn shrewd businessman. He conducted smuggling as a sophisticated business quietly investing in legitimate businesses and being far more subtle and less flashy than most of his former counterparts in Colombia including Ramon Munoz."

▲ ▲ ▲

I could easily see by his whole demeanor how Marco felt knowing he was free from his former contacts in Colombia. I had only my imagination to sense what this meant. I'm positive he didn't think he could not be subject to some blame if a major screw-up occurred somewhere along the line, but his indirect association removed a weight from his shoulders. He was gratified with the arrangement.

26

United States
Washington D.C.

Anna Ralston and Jeanette Libramont were two business women who had proven that they were as competent as any male counterparts or would-be captains of industry. After graduating from Yale University and earning a degree in international business, Anna Ralston attended law school with the intention of going back to her little town of Stafford Springs in upstate Connecticut and opening an office where she would practice law and be content to live a peaceful life. Anna was a beautiful girl in college and had blossomed into a very beautiful woman. Her beauty was certain to be an asset that would propel her in her profession. She was tall---about five foot nine and didn't look her hundred and thirty five pounds, despite her height. With her breadth of shoulder and depth of bosom, her straight figure showed off a svelteness rather than an athletic build with the appearance of one ready to encounter any eventuality. Her shoulder-length blonde hair added greatly to her striking appearance. And when her hair did fall to her shoulders after business hours at the firm, her sexiness was totally apparent.

Jeanette was a woman who had been born in Luxembourg. She had the good fortune of being born into a prosperous family which provided her with the best education that any young woman could be given in Europe. Jeanette had a superior gift of being able to acquire languages with ease and from an early age knew that she would put this gift to great use in the profession she chose. Her father was a wealthy businessman who traveled extensively to the United States, Canada, Mexico, and South America. From twelve years of age Jeanette would travel with her father during the months she was not in school and relished every opportunity to acquaint herself with all aspects of these foreign cultures. While in school, Jeannette was considered by her peers as too serious and too academic, and therefore, a bit of a dull person. But, after college, and with the nurturing that her travels abroad gave her, Jeannette matured into a beautiful woman whose charm and exceptional looks were the advantage she would have to make her way successfully in the world of work and play. Her eyes reflected a coolness which shone and held a steady gaze at the same time. Her hair was a chestnut shade with a bronze sheen. She had a typically classic nose which suggested aristocracy. Though the portrait painter would see her mouth as rather wide, any young male observer would see inviting lips that were nice to look at. Her countenance and stature, similar to Anna's, reflected strong and pleasant womanly attributes, determination, tolerance, sense of humor.

It was fate that Anna and Jeanette would one day come together, each bringing her own expertise to create a page in history that would astonish the leadership of such a world renowned institution as the Church and the masses of people who were totally unaware of the scandal they helped bring to light.

Anna did not become a small home town lawyer; instead she was offered a position in a prestigious firm in Washington D.C. after she passed the bar exam. Jeanette did not remain in Luxembourg after she had attended schools in Germany and France where she majored in history and business and became highly proficient in five languages. Her proficiency in German, French, Spanish, English and Italian besides her native language, and her extensive background in European and American history brought her to the attention of high ranking executives in American banking. Naturally, her father had substantial input in his daughter's progression from schoolgirl to professional. His contacts world-wide would have secured an enviable position for her almost anywhere on the globe, but because of his many friends in New York City and Washington D.C. he was only too happy to see Jeanette take a position in the U.S. In addition, he was well aware of how this could be of advantage to him having her as an intermediary for some of his business dealings.

The aspect of both girls' jobs that would eventually force their relationship was the amount of travel each would do as necessary to their work. The firm Anna joined required her to spend time in Lisbon, Madrid, Zurich and Rome. International law was the specialty of Dempsey, Rodriguez, and Schmidt, LLC, so Anna's time would be divided between the office in Washington and the offices in Europe. She was elated that she would be able to work and travel seeing many of the interesting and charming and romantic places she had only read about or had seen in pictures. The cultural centers of the Iberian Peninsula and Italy would be accessible and give her an educational background that would profoundly influence her life.

Deutsches Bank of New York had offices in several European cities and Jeannette found the best of both worlds in the fact she could conduct banking business, and be able to spend time in many familiar cities where she had scores of friends and acquaintances. Each trip to the Continent would be like going home. The opportunities presented to meet ranking executives in the banking world would broaden her views immensely and prepare her for a career that only seemed real in movies or paperback novels.

▲ ▲ ▲

"Excuse me. Sorry to disturb you. I have the seat next to the window," Jeanette said.

"Oh, okay. Let me just grab my purse. I thought I was in 14B," responded Anna.

Exasperated, Jeannette said, "What a day! I had all I could do to get to Dulles on time for my flight. There was an accident on the expressway and I just missed being locked in traffic by two minutes."

"Lucky. Some times in this D.C. whirlwind of congestion on the road we're fortunate to get from point A to point B. in a sensible length of time. Otherwise, forget it," said Anna.

"Yeah, by the time the cab picked me up at the office I didn't have that much leeway to get here for my flight. Occasionally, someone's looking out for me, I guess. Most of the time I'm frazzled and have to make a run for the gate after I get through security. And then I hope I'm headed in the right direction. Today, I was. Made it to Gate 7, flight 1452 to London."

"Oh, you work in London?" Anna asked.

"No, not really. I'm just there to meet a colleague about some business. Do you work in England?"

"Yes. Some days my work takes me to England. But it takes me to several other cities in Europe as well." Most of my work here takes me to Zurich, but I'm in Madrid or Lisbon or Rome almost as often. By way of introduction, my name's Anna Ralston. And yours?"

"I'm Jeannette Libramont. Wow! You do get around. When I complete my obligations in London these next three days, I'm heading to Madrid to visit relatives. Is Madrid on your schedule this trip? When will you be there next?"

"Well actually, Jeannette, after meeting with my London co-worker, I'm off to Madrid for a meeting," Anna said.

"What is your line of work, Anna?"

"I'm an attorney for Dempsey, Rodriguez, and Schmidt in Washington. Ever hear of the firm?"

"As a matter of fact, I have. I work for Deutsches Bank. The New York office. But I have had business that has involved law firms, and certainly I'm familiar with yours, one of the largest in D.C. isn't it?"

"Yes. Next to Boies, Schiller, and Flexner I believe we are. I'm sure you've heard of them, the firm of the giant bonuses? I had an interview with Cravath, Swaine and Moore in New York, but decided to work in D.C. My specialty is international law. That's what takes me abroad so often. Sometimes I think I travel more than the Secretary Of State. Policies with our good friends in Europe keep me hopping."

After two and a half hours of conversation on the plane, Anna and Jeannette had discussed their jobs, their families and backgrounds. They discussed world events and seemed to be able to offer solutions to most of the world's woes that man faces. They harmoniously agreed on what position governments should take and what policies should be formulated to create a better world. Dialogue between them was easy and casual and most of all enjoyable. Subconsciously each woman was feeling that a permanent friendship could endure long after they alighted the plane and went their individual ways.

"Anna, after you conclude your business, why not meet me in Madrid? After all, you are going there, and we could hang out for some time. Tell you what. I'd like you to stay with me because I'll be at my aunt and uncle's place just outside the city. There's all kinds of room and you'll love my family. I know they'll love meeting you."

"Oh. I wouldn't think to be a bother, Jeannette. I'm sure it would be an imposition for me, a stranger..."

"No way. I think it's a great idea. We'll both be finished with our work and it'll be fun to have a new friend there. We'll chill out for a few days before having to get back to the U.S. Agreed?"

"Okay, I appreciate the offer. We can get to know each other better, and have a relaxing holiday," Anna said, with anticipation in her voice.

Both young women were so comfortable in their view toward one another that the experience of having a respite at Jeannette's aunt and uncle's place for a few days would help to cement a lasting friendship. They clearly felt that it was destiny that brought them together.

27

United States
Boston

TedOD@crestbrook.edu

Ted, after my Board Meeting on the 16th your mother and I will be flying out to meet you. We're scheduled to leave at 7:35 am on a direct flight and should arrive in Madrid early afternoon.

    It will be great to see you since our last visit. I know we communicate irregularly by e-mail, but our get-togethers at the hotel and dinners in the evening are special to your mother and me. I know I don't have to ask about your studies, but are you getting out enough to explore parts of Spain that the family didn't see during our vacations when you and the girls were young? I know the seminary monitors closely, but it lets you guys out from behind locked doors on weekends once in a while to broaden your social skills and travel experiences. You won't be back to Spain for a long time after you leave. You'll study and be ordained in Rome and then the Missionaries will be placing you at one of their schools in the U.S. No telling when you might get another chance to visit Europe after that unless you decide to study for a doctorate and the Order okays that.

    Write so we'll know the exact time we can meet either at the seminary or at our hotel.

You know we always stay at the Ritz. Say hello to Edmund for us. It'll be a pleasure to see him, too. Make sure he plans to spend time with us. We'll look forward to having a great few days together. Any trouble getting out and I'll call the Director on his private line.
    Love, Dad

Spain
Madrid

mvtodriscoll@mindspring.com

Dad, thanks for the update about your trip over. I'm really excited about seeing you and Mother. Yes. They do let us out occasionally to see the sights. I try to take advantage of every opportunity to see all that I can while in Spain for the remainder of time I'll be here. I have to admit, though, that I am counting the months before I get to Rome. Final phase, you know. Edmund is happy you're coming to visit. You know how much he enjoys being with the family and discussing issues of the day with you.
    Looking forward to the 16th. I'll meet you and Mother at the hotel. I'll be there about 3:30.
    Love, Ted

P.S. I didn't realize epistemology was such a bore, but I'm doing very well in philosophy in general. Love reading Aquinas and Duns Scotus.

▲ ▲ ▲

Later, I learned from Marco who probably got his information from Father Alfredo that compared to the seminary in Mexico, communicating with family was not as prohibited for seminarians at del Fontanara in Spain even though the superiors did try to keep the students secluded. The boys were older and further along into their studies, so they were regarded as very serious and intent upon continuing theological courses in Rome which led to their ordination. Unless guilty of some wild and crazy escapade, a student's progress at this point would not be halted by the Order. But that is not to say that Father Alfredo could not for some reason toss someone out. It was a known fact that he even transferred ordained priests from a placement to some other one a bit remote for what he considered a justifiable cause. Having pledged their allegiance to Nuestra Padre, the name Alfredo wished to be called, they had no recourse.

While in Mexico it was a different situation altogether as boys were required to remain away from family and almost never correspond with family members. This seemed like a harsh measure, but one must remember that Nuestra Padre, the Director, had imposed many strict rules which were enforced right to the letter. Many of the students were teenagers and some even one and two years younger. One would think parents obligated to keep in frequent touch with their young sons, but the administration had them convinced or brainwashed that distance or isolation was better for the adjustment of their sons to the seminary. How convenient for Father Alfredo.

It would have been a sorry day for the seminary if Teddy O'Driscoll wasn't permitted to call home or e-mail his family. M.V.T. O'Driscoll would have been on a plane to Mexico in an instant to straighten out anyone who forbade his son a phone call. Old Man O'Driscoll had lots of friends in high places and that included the Church. He would have raised holy hell to make certain things were agreeable to him. Another significant fact was the matter of donations to the Order that M.V.T. made available in the form of sizable checks. Mr. O'Driscoll was not a man to alienate. So the Order didn't.

28

Mexico
Coalcojana

"Father, how much morphine are you taking? You know that your use has gone too far, and the mix with other stuff you take is no damn good for keeping business matters straight. Do what you need to without having it interfere with our operation. But you better back off the morphine in spite of the severity of pain you say you're suffering."

I'm not that addicted to abuse it like he does. Medicinal, my ass. With what I'm doing I always need to keep a clear head.

"I'm in constant pain, Marco, so I need it. You don't know it, but I've got a dispensation from the Holy Father in Rome to use drugs as I see fit for the malady I try to put up with. I have been quite open with him so he is aware of my suffering and has permitted me to use strong medication for the abdominal pain I need to relieve when it becomes so intense."

"I'm only saying don't let it get too strong a grip on you, or it's going to lead to trouble for our business. By the way, part of that last drop I have to see through to some of our people in Georgia. They need to move some of it into Knoxville and up the east coast to New York."

"Don't worry about me, Marco. Damn it all! I've been in the business for a very long time, and I also know how to handle the drugs I take for medicinal purposes. On that other matter, yes. Follow it closely. You can get it through Juarez and then across. Hernandez and Ovieda families can move it without any problem. I like knowing that Jose Hernandez has such sterling credentials that he could move it in plastic bags on top of his car in daylight hours without the police stopping him. He's like a magician when it comes to doing his part. A shrewd businessman, great contacts, outstanding citizen and member of the Movement. He'll never be suspected. And Ovieda. When these two travel together they're damn ingenious."

"That may be," said Marco. " But the operation could never have happened if you hadn't the brainstorm in the first place. Who would ever have thought a man of great renown could get something like this started and all under the perfect cover. A man who started a seminary, began an order of clergy, and all that. When I started with my father and uncle under Ramon Munoz I had no idea where we were taking the shipments when we got to Coalcojana. No one would tell me anything. They said I didn't need to know. If Ramon didn't send me here for you to get me to the schools up north for distribution, I'd never have known who you were."

"We'll have to call it fate, my young friend. But fate is putting mucho dollars in our pockets, or should I say accounts. Which reminds me that I must make a trip to the Caymans presently. Incognito of course. I so admire the level of secrecy at George Town. Usually I have one of my most trusted subordinates from the seminary office to handle my business there, but I will go myself this time to see about the Foundations' accounts as well. If I am not here let me know how the drop at Juarez goes when I return. You can call me from Crestbrook if you like. My best regards to our executive director, Dick Sturm, and principal, John Largent. You and they have done admirable work in expanding Familia Dei with the help of our consecrated. You can give me a full account of membership at all the schools when you can get a report together, let's say by month's end."

"Fine! I'll take care of it. One other thing, Padre. My associates at Crestbrook have made a proposal to me. They want to pay for a new class building for their elementary school children. They are talking about 2 to 3 million. I've spoken to the people up north about it and they welcome the idea. I said I would speak to you to get a final word."

"It sounds like a very good idea. I give my approval. You will oversee the project as it unfolds. Those men can afford it certainly. They rake off enough from what we send up there. They could build two new buildings. Be careful, though, as we do not want to seem like we have too much money that it will stop the flow of donations or disrupt the capital fund drive.

I must have collected at least 30 million this past year alone. I'll never disclose how much I've taken in. The figure would make the heads in Rome spin off their shoulders if they even had the slightest inkling.

29

Spain
Madrid

"Teddy O'Driscoll! Is that really you? What are you doing here in Madrid? I haven't seen you since we left Yale. Oh, my God. I can't believe it's you," Anna said in utter disbelief and astonishment.

"Hello, Anna. What a shocker seeing you. It has to be four or five years. This is fantastic meeting you here. Well, one thing I know is you stay at top hotels when in Europe. I'd never expect to run into a former classmate outside the Ritz in Madrid."

They found a place to sit and began a pleasant conversation for quite a long time.

"Are you a priest now, Ted? I see the collar you're wearing." Anna was a bit dumbfounded as she never figured Ted was the type of young man who would enter the priesthood.

"No, Anna. Not yet anyway. I'm finishing my three years at Seminaria del Fontanara. Then I go to Rome to study before ordination. So, I have a ways to go before you call me Father O'Driscoll."

"Christ, I never would have believed it. Oh, I shouldn't have said that! Everyone thought you and Christy Reiman would be married with kids by now. You two were inseparable for our four years at Yale. Who dumped whom, or shouldn't I ask that? God! Oh, sorry again. Two of the most prominent families in Boston, you and Christy were a match made in heaven. That's okay to say, isn't it?"

"Yes, that's okay to say, but the thought is incorrect. We got along great for quite a while, but I came to realize that marriage wasn't what I wanted, and I didn't want Christy to be misled. You know what I mean. I just thought one day what I wanted to do with my life and I entered the seminary. We had to break it off."

Boy! Anna's better looking now than when I knew her in school. What a beauty she is.

"Holy smokes! I just can't believe it. But I am believing that we are standing here at this hotel in Spain and I'm talking to you." This is excellent. How do you happen to be here?"

He is still amazingly handsome with that smile that's giving me chills.

"My parents are coming in this afternoon from Boston and I'm meeting them. They are here visiting for a few days as it will most likely be the last visit before I go to Rome. What brings you to Madrid?"

"I'm a lawyer and I have a business meeting here at the hotel. This is a convenient and economically reasonable location for a number of countries whose representatives are convening regarding some international legal stuff."

"That's great. How long are you here? Maybe you could have dinner with my parents and me tomorrow if your work is concluded. Even if it isn't you still have to eat, so why not join us. My parents will probably want to stay and dine right at the hotel. It has one of the best restaurants in the city. El Restaurante Goya has the best gazpacho in Spain."

"I suppose I could do that, Ted. I have no commitment until the day after tomorrow. I will be staying with a friend outside Madrid, but until then I'm at the hotel."

"Excellent! Let's say we'll meet in the lobby at 6:00. Any problem call down to the desk. Ok. Have a good meeting. Hope it doesn't last forever." Ted didn't want to seem like he was hurrying her, but he didn't want to delay her from her engagement inside the hotel.

"Bye, Ted. See you at six tomorrow evening"

Whew! Is she ever stunning, and always had the great personality to complete the package.

Fifteen minutes later the O'Driscolls arrived at the Ritz, greeted their son with big hugs and a big kiss from Mom. They were always a loving and demonstrative family.

▲ ▲ ▲

"Mom, Dad, you're both looking great! I've missed you. And I'm so happy you decided to come to Spain to visit before I leave here. We'll have a nice time over the next three days. I've planned a few things that should be fun for us."

"Son, you're looking fit. Must be the great food at the seminary and all the good exercise you get running to classes. Gordon Ramsey still cooking for you guys? Ha, Ha," laughed Mr. O'Driscoll rather obnoxiously at what he thought was a funny.

His mom said, "Teddy, everyone back home misses you so much. You've been gone a long time. It's wonderful to be here with you. We'll have a great time."

"Thanks, Mom," said Ted. "Here, I have something for you. It's been blessed by the Pope and I know it will be meaningful to you."

"Teddy, it is wonderful! Look, Martin, a picture of Ted with the Pope and Father Alfredo."

If it turns out Alfredo's an abuser, I'll rip that picture to shreds when I get back home.

Mr. and Mrs. O'Driscoll had felt saddened when Ted had first told them of his breakup with Christy and about his intent to enter the priesthood. They thought their only son would one day marry the girl of his dreams and provide them with grandchildren just as so many sons did. Knowing that would not happen with their son, they gradually accepted his decision thinking he would join the local diocesan order of secular priests and be in a parish nearby. They had never heard of the Missionaries of the Holy Church Order and were stunned when Ted apprised them of the length of seminary study that would take him to three foreign countries for several years. Of course, they knew there would be frequent correspondence and some visits, but still, so many years away from home.

"Mom, Dad, do you remember the name Anna Ralston, the friend of Christy that went to Yale with us. She's in Madrid staying at this hotel. I met her here and we talked a bit this afternoon. I've asked her to dinner with us tomorrow night. I hope that's alright?"

30

United States
Georgia

Marco found it very easy to coordinate his principal objective of moving drugs from the South to locations in the East and Midwest with the help of key members of Familia Dei. The distribution from the schools was set up around educational conventions that convened at one school one time and another the next. All units came together under the hoax of being ad hoc committees with various educational names under the main theme for the convention. For example, the theme might be "The Three Tiers of Formative Development" with several groups each having a title which would identify it as a participant, and also be intended to divert any attention from its true purpose for being there. The meeting would center on those conducting it: the administrators, members of the Order who were guest speakers and committee discussion leaders, curriculum specialists from within the Missionaries school system and some from the neighboring public and private schools nearby who would be invited to participate. All appearances showed a bona fide symposium taking place.

Marco loved these educational events as they completely threw off any notice of what his involvement was in conjunction with those few members who were present simply to use the school as a point of drug distribution. There were so many people coming and going during the entire days of the meetings that no one, not even the cops directing traffic at the main entrance to the campus, would be cognizant of anything resembling illegal trafficking in drugs. It was an amazing set up. The cover was perfect. Inconspicuous as hell! And it worked magnificently every time.

Upon hearing this from Marco, I was reminded of a story in the past of a mafia meeting that took place in northern New York State where Mafioso from all over came for an organizational gathering. They thought that no one would notice sixty big black Eldorados descending on a farm location in the middle of Appalachia. It was simply a barbecue, hot dogs and hamburgers and beer. But they were noticed and all types of law enforcement surrounded the place and made arrests. Marco and the intellectuals in his band of outlaws were far more savvy than one-hundred guys in black suits and white shirts of the planning and precautions they had to put into play for their operation to succeed time after time. Just as the secret service has an advanced party taking all necessary steps to ensure safety before a dignitary arrives, Marco was far better remunerated to make assurances that his cargo would be safe and no one got arrested.

▲ ▲ ▲

"Being a Colombian national and having a work visa to Mexico, how did you get into the United States?" I asked Marco.

"How do you think? That I just drove across the goddamn border? You forget that when you're connected to a cartel there's all kinds of documents, illegal of course, that give you free movement from one country to another, but not the U.S. I had the Order take care of everything for me. They made sure I got the correct documentation for entry into the United States with an H1b which allows me to work in the country and go back and forth to Mexico. The only restriction was that I can't be gone longer than six months at any one time, and that's no problem. Father Alfredo took care of all the necessary arrangements for me to be hired at Crestbrook and be able to travel to the other schools and the sem in Connecticut."

When I reflect on this I think the U.S. is probably the easiest country to enter either legally or illegally. They have little idea who is coming in and what they're capable of doing. Too damn trusting. But lucky for me.

"No one at a border ever asked any questions?" I asked. "I'll tell you I don't think it would have been the same if you were crossing from Canada, particularly from Fort Erie to Buffalo. Those guys in Customs and Immigration there scrutinize incoming pedestrians and traffic like crazy. Better that you avoided flying into Pierre Trudeau in Toronto too. The agents there really get to the nitty gritty when they sense anything. That's not to say you would have had any problem, being the cool headed criminal you were."

"Thanks, but I always regarded myself as a cool businessman. Buying and selling was the name of the game. I learned very early how to handle myself and sound convincing to authorities whenever I left the country and returned. I had the benefit of not looking like a Colombian or sounding like a Hispanic to Americans, so I never was looked at in a suspicious way. Besides, my documentation was always in perfect order that no one would question me or my purposes. I never experienced trouble or being detained at any border crossing. Maybe just luck, but I don't think so."

▲ ▲ ▲

Marco may have sounded cocky or arrogant to me when he said this, but I did have to agree that from the American view he was a good looking guy that could easily have passed for anyone's brother. He always dressed like an American businessman, so he didn't give any vibes that he was anything but a young man going about his work to make a living, and if he ever needed to show customs and immigration officials pictures of his blonde wife and light skinned children, he was waved forward after his credentials were checked and verified.

31

Mexico
Coalcojana

LYNX@crestbrook.edu

Marco, I do not want you to forget about the report you are to give me by the end of the month. I suspect that all went well at the conference in Madison. Be aware of the arrangements for getting the money sent through proper channels to the Gonzales Foundation so there can be no possible trace of the funds. The U.S. Superior, Father Mark Daly desires to confer with you and the executive directors of the eastern schools at a meeting to be held at the Double Tree Hotel in Buckhead, Georgia. The directors will fly or drive in for the meeting. Make all arrangements for it. Get back to Father Mark and send notices to the E.D.'s. Plan to be in Coalcojana the first week of next month. As usual, fly into Mexico City. There will be a car waiting.

L.

latente@sem1.edu

Yes, L. All will be taken care of. Funds from delivery in Madison are secure in proper accounts of Foundation. Packages were divided and distributed. Members traveling cautiously to home bases. All went better than planned just like last time.

See you in Mexico.

Lynx

▲ ▲ ▲

I was told by Marco that e-mail was the means of communication for expediency purposes when merely messaging. When the trade was included in the message, however, everything was encrypted using a system devised by Father Alfredo that used parts of the gospels, epistles, and psalms of the Bible. For example, the above correspondence of Father Alfredo used St. Paul to the Philippians, chapter 4, verses 4+: "Your kindness should be known to all. The lord is near. Have no anxiety at all" and from Luke's gospel: "His winnowing fan is in His hand to clear his threshing floor and to gather the wheat into his barn." Also cryptically included were words from a letter to the Hebrews, 10:5+: "Sacrifice and offering you did not desire, but a body you prepared for me."

Marco's response was from the Book of the Prophet Zephaniah, 3:14+ which states "The Lord has removed the judgment against you, he has turned away your enemies; the King of Israel, the lord is in your midst. You have no further misfortune to fear." Also, from the Book of Micah, 5:1+, "He shall stand firm and shepherd his flock."

▲ ▲ ▲

Interestingly to me, were several of the well-known Biblical phrases they used to transmit messages, such as "I shall not want," "verdant pastures," "my cup overflows." "manna from Heaven." Cleverly encrypted meanings showed clearly in "slaughter the fattened calf," Luke's gospel, and I liked the ones Marco showed me in another message from Psalms 126:4-5:

"Restore our fortunes, O Lord, like the torrents in the southern desert. Those that sow in tears shall reap rejoicing." And from St. Paul to the Philippians, 3:8+ which says: "Forgetting what lies behind but straining forward to what lies ahead, I continue my pursuit toward the goal."

Also, code names (Latente, Lynx) were always used. Marco was extra cautious at times when he was to communicate with parent members of Familia Dei who were his committed cartel compadres. Some of the clandestine messages to the cartel were Isaiah, 40"1+: "Every valley shall be filled in, every mountain and hill shall be made low; the rugged land shall be made a plain, the rough country, a broad valley." Another strong encouragement to the cartel was Jeremiah, 1:4-5: "For it is I who have made you a fortified city, a pillar of iron, a wall of brass, against the whole land….They will fight against you but not prevail over you, for I am with you to deliver you." On the surface, all nicely packaged memos to the men that simply appeared to be the holy writings of a religious man. E-mail was always used to correspond with the Order's Director-General in the U.S. and others of the Order as there was never anything besides F.D. business that was sent. The radio link-ups were usually the means when certain narco business was transacted.

The communications system that the cartel in Mexico used was quite a sophisticated radio network that involved hidden radio antennae and signal relay stations connected to solar panels. Facilities were linked to radio receiving cell phones and phone devices. Throw away phones that could not be detected or transmit any conversations that could be retrieved were used. Also, all conversations that required it were encrypted, and if intercepted, it would be too late to decode to halt any intended activity.

32

**Spain
Madrid**

JL@deutschesbank.com

Jeannette, I will be waiting in the lobby of the Ritz. I will say goodbye to my international colleagues at 7am and be waiting for you. Anna

AR@DRSfirm.org

Anna, having exchanged e-mails made this easy. I'll pick you up at the hotel. I'm leaving my aunt's now, so I shouldn't be too long. The Ritz has great biscotti at that little kiosk between the front entrance and the hallway to the shops. Grab one for me and bring a cup of coffee too. I haven't had anything to eat yet and I don't want to stop before getting to Madrid. Thanks. Jeannette

▲ ▲ ▲

"Hi, You weren't waiting too long, were you, Anna? I made good time getting here. Not much traffic on the country roads, so I cruised right along."

"Hi, Jeannette. No. I just walked outside figuring you'd be here any minute. You did make good time. Here's your coffee and biscotti. I had mine while I was waiting. Can you drive and eat at the same time?" She was quick to notice that Jeannette had either rented an upscale sedan that was obviously very pricey, or that she was driving an expensive Benz that belonged to her uncle.

"You ought to see me back in New York when I'm trying to deal with coffee and something for breakfast on the subway. When I get a seat there's no juggling act, but when I stand, that's trouble."

"How far do we go to get to Pina Grande?"

"Not far. About 22 kilometers, that's about 35 miles, I think."

"You know, I have to tell you something interesting. Two days ago I met a guy I knew at college right outside the hotel. He was waiting for his parents to arrive from the States. Last night I had dinner with them and spent a pleasant evening. I could not believe that I ran into him right here in Madrid. He's a seminarian at some place he mentioned here in the city. I hope you don't mind, but I got into some conversation about your uncle who's a Cardinal from Luxembourg. I mentioned that Ted should go to see him when he is in Rome. I didn't overstep did I, Jeannette?"

"That's cool when something you'd never expect happens like that. What's this guy like? A real geek?" asked Jeannette. "And I don't mind at all, Anna."

"Oh, my God, no! He's a dream. I knew the girl well that he dated all through school. She was gorgeous. I never asked Ted why he and she broke up, but he did say he simply had a calling to be a priest. I never would have guessed it." I thought this was pretty amazing."

"Yeah, I guess these kinds of things happen. Well, just a short distance from here, Anna. Do you have someone that you're dating?"

"No. There are a couple of guys that I've met through work that I've gone out with, but no one I'm hooked on. And, of course, I don't want to even look that way at any of the lawyers in the firm. I believe that kind of involvement wouldn't be good. The workplace romance, you know. Do you have anybody special in your life, Jeannette?"

"No. I haven't had time for that. I've been so damn busy at the bank; I haven't really had an opportunity to nurture any kind of relationship.

Right after college, though, I met a great guy named Lew that I thought was someone I'd like to get to know a lot better. You know, one of those guys you feel has potential. But that wasn't going to work out. I was just getting started and he was entering medical school way out on the west coast. So, I just let it go. Here we are. We have arrived."

"I can't thank you enough, Jeannette, for inviting me here. It's a gorgeous setting to relax and have some fun for a couple of days. I'm ready for a tall glass of sangria."

"We'll have a blast. The beach down from the house is one of the best in this area, and my Uncle Dominique makes a super sangria."

"How do your aunt and uncle happen to be in Spain, Jeannette?"

"During the war my aunt's parents fled Luxembourg when the Germans were conscripting men whose mothers were German. I had several relatives that were taken from France where they went to get out of Germany thinking they were safe. My aunt and uncle have been here for many many years having escaped detection and incarceration by the Germans. They were safe in Spain and have adapted quite nicely to the area where they raised their children. I came here often with my mother to spend vacation time from school, and loved seeing my cousins and playing with them as children."

Just thinking of them and the good times I spent with them is wonderful. I have such great memories.

33

Italy
Iles d'Arda

"How did you get to know Father Alfredo that well, Marco?" I asked.

"You mean after Ramon sent me to him in Mexico?" he said.

"Yeah. How did you become a favorite, so to speak?"

"Well, for some reason I can't explain, I felt a closeness right from the beginning of our alliance. It wasn't the drug business or the operation that I was so drawn into the fold, but something else. What I mean is that I felt like Father Alfredo was somehow a part of my life, or was to become a meaningful part of my life. I don't know why. He accepted me as one of Ramon's men, but came to accept me as an essential part of his cartel. I was an essential part, and surprisingly at the beginning there was no mistrust or anything. That just doesn't happen. Not in the business we were in."

"Yeah. That is unusual. But you're saying that you felt some type of bond right from the first. Maybe it had something to do with him knowing you were a smart kid and you were going to oversee the distribution to the north through the schools." I was just surmising and trying to dig a little deeper for information.

"No. He didn't just know that because he didn't know me. It was his idea to plan all that out afterward. His idea was to place me in Georgia at Crestbrook and to educate me in the ways of Familia Dei so I'd have a legitimate reason for being at the school and getting in deep with the members who were going to assist me in running cocaine and marijuana to the East Coast and Midwest. It's almost like a guy who needed a brother that he could trust with his life to be a part of his operation. You know what I mean?"

▲ ▲ ▲

I was amazed at how he expressed himself. It was as though he had never thought about the relationship he had formed with one of the most powerful men in Mexico, a priest who began an Order, a priest who founded seminaries in Mexico and Spain, a priest who was a capo of a cartel that ran drugs into the U.S., a priest with incredible influence in Rome. I began to think that there was something he was not telling me that related to his association with Father Alfredo. But, I was simply hearing his story as he wanted to tell it. I couldn't help but wonder if he was not connecting all the dots for me for a good reason, or if it was just my intuitive mind thinking there was more to his story than he was relating at this point.

At the same time I thought Marco was numb about his relationship with Alfredo. I thought of my own situation with Marco and these thoughts gave rise to some immediate suspicions, Why am I really here at Iles d'Arda? What is it that Marco has to tell me about the past? Perhaps, it was time to get some straight answers now! I'd wait for the right moment and question him.

34

Italy
Iles d'Arda

Marco continued his story.

"The number of men ordained was thirty. Sixteen of those were of the Missionaries of the Holy Church. They had completed the final years of study in theology in Rome and were now ready to be assigned to various placements in the Order. Father Kelley and Father O'Driscoll were sent to the United States to serve at Crestbrook Academy in Georgia, one as a student counselor and one as the chaplain for the entire student body. Both served as confessors for students as well as for administrators and staff. It was not required that any one avail himself or herself to these priests as his or her confessor, but they were there for spiritual needs if they could be of service. The chaplain's function was to say masses daily and provide a schedule of formation classes and activities for the students, and be the spiritual director. Father O'Driscoll had his office in the school building where students knew they could enter to talk, and where he was visible during the day. With a good sized student population that Crestbrook had, the good Father was kept quite busy as counselor and also as a teacher of religion who taught one section of students. One year he might teach middle school, the next could be high school, so he got to know all the students by name.

"Both clergy were members of the administrative board. They would sit with the executive director, the principal, the assistant principal, both level coordinators, a lay person, and the priest in charge of all the Missionaries schools who was only present for budgetary matters, and myself. All of us lay people were members of the Familia Dei Movement within the Church.

"I have to tell you right now that none of these people knew about or were a part of the drug distribution operation that I and other people connected to the school were involved with. I cannot mention who the parents were, but I told you before that they were money people from Mexico with the closest ties to Father Alfredo. One might suspect that the two priests at the school were knowledgeable because of their years at the seminaries in Mexico and Spain, and because they had brought the question of pedophilia at the seminaries to the attention of the Director at del Fontanara when they were students there. I feel it is imperative that you know these men were not attached in any way to the illegal activity which I conducted for the cartel in Mexico. The Executive Director, Dick Sturm and the Principal John Largent were completely in the dark, and for that matter, about most things. They were clueless to most activities that went on outside their office doors. Inwardly, I was often surprised that a couple of the sharper minds at the school never picked up on things that should have seemed obvious at the time. I guess it's merely because the others and I carried out our mission without anyone detecting a flaw."

Bravo for me and my leadership. There goes my humility again.

"But ours was the business where there could not be a flaw. Our everyday lives were a ruse. The penalty for playing things loose and getting caught, or becoming suspicious, was severe for all involved. And that includes innocent family members who didn't have the slightest inkling that a spouse or father or brother was a major part of a criminal enterprise."

35

United States
Georgia

I wanted to ask someone qualified to answer the question that has been burning within me since I began to learn about the man who was the boy that came to a life of deceit and crime. Was it a part of his DNA that made him what he became? Or was it merely greed? How could a boy enter the seminary because he had a vocation to become a priest and devote his entire life to a loving and merciful God, and then turn into a callous criminal of the worst kind? The kind that takes advantage of and abuses a defenseless human being, a child, and the kind that becomes a capo providing harmful, life-threatening drugs to weak members of society. What turned him from doing good works for his fellowman and practicing the vows of charity and humility and undying faith? This I wanted to learn about Father Alfredo.

Much later, a psychiatrist friend of mine who practices in Atlanta explained it to me. I had told Doctor Odak the whole story, and she responded: "Criminal minds have certain defects with capacities for conceptual thinking, deliberation, awareness of options and alternatives, and choices that show self-restraint. It is most likely that Father Alfredo had a hyperactive amygdala and an abnormal functioning prefrontal cortex which meant significant interference with the operation of other cortical areas that would allow proper behavior seen in the average normal person. He, like most criminals, lived in a private world driven by inner tendencies and emotional perceptions which explains why he had so little regard for the interests and well-being of others and was unable to assess the consequences of his conduct. Why was he not concerned about the possibility of arrest and incarceration? He was a criminal who discounted the possibility of failure which lead to hyperoptimism and disregard for risks. As a pedophile he experienced perpetual anger and fear. He tried to overcome rejection by exploiting young seminarians. His domination of the vulnerable was the expression of the anger and fear he felt. In his mind he was not culpable of having inflicted any harm because he was demonstrating affection, concern, love.

"The criminality connected to the drug trade was solely motivated by greed and the desire for continued power both in the society of Mexico's elite and in the Order. This power extended itself to his acceptance and high regard and respect by the Vatican and even the Pope himself. The flow of money into Father Alfredo's accounts was tremendous and his manipulation of several Cardinals with that money was the impetus that drove him. He was an icon and would do nothing to tarnish that image. He was the emperor of his realm and it made no difference that the money was filthy and the money destroyed lives.

"A need for acceptance and a need for power were the consolation that assuaged his inner fear and anger and brought self-gratification to him. For the detriment to so many souls afflicted may he suffer eternal damnation, in my opinion."

It made perfect sense to me after Dr. Odak explained it so precisely.

▲ ▲ ▲

In one of my previous sessions with him, Marco had told me, "Father Alfredo had been described by a person of prominence in the Order as a man who manifests a weird aloofness that appears to be a dominant part of his nature. He is a gnome of a man whose anger I have seen aroused because of that. He tries not to show his inner deficiencies, but when challenged he displays a conduct that reveals a turmoil within. I have seen this many times when a subordinate failed to meet a standard that Father Alfredo had established.

While one may demonstrate anger over displeasure, Father Alfredo showed an inner volcanic turbulence.

"I remember an incident when I left Atlanta for Coalcojana to attend a meeting. I really believe that Father Alfredo reacted spontaneously and without regard to the appearance of his actions, but he gave a display of uncontrolled emotion that was unwarranted. A young priest who was on the faculty failed to have Alfredo's invocation ready for the opening of the meeting. Father's shouting astounded all present, but the slap that he struck on the priest's cheek brought everyone to his or her feet with a gasp that reverberated throughout the entire chamber. Alfredo turned, faced his audience and began to pray. At the end of the prayer jaws were still dropped. The person in the Order who was a trained psychologist said he knew this to be true, and that he had counseled Alfredo for years, seemingly to no good end."

▲ ▲ ▲

Father Alfredo was well defined, I thought. I wondered if he had ever considered psychotherapy.

36

United States
Georgia

Viktor Gonzales said, "Marco, as secret as things have been, there's a suspicion that we are being closely watched. Brothers Nicco and Tony Perez that work the streets have seen cops who just seem to be watching. I don't know how they can suspect anything coming from the school as we're not moving anything from there, but the guys said they sensed something when they were moving up the I-75 toward Chattanooga. It was a long way from there to Memphis and they weren't stopped. Do you figure we'll be played with until they have enough to close in? You know they always want to get the top dog when they think they got all the information they need. I don't see how they can tie anything back to you. And when the operation has movement, I'm always at my office. I'm not thinking they could think a V.P. at Hartwell & Smith could be implicated in anything illegal like transporting drugs. The only thing they'd be able to get me for would be those donations to our friendly congressman, but that's not connected to our enterprise."

Mr. G., as Gonzales was sometimes referred to, was a reputable member of two or three community organizations, a Familia Dei member through Marco's group at Crestbrook, and a big shot at Hartwell & Smith, a company that had been in business for over forty years and had offices in four southern states and two offices in Mexico. At one of those in Mexico is where Mr. G. got his start. He was smart and had a degree in economics and was sharp enough to rise in position and ultimately get a promotion to the Atlanta office. When he came north he had no problem fitting into an area where many of his countrymen lived either legally or illegally. Because of his connection with the Familia Dei Movement, he was on a friendly basis with Father Alfredo and other priests in the Order and also knew Marco. He wasn't aware of just what Marco's position was as he saw him as a liaison between the seminary in Coalcojana and somewhere in Georgia, presumably one of the Missionaries' schools. At the time of his move to the United States he contacted Marco and this is how they became better acquainted and how Mr. G. got involved in the drug trade. Why he wasn't content with his position at Hartwell & Smith and the money he was making as an executive, is inexplicable. But greed being the motivator it is corrupted the man. He saw the opportunity for lots of money, and money he could keep hidden in accounts in Mexico. He wouldn't want to be noticed at his business place as living too high a lifestyle.

Mr. G. had a beautiful house in Tenexpa, Mexico where he would go when he went on company business. It was far enough from the office that he could enjoy the good life without anyone knowing anything clandestine about him. All his co-workers knew he was knocking down a respectable salary so they would have no suspicions about his having a much better than ordinary house and the trappings that went along with it. His child attended Crestbrook and his wife was very complacent and comfortable as a housewife living in Georgia. Saying that she was happy and content was more for the sake of her children living in Georgia and having friends and sports to play. She was actually indifferent to the community and feigned contentment. They very rarely accompanied him to Mexico when he went. Mrs. Gonzales said there was nothing down there for her any longer to warrant a long stay except the ocean and the beaches which she loved. But she did check on their home occasionally, and attended various events and specific parties with her husband when a wife by her husband's side was expected.

Marco added, "Mr. G. and I became very close friends before I, more or less, reeled him into our organization. Upon first coming here he was eager to help me with activities of Familia Dei and becoming a part of the Crestbrook family. He offered what time he could to promoting our Movement and even showed interest in assisting our baseball coach with the young students. Needless to say the money I talked about was too overwhelming for him to resist, especially as I minimized the risks that were involved in earning it. It was he who suggested one day that two of his closest friends whom he trusted with his life, as they spent their childhood growing up together in Mexico, could be enticed to join the cartel. The allegiance we had to each other is what made the wheels turn and the machine hum. It seems true that when enough money is involved devotion to the cause is insuperable."

It sickened me to hear him speak this way. If he had any beliefs in what he purported to be through the Familia Dei Movement, how could he pollute the lives of others who supposedly had those same beliefs? Perhaps, I thought, it goes to further support the psychological analysis of his mentor, Father Alfredo. The idea of the prefrontal cortex being so disturbed that it prevented rational thinking and the generation of good and right decisions. The criminal psychologists and psychiatrists could examine these cases and draw proper conclusions I am compelled to believe.

37

United States
Washington D.C.
New York City

JM@deutschesbank.com

Jeannette, I had a wonderful time with you and your relatives, Dominique and Josephine, in Pina Grande. It was relaxing to forget about work for a while and just enjoy the walks on the beach and the cool evening breezes as we sat in conversation at such a resplendent table of excellent food and drink. Better than any resort I've been to. Now that I'm back in Washington I will get started working on a case that will take me to South America in a few weeks. This was highly unexpected as I didn't know there was activity there that my firm was to be involved in. I'll fill you in later with anything not top secret. I'm so happy that we met and shared time and some of our history. By the way, you recall my mentioning a former classmate who is a seminarian in Madrid? When I got home I had a notice to call his father. It seems he has something he wants to confide in me. I can't imagine what, as we never touched on a subject of consequence when we had dinner at the Ritz. Oh, well, I'll see what it's all about when I respond to his message. Bye, bye for now.
Anna

AR@DRSfirm.org

Great to hear from you, Anna. I'm happy that we befriended each other and have things in common. Darn! I wish that your firm had business in Luxembourg where I could meet you when I'd be home for a time. I have vacation time over Christmas if you can get away too, and would like to see my little country. I know your family will expect you home in Connecticut, but anyway it's a thought for the future. You'll have to let me know when you might be in New York so we can meet up and spend some time. I'll do the same for Washington. I find it very interesting that you recently heard from Ted's father, and I wonder what it's all about. You'll have to let me know. There's nothing of great interest happening at the bank right now, so it appears I'll have a quiet time until something brews that takes me away from here. Don't you know, I love excitement in the banking business. Talk to you later.
           Jeannette

38

United States
Washington D.C.
Boston

mvtodriscoll@mindspring.com

Mr. O'Driscoll, I got your message when I got back from Europe. I'm sorry for the delay in getting back to you. I know it's been quite some time and I hope you didn't think I was ignoring your correspondence. It was very kind of you to have me to dinner with your family. I thank you again for your graciousness and generosity. It was a lovely evening that I had with you and Mrs. O'Driscoll and Ted.

You mention that you want me to correspond with Ted about a matter of grave importance regarding occurrences of pedophilia in the seminaries at Coalcojana in Mexico and del Fontanara in Spain. Though I completely understand the significance of this to you, I'm not so certain that I can be of help. Because of the nature of my work, I would suggest that you solicit the help of an attorney within your company who can direct you to a better source for what you need. I realize you contacted me because of Ted's and my friendship, but you would be better advised to seek someone who could handle this case.

Anna Ralston

AR@DRSfirm.org

Miss Ralston, I apologize for the misunderstanding. I was not requesting your help in this matter as an attorney. My intention is that you could better speak to Ted and advise him with your legal background. For one thing I get too riled when Ted tells me about superiors molesting young seminarian boys. I think you could discuss what needs to be done within parameters of the law in a calm and cool manner which would make sense.

    I know he would follow any instruction as to the course to take. You do understand that there is fear and apprehension on his part because of who this man is that he is accusing. He has a position of authority and has the support of the Church. It's a David and Goliath thing. Please be apprised that Ted's time in Madrid is short, and that he will be going to Rome for completion of studies before his ordination. I know the process will be extenuated until after he and Edmund are ordained, but I feel strongly that our pursuit of justice for those abused seminarians must be tenacious no matter how long it takes. However, my writing to you is more in reference to part of the conversation we did have during dinner, and that is your mentioning that a friend you were staying with said she has an uncle who is a Cardinal in the Catholic Church from her home diocese. I think a connection like that could benefit Ted in what he feels he has to pursue. I would be indebted if you would share the name of the Cardinal and more or less lead the way to an introduction through your friend Jeannette. Will you please do this? I am hoping to hear from you.
    Martin O'Driscoll

mvtodriscoll@mindspring.com

Mr. O'Driscoll,

    I have spoken to Jeannette and explained the circumstances of your request. I have also spoken to Ted and apprised him of our correspondence. He said he would appreciate my making the connection for him. Jeannette is in touch with her uncle and will explain to the best of her ability. We talked and we believe that it will be a hard sell in as much as her uncle is going to require an abundance of concrete evidence before he can even offer a suggestion, if he is disposed to. Ted and his colleague, Father Edmund, will have to amass a plethora of information and documentation if something like this is going to fly.

    Asking for a Cardinal's assistance may be going out on that proverbial limb. As a lawyer I know how difficult it can be to have someone intercede with a higher-up, and in this case we're speaking about the Roman Catholic Church. My hope is that with the number of world-wide cases of pedophilia by such a large number of priests enough very specific evidence and proof will encourage Cardinal Lorentzweiler to intercede. The other thing that makes this an uphill fight is the popularity and reputation that Father Alfredo Legados has in Mexico, Spain, and Italy. Though the Missionaries of the Holy Church is established in the U.S. there aren't that many Americans and American Catholics who are very familiar with his Order. Though I don't have much time to devote to this matter because of my professional and personal responsibilities, I shall try to assist in any way I can.

    Anna Ralston

Thomas Rath

AR@DRSfirm.org

Miss Ralston, Thank you for the attention you have given to my request. I enormously appreciate your contacting Miss Libramont to see what she might be able to do. We understand completely the necessity of having the right evidence to be convincing for the Cardinal. The investigation of the allegations will be most accurate and complete. Be assured that I will use every influence within my power to solicit the help we need to attain the truth. The political atmosphere today is one that has every American parent wary of people in powerful positions who may be detrimental and dangerous to their young children. Justice must be served even when it comes to proving the guilt of religious leaders and seeing to it that they are prosecuted in a court of law and appropriately punished if found guilty. I am sincerely grateful for your willingness to be of help in light of your schedule and responsibilities.
    Martin O'Driscoll

39

Luxembourg
Esch

Jeannette and her uncle spoke in their Letzebourgesch language.

"Jeannette, den Idee ass absurd! Ma weast Du wat fir eng reputaschen den Mon huart?

("Jeannette, that idea is preposterous. Do you know the reputation of that man?)

"Awer gewess absurd, Mony. Waest Du viefiel nummerin fir Pedophilia sachen et get wo Pastoren matt gemacht hun an den letzten decaken?

("Hardly preposterous, Uncle. Do you know the number of cases of pedophilia that have involved priests in this past decade?) How many of them have been defrocked and punished with penitentiary sentences? Of course, you do. You're totally aware of these. And you know that there are cases pending, and some that will never be brought to light. And the vast sums of dollars that the Church has paid to proven victims."

Disgruntled, the Cardinal responded, "Father Alfredo Legados has been a priest for so many years and has directed two seminaries of great reputation. Why hasn't any charge of this sort been brought out before if he is a perpetrator?"

If allegations against Alfredo are true, it could mean ruin for several in Rome.

"Why? Because he is so certain he is not guilty of any crime like this; he doesn't see it as a crime. And besides, he has been protected from investigation when scrutiny of his behavior has been thwarted by members of the Curia," Jeannette said with pure conviction and absolute disgust for the subject of this conversation.

"Yes. I do know of the money he has brought to the Vatican and of the charitable donations he has made to several of the Cardinals of the Spanish speaking countries. He has been exceptionally generous with the money he has attained through the wealthy citizens of his homeland in particular," Cardinal Lorentzweiler acknowledged.

There have been some in Europe, too, who must be indebted to him I'm sure.

"I plead with you for help within the bounds that you can stay. But you must influence the Pope to look into the allegations that the two young priests have taken to the Church authorities. What more evidence do you require than the testimony of the two men who went to Father McGlynn in New York. You spoke to me of that at the time, but nothing was done. Father McGlynn initiated the proper action with his letter to the Holy Father. The Curia must act, and not provide a shield for such a dangerous man as Father Alfredo Legados. The Cardinals cannot be blamed for having taken gifts in the past from a child molester who sought merely to manipulate them knowing that the day would come when he must face the consequences for his sins."

"Jeannette, Father McGlynn's letter had been received, but without substantial support. The others who say they were abused as seminarians must come forth to give testimony. Fathers Ted O'Driscoll and Edmund Kelley have done a great deal to investigate the rumors they were aware of as seminarians, and have conducted a thorough investigation. You made me aware of the assistance Mr. O'Driscoll gave to his son's difficult work in attempting to attain the truth."

"Yes, now what can you do? What will you do?" asked Jeannette emphatically.

"I will go to Rome and speak to the Pope. This is a critical matter and it's not one that the Church will be happy about, but the facts must be regarded and more facts gathered. The Pope himself has the power to judge and determine whether or not this will go forward. I would tell you, my niece, that those young priests and their superiors they have entrusted with documentation will appear in Rome when this case is brought forward for trial. This will not be easy and they must be fully prepared. If your young lawyer friend has taken testimony from victims, which is part of the evidence Father McGlynn has sent, I am certain she will be subpoenaed to the court as well."

"Yes, Excellency, Anna is aware that her presence is expected for her participation. Upon hearing the evidence in this case that Father Ted has collected and the depositions she will have recorded, she will be prepared to persuade his Holiness. She is a seasoned attorney used to the courtroom and its proceedings.

"I'm disappointed that Anna was unable to come to Luxembourg this Christmas for a visit. I had asked her to come, but as the season drew closer she had too much on her plate to get away for even seven days. I wanted her to meet you for this conversation as she would have been much better at stating the case in asking for your intercession. I know you will do all that you can, and that fairness will prevail when a bad priest is brought to trial before the Pope. I'll be very happy to introduce Anna to you at the time of the trial. I know she will enjoy our time in Rome together, too"

Cardinal Lorentzweiler ended his visit with his young niece saying respectfully, "Jeannette, meng niece, ech wais ouren Hergott werd seinen Segen gin pour wat Du machst pour all den yungen Pastoren an Du helfst ihnen fir zurrueck an die Ecole an Georgia.

("Jeannette, my niece, I know that God will bless you for what you are doing to help those young priests back at that school in Georgia.)

"Ma wenndat so muss sin dat Pater Alfredo well guelitsche git, seng paine muss kommen an all Welt muss well wessen dat Eglise muss alles machen pour protection fir die Unchuldigen von den Taten an den rueoklosen Monnen.

("If it is to be that Father Alfredo Legados is found guilty, then his punishment must come and the world must be made aware that the Church does everything to protect the innocent from nefarious deeds of nefarious men.)

I realize her intentions are noble, but I can only pray nothing comes to light that might implicate some members of the Curia. God's will be done.

40

Mexico
Coalcojana

A conversation took place between Father Alfredo and Father Jose Morelos. the man now in the Director's position of the sem who up to now played a minor role at the seminary, but his unquestionable devotion to Alfredo has made him somewhat of a confidant.

"I must send out a communiqué professing my innocence and protesting the accusations made against me. I'm restrained at this moment from silencing the priests in America who have spoken against me in this dreadful way. The Vatican has informed me of the charges and the preponderance of evidence they say they have to prosecute me."

Morelos responded, "Well, what the hell. I've only known you in one capacity and it's as the director of a seminary. I don't know what you did in the past, but you do. It looks like you're going to have to answer for it. What's your defense?"

What in blazes was the moral compass guiding this man? I never took him for being a stupid ass.

Attempting to sound self-assured, Alfredo said, "I'll speak to Cardinal Bisenzio and Cardinal Molinella and ask them to speak to the Pope and dismiss any charges before they are even brought to him formally."

"But that letter has already been sent to the Vatican from Father McGlynn in New York." said Father Morelos." I think you have delayed far too long."

He doesn't appear to sense the magnitude and severity of this situation. Can his head be that deep in the sand?

"That has already been rejected. They didn't believe Father McGlynn and his bishop who formed the charges against me, so that doesn't matter."

"Yes, but the priests at Crestbrook have been in collusion with Father McGlynn and have been in contact with the Director in Connecticut. They have new evidence and say they have depositions from older men whom you molested when they were young boys at Coalcojana. It's these men who McGlynn and his bishop are interceding for."

"I'll get a formal letter to rebut the charges to the Order. My priests have sworn not to speak against me or the Order; therefore, they will be convinced of my innocence and be appalled that I must defend myself against allegations like these. I'll deny any accusation. I don't know how anyone who knows the extent of my love for all who have attended the seminaries could think I'd be a perpetrator of young boys."

"I'll do that to be on the safe side, however; I will write to my loyal friends in the Curia to try to nip this in the bud."

"For your sake, Father," said Morelos, "I hope they remain loyal to you. As long as you have funded their causes and needs, they were on your side. But, I fear, 'When in Rome do as the Romans do' will be the mantra you're going to face. They will side with the forces of Cardinal Salvacco who have the Pope's ear."

Salvacco is nobody's fool. He's sure to have readied his battalions.

"We'll see!" said Alfredo.

"Actually, Father, with a new case of significantly more evidence brought against you, I don't think the charges will be excused as they were before," said Father Morelos. "I don't have all the facts, and I don't know the truth, but you are being summoned to Rome, so rather than proclaim innocence to us at the seminary, I'd suggest you prepare a solid defense."

There's no damage control he can affect at this point. I'd wager my life on it. He knows I'll have to stand with the Order when I see he's dead in the water.

41

Mexico
Coalcojana

LYNX@Crestbrook.edu

Marco, what the hell is going on? I'm being charged by a conspiracy of my own priests with the heinous crime of being a pedophile while I was in charge at the seminaries. The two names that have arisen are Father Ted O'Driscoll and Father Edmund Kelley. Who have they spoken to that have made these false claims against me? I want you to find out what they know, whom they have that will testify, and who they have doing investigative work; in other words get to their computers and get information. I know they must be consulting a lawyer. I know they have someone who has gone to see Father McGlynn in New York. This whole mess is bad enough, but I can't allow it to disrupt the operations of the cartel. If all this ends up in Rome with whatever evidence they say they have and it's overwhelming, I'm in for a tortuous trial and condemnation. The Order will be seriously affected and the Pope has the power to completely dissolve it. This cannot happen! I've worked my entire life building the Order and the cartel. Get on it immediately and keep me informed.
    L.

Latente@seminaria.edu

Father, I've been able to secure data from the priests' computers and have recorded every e-mail. My discovery is that you will have to do much to combat the charges they are bringing to their authorities in the Order and the Church. They have several witnesses. I've read some of the damning testimony that has been presented to Father McGlynn. They have a lawyer working for them in Washington who had been contacted by Father O'Driscoll's father. I've read the exchanged e-mails of the lawyer and of O'Driscoll as they were copied to Father Ted.

I also found out that both priests here had brought these same allegations to the Director of Seminaria del Fontanara when they first arrived there from Mexico. They backed down at that time. They feel they have enough documentation and witnesses now to proceed with their charges against you. There are numerous references to the number of abuse cases that have been uncovered and tried during the past several years in the U.S. and Europe. I think this gives them the courage to bring proceedings against you. The lawyer is a woman named Anna Ralston. She was at Yale the same time Father Ted was there. That's the connection. A friend willing to extend some legal help, and she took the testimony from the witnesses you will have to confront.

Lynx

LYNX@Crestbrook.edu

I want you to be here in Mexico before such time as I have to make any appearances before a tribunal or be in court either here or in Rome. I want you to be ready to follow my orders which will be very specific as to how to handle the things that will be absolutely necessary. I will no longer be open to receiving e-mail. Any damaging data on my computer will be obliterated, and the hard drive will be destroyed. I suggest you do the same to yours in case you have incriminating information stored. We have always been careful to use code, so I'm not concerned that anyone could decipher anything related to the cartel, but there's no sense taking any risks. Destroy everything! I can't speculate as to the outcome of this situation, but I know the course I have to follow. Be ready to avenge the torment that these people want to put me through. And know that you will be acting to protect yourself as well. Immediate action is needed at this point to combat these maligning bastards.

 L.

42

Italy
Iles d'Arda

"Was your life merely wrapped around the work at Crestbrook and distributing drugs to centers in the U.S.?" I asked Marco at one juncture of the story. "Were you constantly alone?"

"No, of course not. Do you recall my telling you that it was normally a group of women who were the start-up people of the schools, the ones who sought out locations and determined leases or rentals of the properties and sometimes purchases? In the case of Crestbrook in Georgia the school began in a basement. It grew to a 110 acre campus that was valuable property off a major highway. Today, that acreage alone without the buildings is worth three times what the Order paid for it. It was a great investment if ever the Missionaries of the Holy Church has to sell it.

"I became interested in the older daughter of one of the women and began courting her about two years after I got to Crestbrook. We dated for a few months and then got very serious about each other. We attended Familia Dei meetings and functions regularly; she was a tremendous help in the organizational aspects of the Movement in Georgia. There was no way I could tell her anything about my connections in Colombia and Mexico. I just led her to believe that my travel back to Mexico periodically was to confer with Father Alfredo and the Order about the Familia Dei Movement. She never became suspicious of what I was doing even when I'd tell her I had to go to Coalcojana and even when I would meet privately with Mr. G. and others, or when we would go to the "set up" conferences and meetings at the other schools.

"Sarah and I did get married. The whole school and Mexican community knew we were together and expected an engagement announcement closely followed by a wedding date. They got their wish. This was the right thing for me to do. We truly love one another, and it became easier for me to go about my illegal activity without her questioning me after our first child was born. And even easier after the next ones arrived. There hasn't been one time that I slipped up and said something or left something around that would arouse suspicion. I was able to keep family and religious life completely separated from my life of crime."

If I just could tell you how often I wish I could have met Sarah first, but I never would have had her if my other life had never been.

▲ ▲ ▲

I was satisfied with his answer to my question. He must have been quite clever to keep his double life so completely secret. I would have thought that over time it was impossible to not screw up. But realizing that his position put him in such close contact with so many priests of the Order and a vast number of Familia Dei members in Mexico and several regions of the North quite distant from each other, he could hide many things from his wife, colleagues and close friends. For a man who grew into the person he was and having a limited educational background, Marco attained a definite level of success. He was a spiritual leader at the same time he was a shameless criminal. Angel on one side; devil on the other. I might be willing to accept that this juggling act could persist for a length of time, but would figure it couldn't endure for a lifetime. Well, actually it didn't, or he wouldn't be telling me his story now. But one must be impressed by the number of years he pulled it off. Even with lots of help and many cover-ups to camouflage his activities, the guy showed remarkable ingenuity and craft. He managed to conceal anything that would cause mistrust, and he limited any use of narcotics to his visits to Mexico. Never once did he appear glassy-eyed or out-of-it in front of Sarah because she could discern any change in his demeanor immediately as a wife definitely could.

Where his story was going I couldn't even guess. Who else besides his mentor in crime, Father Alfredo, might be implicated in some way, I couldn't speculate upon. I simply knew I was privy to a narrative that would be the most satisfying to me as a journalist that I would ever experience. Hell! If I write it well enough, I might pull off a Pulitzer. But that was all secondary to me at this point because I found myself becoming intrigued by the reality of the story, and this is what was moving me forward. I could only ask myself if the story I was recording was a movie or TV script that I had experienced somewhere in my past when I might have been addicted to terrible American filming, and before Netflix came across my screen for eight bucks a month.

43

Italy
Iles d'Arda

Marco went on. "What I understood is that several professional men had come forward giving testimony that they were sexually abused by Father Alfredo in Coalcojana and Madrid. All of the men are Mexican. Three college professors, a current priest, a scientist or engineer, a lawyer, and a teacher, all well-educated men had made the serious accusations and had legal representation. Other priests had taken up their cause and had written letters to the Pope. My belief is that a parish monsignor on Long Island had written and gotten no response from Rome. These men were coming forward because they claim they had letters previously written seeking an investigation which was ignored by the Pope, too. The Pope had been a staunch defender of Father Alfredo through the years and I would expect that he would offer whatever protections he could to ward off any attackers of Father Alfredo and the Order.

"Father saw this onslaught of accusations by these men as a conspiracy. I thought it would eventually be thwarted when the Order's law firm shaped its defense. Father Alfredo was concerned that the Papal Delegate would establish a commission to hear the charges and make necessary determinations. The statement says that the Commission will seriously study the recent allegations regarding Alfredo's conduct, and will address consequences that have affected the victims. The General Council of the Commission is normally four priests, but I was not surprised to see that the Papal Delegate appointed six to the Council. Not a case of the more the merrier, but the more brain power to construct a definitive response and settlement to the issue."

With all of this information that you gathered from the computers, what did you do?" I asked Marco.

"Immediately, I left for Veracruz where Father Alfredo had gone to lecture to confer with him and take instruction from him. That was all."

"Did either Father Ted or Father Edmund discover that their computers had been hacked?"

"Nothing was ever said, and I'm sure that something would have been, if they had any suspicion. Most likely blame would have been cast in the direction of one or a couple of older students thought to have slid into their offices and messed with some stored data such as an upcoming test or exam to be given in class. Besides there was nothing to become suspicious about, and they weren't the type to keep their guard up. My experience with them aside from instructional and religious duties was they were happy-go-lucky sorts who enjoyed their lives living more as secular priests and enjoying that kind of freedom than members of an Order. Their interaction with students and parents seemed to be at their center of interest. They weren't the suspicious types who would conceive of me, a trusted colleague, hacking their computers."

This was a second occasion where questions entered my mind and I wondered if I was being played by Marco the way he regarded the two priests. Was I as naïve as they? By this time he hadn't alluded to the reason he requested my writing talents. I didn't have a good feeling about what I was going to hear as my suspicions increased.

44

United States
Long Island, NY

"Miss Ralston, I thank you for leaving other important business in Washington and coming to my parish to take care of the legal necessities so we can proceed with documenting the accusations against Father Alfredo. I'm eternally grateful to Mr. O'Driscoll for having contacted you in regard to this grave matter, and I know the extreme concern he has for seeing that his son is well advised in this case. Your assistance will give him support he needs. It is not a light responsibility that we all feel having to proceed with a case such as this. However, the harm that has been done is irreparable and must be atoned for. You will understand that better after you have heard and questioned and recorded the remarks of the victims who have suffered for a long number of years. I decry the injustice they have been served."

"Father McGlynn, I feel as you do about the need for justice for these former seminarians who have felt much pain over the years. Recompense is in order if, indeed, we prove our case in Rome. While in New York I do intend to see a good friend who is actually the one person who set all the wheels in motion. I refer to Jeannette Libramont who contacted her uncle, Cardinal Lorentzweiler, in Luxembourg to intercede for us with his Holiness at the Vatican. Also, I am fortunate that I work for a firm that has allowed me to enter this case. It was originally intended that I go to South America as part of a team, but Mr. Dempsey altered schedules.

"The firm saw this as an opportunity for me to extend my legal prowess in an entirely different aspect of international law. We defend policies, treaties, resolutions and declarations that nations recognize as binding upon one another in their mutual relations with one another. This case will be adjudicated in a jurisdiction quite different from what I'm used to, but I have no disbelief that the Commission in Rome will see this as a heinous crime by a member of the Church who must be made accountable.

"The impact that an important person such as a businessman like MVT O'Driscoll can have upon persuading a firm to assist him is impressive. And needless to say, Mr. Dempsey, Mr. Rodriguez and Mr. Schmidt felt that impact. Occasionally it is regarded as an honor to comply with the wishes of a person who can exert a great deal of strength in the political world. And I do have to give Mr. O'Driscoll credit that he only desired to influence help from a legal organization, rather than go to allies in Washington which could have made this a political issue.

"Shall we proceed, Father McGlynn?"

▲ ▲ ▲

Anna Ralston began listening and interrogating each of the petitioners for justice. She heard essentially the same identical story from each man, only in different words, but with similar emotion that exhibited deep felt stress. She heard how innocent and impressionable young boys were forced or cajoled into performing despicable acts by a contemptible man. Several of the men said Father Alfredo told them he had permission from the Pope to seek them out sexually for relief of physical pain. These were well educated, professionally successful men who wept while they said they were still plagued with memories of the events that took place. Their affidavits asserted that Alfredo had molested more than thirty boys over two decades.

When Anna asked what the specific inappropriate behavior was, the response was uttered with embarrassment. Father Alfredo would summon a boy to his room at night while he was in bed acting as though he was in tremendous pain, and ask the boy to massage his stomach. The relief would be in the act of masturbation, mutual masturbation. Anna was appalled hearing of this victimization. She had difficulty remaining composed as she thought about one's own younger brother, picturing him in that room being abused by a corrupted man which would leave permanent scars that would remain unfaded well into his manhood.

One of the affidavits included testimony that a twelve year psychosexual relationship existed between Father Alfredo and a boy who is trying to comprehend as an older man how it could have happened. He contends that in his innocence he was lead to believe by Nuestra Padre that what he was doing was not just good, but justified. He stated that the priest would bless him, "In nomine padre, et filia, spiritus sancti" after the ordeal to let him know he was cleansed of any sin. Later in life this man attempted to find some peace of mind by writing that what Alfredo did to him contradicts every belief of the Church and of the Order in which he was ordained.

Anna was truly disturbed by what she was hearing. It made her nauseous to think that years later these stories could be so graphic in their minds. Her mind went to the thoughts of the pedophilia cases that were disclosed so often over the past years. It seemed epidemic. Little did she know that she would be steeped into a situation like this when she recalled the Archbishop of a major New England city being an upper echelon member of the Church defending a priest who had been accused of child molestation. Though a much younger woman at the time, she remembered the repulsion of parents and entire communities and that city being so near her home state. She realized, of course, that pedophilia was a curse that knew no borders for it seemed at the time it was raging through the Church in many parts of the world. How close she was to that thought now as she encountered stories of victimization that occurred in Spain, Italy, Mexico. It was an absolute mystery to this young woman how these perpetrators could conduct religious affairs of the Church on an everyday basis without such pangs of conscience racking them every hour of the day. Even to contemplate the conflict they must suffer living in a confused and sick, perhaps demented mind was unimaginable to her.

Anna said, "If there were pleas for help that were sent to the Vatican before, and they were unanswered, they won't be this time. These allegations are substantive and condemning, and will reach the highest levels where their best Canon lawyers had better be ready for argument."

▲ ▲ ▲

Father McGlynn presented a letter with a group signature of five names to Anna that came from an address in Wisconsin that stated: "We are aware of the case you are preparing and attest to its urgency in order to reprimand a reprehensible pedophile. We hope that our statement can enhance your position in court and bring Father Alfredo to the punishment he deserves. While studying at the seminary in Coalcojana we knew there were a select number of Mexican students referred to as "the apostolic schoolboys" who enjoyed the favor of the Director. We Irish and American seminarians felt our treatment by the Director General and professors to be lesser than that awarded to those from Mexico. The favoritism shown to them was apparent and the resentment we felt was ongoing. It was something which we did not comprehend at the time until rumors became rampant that these select students were the victims of sexual abuse, or what we called illicit sexual favors. Studying for the priesthood is much more than a solemn pastime, and when we became aware of such criminal events taking place in a holy and religious environment, we felt that the walls were caving in. The most unfortunate occurrence was our failure to do anything about it. Two seminarians, we later learned, had the courage to speak up, and when they did, they shipped out to Madrid and their efforts to right wrongs were repelled. Our inaction was attributed to the notion that we couldn't be certain and we were too young (and stupid) to do anything about it. Needless to say, our consciences have been guilty ever since. We pray that this announcement bolsters your position and gives us some sense of exoneration."

This pronouncement came at a crucial time for two reasons. Though these men were more than reluctant to take action when their position as students was untenable, they now demonstrated that they were truly God's soldiers in desiring to right wrongs and make the world a better place. Anna felt that they would be forgiven by a just and angry God. She also knew that their statement of truth would lend weighty support for the case she was to present, as she had no doubts she was to face sturdy confrontation by an obdurate and arrogant opponent. The letter was signed, but it specified that it be put into evidence where only the Commission's six member General-Council would see the signatures. Otherwise, they were to remain anonymous.

▲ ▲ ▲

DDempseyesq@DRS.com

Mr. Dempsey, I have affidavits and all other documentation that I need to pursue the abused seminarians case vs. Father Alfredo Legados. You will see the vast number of times the word "pederasty" is used by these men. It sickens me. Copies being sent for your perusal. I'll be returning to Washington tomorrow when we can confer and adopt a strategy.
    Anna

45

United States
Manhattan, NY

"Yes, Jeannette, I met with Father McGlynn at his parish on Long Island and took the sworn affidavits from the plaintiffs in the case against that priest in Mexico. The experience was just incredible. It will be awesome for me to represent these men in Rome before the General Council that Cardinal Salvacco formed. We can talk more about this later. Let's have dinner first," said Anna.

I need some small talk. Something to get my mind going in another direction even if only for one evening. Being blown away by what I've heard, I need some relaxation.

"I suggested this restaurant because it isn't too far from my office, and it's very close to the airport for you to head back to Washington. Time to relax and have a cocktail to unwind a bit before we discuss this recent event in your life," Jeannette said.

"Sounds good to me. What will you have to drink? I'm ready for a delicious cosmopolitan."

And I know I'm having more than one. That's a given with the way I'm feeling.

"Seeing we're in Manhattan, I'll drink to our being here with a manhattan. Love the town and love the drink."

Anna said, "I'd be in Venezuela right now if I didn't get that message from Mr. O'Driscoll just about pleading with me to handle this situation which I have labeled "Sems vs. Satan." I don't think I would have gone along with it if it were not for Ted's involvement."

"Well, Anna, you did the right thing; I believe that because of the nature of this case against an alleged pedophile that brought all kinds of misery to people. And I believe, too, that you are the perfect lawyer for the task to bring that bastard to justice. His sins aren't just something that he can confess to another priest for absolution, and have no accountability for. I know I'm prejudging him, but all those men couldn't be accusing him if he wasn't guilty of something, and I mean something reprehensible."

One more drink and I'd be saying fucking reprehensible.

"Jeannette, I just had a thought flash into my brain as I was listening to you."

"Tell me!"

"When I meet with my boss, Mr. Dempsey, tomorrow, I'm going to suggest that he allow me to take you to Rome with me as an interpreter. God, Almighty! Who else, and who better when you speak both Spanish and Italian as well as you speak English. This will be terrific and such a magnificent help to me. I know I'll encounter a lot of unfamiliar language from the Council members that I'd have to wade through and hope not to misunderstand. This way you will make certain that clarity is brought across the table to me. Excellent idea, or not?"

"Well, sure, I'd be all for it, Anna, but you're forgetting I've got a job here in New York with my bank. Can't just up and hop on a plane, you know."

"C'mon. We're smart enough to figure it out, and know how to get around that. Influence, using influence, my dear. That's how the world works. First, I'll talk to Dempsey, then we get a hold of Father McGlynn who'll confer with his bishop who will place a call to Mayor Kocher who will call the president of Deutsches Bank, and you're in. Sound okay?"

"Yeah! Why not give it a try? I'd really like to be of help in some way to condemn that goon."

While draining her glass: *I'd love to be a partner in bringing about the collapse and destruction of that wicked and diabolical monster.*

Wherever God erects a house of prayer,
The devil always builds a chapel there;
And 'twill be found upon examination,
The latter has the largest congregation.
                              (D. Defoe)

46

Mexico
Coalcojana

"Marco, the heat has been turned up considerably. I've gotten word from Connecticut that more letters have been sent to the Vatican and that McGlynn and his bishop in New York have the sworn testimony from my accusers. They have met with a lawyer that Father Ted O'Driscoll's father got, and put things into motion against me. I was right about that, knowing they had hired a woman lawyer.

"I've put many things on hold with further drug shipments, and the Colombian cartel isn't real happy. I've been doing a balancing act for a long time and I'm getting too old to keep it up. But I'm into it, and can't escape regardless of how I feel."

"Father Alfredo," Marco replied. "I could take more responsibility and lift the pressure off of you. I could see to the operation here in Coalcojana and still maintain control of the runs from Georgia. With Mr. G. and the other associates up there we can continue and increase the number of drops in the U.S. That would more than please our friends in Colombia."

"Listen, my son," Alfredo said. "We take care of first things first, and that means I've got to get free of the allegations that are being viewed by the General Council at the Vatican as we speak. I've been called to Rome. I have others in place, some trusted Cardinals, who will exert pressure on a couple of those who oppose me who are the most vulnerable. If it works out that they have a change of heart, perhaps it will persuade the rest to back down and say they were mistaken. But I can't be certain that will happen, so listen to what I want you to do. Get to Italy. There you will meet a member of the Italian cartel who's going to be with you. You'll remember him, Giuseppe Vilardo. He will expect to see you in the coffee shop of the hotel the afternoon you arrive. The pretense will be to conduct business for Familia Dei on behalf of the Order. Check in at the usual hotel, Gran Melia Rome, not at any of the residences of the Order. You are going to have to secure a car that you will use for the accident. Plan for that. Vilardo knows the streets and roads so he'll do the driving. Afterwards, be in the company of the Order as the police will get to the scene quickly.

"I'm not concerned that anything will go wrong if you do this job correctly, but I must be prepared for the next step just in case. I will tell you how to get it done, so you can plan it out. That is why I sent for you at this time."

▲ ▲ ▲

Marco said, "I wasn't sure what kind of plan Father Alfredo was constructing, but I knew that his telling me to go to Italy implied that I'd be taking someone out. I knew it wouldn't be any of the Cardinals, so I figured it would be someone going to testify against Alfredo. I didn't think this was a good move because any accident or murder that involved a witness would look bad to the Commission that was judging the case against Father Alfredo. They just might think Nuestra Padre was behind such a plot. But it wasn't my position to question Alfredo, but to comply regardless. There were many times before like this that I felt I had taken that vow to hear no evil, see no evil, speak no evil when it came to loyalty to Father Alfredo.

"At this point I can say to you that in retrospect I don't know why I just didn't go back to Georgia, pack up my family, giving any excuse I could conjure up, and take off for parts unknown. That was my thought at the moment, but I knew that once you're in as deep as I was, this kind of thought is an instantaneous reflex of revulsion, and dismissed from the mind as quickly as it entered.

"I packed some clothes to make it look like I was a religious man devoted to a noble cause and organization traveling to Europe to confer with the holy men of a revered Order to spread the good work of the Church. One respectable layman pious upon appearance. I would await word from Father Alfredo and then fly to the Leonardo Di Vinci Airport. Being fairly familiar with the city and a large radius around it, I would have time to mentally put a plan together. I surmised that what Alfredo would want us to do wasn't going to involve the use of guns so as not to draw attention to us. The designated hit men in the cartel used silencers before when a kill had to be made quickly and quietly, but I figured Neustra Padre would have something else in mind especially when he said, "Get a car." When I did get his message, I was right."

What an idiot I am. Asshole is a better word.

Recalling this point in his life, his anguish caused by a sense of wrongdoing was evident to me.

47

United States
Washington, D.C.

"Welcome back, Anna. From the materials you sent we can see the great job you did, and also know the hours of work you're going to expend preparing for the presentation before the religious Commission at the Vatican. I have spoken to Bob Rodriguez about his assisting you; after all he is a partner and has credibility that the opposition will respect. He grew up speaking English and Spanish so he can be of great help when confronting Father Alfredo in court."

"Thanks Drew. It was an ordeal which I didn't think would affect me so emotionally. The testimony I recorded from those victims was incredible, and at times I had to excuse myself to leave the room and recover my composure. I've never experienced anything like it.

My reason for drinking one cosmo too many at dinner with Jeannette. First time I've gotten a bit loopy in quite a while.

"I don't think Bob will have to leave the office here to accompany me to Italy because I have another suggestion, if you'll allow me. My very good friend, Jeannette Libramont is accomplished in both Spanish and Italian, and I have asked her if she would go to Rome and translate for me. If you have no objection to this, I would want your approval. I feel very comfortable with Jeannette and really don't require another attorney at my side. I do appreciate your offering Bob's assistance, but he does have legal responsibilities at the office. What are your thoughts about that, Drew?"

"Well, it doesn't matter to me. It was just a suggestion that I thought would help. If you're comfortable, as you say you are, with your friend Jeannette, then by all means do what you think is best. I trust your judgment without question, so I know she will be a major asset, and that you will be successful in presenting the evidence and building a strong case."

"Thank you. I hope I show the confidence in myself that you have in me. I will not embarrass the firm; you can count on that."

"Well, Anna, map out a strategy. Come on strong because from my experience there aren't too many men in the Church who have shown great acceptance of a woman when it comes to litigating a case. And this is one of their own, so they will throw everything they have against you. I've not seen it personally in this arena before, but I don't think it will be that different from the military. Some high ranking officers have given women a rough going-over at times to show their superiority. A bunch of Cardinals who have studied Canon law and have legal credentials can be tough competitors and real jerks, too. Not that there aren't some fair-minded men who are uprighteous, but be prepared and watch your back."

"I will."

Seems silly to think I have to watch my back in a room filled with Roman Catholic Cardinals. Drew must mean the civilian lawyers.

"The good thing is that you've got a lot of power on your side with Father McGlynn and his bishop behind you along with those incriminating affidavits. That's a lot of big guns and ammunition."

"I'm not too worried, Drew. My instincts tell me that the Cardinals are reasonable men who seek justice even though they may see the necessity of shielding one of their own. Reasonable and intelligent describe those who recognize grave depravity and know they can't support guilt."

"When will you be notified as to where and when?"

"Father McGlynn will notify me as soon as he gets a response from Rome. The last time his missives went unanswered, so he knows they take their good old time. But he feels that with the arsenal we have, a large number of priests over a span of two decades, I guess, Rome won't drag its feet and hesitate with a response. I hope he's right as I want to get into this quickly and get it behind us. I'll be anxious to move on. I was a bit disappointed that I wouldn't be joining the team in Venezuela to ply my diplomacy talents working on the Chavez thing."

"Oh, don't worry! That's going to last a while." You'll have time to work on that, I'm sure. With Chavez's illness and maladies that occur periodically, I know everything down there will drag out. You'll have time. Regardless of who's in power, the U.S. will always have its international issues, and they'll never be resolved by diplomats within the frame of a decade, I can assure you, Anna."

"I'm not certain that's good to hear, Drew, but it tells me I'll most likely get there someday."

"I know so, Anna. Get home now and get some rest. These last few days have been super taxing on you. In the upcoming days you'll need all your physical and mental strength to go head to head against your opposition in Rome."

Anna left the office and her meeting with Drew feeling better knowing she had his full support. There was no doubt that turmoil was stirring inside her, but her level of confidence was higher and would sustain her. Now, she thought, if Jeannette is able to assist her, she will feel the power she'll need to exert to overtake any barriers placed in her way. She was ready.

48

Italy
Iles d'Arda

Marco told me that he returned to Crestbrook to continue with his duties at the school. He always sensed that the Executive Director, Dick Sturm, wondered about some of his trips back to Mexico, but only spoke to him about his Familia Dei activities. Marco had told Dick that he was a direct liaison between the Order and the members of the Movement in Mexico and the members in Spain and the U.S. The executive director never questioned what Marco told him for he knew that everyone at the school including him was subject to the commands and demands of the Order. (More than once was he called on the carpet before the Director even though he was an extraordinary leader.) Dick, knowing the close contact that Marco had with Father Alfredo whom they all regarded as a saint, felt that Marco held the most important place in the Movement and naturally would be at the beck and call of the Director Generals of the seminaries in Mexico or the U.S.

Marco was never derelict in his duties at the school and always managed to be where he was supposed to be when various activities or programs or special masses, or whatever were scheduled. He actually had no part in the academic life of Crestbrook. No curriculum work per se with administration and faculty. Everything through the religious program came from Familia Dei and that was mainly inspired by the Order and the supposedly great writings and pontification of the founder, Father Alfredo Legados. Though he took an inferior part in discussions when administrative meetings were held, Marco rarely offered opinions about core subjects. His contributions were almost exclusively relegated to the religious educational sphere which hinged on Familia Dei material. Essential to the position and function he was to provide, he had undergone a thorough and methodical grooming process. Alfredo saw very early into the type individual Marco was and knew his innate abilities would carry him forward.

The photocopier in the teacher workroom was the only tool that Marco used. He constantly ran materials off in huge numbers that were peddled to fellow members of the Movement locally, or to the other Missionaries' schools or were mailed to Mexico. To the faculty who were not Familia Dei, Marco seemed a loner. He ate lunch in his office and he seldom conversed with faculty and staff. His wife and children were only seen on campus in the morning for 7:30 mass. They appeared to limit conversation with their friends after mass, and then departed for home. Only Mr. G. and a few other men seemed to huddle with Marco and talk and smile when conversing.

As Marco looks back he wonders why he did not feel hypocritical on all those mornings, but seemed to be insensitive to his surroundings. His secrecy was obvious in another way which was more than certain to blanket his underground activities. He and his wife had several children. This was a requirement of sorts in that the Familia Dei Movement would never condone contraception of any type except that tried and failed method of the church called "the rhythm method." It almost appeared a joke on the campuses of the Order's schools that male faculty members at their reproductive stage of life were expected to have wives continually pregnant. It seemed like a contest was being held as to what couple would have the greatest number of children. After one wife gave birth, the next one was noticeably pregnant, and after she had her child, another wife conceived. Interesting to be sure, but the process kept all members united and seemingly happy. I asked how was it possible to endlessly propagate and live on a teacher's salary. This was a major concern for the ordinary couples, but Marco had no trouble as he had a very reliable source of secondary income.

141

And it was quite abundant. Marco had substantial accounts mainly in banks in the Caymans so he wouldn't one day be concerned that his 401K looked low and feeble when a downturn affected the economy. He knew the healthy situation he would enjoy when he felt like retiring to a beautiful ranchero on the Gulf, providing, of course, that he hadn't been killed, and his wife was willing to move there. Why wouldn't she be? The kids would be raised, educated, and on their own by that time. He contemplated a very pleasant future life if he made it that far without a serious problem, such as getting shot, or serving a prison sentence when something went terribly wrong after he was arrested. And, of course, he never considered the possibility Sarah would be anywhere but at his side.

49

Colombia
El Ritero

"Marco," pleaded Arturo, "we want you to come home as quickly as you can; our mother is very old and frail. We have kept you informed over time of her illnesses and condition, but things have worsened and have reached a critical point. Her doctor says that she won't have much time to live. He doesn't offer hope, and says he can't rely on a miracle."

"Why haven't you called me before now, Arturo? I've tried to stay in touch with all of you. I know I haven't been home in a long time, but I have called often. I spoke to mother a few weeks ago and knew she wasn't well, but not at the point of death. Can she talk on the phone to me?"

"Marco, Mother is very old and the stomach problems have gotten worse even in this past year. She was a rugged, tough, old lady still doing her chores and cooking and tending to the vegetables in the garden, and she has been quite robust, but the stomach disease seems to have taken such a hold on her that the doctor says she will not get over it, and she might die soon. She has pancreatic cancer and there is no cure for her. The doctor says that many people much younger succumb to this horrible cancer."

"Mother has lived a long life and a good one. She is especially proud of her three children who stayed close to home and brought her much comfort. I know I have disappointed her because I left El Ritero so young, and she did not approve of my being in the cartel when Ramon Munoz took me in. I will try to get home with my family to see her soon. I have to see Father Alfredo in Mexico, and then I will come home. Please tell mother that she will see me and she will see her American grandchildren pronto."

"I am glad to hear you say this, Marco. Mother has spoken of many things to us and said that there are things she would like to tell you that she has not mentioned to anyone before. Perhaps there are things in the past. Perhaps she wants to say she forgives you for going away. She has been a good woman and has worked hard all of her life, and feels that now is the moment to express true feelings from deep inside."

"Thank you for calling me, Arturo. I will be home as quickly as I can."

If Mother despised me I couldn't blame her at all. I left home early and she was saddened by it. I haven't been the kind of son she hoped I would be. Unlike the story in the gospel I was the prodigal son who didn't return, but remained prodigal in her eyes.

50

United States
Georgia

AR@DRSfirm.org

Anna, I will be leaving Atlanta on Monday for Rome. I'll see you there. I heard from my father that all went well when you were in New York with Father McGlynn and the bishop. Fortunate for you that you will be traveling with your friend Jeannette to Rome. I'm confident that the case you present will be convincing. The Order in Mexico and the Director in the U.S. are quite disgruntled that I am going to Rome to testify. I was ordered to do so, as you undoubtedly know, by the Commission, so they can be angry about it. Father Alfredo sees me and Father Edmund as traitors, but if we are successful with the charges we are bringing, and Alfredo is given much more than a reprimand, he won't be thinking of me or transferring me from Crestbrook. Hopefully, his punishment will remove him from his position in the Order forever. We'll discuss what we think an appropriate punishment is after we face the General Council. Have a good flight and I'll see you in Rome. I'm staying at the Gran Melia Rome, Via Del Gianicolo 3 which is less than a half mile from the Vatican. I wanted a place which would be very convenient.

    Father Ted O'Driscoll

TedOD@crestbrook.edu.

Father Ted: OK. I leave here for New York to meet with Father McGlynn one more time. I am very fortunate that the wheels that were put in motion gave the ok for Jeannette to fly to Rome with me and act as my interpreter. I know your father went over many of the details. Also, the Commission has guidelines that they will regard in reference to punishment apropos to the crime, if we get a conviction. Won't worry about that right now. Jeannette and I are staying at the Gravina San Pietro, Via della Cava Aurelia 17. See you soon and remember Jeannette and me in your prayers.
    Anna

51

Italy
Rome

Cardinal Salvacco convened the meeting of the Council in order to discuss the case of the Seminarians vs. Father Alfredo. He was adequately prepared to catechize Alfredo.

"Members of the Commission, we know the charges being brought against Father Alfredo and we know the men who are making those allegations. We will have to hear the evidence and see all of the documentation to render a verdict. I know that some of you are appalled that this is happening to a man who has been so revered and honored in the Church. Why, he has been a favorite of the Holy Father for several years, and has been admired for his significant contributions to the Church. Many of us in the Curia have benefited from his enormous generosity over the years, but, I must insist that we view this case with open minds and an ardent desire to seek justice for Father Alfredo and the victims who have suffered, if Alfredo is found guilty. I must remind you that these past years have not been good for our Mother the Church with the large number of pedophiles who have been found guilty and made to leave the priesthood. The entire Catholic community has been enraged by all of this, so we must respect the fact that we will be being watched and our judgments closely scrutinized. Remember that many of the faithful have decided to stay away from practicing their faith because of the disgust they feel at having been deceived by men they have trusted. If we are satisfied that the evidence and testimony leave no reasonable doubt as to Father Alfredo's guilt, we must issue a condemnation of his acts. Some of us have had a legal education and these Cardinals I will lean toward to make sure we do not falter in any way from legalities.

"I want everyone made aware that an attorney from Washington is the spokeswoman for the former seminarians and will be presenting their case. My understanding from Father McGlynn is that this woman is not a seasoned courtroom prosecutor, but she is incredibly bright and more than capable. Father has assured me that she can adequately handle herself before a judge and jury. When the Director-General in Connecticut spoke to her of the allegations as preposterous, she took thirty minutes to perfectly refute everything he said and had him apologizing for obstructing the basic Constitutional rights of eight Americans who happened to have been studying for the priesthood as seminarians.

"One or two young priests of the Order will also be giving testimony. They, you will recall, are the men who intended to bring charges against Father Alfredo several years ago when they were studying at Seminaria del Fontanara in Spain. I have no idea what direction they will be coming from in their planned attack, but we must evaluate their positions and evidence as strongly as we will the lawyer's. Gentlemen, we seem to have come to a critical time that requires us to be as judicious and candid and astute to ensure fair treatment of all. Pray for the Lord's blessing and guidance to see us through this case. This is a most trying time for the Church. That we all agree on."

▲ ▲ ▲

There may have been some discussion, certainly some dialogue, between members of the Council, but it centered around their role as judges and coming to a verdict that would send a strong message to the priests and Orders of the world, as well as to the millions of Faithful around the globe. There may never be such a tribunal formed again with the gravest of responsibility as this case will demand. They could not fail, and with the strength of the Almighty supporting them, they would not.

52

Colombia
El Ritero

Arturo and Ricardo met Marco at the Jose Maria Cordova Airport in Medellin. They and their families were elated to see Marco home in Colombia. The greeting was warm and cordial and light conversation took place. Arturo known for his piquant wit good naturedly brought up an incident from their early years which allowed moments of laughter. Then he got serious.

"Marco, we're happy to see that you have come home to visit and to see your dying mother," said Arturo. "Where is your family? Your wife and the children? They did not come with you?" he said in disbelief at not seeing them pass through customs and immigration at the airport.

Ricardo spoke up, "I do not see anyone with you, Marco. Where are they; you said they would come to visit with you." He too indicated his dire disappointment to his brother.

Politely and respectfully, Marco greeted all of his family members expressing his feelings towards each one of them. Then addressing Ricardo and Arturo, he said, "Brothers, I intended that we would all come, but realizing the urgency for me to see our mother before anything would happen to her, I decided to hurry and get here quickly. Sarah and the kids will arrive here in one week. Also, Ricardo, when you called and told me of our mother's impending death, I said that I had to go to Mexico first to confer with Father Alfredo about Familia Dei business. I was only there for a short time before I got here, but I came right away as soon as I could leave Coalcojana."

"We are disappointed and Mother will be too. She wanted to see her grandchildren from America. But we are glad you are here now, and that we will see the family in a few days. I know her spirits will be much better then, Marco," Ricardo said.

You better not be lying to us, Marco, or I'll break your neck if you disappoint your mother who is so ill. You've been a disappointment to all of us at other times when we had expected you to come home to visit.

"Yes, I would rather that my family was with me, but it had to be this way."

Why the hell is he looking at me like that?

▲ ▲ ▲

When Marco arrived at his mother's house, she greeted him warmly and said, "Marco, Ricardo and Arturo have told me that you were coming to see your family. I am happy you are here to be with me during my last hours. The doctor says there is nothing more he can do, and that the hospital offers no cure for me. This cancer I have had for a time, and it has gotten so much worse I can only wait until it takes me from all that I love, and then I must look to being in paradise with God. I have had a good life and I am old, so I do not lose faith, but these days have strengthened it to make me more ready for death and eternal life. Your father did not know the comfort of having time to repent and express his desire for forgiveness and ask the Lord to save him from damnation for the evil things he did during the last years of his life. I have spent hours in prayer begging for the salvation of his soul, and that he repose in the presence of the Lord for all eternity. I have always prayed for you, my son, that you would see the right path to follow. You are so connected to the Church with your work every day at the school and with the Movement that you honor so greatly. You are attached to the priests and their work and especially to Father Alfredo who has been like a natural father to you.

"On my death bed I will confess my sins to God and I will confess my sins to man. There are things I must say before I die that can be said at that moment alone. My family and yours should be standing with me for all to hear. There is one mortal sin in my life that I must reveal, and beg forgiveness because it has been so burdensome for most of my life. I will do all I can to resist falling into a coma and not being able to speak my final words."

Consuela Montoya was a very religious woman throughout her life. Even in times of hardship she never wavered in her faith, but maintained trust that the Almighty would guide her and her family. She was fervent in her prayer that she spent a lifetime repeating hoping that her soul would be saved and that the souls of all whom she loved would one day share in the blessings of eternal life with her savior. Now that her life on earth was coming to an end, her wish was that Marco would see the necessity for repentance as she knew intuitively that he continued to move in a shadowy world. He was the son who was constantly in her thoughts. The others were good children that she knew were God-fearing and devout.

53

Mexico
Coalcojana

Marco did see Father Alfredo in Mexico, and only for one main purpose. Aside from discussing cartel business, Alfredo got right to the point regarding his situation as delineated by Cardinal Salvacco so clearly when he apprised Alfredo of the allegations being brought against him. Alfredo already had constructed his plan as to how he would settle with his aggressors who would be in Rome to bring the case to court. Salvacco demanded that Father Alfredo be there to hear the case prosecuted, and to respond in his own defense. He was told by the Cardinal that a lawyer would be unnecessary as the merits of the testimony and evidence would be evaluated by the Council who would deliberate and render a verdict, and a sentence if warranted. But he knew that Alfredo had already hired an Italian lawyer to consult with and had a lawyer from his Order. With Alfredo facing such charges the Order would see that he was adequately represented.

▲ ▲ ▲

Marco didn't like Alfredo's plan for retribution, but he would carry it out because of his loyalty to the man, though he would be very concerned about being a part of a crime in Italy. Torturing and shooting someone in Mexico was not a problem, he said, and shooting a rival cartel member in the U. S. he could always get away with. But Italy frightened him.

His travels to Italy had always been pleasant whether on business for the Order, or just to enjoy the magnificent city and the cultural and religious aspects of it. He loved the museums and could explore the grandeur of the Vatican treasures for days on end with a vitality that reinvigorated his life and his appreciation for the artistic talents of the masters. Why now did he have to become immersed in the sordid side of life at the behest of his mentor who in all likelihood was completely guilty of the crimes he was being summoned to answer for. Though confusion and consternation clouded his mind, he was as reliant as a Swiss-made clock when having to do the bidding of the rapacious man in Mexico.

▲ ▲ ▲

I suspect this dichotomy is as difficult for another as it is for me to understand—the loyalty of the man to his mentor versus his fidelity to his God. To the common man the distinction is so great there is no question as to how Marco should behave, but the common man is quite separated from the type of life Marco was immersed in. I questioned the kind of moral compass that he was guided by for up to this point I felt he expressed too little penitence.

54

United States
Georgia

TedOD@crestbrook.edu

Ted, when you get to your hotel you will be receiving this mail from me. The pressure has mounted as they say. The whole Order is ablaze with anger for us and for Father Alfredo if he is found guilty. There are those who are staying loyal, but a significant number is plainly perturbed (not a strong enough word) at the thought of Alfredo being accused of pedophilia. Where were some of these yokels when rumors were going around years ago? Everyone is wondering how this will play out, and they are amazed at the high level this has reached. Listening to others, I hear them say that this should have been handled silently and within the Order. It seems that when the eight priests and the former priests came together, and Father McGlynn took the case to the Vatican, it angered many in the Order. I wish you good luck speaking before the Council. I wish now we had been able to go further when we were in Spain and disregarded what we thought was so much to lose. In retrospect being expelled or having ordination delayed or denied would not have been so great a price to pay to my current way of thinking. My prayers are with you and with Ms. Ralston.
    Edmund

ek@crestbrook.edu.

Edmund, I got your message after I got my computer connected to wifi in my room. I figured that there would be pandemonium within the Order. That doesn't surprise me at all. There are many men loyal to Father Alfredo, but once the Council delivers a decision the outcome will alter the views of many. Not one will want to remain steadfast with him when they hear that the charges are true, and I can hope that the Council hands down a penalty that will be severe and remove Alfredo permanently from the Order. I hope the Pope will not want to conduct a widespread investigation of the Order because that could be too debilitating, and that the signal sent out to the faithful around the world could ruin everything that many good priests and laypeople have built over the past years.

Anna Ralston arrived yesterday with her friend Jeannette Libramont. I will see them later this evening. I want to hear what Anna can tell me about the depositions that she took from the men in New York. I'm sure she will confide in me some of the material she will put into evidence. I have a good idea just how devastating it will be, as my father indicated to me it was, when Anna spoke to him before she left Long Island for Washington.

I need to speak to Marco. I would convey a message through you, but I would rather deal with him directly. Will you please ask him to e-mail me ASAP? Thanks

Ted

TedOD@Crestbrook.edu.

Ted, Marco is not here at the school. He has gone to Mexico. I spoke to his wife Sarah and she said he left in a big rush to Coalcojana. She found tickets for her and the kids to fly to Medellin, Colombia, and said they are to meet Marco at his

family's home. That's all I know. I'll try to reach him and have him respond to you.
    Edmund

ek@crestbrook.edu.

What do you mean he's in Mexico? Why is he there, do you know? He is supposed to be in charge of all the classes and even the Familia Dei meeting scheduled for Thursday afternoon. There must be something secretive that he's up to. He was just down to see Father Alfredo last month. What could have come up that would take him to Coalcojana in such a hurry? I'm angry that he did not consult me about any of this, especially the extra time he'll take in El Ritero. Who knows how long he might remain there?
    Ted

TedOD@crestbrook.edu

Father Ted, I got Edmund's message. I forgot all about the schedule for this week even knowing that you will be in Rome for a few days. I sincerely apologize. Father Alfredo and Father Morelos at the seminary sent for me, so I left home immediately. As I have told everyone at the school, my mother is close to death and I have to be at her bedside with my brothers and sister. Please remember her in your mass and in your prayers. I'll see you when I return to Crestbrook.

    As far as I know John Largent has made arrangements for all the classes that both you and I will be missing, and he will conduct or cancel the FD meeting. He feels that the members led by one or two of the Consecrated can handle the meeting. They all have you in their prayers and hope for closure to the proceedings at the Vatican.
    Marco

▲ ▲ ▲

I had asked Marco if he had knowledge of the child abuse allegations that were being brought before Alfredo. He only stated that he was aware of the rumors. Of course, he couldn't let anyone know what his involvement with Alfredo Legados was. His was a business relationship dealing with drugs, and he didn't poke his nose into any of the seminary's affairs, or the people who ran the place. He said that Alfredo never said a word about being a man who liked to fondle young boys, but when he was informed by Alfredo of the charges, and that he was going to be a part of a get-even scheme in Rome, it was the first that he felt Father Alfredo was guilty as charged.

I didn't know whether to believe him or not. But I couldn't see how he did not know. He was closer to Father Alfredo than any other person. In the business relationship between Marco and Father Alfredo, one could understand loyalty and commitment, and whatever else to keep an enterprise running smoothly, but on a personal level, I didn't see why Marco felt anything but disgust and repugnance for the man, if only for the reason that Marco had children of his own whom he would defend until dead, if anyone tried to harm one of them.

55

Colombia
El Ritero

"What? What do you mean you have to go to Rome?" Sarah shouted at Marco when he said he would be leaving her and the kids to go to Italy. "You told me that we would be spending a week here, especially because your mother is so ill. If you knew you had to leave why did you have the kids and me come to Colombia? I never would have agreed to it. You could have come to see what state of health your mother was in, and then left. Why are you going there?" Sarah was generally a placid woman, but this was one occasion where she exploded. Naturally, the kids were far out of earshot when she went on the attack, but the children were not impervious to the rancor between their parents.

"I've gotten instructions from Father Alfredo. He needs my help at the Vatican. He is facing some charges that are being brought, and he feels I can be of help." Marco appeared weak facing his wife and trying to justify his intentions.

"What do you mean? How can you help him? You're not a lawyer."

"I can't tell you that. There are some things about my connections in Coalcojana that you do not know about, and it's better that you don't. Don't press me; that's all I can say right now." Seeing how adamant she had become, he felt he had to come on stronger.

Oh shit! This is going to be a showdown I'm not prepared for, but if ever I deserved a tirade from her this is it.

"Don't press you? You tell me that, and I know something's not right. You're involved in something illegal, or else you would be able to tell me."

"Just let me take care of what I have to, and later, back home, we'll talk. But, it's critical that I leave tomorrow for Rome."

"Tomorrow!" She was incensed. "You're a son of a bitch, Marco!"

▲ ▲ ▲

That's how it was left. Not a good situation for Marco. As bad as he felt at this confrontation, he said there was no way he could bring himself to tell Sarah anything about his relationship with Father Alfredo and the cartel. He bought himself some time before he would be back in the U.S. and have to face her. Until now, his wife only knew how deeply steeped he was in the Familia Dei Movement which required him to travel often. She suspected that this trip was for the Order's business, too, if he was to be of help to Alfredo.

The next day feeling miserable and hypocritical he did leave after saying his goodbyes to all family members and some close friends who were at his mother's bedside. All were startled at Consuela's condition for she was much improved. Perhaps, the wonderful effects of her family's presence and prayers were factors that brought noticeable vitality to her aged body. But this resurgence of strength and favorable condition was temporary and could not last for long her doctor said. He had known from test results that the cancer had spread to other organs and it was only a matter of time before death. He could not foresee any miracles taking place to add years to her life, or even months.

56

Italy
The Vatican

After the proceedings and court business came to a conclusion, Cardinal Salvacco approached Anna to express his gratitude for her courage and expertise.

"Thank you, Miss Ralston," Cardinal Salvacco said. "These past two days have been the most difficult and trying days we have all had to endure. They have been unpleasant and heart wrenching. For you to present, and for us to hear the kind of testimony from many who have suffered so long a period of time has not been easy, and it will stay in our minds for a very long time. For one of our members, ordained for many years in the sacred priesthood of the Church, who was accused of merciless crimes against children, scornful predations, we members of that priesthood are deeply wounded and humiliated.

"To Father Ted O'Driscoll and Father Edmund Kelley and Father James McGlynn we are eternally grateful for their testimony, and the righteous indignation they have always felt that brought this case to the General-Council to be heard. It may have been more emphatic if Edmund was present, but Father Ted was more than effective in his presentation. We are grateful, too, that five of the Missionaries Order in Wisconsin who were witness to the abuses inflicted upon fellow seminarians came forward through their letter to support allegations against Father Alfredo. The Council will continue discussion, deliberation, and examination of all evidence presented and will construct an announcement that will first be given to His Holiness, and then made public to the Missionaries of the Holy Church and to the Faithful throughout the world.

"Again, the Church expresses its gratitude to you as do I."

▲ ▲ ▲

After two days of discussion and deliberation by a plenary session of the Cardinals, the General-Council felt it could convene a final time to render a verdict. There were not any doubts in the minds of the members. Upon weighing the convincing and damning testimony, it would be definite that a unanimous judgment was to be recorded.

Cardinal Salvacco began, "Members of the Council, we have heard and pondered the evidence, damning beyond belief. Testimony clearly reveals the trauma still felt by the plaintiffs, and it does appear that these men are all truthful in the narrative they tell. We are obligated to come to a conclusion as to the punishment we must weigh appropriate to Father Alfredo's crimes, not merely for the violation of the sacred vow of chastity, but mainly and more significantly for the harm it has done to these men."

Cardinal Rizzoni added, "I was horrified to hear Father Miguel say how he was actually imprisoned by Alfredo for not complying with his directive to commit an unlawful sex act. I felt the adrenaline rage through me as I listened. I stifled every impulse to openly rebuke him at that moment. It's unthinkable that young boys of ten and twelve years would feel the need for self-flagellating as a way of transferring guilt to themselves for the sins of Alfredo. How he could inflict such mental torture is another crime he must be held accountable for." In the recent past Rizzoni had been involved in two cases where parish priests had been suspected, tried, and found guilty of abusing some boys in their respective CCD classes. He was shaken more than others on the Council during this period.

In their deliberation Alfredo's background was revisited, too. He was a man who came from a long line of priests many of whom rose to bishoprics in Mexico and were strong defenders of the Church. Some of these forebears dated back to the times of the Mexican Civil War.

Father Alfredo's fundraising abilities were also discussed. Though forewarned that this was not to be an influence in determining his guilt or innocence, it was only brought up in regard to what his affluent benefactors would do if he were found guilty. Would they turn their backs on charity? Would contributions to the Order cease?

Cardinal Kawamata of Japan said, "I was mortified to learn during the proceedings that Father Alfredo was so dependent on painkilling drugs. For all the years I have known him I was never aware of the divided personality of the man. He has managed to keep his addiction hidden from us, and I am sorry to say I do not believe his reasons for his drug use, some of which are absolutely absurd. My head throbbed as I struggled to remain neutral and unbiased during the proceedings."

Agnus Dei dona nobis pacem.

Cardinal Bjornlunda of Sweden added, "I am confounded to think that he used young seminarians to go to local hospitals, and to the good nuns to bring morphine and syringes to him. One of the plaintiff's affidavit stated that he was coerced to inject Alfredo many times with addictive drugs that he was dispatched to the apothecary to fetch. Alfredo actually encouraged the breaking of the law, not just by the boys, but by the nuns and druggists by supplying illegal substances. I anticipated contrition but we received only unmitigated sarcasm during his defense."

One of the Cardinal's closest Vatican aides, Father McNeill, when privy to guarded information, told the Cardinal in his best example of dysphemism that Alfredo was a nefarious desperado and a lascivious renegade. The Cardinal always admired McNeill's ability to delineate people by linking appropriate adjectives and nouns.

▲ ▲ ▲

Obviously, the Council members would be shocked senseless to learn of Father Alfredo's longtime activity dealing in illegal drugs? If they knew his addiction to drugs was far more severe than simple reliance on those he claimed to take for medicinal purposes, the Cardinals might have insisted he be sent away immediately to obtain help. His snorting cocaine was somewhat recreational, but then a good portion of his day was devoted to recreation. If Marco could have testified to reinforce the stories he was so familiar with in those sworn affidavits, there'd be no question in their minds of Alfredo's illness and his need to be sequestered in a health facility.

▲ ▲ ▲

"Another infraction we must consider is that Father Alfredo refused ordination to a young man who demonstrated the moral fortitude to report his evil conduct," said Cardinal Salvacco. "Then, I might ask, who would these men have gone to? And then, for a young seminarian to acknowledge that he had engaged in sexual misconduct was considered sufficient grounds for dismissal from the seminary. It is no wonder some seminarians denied any actions that would implicate them in wrongdoing.

"I believe the signed affidavits are proof enough, and all we need for a decision made in good conscience. I realize, too, that the letter from the Jesuits in Spain fully supports the accusations. Their involvement in this case cannot be taken lightly. The Jesuits may have an axe to grind from times long ago against the Missionaries, but nonetheless my suspicion is that someone came forward to their Superior with credible information to incriminate Father Alfredo. We have more than sufficient material to cast a decision of guilt.

"Cardinal Kawamata, as Secretary of the Council, please formulate an official document of gratitude to send to Miss Ralston at her firm in Washington and the same to Fathers Ted and Edmund at the Missionaries of the Holy Church main seminary in America. Also acknowledge the participation of Father McGlynn and his bishop in New York. I will personally write to each of the plaintiffs. This day we owe much to them all for their courage to stand steadfast in conviction. The justice we've experienced would never have been known if their testimony was not so convincing. The sacrifices these good and noble people made were to condemn a lecherous individual, and also to free the Church from him. We are grateful to them all. Luke 14:7-14 comes to my mind at this time."

57

Italy
Rome

"Well, I'm glad that's finished," said Anna. Jeannette replied, "Your presentation to the Cardinals was nothing short of brilliant, Anna. It was a joy beyond belief watching you deliver those sworn testimonies in such artful and precise language that I've ever heard expressed. I don't know what those Cardinals expected to hear, but I'll tell you clearly they were greatly impressed. The manner in which you responded to their questions, especially when one or two of them intended to throw you on the defense was pure Ted Olson at his best."

"Well. I'm glad you think so, Jeannette. I'm satisfied with the outcome. When Cardinal Salvacco made his final pronouncement I knew the voices of those eight men were heard. I don't know what I would have done without you being there. When some of the Cardinals spoke in Italian knowing I don't speak Italian, they were practically torn out of their cassocks when you translated for me, and without hesitation I could respond intelligently. You were a life saver, Jeannette. These past two days I'll never forget as long as I live." The relief Anna felt showed itself on Anna's face.

"I was totally blown away by the way Father Ted handled his part," said Jeannette. "He had names and dates and places and times that he had recorded in the past when he and Father Edmund were students. His information was very accurate and not anything that the Council could subordinate to inessential or unsubstantiated hearsay or hogwash. Father Ted was right on target. I wish Father Edmund could have been here to personally testify and witness the proceedings."

"At the moment we can only wait until the Commission decides Father Alfredo's fate," said Anna. "I have faith the decision will be to impose an extremely harsh penalty that he rightly deserves. Anything less than harsh is unacceptable, and would be a slap in the face to each of the victims. Cardinal Salvacco's final words to us pointed to his belief that Father Alfredo would receive a sentence that would, with God's help, thwart any future transgression of this nature by a man entrusted to God's work on earth."

"I'm certain your assessment is correct, Anna, for that's exactly what I understood his meaning to be. He was quite straightforward. He handled the entire proceeding with the sharpest precision."

"Let's make our way back to the hotel to freshen up. I'd like to put in a call to Mr. Dempsey to let him know the outcome at this point," said Anna. "I don't want to get ahead of things too far before the Cardinal makes an announcement, but I feel I owe my boss a call."

"Okay. Let's celebrate what I think we can call success with a nice drink and a wonderful dinner. I feel like a refreshing glass of Chianti. Is Ted, I mean, Father Ted, planning to meet us? Did he say anything to you?"

"No. He only expressed his delight at how the Council reacted to his testimony, and was excited to think that at long last Father Alfredo would get his due. He was happy for all the victims, the earlier and the later ones that they were finally heard, and can now truly feel absolved. He was planning to go straight to his hotel and try to get a good rest. I guess he'll be going to the airport early tomorrow morning. He mentioned to me his great annoyance with Marco for having left his post at Crestbrook, so he's in a hurry to get back to Georgia and have it out with him."

"Who's Marco?" asked Jeannette. "I don't know that I've heard of him."

"He's the right-hand man of Father Alfredo who was given an administrative and teaching position at Crestbrook," said Anna. "He's very high up in the Familia Dei Movement and has much control of it in the U.S. Somehow, he's quite a powerful figure in the Order, too, but he's not a priest. Father Ted had hinted to me that there are some suspicions he has about Marco's relationship with Father Alfredo and the Missionaries as well as with several wealthy and influential Mexican-American men in Metro Atlanta.

"He told me that there's not a lot of trust that he has in this man. Thinks he's a scoundrel. However, Marco appears to have certain people in his back pocket, the Director General of the Missionaries and Crestbrook's executive director and principal.

"Anyway, let's be on our way and enjoy the time we have here in Rome. Who's to say we can't revel a little bit in this glorious city. I know we won't hear anything for a while from the Cardinal."

Even though I'm confident, I'm still feeling a nervous wreck.

Satisfied with this information, Jeannette said, "The car is parked in the ramp across the street. Nice having a little Fiat to drive around the city, and our hotel is a short distance away. Why not ride up to that neat cozy trattoria called Quanta Bosta that we passed yesterday on the way out of the city before we go back to the hotel? I think it was off SS2 toward Formello."

"Sounds good to me. I'm famished, and am craving a great filetto di manzo. Let's go," said Anna cheerfully.

The two friends left together and were in great spirits feeling satisfied with the results of their work over the past several days, and hoping to relax and enjoy each other's company for a couple of hours before settling in their hotel for the night and taking a flight back to the U.S. the next afternoon.

From the heights of power
To the depths of depravity

58

Italy
The Vatican

Cardinal Salvacco began by summoning Father Alfredo to the Commission. With asperity he spoke.

"Father Alfredo, the evidence brought against you was overwhelming, and the evidence is incontrovertible. The prosecution of the case against you was impeccable in its completeness and clarity. The number of witnesses who spoke against you was remarkable and their testimony was more than compelling. There was no defense on your part as you tried to persuade us of your innocence. You were feeble in your arguments. They were shallow and consisted of lies. You have lied in the past during all the years that you were building the Order, Missionaries of the Holy Church. The Church that you have betrayed has bestowed praise upon you and your work over the past decades, and you have repaid that homage with a deceitful and hateful life. You have been the cause of serious affliction on the many people who entrusted themselves to your care and supervision. You have been the source of the mental and physical scourage they have felt over their lifetimes. You have been the devil incarnate all the while pretending to be a pious minister of the faith. Your false generosity was a devious means to an end as your intention was to corrupt. Unfortunately, many who accepted your generosity for the wrong reasons were those duped into coming forth to aid in your defense. But, thankfully, they too turned their backs when the truth about you was proven. Your arrogance has shown your unwillingness to be penitent. You have insolently resisted our attempts to discover truth. You are polluted beyond any possibility of redemption, but we pray for your soul because we believe so powerfully in the forgiveness of the Lord, and we hope for your salvation.

"Though there are some who would spare sentencing you with the penalty you deserve, which to me, personally, would be to send you to the depths of hell, all members of the General Council acquiesce that your punishment will be most severe, We have deliberated for many hours; we have sought counsel from astute colleagues; we have consulted His Holiness the Pope; we have approached civil law enforcement authority, and we have prayed with fervency to come to judicious punitive action befitting your crimes and sins. No sinful deed that any member of the Church has been found guilty of comes near to being as reprehensible as the one for which you will be punished. The perfidy you have orchestrated against your church demands a harsh sentence. I can only pray that never again will the Commission of Cardinals be called to session to deliberate a case like yours."

I'm worried that there are more like you out there who haven't been caught, and I worry much more for the Church when they are found out. The acts committed by these terrifying men are inscrutable to decent- living people.

Cardinal Salvacco ended his disparagement of Father Alfredo and walked quietly from the room without allowing the priest any opportunity to speak. This was a dark moment for the Cardinal. He thought he heard Alfredo mumble something about an appeal, and this prompted the polyglot Cardinal's thought in French: *A quoi sert tout cela?* (What's the point?)

You've got no grounds for an appeal; also the Holy Father will never accede to that.

59

Italy
Outside Rome

"I got the call from the patrolling officer thirty minutes ago. Any idea how this happened?" asked Captain Lorenzo of the Rome carabinieri.

"The officer who was first on the scene said he saw the lights streaming from the ravine and pulled over to investigate. He was awestruck to see the car at the bottom. It's not a deep fall over the cliff from the road, but deep enough when an automobile is moving at a fast rate of speed, is struck, and rolls over a few times. You don't expect that you're going to find the driver or passengers fully intact," said the Lieutenant.

Any bodies in that wreck have to be badly mangled. This is the worst I've seen along this highway in a long time. The guy in this one has to be dead.

"Let's get everyone who needs to be here to investigate. Tape off the entire area. Stop and re-route all north bound traffic, not that there's much at this time." The coroner and his forensics team should be arriving to lead the investigation. Meanwhile let's go over the scene. I want to see the tire tracks and gather some thoughts about this accident," the Captain said. "We have to find the bastard who caused this."

"From what I can immediately speculate there were two cars involved in this accident. That can be verified or not when that car gets lifted out of there for a thorough check. But, I'm guessing that the Fiat was sideswiped or deliberately struck; the driver lost control, naturally, and it careened over the embankment. That's my initial thought. I've seen these things before and that's what it looks like to me."

It was obvious that this was a terrible accident scene, and with no other vehicle damaged and parked on the roadside, the Captain's surmise that the car to be pulled from the ravine was sideswiped was accurate.

"The rescue team has been down there for a while now. They're just coming up with the bodies," Lieutenant Giancarlo said. "Such a small auto. I don't see how there could be survivors. Anyone in that vehicle must have been crushed to death."

"Let's get out of their way so they're able to position the gurneys. Are they both dead?" asked the Captain in a hushed voice when the men brought two bodies, broken and bloody, to the waiting ambulances. Considering the short amount of time it took to extricate the people from the car indicated to him that there was hope they were alive.

"No," responded the medic in charge. "We have two females, young, looking about mid to late twenties, or not much older. They are in very bad condition from what I can tell of their injuries, but luckily, they are alive. Lots of blood all over them. How they survived death in that little car is actually amazing. Someone was certainly looking over them."

"Thank God! Deus non fortuna," said the Lieutenant who was a young man himself. "Get them to the hospital as quickly as possible for urgent care. We don't want to linger here and have anyone die. This scene is ably protected now so that the investigation can thoroughly get under way."

"Record all the data, Lieutenant, and I'll see you back at the precinct later, and I would say "Deus et fortuna, Lieutenant"

"Alright, Captain, I'll be here for a while to see that everything gets wrapped up without any investigative errors being committed, or any dumb oversights."

The captain turned to head toward his cruiser, and the lieutenant with two other officers took charge.

About 170 yards up the road: "Sorry, Sir. Stop right here! Traffic is being diverted because of an accident up ahead. You will have to turn back," said Lieutenant Giancarlo. "Oh, Father! Mi scusi. At first look I didn't see your collar."

"Is there anything I can do to help, Officer?" said the priest.

"I'm not sure, but I know the victims of the accident are alive for now. I don't absolutely know their condition except they are critical and have to be rushed out of here. One second, Father. Captain, before you leave, there's a priest in this automobile. Can he see to the spiritual needs of the victims if they are conscious?"

"Yes, Lieutenant, of course. Take him to the women," the Captain said.

These women are very fortunate he's here if these are their final minutes on earth. Not everyone gets a chance to repent and ask forgiveness and mercy when their time is up. I hope they can respond to the priest.

60

Italy
Rome

Knowing that communications were safely encrypted, Marco needed to reach Father Alfredo immediately to inform him of their success: two dead in a horrible collision. Alfredo wanted to be certain that Marco had exact instructions to get out of Italy ASAP.

Latente@Seminaria.edu

Father, the mission has been accomplished, Marco said. We hit our mark just as you instructed me. The stretch of road was fairly deserted at the hour we struck them, so I know there was no one to witness "the accident". We followed them as they left the bar and ristaurante, and Vilardo knew the exact spot to send their car flying down the embankment.

    I suspect the Council was not in your favor or you would have called off the plan. What's the next step, or don't you know yet? I hope the Commission didn't dig any deeper into other matters that concern us both.

    Lynx

Lynx@crestbrook.edu

No! Matters did not go well for me. The bitch of a lawyer had an onslaught of evidence that was extremely damaging to me. I confessed nothing, and will still maintain my innocence. Those whom I felt I could rely on for support ran from me like timid dogs with tails between their legs when they heard the testimony of the eight former seminarians. Salvacco was in complete charge and he led the attack after hearing the evidence presented. I thought I had the advantage speaking Spanish when I spoke, and when I questioned, but I was caught off guard by a woman friend of the lawyer who is fluent in several languages. While listening to them all as they persecuted me, my mind was straining for revenge. Knowing the plan that was in place brought me pleasure as I watched that woman in the room, and knew she would not fly back to America sitting upright in coach. They both would be taken back outstretched in wooden boxes. It was the only relief I felt. It will be some time before I hear anything from the Council, but they have assured me that the penalty given me will be weighty. In the meantime I will plead for an audience with the Pope, and do what I can to have him intervene in the punishment phase of the case. I think that if I can persuade him to do that, the Cardinals will yield from their adamant position and extend leniency to me.

I will be looking at *El Espresso* for the report of the accident. What a shame that two beautiful women from America crashed their vehicle while traveling in Italy, and will return to their country in body bags. Justice prevails. Revenge is oh so sweet! You, Marco, return to Georgia and get back to normal life to avoid any suspicion that someone may form because you are here in Rome. I know that Vilardo will blend into the countryside and remain there safely. He has friends who can hide him for a time. I don't want the police to think they have anything but a horrendous accident to investigate. Vilardo can be trusted not to act stupidly.

L.

61

Italy
Rome

"My Jesus Mercy! Captain, I know these women," said the priest choking on the words, "Oh, no. I can't believe this has happened! They are colleagues of mine who came to Rome to prosecute a case at the Vatican. I've got to give them the last rites now in the event they don't pull through this tragedy. I'll ride in the ambulance. Please, we must get them to the hospital immediately. I can't believe that this has happened! Captain, my name is Father Ted O'Driscoll, and I'm of the Missionaries of the Holy Church Order. I'm from America as are these women. What do you know of the accident, Captain?"

"I only have a suspicion of what might have happened, Father, but it is obvious that they were struck and forced off the highway. It wouldn't take too much to knock a small vehicle like theirs out of control and have it careen off the road."

We'll get the rotten bastard responsible and not having the moral decency to stop if it was truly an accident.

Trying to focus on his responsibility, but with a multitude of thoughts cluttering his mind, the priest said, "Captain, if your assessment of the accident is correct, I think you will be investigating a murder if one of these women dies. I can tell you I have a legitimate reason for saying that."

'I hope that will not be the case, Father. We have to safeguard their lives so we can question them the first opportunity we have when they recover. After ministering the last rites to them and seeing them to the hospital, please find the time to come later to my office on Vittorio Vespucci so that we can talk. I know the hour will be late, but it is important we discuss what you know. I need to hear why you would think that this is more than just an accident. I need what information you have," the captain said with an inquisitive and puzzled look as he didn't expect to hear anything about a possible murder attempt. He was nonplussed to say the least.

Very early next morning the doctors at St Nicholas Hospital reported to Captain Lorenzo that one of the women, Jeannette Libramont, had internal injuries so severe she could not be saved. Dr. Luigi Lombardo told the Captain that Jeannette was rapidly declining from her injuries. She had lost a large volume of blood and had received several transfusions. Operating proved unsuccessful. All attempts to save her were hopeless, and she will die without ever gaining consciousness.

Later in the morning, Lorenzo, knowing what the investigation had possibly now become, called Cardinal Salvacco at the Vatican.

"Cardinal Salvacco, please. This is Captain Lorenzo with the Rome police."

"One moment, Captain. I'll connect you," said the receptionist in a very subdued and pious tone.

"Captain Lorenzo. Cardinal Salvacco here. How may I help you today, Sir?"

"Your Excellency, I would not disturb you but for a very serious reason. There was a terrible accident last night that involved two persons who were at Vatican City regarding a case that you and the Commission were hearing. This is indeed unfortunate because the accident now involves a fatality. I have spoken to Father Ted O'Driscoll, Your Excellency. He has told me the reason that Ms. Ralston and Ms. Libramont are in Rome. I've been notified by the physicians at St. Nicholas Hospital that Ms. Libramont has not survived. The injuries she sustained were enormous.

"I believe I should come to your home to speak privately about this situation."

"Of course. First, let me say I am horrified to hear this from you, Captain. I just wished both women well yesterday when we parted. They were to fly back to the U.S. I will expect you at any time today it is convenient for you. I'll inform the Curia to begin prayers and masses for the women, Captain. What is Ms. Ralston's condition?"

"She is still not conscious. Her condition remains serious."

"I shall be about 3:00 this afternoon, Cardinal if that is agreeable. I'll see you then. Goodbye."

"That hour is fine. Goodbye, Captain." The Cardinal's face turned ashen; he sat slumped in his chair with his face in his hands and began to pray in English. "Our Father . . . forgive us our trespasses as we forgive those who trespass against us. . ." It was what he had to do after being stunned by the saddening news.

62

Italy
Rome

ek@crestbrook.edu

Edmund, I have terribly bad news. Anna Ralston and Jeannette Libramont were in a car accident last night. They're in real bad shape and it looks like Jeannette might not survive. I gave <u>extreme unction</u> to them when I saw how seriously they were injured. It was just plain coincidence or divine intervention that I happened on the scene of the crash because I changed my mind and decided to join them at the trattoria where they were going for dinner. It appears that another vehicle may have sideswiped them and forced their car off the side of the road. Listen, I can't leave Rome until I find out how they are going to be. I have a theory of what could have happened, I mean, who could be responsible for the accident. If I am correct, it wasn't any accident, but a deliberate act to kill both of the women. I'm sure you know what my thinking is. I met with the police late last night and explained everything I know.
    Ted

TedOD@crestbrook.edu

What a shocker to hear! I can't believe what you said. All of you were so overjoyed at how the proceedings went before the

General-Council, only to have that joy darkened by a tragedy like this. My prayers and masses will be for Anna and Jeanette. I'll have the students and faculty offer their prayers for their recovery. Don't worry about anything here, Ted. I'll see to it that everything is covered appropriately for you. Have you seen Marco at the Order's house?

Ed

ek@crestbrook.edu

Father, thank you. Prayers are what 's needed because only God can help us here. To answer your question: No, I haven't seen Marco, if you mean, have I seen him to speak to. If he had known I was staying at the Gran Melia Hotel, and not at one of the Order's residences, you can be sure he would have avoided me. Marco is who I think is behind the "accident." It's my theory that he and Father Alfredo had something to do with the car crash. In fact, I'm convinced they're behind it. I've got to speak to the police captain later this morning, or by early afternoon, and tell him what else I know. I have no idea what may evolve from this point, but I will fill you in later.

Ted

Feeling languid after writing, Father shut down his computer and sat pensively for a few minutes with his face turned to the small crucifix that he had placed on the desk where his laptop rested. Focusing on the image of Christ on the cross, Ted brought to mind the names and faces of the people he knew who were severely affected by Father Alfredo and who endured hurt and suffering. In the darkened and quiet room he fervently clasped his hands and began to pray until the weariness of the day's and night's events forced his eyes to close in sleep.

63

Italy
The Vatican

"Welcome, Captain. Come right in," said Cardinal Salvacco. "I have been so disturbed all night long by the tragic news of the accident. It is difficult to repose when one receives such tragic information about persons recently met, and to know now that one of them has succumbed to death."

"Yes, Cardinal, and I thank you for seeing me so soon after my request, but urgency is a real priority. I'm trying to piece things together to see if I can quickly resolve last night's disastrous event."

"May I get you anything to drink as we begin the conversation, Captain?"

"Thank you. I would like cold water, please. I have spoken earlier with Father Ted O'Driscoll of the Missionaries of the Holy Church who testified at a hearing that centered around the crimes of Father Alfredo founder of the Order. Father Ted arrived on the scene of the accident simply by chance, and after composing himself upon recognizing the victims, happened to mention that the accident may have been an intentional act to commit murder. Of course, my ears perked up at his announcement, so I was intent upon learning what information he might have. One of the things he thought to be of importance occurred when he was leaving his hotel for the Vatican. He said he glanced in the direction of the café and thought he saw someone he is very familiar with. He saw two men talking and thought he saw Marco Montoya, a close colleague of Father

Alfredo. Father was hurrying to get to the Vatican so he did not stop. He thought he must have been mistaken because he knew Mr. Montoya was in Colombia with his family visiting his sick mother. We will check the surveillance cameras just to be sure. Are you familiar with Mr. Montoya, Cardinal Salvacco? We talked at length about the proceedings you had led here for a few of days, so I am aware of the specifics of the case."

"I do know that Marco Montoya is connected to the Order as he is a significant man in the Familia Dei Movement which as you know was begun by Father Alfredo. It is good, Captain, that you have specifics of the case as that saves a lot of time. Go on, please."

"What I need to know, Cardinal Salvacco, is what you can tell me about Father Alfredo. You know what I mean?"

"Yes, I do.

From recent discoveries about the man nothing would be too astounding in terms of what he might do to perpetuate his own designs.

"You are wondering if Father Alfredo could be behind the accident, or if he's implicated in some way. You know from Father Ted what the conclusion of the trial was. Yes, I believe I can say that Alfredo could have engineered an unfortunate accident to occur to a person or persons that did much to convict him of the crimes he was charged with. The Commission which tried the case came to agreement that we never truly knew the person that Father Alfredo is, and because you are asking me, I would never doubt to what ends he might go to avenge someone whom he feels inflicted great harm to him. I would say directly that Father Alfredo is the person you need to interrogate. Remember that he has a vast number of friends and followers and many dedicated priests at his Order's churches in Rome. I said that he may be the architect behind the attempt on the women's lives, but he would not pull the trigger, or in this case, drive the car. There are many people who have come under his influence over several years."

"That is direct enough, Cardinal. Thank you."

"I will add that the General-Council has not made public what Father Alfredo's punishment is, but all concerned know that it is most severe. I will tell you secretly, Captain, that Alfredo will not be seen publicly again unless he leaves the Church, which I doubt he will. It will be the result of your investigation that determines whether or not Alfredo will ever be seen publicly again," said the Cardinal with an air of complete determination.

"I ask for your prayers, your Excellency, that I can resolve this matter expediently," said Captain Lorenzo.

The captain left the office of Cardinal Salvacco with much on his mind as he had acquired the information which would direct his actions for the next hours and days. He wondered whether his job now would be easier or more difficult depending on how Father Alfredo might plan his confrontation and defense. Everyone knows perfectly well how contumacious Father Alfdredo is. STUBBORN INSUBORDINATE

64

Italy
Iles d'Arda

Marco continued his story.

"The newspaper *El Espresso* reported that the stolen car had been reported to the police an hour before it was found abandoned on Via della Pisana toward the A90 about three miles from the scene of the accident. I got back to the Gran Melia Hotel and waited to listen to the 11:00 newscast on television. In the meantime, I went to the lobby bar and had a couple of drinks before I returned to my room. I was confident that the entire plan was working to perfection.

Why wouldn't it? Alfredo was the master architect behind it, and Vilardo and I pulled it off without a glitch.

"The flight back to Atlanta was scheduled for early morning and was part of a round trip ticket so there was no time that had to be spent hunkering down at the hotel. I immediately left for the airport and was soon on my way home. At this point I only calculated that both women in the car had been killed; the newscaster did not mention that anyone survived the crash with so many life-threatening injuries. I figured that both were dead and there were no witnesses, so I was in the clear. I showed no remorse and even now have no pangs of conscience; I was simply fulfilling my responsibilities in getting a job done. I got back home the next day and looked forward to a browbeating from Sarah whom I knew I had abandoned with the kids in Colombia. I was expecting the worst, but knew I would get over it fast when I returned to

Crestbrook and resumed my duties. Getting my mind back to work and on my daily routine would be welcoming.

"I had no further contact with Father Alfredo. I wouldn't have any until Alfredo was back in Mexico. And I didn't know when that might be."

▲ ▲ ▲

I found it hard to believe that he was so callous about what had taken place. Not being completely heartless, he said he did feel some emotional impact, but he soon returned to thinking about tomorrow. Deliberately murdering two people whose only crime was to bring to justice a man, a pedophile, who had violated his trust as a priest in teaching and supervising young seminarians I found despicable. This, he felt, was justification for following Father Alfredo's orders to avenge the legitimate actions of two women trying to secure justice and safeguard the rights of future boys who would enter the seminary.

Marco told me that he was perplexed when he heard that Father Ted was not back from Italy, and might not return for a while. He was informed by Father Edmund that Ted was remaining in Rome and keeping vigil at the room of Anna Ralston who was slowly recovering from her injuries sustained in the crash. Marco said he became very nervous about this, knowing that Anna was alive, and his not knowing if it was possible Anna could remember anything about the accident that she would tell the police. He was very worried as to how the investigation might go if Anna regained consciousness because one could never be absolutely sure she did not see him or his accomplice when they ran her off the road. He said he was very rattled when he heard about Anna.

I left the prison early that day. I felt I needed a real break from the story to immerse myself in something wholesome. I got back across to Rome and walked about the Capitoline Hill. I went to the trapezoid Piazza del Campidoglio and the Cordonata, beautiful structures designed by Michelangelo. After enjoying the magnificent sculptures and paintings housed by the museums, I walked to the Tarpeian Rock to view the Forum lying below. I had a half bottle of red wine to accompany a fabulous plate of ossobuco alla piemontese at a ristorante recommended by a guard at the prison, and took a taxi back to my hotel. I turned on the TV and couldn't avoid hearing reports of crime and accidents and killings in the city. For a minute I thought I was back in Atlanta. It was impossible for me to rest just thinking about Marco's attitude toward murder. Then it struck me! Murder! Just maybe my thinking that Marco had been using me went in the wrong direction. Maybe my brother was murdered and Marco had some involvement with it. I'll finally get some answers. I was bothered by this thought for days and wondered how many unlucky souls had been the victims of a two-sided man who appeared to be living a happy and charming life. Marco was a man capable of reprising his role as religious leader one time and then reprising his role as ruthless lugarteniente another. A modern day Jekyll and Hyde. Yes, Alfredo was correct when describing Marco as a Proteus figure.

65

Italy
Rome

"Lieutenant Giancarlo is our best interrogator," said Captain Lorenzo, "but after hours of questioning, Father Alfredo revealed nothing that would tie him to the accident/murder. He maintained his ignorance of any knowledge about it. I know from what you said, Cardinal, that Alfredo is quite an accomplished liar and deceiver, so we will keep pressure on him and use tried and true tactics until we're absolutely certain that he was not part of a plan to kill those women. We're not mentioning the name Marco Montoya to Alfredo until we think we have something."

And when we do he'll be slapped damned hard across the head with his own dusty and worn huaraches.

"Captain, I will see to it that Father Alfredo does not leave the country before such time as you are finished with him. Even if he were to leave for Spain, or go home to Mexico, I can get him back to Rome for you to pursue questioning of him, but I know he will not be departing any time soon unless he should yield to death. When you are satisfied as to his innocence he can leave for home, but he will be sequestered by his Order in Mexico. At this time I will be calling him in to mete out his punishment decided by the Council. I'd like you to remain here to observe."

"Monsignor, call in Father Alfredo, please."

In a firm voice with a strong hint of anger, "Sit down, Father." said the Cardinal. "I know you attempted to have a conversation with His Holiness. After you were tried, I spoke to the Pope and informed him of the results of the trial. He and the members of the Council condemn your crimes; the Church in general condemns your crimes. Very simply and directly, we are all in agreement that you will be banished from active ministry to live a life of prayer and penitence. For the remainder of your life you will reside in seclusion at your Order's guest residence at one of the seminaries. You will be permitted to go home to Mexico for the purpose of settling any affairs of the Order. You'll be confined at Coalcojana until you hear from me about returning to Rome. We'll decide if you remain here permanently as the Council decreed, or if the members allow you to spend your final years living in Mexico. The Curia with the Council is contemplating the dissolution of the Missionaries of the Holy Church and confiscating the properties and accounts of the Order. They do have that authority as you know.

"Also, be apprised that the General Council has formed an ad hoc committee of five bishops from five different countries to continue the investigation into your past. Despisedly, your Order has not been as cooperative as it should have been, particularly with its leadership hiding your corrupt and randy life. Very few came forward to speak anonymously and verify your activities. The results of the bishops' inquiries will determine if you receive additional punishment regardless of your advanced age. Let us hope they discover nothing more. Have you anything to say to me?"

An unexpectantly sedate Alfredo responded with disdain, "Cardinal Salvacco, though I dispute several of those charges, I feel I have no choices. I have already written an apology for what I have been accused, as I have no recourse to your decision. Upon hearing my sentence, I can only ask that you do nothing to dissolve the Missionaries. Over time the pious and Godly priests of the Order have done magnificent work in the name of the Church worldwide, and will continue to build schools, establish universities, open mission fields, and perform other great works for the benefit of mankind. I plead with you not to disrupt the Order, and to leave the coffers for the Missionaries to be solvent for their work."

I can only hope Salvacco and other morons at the Vatican never uncover the money they don't know about. They'd take every last dollar.

Captain Lorenzo received a call on his cell phone and interrupted Father Alfredo by saying, "Cardinal, I have been called to the hospital. I'm sorry, but I must leave now. If there is anything further that you find out upon inquiry, please do not hesitate to summon me to your office."

"That's all I have to say, thank you," said Father Alfredo.

"I believe our business here is completed, Captain. I will comply with your request, and I assure you that if Father Alfredo can recall any substantive information he, too, will be happy to talk to you. Isn't that correct, Father?"

"Yes, of course, Your Excellency," a disgruntled Alfredo responded.

Oh, don't worry about that, Cardinal. I have nothing further to say at this time, but I just may have my day in the near future.

▲ ▲ ▲

Captain Lorenzo was not a religious man. He had his beliefs having been raised in the faith of the Catholic Church, but was not pious to any extent. In fact, he could not recall the last time he attended mass, but could recall that the last time he entered a church was on an occasion to investigate a crime. A robbery where some sacred icons were taken from the Church of the Holy Redeemer.

When he left the presence of Cardinal Salvacco and Father Alfredo, he saw the distinct dichotomy of good and evil, and contemplated the two. Driving to St. Nicholas Hospital he wondered how two men of the Church could be so unalike. Both were educated in the teachings of Christ, but one had lost his way in the darkness of sin while the other lived the life of Christ. He drove on philosophizing about the mystery of mankind and recalling a phrase his father used to say especially as he got older: *Dagliu Avvocati e Medici mi salvi Dio.* (God save me from doctors and lawyers.) Lorenzo now thought that perhaps bad priests should be added to the phrase, something he never contemplated before. Oh, he was aware that bad ones existed from past times up to the present, but his recent experience with the likes of Father Alfredo brought him to this generalization for which he hoped God would forgive him.

66

Italy
Rome

Shortly after the accident, Father Ted felt it was not too late an hour for a necessary phone call to be placed to Luxembourg.

The priest who had stood by her notified Jeannette's parents in Luxembourg of her condition and asked that they not hurry to Rome until her status changed either for the better or the worse. He attempted to sound very hopeful, but he did not tell them the extent of her injuries which may end her life. He wanted to offer some hope of her recovery slight as it may be. "Everything possible is being done for her," he told them. "But the doctors aren't certain that she can pull through. We are all continuing to pray that we'll see a significant difference in her condition by morning."

When Father returned to the hospital next morning, Captain Lorenzo gave him the sad news. Captain Lorenzo said to the Lieutenant, "I had the most unpleasant task of informing Father O'Driscoll of Jeannette Libramont's death. He was badly shaken after hearing that news. I knew he needed time to pull himself together as he had found a respectable friendship with her and her good friend Anna Ralston, so he was emotionally affected."

Afterwards, all Father Ted could say was, "Jeannette's parents will be horrified to hear that she didn't pull through. When I first notified them, I didn't want them to lose hope of her recovery. Now they have to be told their daughter is dead."

This has got to be one of my worst moments; one of the worst for a priest. How do I bring comfort with mere words that will be empty sounds to these dear people?

▲ ▲ ▲

"It seems we now have a murder we're investigating," Captain Lorenzo said. "What is Ms. Ralston's diagnosis presently, Doctor?"

Doctor Lombardo answered directly: "She has stabilized nicely, and is out of danger of death. Her injuries are very severe, but she will recover with time and continued medical attention. I'm optimistic that she will not suffer any serious life-long problem after she heals."

"Is she able to converse with me? Is she coherent? Or might it be too early to try to elicit information about the crash?" Lorenzo asked.

"I really think it advisable to wait a while longer, perhaps two days. I will call you as soon as I see she is well enough."

"Doctor Lombardo, is Father O'Driscoll still in the hospital, or has he left to inform the Libramont family?"

"Yes, he is still here. He hasn't left the hospital. I believe he went to the chapel. I'll summon him for you, Captain."

"May I use your office to speak to him privately?"

"Of course, Captain."

67

Italy
Rome

"I know the anguish you are feeling, Father, for your two friends," said Captain Lorenzo. "I am sorry they were so badly injured, and I am sorry that you must experience the pain they have suffered. I want you to know that the Rome police and the special police agencies will do everything possible to solve the crime that has been committed. The other car has been found and it was perfectly clean. No fingerprints or other forensic evidence was discovered. Whoever drove that vehicle knew what he was doing to keep any clue away from us. But there is one small matter they did not consider, and that is they left the car on Via Cimato across from a bank building which has cameras on each corner of the building hidden by the gargoyles. The film is being looked at carefully, as is the film from the Gran Melia Hotel's camera. We will be working this case diligently, and I hope that Ms. Ralston will be able to tell us something that we'll be able to go on to find the driver that forced them into the ravine.

"Doctor said you spoke to Ms. Libramont's parents. That was good that you informed them that her condition was critical and she might not pull through. Because of her death I will follow up explaining what has transpired and express my condolences, and also apprise them that a murder investigation is underway. If you have already called the Libramonts with the terrible news, they may be expecting a call from me. If you have not, I think their sadness might be lessened when you do call. Better that you speak to them first before I do."

What a profession! Always the messenger carrying horrible news to good people. Never in their imaginations could they believe their daughter would be killed. Only to think of my own child.

With head bowed and downcast eyes, Ted dolefully replied to the Captain, "I feel such an obligation, Captain, because I'm the one who brought the two women into this situation. It's my fault they are lying in this hospital, and that one of them has died, and at such a young age. I wish I had never run into Anna in Madrid so long ago that my father would have asked for her help on my behalf."

"Father, you can't look back now. We have to do all we can to make Ms. Ralston's life better, and all we can do is offer our prayers for Ms. Libramont and try to comfort her parents."

"Captain, what about Father Alfredo? Did he give you anything that you can go on?"

"No! It was not the right moment to question him about the accident. The Cardinal summoned Alfredo to tell him his punishment. I was present to observe the man and his reactions. I asked if he was informed about the accident, but he was adamant that he knew nothing about it. He offers his condolences to the women and their families. Why is it I do not believe the apostate? I will be speaking to him, Father. Of that you may be confident."

I know he's a major player behind all of this tragedy. I'll get him, and I make this a solemn promise to the parents of Jeannette Libramont. They will not have lost their daughter and see a guilty man go free.

68

Italy
Iles d'Arda

Marco said that the five bishops continuing to look into Father Alfredo's past as ordered by Cardinal Salvacco did not have to wait long to approach the General Council through Cardinal Salvacco. When the Cardinal did in fact halt the flow of much of the Missionaries' money, and when Father Alfredo had no further access to the Order's money by his isolation, he had no freedom of movement and could conduct no financial business. He felt helpless.

In their report to the Cardinal, the bishops said they were approached by women who claimed that Father Alfredo had fathered their children, and that he was their sole source of financial support and had been for several years. With Alfredo's departure from active daily operations of the Order these families were without income because checks were not being sent to them. They objected to the halting of funds from the Order, and claimed they were entitled to continued support. These families demanded further compensation to see their children raised and educated and to see the mothers through old age.

The bishops raged with indignation to learn that Alfredo had fathered children by two Mexican women and one Swiss woman. The discovery yielded six children in all, the oldest being nineteen or twenty. The bishops' ire was equally provoked by the fact that within the Order there were no statutes making any kind of fiscal transactions illegal. There was no reporting of sums of money; there were no records of who received large sums of money; there were no written statements explaining how Father Alfredo circulated the money. They believed this to be most unethical, and demanded that Cardinal Salvacco haul Alfredo back to Rome to explain these matters that were presently uncovered.. Confronted by three families who could prove that the children were Alfredo's, the Order, the Council, and the Pope were shocked and bewildered over the man's lack of sanctity and sanity. It was scandal after scandal, not just pedophilia, but an added sex crime by one who has taken the vow of chastity.

Marco said, "At the time of first being accused, Alfredo said he would never admit to any wrongdoing, but this stance changed. When having to face all of this, Father Alfredo told me that he admitted to everything. He didn't care that the Church was about to disclose all of his sins publicly for he was already sequestered and this was his punishment. The cartel was still his. And with this he could operate with impunity. His clerical life was ended, his religious interests had ebbed. "Non sum qualis eram!" (I'm not the man I was) he wrote in a message to me. But what he didn't know was that his every act was being monitored. The cartel was alerted to Alfredo's having channeled millions of dollars to secret off-shore accounts in the Caymans as well as to Switzerland. In fact, he used cartel money during the years to maintain the support of the families who arose out of nowhere and brought added woe to his life. Without compunction he stated that he was proud of the paternal blessing that came into his early life, and that he felt elevated from the basic level of life. This sentiment vexed even the last of Alfredo's supporters. His audacity was reprehensible.

"There was strenuous opposition within the cartel as to how things were being run, and it seemed a matter of time before there would be a rift that created factions. Father Alfredo was old now. Even Chuko of the Nagella Cartel was fifty and this was like one hundred in cartel years. With the negative publicity that emerged during the charges leveled against Alfredo, and the conviction of guilt by the General Council, and the Pope's declaration of his guilt, and the punishment that was tantamount to exile,

Alfredo's days were over as the head of anything. The realm of the beast would be no more."

I actually saw this as a big opportunity for me, but I knew enough to keep this thought to myself. I didn't want to be a fatality during the early stages of a power-grab.

69

Italy
Rome

"Anna's out of the coma, Father, and I think she's going to recover just fine," Mrs. Ralston said with a guarded cheeriness in her voice. "The doctors have been very encouraging most of the way through this ordeal and have always shown much hope that she will be okay. Thank God for that. She has been given the best of care, and most important, Father, have been your prayers and your being here for her. I don't know what we would have done without you." Tears blurring her eyes.

"Mrs. Ralston, you can't know the feelings I've had thinking I was the one who placed her in this situation," said the priest with remorse.

"I wish you wouldn't feel that way. Anna wanted to do everything possible to help when your father called and told her of your need. You were great friends in college and she wanted to be your friend now. That's how Anna is."

Father Ted said, "I couldn't be more thankful to God for bringing her through, but I can't imagine what Jeannette's parents feel. I'm so sorry they lost their daughter, and Anna lost so loving a friend."

"I know. I was so saddened when they arrived here to take her body back home to Esch for burial. They flew to Rome immediately after you phoned them which was shortly before or after Captain Lorenzo spoke to them. They left in great haste without seeing anyone, but did inquire about Anna's condition. I can only pray that Captain Lorenzo gets sufficient leads to find the one responsible for her death and sends him to prison for the rest of his life." These last words were spoken with rancor.

"I hope that, too, but I think time is running out. The Captain would have told us if there were any new leads that he was following up on. I hope he's playing it close to the vest and has information that he's working on, but is keeping it to himself. He seemed determined to solve this case judging by the number of officers working it. He told me how intent the Force is.

"And I'm not surprised that Jeannette's parents were so grief stricken that they didn't want conversation with anyone, but desired more to leave for home. I don't feel slighted at all. I understand completely."

Sounding full of hope, Mrs. Ralston said, "If just for Jeannette's parents' sake, the police have got to find the killer. Oh! Here's the doctor."

"Doctor Lombardo, how's Anna doing? Is she able to see us and talk to us?"

"Yes, Father, you and Mrs. Ralston can go in her room and see her. She's a bit groggy, but will be coherent in conversation. I'd just ask that you don't tire her out by staying too long. She'll probably close her eyes when she feels sleepy or too tired to talk any longer."

"Thank you, and thank you for the superior care you gave her, doctor. I don't know how I would have handled all this if I didn't think she was in the best medical hands," said Mrs. Ralston.

"Well, you're welcome, Madam. We have a great staff of doctors and nurses at St. Nicholas Hospital and this is one of the best in Rome," Doctor Lombardo said with pride and with every attempt to sound humble.

"Anna, darling, I, I," stumbled Mrs. Ralston.

"Hi, Mom, it's okay. I know."

"I'm just so relieved and happy that you're here and doing so well." She knew she had to repress any tears for Anna's sake.

"Hi, Anna," said Father Ted. "We had no idea how long you might be in a coma before coming to. Your mother has been here holding your hand and praying for your recovery every day and night since she arrived. You've been through so much, but the doctor says you're going to be one hundred percent in a short time. You'll be out of the hospital and heading home as soon as you can get on your feet. Thankfully, you suffered no internal injuries that were life threatening."

"How is Jeannette? Where is she? How is she? Is she okay, Mom," asked Anna in a strained voice.

As softly as she could speak the words, she said, "Honey, Jeannette's injuries were so severe she didn't pull through."

"Oh, God, no! I can't believe it!" cried Anna.

"Everything that could be done for her was done, Anna. The doctors and nurses diligently tried everything to keep her alive, but they were unable…"

In a pitiable shriek Anna cried, "This is the worst day of my life. I don't know how I can ever get over her death; she was so special a friend to me. This is horrible."

"I know, Honey, but she's in God's hands now, and I'm sure, in a better place. If she survived somehow, she would have been a different person. The head trauma she suffered was horrible. She never regained consciousness from the moment her head was struck, so she didn't suffer at all while she was in the ICU."

I can't be thankful enough that it wasn't you that was killed. I don't think I could cope. Jeannette's parents are suffering so.

Anna closed her eyes, lay in silence, tears wetting her cheeks, which signaled to her mother and her good friend it was time for them to let her grieve. Outside Anna's room, Mrs. Ralston and Father Ted sat in the visitor's lounge and talked for a few minutes. With great concern for her daughter, Anna's mother said, "Father, I don't know how Anna's going to hold up after this ordeal. I know she'll feel responsible for Jeannette's death. I only hope I can console her."

Attempting to give reassurance, Ted comforted her saying, "With our prayers she's going to show surprising resilience, and though the emotional impact is so heavy upon her now, with some counseling she will be fine. I'm confident of that."

God, I hope I'm right about that.

They said goodbye to each other and Mrs. Ralston returned to her hotel to rest and await her husband's arrival. Ted left the hospital also. He intended to spend a little time with a philosophy professor at the university from whom he had taken courses when studying in Rome, but was too distraught to attempt being social with an old friend. His emotions told him he needed time for contemplation, so he decided on quiet time at one of the alcove chapels in St. Peter's Basillica where he knelt and prayed for several hours. Along with the prayers that he whispered to himself, he could not erase the thought that he was indirectly responsible for so much that has happened.

70

Italy
Rome

"Excellent work, Lieutenant! We'll get those bastards now," said Captain Lorenzo feeling exhilaration for a very positive investigation. Both films confirm that Father O'Driscoll was right about Marco Montoya being in Rome at the time Ms. Libramont was killed. The camera facing Via della Pisana from the bank clearly shows Montoya. And look at who else we've got, Lieutenant. Best of all we've got Giuseppe Vilardo on video, too. The film from the hotel offers conclusive proof that Father O'Driscoll did, indeed, see Marco Montoya at the Gran Melia café. We've been tracking that narco rat Vilardo for a long time. This was almost too easy. Let's get Vilardo in and see how he's connected to the priest and Montoya. This is interesting to me. I've only known his connections to be with the cartels in the Mideast who transport their drugs to Europe through the dons in Corsica. My guess is he'll be obliging, and want to make a deal knowing we got him on a murder charge. Finding him is the first step. And the second will be my ripping that fucking talisman he thinks is so sacred off his goddamn neck."

"Are you going to call Interpol to relate what we have to the American and Mexican authorities," asked the Lieutenant.

"No. Not yet. I want to get Vilardo wrapped up first." Those other two we'll get with his help."

"Yeah, but what if the priest, Father Ted, says something to Montoya? You know they work together at that Christian school in Georgia."

"No. He and I have talked about how this will be handled. Father Ted knows how to play this. He gave us the lead that Montoya may have been in Rome, so we could follow up with the cameras. I'm going to call him immediately and tell him we got the killers on tape, so he has to be cool as far as his association with Montoya, and to be patient. He's a smart guy and wants nothing else but Ms. Libramont's killer or killers to be caught."

"Captain, I'm thinking now that Vilardo is connected to Montoya and Father Alfredo and it's all about drugs. We're going to have quite a case in front of us. After you get Vilardo to crack, we've got to get the Mexican government to extradite the priest, and that might be impossible knowing how he's been supported by the police because of the bribes he's given. I'm afraid they don't see him as pernicious as we do. It's well documented how venal they are. It'll be easier getting Montoya here. The Americans will be happy to hand him over to us knowing he's wanted on a first degree murder charge."

"Yeah, I agree," said Captain Lorenzo confidently, "but I think we can exert enough pressure on the Mexicans to hand Alfredo over, if we have to. However, we won't rely on their cooperation because I'm going to get him here through the Vatican. Cardinal Salvacco will do our bidding, and Father Alfredo won't know the real reason he's really being called back to Rome. He'll discover that the penalty placed on him by the General Council of the Curia is small compared to the charges he will face in criminal court: accomplice to murder and drug dealing. He'll be convicted. He won't find himself in a cloistered church environment, but in an eight by eight foot cell for the rest of his life which probably won't be too long, but long enough to bring him misery."

His ministerial days are finished. Maybe they'll let him hear other prisoners' confessions and help them save their souls.

The Captain thought for a moment about the importance of how a tragic incident would lead to the Rome Police Department breaking wide open a huge drug operation that extended from the U.S. and Mexico to Europe. He felt a sense of spirituality down deep, and silently offered a brief prayer for the young woman whose life was taken away from her by men with avarice in their hearts.

"Lieutenant, go and get Vilardo. Find him. Take men with you and be very careful. Bring him in for interrogation. The process begins now. You know where to look. I don't think he can know that we would have any reason to arrest him, so he won't run, but be cautious. He's a halcone who would like to think he would die for a cause. Meanwhile, I'm going to the hospital to check on Ms. Ralston and see if there's anything she remembers that will help us. She's been through quite an ordeal, but perhaps there will be one thing she can add to what we already have. It doesn't matter too much if she can't recall details because we've got all we need right now with the video evidence, but it does no harm to ask. The doctor notified me, as I asked him to, that she is doing exceptionally well. It's surprising how a car crash will allow one person to walk away with injuries that are not life threatening and another person sitting beside her to be so badly banged up that she dies within hours. When your time is up, you can't escape it. Well, I'll see you later. Get that scum Vilardo back here, Lieutenant, and then we get to work."

▲ ▲ ▲

When Captain Lorenzo left the hospital and got back to the precinct, he sat at his desk and subconsciously let his mind flow to past homicide cases. He had worked all types of murders during his lifetime as a cop, and sat philosophizing over what makes a person take another's life. Morosely, he brought many reasons to mind, but could not think of any sound rationale for any one of them. Just as quickly, the realization of being confronted with another crime to investigate and solve entered his brain. A surge of energy coursed through him. He knew he would bring the killer of Jeannette Libramont to justice. Time and patience and purpose he understood better than most people.

71

Italy
Rome

"Mom, Dad, I feel so terrible that I can't express my feelings just thinking about Jeannette. If only we had not decided to go out, and instead went to the hotel as we originally planned, this might not have happened," Anna said to her parents. "Father Ted told me that it was no accident, but someone intentionally wanted to kill us both."

Neither of us has any enemies in Italy. Who would attempt to murder us?

"Anna, if this was an accident you couldn't have foreseen that it would happen. If it was an intention to kill you both, those men would have done it another time and in a different place. They are evil. I know the police will find the ones who did this. But don't blame yourself for it. You and Jeannette did the natural thing that two young girls would do after enduring those two intense days in that court setting."

"Where is Father Ted? Has he gone back to the U.S.?" Anna asked.

I hope he hasn't left yet. There are so many things I'd like to say to him. Things I need to say.

"Yes. You don't remember much, Honey, but Father spoke to you soon after you came out of the coma. You were coherent and talked for a while, but you evidently don't remember that he said he would be leaving Rome. He was not about to leave before you regained consciousness, and he heard from the doctors that you would be perfectly fine after much rest and recovery time. He said he would be calling periodically to check on your status."

Mrs. Ralston still had a mother's instinct that there was something deeper between Anna and her close friend, Father Ted. Anna's father was impervious to what his wife saw as obvious.

"It was great having him here, Mom, even at times when I didn't know he was here. He has been a real friend, and I don't want him to feel like he was responsible in any way. I'll miss him."

"Yes, Anna. You will miss him. I know that because I have sensed that you wish your relationship with him could be more than friendship. But it can't be, Dear. Father Ted's a priest devoted to the Church, and if he felt a certain way toward you, it would have to be feelings he cannot respond to. He's a good man and a good priest, and that's how it is. If you would hope for anything more, you must suppress those feelings. I say that I sensed something when I saw the way you regarded him whenever he was present, and I've read between the lines when you have talked about him in the past. Perhaps you didn't think anything was obvious, but I could tell what your emotions were. He's a handsome man with so many great characteristics that are simply admirable, but he has made his commitment to serve God, and that's the way it is."

"I know, Mother, I know," Anna said sheepishly.

A stream of thoughts went through Anna's mind.

My mother was one able to detect things I thought I kept positively well-hidden. In this case she was right. There was something special I felt for Ted O'Driscoll at the time he was so serious about Christy Reiman, and it sprang up again when we ran into each other in Madrid at the Ritz. Through the years I suppressed it pretty well I thought, but some things don't go unnoticed by watchful mothers, and mine evidently was very watchful. I have no idea what Ted was feeling, or even if he ever felt anything. I can't presume he did because he went on to become ordained, and appears to be content and happy with his life. I guess it was just me. But I'm not shocked that Mother picked up on it. She's always been so observant.

Mrs. Ralston continued, "Anna, you're lucky to be alive. You have a nice life with a tremendous job and lots of good friends. You have much to be appreciative of, and I know you are, Dear. I'll be happier when the doctor releases you from the hospital and we can get back to Connecticut and resume our lives until the time you go back to Washington to work. Your father and I are so proud of what you did, and rejoice that we have our daughter."

Anna said, 'I'll be glad to leave here, too, go home to rest for a while, and then go back to work where I can get my mind on other things, though I'll never get Jeannette out of my mind. Drew Dempsey and the other partners have been tremendous through all this. I really owe them and the firm a great deal. It's such a magnificent feeling when people like that are there when you most need help. Did you see that bouquet sent by my office, Mother?"

"Yes. I do see it, Darling. Absolutely beautiful, isn't it? And what a beautiful and thoughtful note of love and encouragement attached," Mrs. Ralston said.

She had become quite weary after so many days of worry sitting by her daughter's bedside, continually wondering what the outcome of Anna's injuries were to be. Now that she was confident Anna was on her way to a full recovery, and also confident that Anna understood what her relationship with Ted O'Driscoll had to be, she was ready to go home. Inwardly, she longed for the comforting surroundings of her Stafford Springs home. Living in a hotel suite that had fine adornments was not the same as being home, so she was ready to see her daughter fit enough to board a plane for home where Anna would rest and recuperate better than in the hospital bed in St. Nicholas. She and her husband more than once expressed their gratitude for the remarkable care their daughter had received, but felt they couldn't be completely at ease until Anna was under the care and supervision of the doctors known back in Connecticut.

72

Colombia
El Ritero

Marco told me he received an urgent message from his brothers that their mother had had a relapse and was now in peril of death. He knew he would not go to El Ritero again to see her. The visit he made earlier, and the week that Sarah and his kids spent with his family would be the last time that they saw his mother. Old Consuela had said that there were things about her life which she had told no one, and which she had held secret for a lifetime, but which she felt obligated to confess before she passed on to the kingdom of God. Besides the strength of her family at her side, the morphine drip was all that alleviated the agonizing pain she was suffering. The pain of her illness became so excruciating during her final days that she decided to write a letter to Marco; she would not have the stamina to speak at any length on the telephone to him, so taking her time to do so, and in complete solitude, she wrote.

▲ ▲ ▲

He showed me the letter which he took from between the leaves of a book he was holding. It must have been the most difficult thing this woman ever did in her entire life. I have been a journalist for my whole professional life, and being that, I have always strived to construct the best stories in the most eloquent prose that anyone who loved literature would enjoy reading. It is always gratifying to know that the words I put together to report a news event or narrate an account of something were the most expressive and descriptive and thoughtful that entered my mind. But with Marco's translation to English of his mother's letter, the simple expression of her emotion came through in very impressive language that was direct and heartfelt. Not flowery nor ornate, but sincere.

▲ ▲ ▲

"Marco, I have loved you with all my heart since the moment of your conception. Your birth as my oldest child was a joy that entered my body as yours left mine. Through the years of your childhood I felt the good Lord blessed me abundantly. You were a good boy to me and to your father, and you helped always with the work at home doing daily chores and with your siblings. I was so sad and felt lonely when you left our village at a young age to go to Medellin. The choice you made upset me terribly. I knew you were making a very bad decision. It is not what I wanted for you, and I was angry with your father for letting you go. I knew it would lead to bad things in your life, and maybe even lead to your death at a young age. I have loved you as I have loved Ricardo and Arturo and Rosita, but you were a special child. It is with a mixture of joy and sorrow that I say to you what no one knows except me. I was so young when I married your father, but we loved each other more than we could ever imagine. My Fernando loved me as a young girl, and said he always hoped my parents would allow me to marry him. When we married we had a baby. You are that baby. Your father loved me and his baby and he loved us right to his early death.

"You know that my brother went to the seminary in Coalcojana at a young age because a priest came to El Ritero and recruited boys to study for the priesthood. The priest who is Father Alfredo Legados is the man whom you have become so close to over many years. The Familia Dei Movement you belong to and the work at the school have brought you together. Father Alfredo was the young priest who came to our village. He was there for many weeks and he came to our home often, mostly to talk to my brother about the seminary. He knew it would be hard on my mother and father to be without their son to help do the work. Marco, Father Alfredo saw me sometimes when he came. I committed a sin with him that I was ashamed of for a long time, but I was never ashamed of having my son. When I knew that I would have the child, I begged my parents to allow me to marry my beloved Fernando. I did not tell him or anyone else that I was pregnant. A while later I told him that he and I were going to have a child, and he never questioned it, but accepted it proudly, and I let him believe that you were his boy. I never told my husband the truth. I could never tell you before. It was not right for me to tell you, but now is the time for you to know. I want you to forgive me. I was very young. Our marriage was good and happy. Your life with Fernando as father was good. Forgive me."

▲ ▲ ▲

Marco was struck hard and shocked when he learned who his father is. It was like the proverbial ton of bricks that hit him. He said that he forgave his mother and felt she was brave and good to tell him the truth. He could not hate her for this, but said that what she kept from him was not as bad as what he kept from her. Consuela never knew either from her husband, or her son, that Marco's real attachment to Father Alfredo was not just the Order, but the cartel. This knowledge, he thought, would have depressed and killed her long ago. It took much time for him to digest what he had read for what was churning within was the thought of Alfredo not knowing he was his son. Consuela died after she finished the letter, confessed her sins, and received the last rites from the village priest. Two of her sons and her daughter mourned the loss of their mother. Sadly, Marco was far away.

▲ ▲ ▲

Marco told me that one of the saddest days of his life was when he got the news that his mother had died. He was sorry he was not in El Ritero to be with his family when it happened; he was sorry he did not have a last goodbye even if Consuela was not conscious. He was sorry, too, about what his mother told him in her letter. Coming this far along with him as he told the story, I couldn't help but feel the anguish he felt. Regardless of circumstances, when you come to know a person who is confiding in you the narrative of his life, there is an empathy that comes naturally. I put myself in his place to sense what emotion I would have experienced not being present when my mother or father drew the last breath of their conscious lives. The tears flow hard in just that sorrowful second as memories flood the brain. Memories of early years and later years, and that last week when you know the end of a lifetime is imminent.

▲ ▲ ▲

Consuela Montoya had a good life. There were times of strife where "life ain't been no crystal stair," but with the immense love in her heart for her family and her husband, most of life was good and happy. She never had much, and even when Fernando did bring more money home, money she felt was so tainted, she was generally loath to really appreciate it. Marco had sent her money, but not knowing its true source, she often wondered if it could be used for good. After Fernando died too abruptly in a hard and bitter battle, Consuela always questioned the origin of the money when Marco sent it, but prayed it was what he and Sarah could afford to send from his salary at Crestbrook and investments he said he had. She had been unaffectedly simple her entire life.

Thinking of what was to follow, Marco was completely distressed and wondered how he could possibly assume the strength and courage to face it, knowing he had no choice, but to be completely open in facing Sarah, and then with anger and bitterness facing Alfredo. This was to be the two most important confrontations in his life. Others that brought him near to death were not as meaningful as these would be. He feared both. He didn't know how he might approach each encounter, but that he inevitably must, and neither was a situation he eagerly looked forward to. His encounter with Sarah would be devastating. His truthfulness was certain to turn her away from him forever. His anger at Alfredo and feeling of betrayal by him were sufficient to give Marco the ferocity that a face to face hostile clash demanded. It was inevitable. I asked him if parricide had entered his mind.

73

Mexico
Mexico City

Captain Lorenzo and agents from Interpol contacted the Mexican government to acquire background information on Father Alfredo Legados. They were judicious in their approach of the authorities knowing that Alfredo had long been in the favor of high ranking officials who had been supporters of the Order, and also recipients of bribes. The Captain knew very well how susceptible to accepting money for favors many public servants are. There are good and there are bad like anywhere in the world, but he was fully aware of the number of corrupt government officials in Mexico who appear to be legitimate, but are not. It would be a challenge to make the correct connections with authorities who had the right intentions to bring down Father Alfredo, and Marco if he were in Mexico when the agents moved in on them.

An officer whom the DEA said would be the right man to involve was Colonel Renaldo Segoyas. The DEA had Segoyas's cooperation in the past when they went after killers in the Guadalajara Cartel who had kidnapped two American businessmen. Segoyas was loyal to the cause of bringing to justice those who were bent on corrupting society, so Interpol would have his expertise as well as his forces to aid in an arrest or attack.

The plan was for Captain Lorenzo with the Interpol agents to meet with Colonel Segoyas giving him complete details of the murder of Jeannette Libramont and the intended murder of Anna Ralston.

Realm of the Beast

Information concerning Marco Montoya and his association with Father Alfredo, and their connection in Italy with a major drug gang was given to the Colonel. They needed to figure out the best plan of attack to get to Alfredo and wrap him up for extradition to Italy. Previously, Captain Lorenzo thought the easiest way to insure Alfredo's trip back to Italy was through Cardinal Salvacco, but he decided against this measure because he thought that Alfredo might ignore the Cardinal. Operating through the law was to clearly indicate to Alfredo that some very serious charges were being brought to bear upon him, but it still might be tricky getting him out of Mexico. The Italian authorities working with Colonel Segoyas had what they needed to get Marco, and knew they'd have no trouble having him sent to Italy, but they wanted to set a trap to bring Marco to Mexico, and then get both him and Father Alfredo on a transport to Italy.

It was always easy to get Marco to Mexico through some matter that involved him in the Familia Dei Movement. Because there were several things planned to take place almost simultaneously through the InterAmerican Catholic Association, it was reasonable to expect that he was to be a significant part of the festivities. Mano Amiga was dedicating two new schools for the underprivileged in Central America and a convention of Familia Mexicana was being held in Mexico City. These events were to convene hundreds of Familia Dei members, and Marco Montoya would be a major presenter at the convention. When Captain Lorenzo conversed with Father Ted O'Driscoll, Father told the Captain the schedule of FD activities, and that Marco's participation with other members of the Order and Misters Largent and Sturm was definite. Besides Montoya, the principal and executive director would be making speeches to commemorate the new schools, so it was anticipated all were traveling together and flying Delta Airlines to Mexico City.

The Captain figured that this was an ideal situation with no one suspecting a police presence, and with no interruption to the dedication or convention, allowing the Mexican authorities to sweep down and make the arrests. Colonel Segoyas then will surrender them to the Italian police and Interpol who will take them into custody on board a private aircraft to be flown to Rome. All of the proper documentation will be in the hands of the Colonel who will answer any questions that might arise.

The only problem that seemed like it would disturb the workings of the plan was that the colonel was not certain he wanted to let Father Alfredo and Marco leave the country. He was aware of Father Alfredo being a major player in the drug movement in Mexico, and knew of his connections with Colombia, and he felt that if Alfredo was going down, he wanted to be the one who brought him down. It was a matter of his ego being bruised if he wasn't seen as the knight in white saving his country from shameful drug activity. Captain Lorenzo tried to assuage his ego by saying that any credit that should come from this bust could be evenly distributed. He'd later make a statement attesting to the ingenious police work and courage of the Mexican force led by the brave and stoic Colonel Segoyas that brought two murderers to justice and devastated a drug operation conducted for years behind church walls. Lorenzo's only care was to send two murderers to prison. There was no glory that he expected for just doing his job.

Apologia pro vita sua
(Apology for his life)

74

United States
Georgia

Soon after hearing of his mother's death and learning who his biological father is Marco was confronted by Sarah. She was still more than greatly distressed over the time in Colombia when Marco left her and the kids and flew to Rome supposedly on vital Familia Dei business that could not wait even with his mother so close to death. She wanted to have it out with him, and she was going to.

Listening to Sarah go on and on, Marco felt so emotional and so overcome with remorse for the things he recently did, he made the decision to tell Sarah his whole story. He knew that even her undying love was not going to be strong enough to allow her to continue living with a criminal, but he had to speak. If she thought that his abandoning her in El Ritero was a crime, she was in for the shock of her life. This conversation with Sarah was the only mention of her and his family, and the truly ill-starred fate of them all that Marco said he was about to tell me. I was not to bring up anything, not a single word regarding his wife and family, and this matter, or he would end the documenting of his life. I agreed.

I don't think there was another moment when I felt as sorry for Marco as I did at this time. Anyone with an ounce of empathy could understand the turmoil within him and the loss he was to suffer. He spoke and I just listened intently.

▲ ▲ ▲

Marco said, "Where do I begin? Do I go back to my conception which is a story I just found out about through my mother's letter? Maybe I should end with that. Hell, what's the difference. Sarah, my mother wrote me this letter. I want you to read it."

The grimaces and facial indications of disbelief were apparent after each paragraph she read.

"This is a total shock," she said, after reading the letter. "It is unimaginable to comprehend the emotional impact this must have had. You kept your feelings well concealed, Marco. I never noticed you acting differently; you didn't change in front of the kids. I know how you are affected by this, and I don't know how to react."

"It's not something that will cause me to be different from what I am, Sarah. I accept it just like someone who is told that he is adopted and he has lived half his life not knowing it. It's a kind of revelation that can either hurt endlessly or one that just is. It's not the thought of someone else being my father; it's the realization that a man I have served for so long and know so much about is my father. I will tell you so much more about him you don't know."

Oh, God, help me get through this. And even when I do, nothing will ever be right again. This is really the end of my good life. How can I even ask God to guide me through this?

▲ ▲ ▲

Marco told her about the Cardinals' investigation, and the number of women Father Alfredo had relations with, and the number of children who have come forward proving that they are his offspring. This was heavy intelligence for her to receive all at one blow. But there was more to come, and Marco said he had all he could do to muster the guts to tell her. He was obviously sweating profusely with his body tightened by the knots in his throat and stomach.

"My life hasn't been just what you've seen since we're together, Sarah. There's a part of me that I've kept secret these few years, and it's because I did not want to lose you if you knew everything about my past. I was afraid if you did, you would walk away from me. As it is you will probably decide to do that now, and this rips me apart."

"What the hell are you talking about? Is this some riddle?" Sarah asked.

"No. It's the truth that I need to be open about because things have happened which will inevitably change our lives." Anguish was visible on both their faces.

"You better tell me everything; I'm feeling this is going to be more than I can withstand," Sarah said with a heavy heart.

"How would you feel if you found out that you weren't who you thought you were? That the man you grew up with loving every day was not your father. You can't feel what I feel, knowing that Father Alfredo who has been my mentor, who brought me into the Familia Dei Movement, who got me this position here at Crestbrook where we met, and who has given me opportunities that I never would have had as a kid and as a man is my father."

"What do you mean? What opportunities? I have believed that your life, our lives, the children's lives, have been all that you wanted them to be. That there were no other things that mattered as much. Material things have not been important to us like the satisfaction you derived from working within Familia Dei. And being deeply rooted in the Movement."

"It has been all of that, Sarah, but what you don't know is that when I travel to Coalcojana it's not always about the Order's business. I've been living a double life. I hate confessing this to you, but I've been involved for my entire life in another organization, one that's illegal and criminal. I've been a member of a cartel in Mexico."

Sarah cried a horrible scream and through a deluge of tears shrieked, "What! I do not believe this. It's insane. It's something utterly absurd."

Has he lost his mind, or am I not following this correctly?

"No, it's true. I left El Ritero when I knew that I could belong to Ramon Munoz's cartel and have a better existence than by staying home working the land and raising animals. That was not what I wanted."

"Tell me, Marco, this is unreal, a nightmare I'm having. It's ridiculous. I've known you long enough that hearing what you're telling me is not a part of you. It can't possibly be." Her heart had sunk to an unimaginable depth.

"It is, Sarah. I left the farm and became involved with the drug trade. I was sent to Coalcojana to work closely with Father Alfredo who was a capo in the cartel. He set me up in everything, gave me the cover I needed through Crestbrook to distribute drugs in the U.S., gave me the contacts through well-to-do Mexicans who were members of Familia Dei and had kids in Crestbrook. These men and I were responsible for getting drugs to the East and Midwest schools for distribution to the streets. I was at the entrepot of the drug trade between continents. You know the educational conferences I attended? Most were all bogus meetings, cover-ups, jumping points for us to distribute."

Sarah furiously interrupted, "Our life-style has been simple. We've lived on your salary from the school. That's all the money we've had. I subbed in the school for extra money which wasn't much at all. We got along just fine with that."

"The money is hidden in accounts off shore, Sarah. For the kind of risks I've taken, I've got money put away in the Caribbean and the Cayman Islands."

"I can't handle this, Marco," said Sarah with evident distress and misery. Syncope almost overtaking her. " You're sitting here telling me something you saw on television, or that you read in some novel. This is not your life I'm listening to. Something this astounding is seen on "Mysteries of the Underworld" or some kind of mafia story. This is too much to possibly believe. Should I start laughing now at how you've been so entertaining with a far-fetched story you contrived?" A barrage of expletives exploded.

"Sarah, believe it. Believe me. My life has been hidden and has been a lie."

I know what this all sounds like to her. Why can't she tell from my expression that I'm telling her the whole absurd truth? I can't bring myself to tell anything of Italy.

Thomas Rath

▲ ▲ ▲

Marco told me that when it did sink in that everything he was telling her was a fact, Sarah left him. She and their children went to live in Suwanee with her mother and father where she stayed for a time. After the divorce Sarah's parents gave her their summer home on a quiet lake in the Chattahoochee National Forest Preserve near Panther Lake along Old Historic 441. She had to get far away. She had to deal with the kids alone. What Marco had unloaded on his wife was too much to bear, and she knew she could not stay with him. Seclusion would offer her solace.

This was the lowest point of Marco's life, but his life is what he made it to be. He left for Mexico where he would remain a short while before he would leave for Italy and be arrested for murder and attempted murder and stand trial along with Father Alfredo. In writing this, I've taken the liberty to abbreviate much of the dialogue I had with Marco. It's unnecessary to get into the emotional and psychological parts because most readers can understand the internal gnawing away that Marco felt. But I did find it interesting that being what he was, he was passionate in his love for Sarah. He told me that there was a poem she used to say to him each time he had to leave her and the kids and be gone for a while. It continuously streamed through his mind. Hardened by the life he had lived, Marco was not lachrymose by any means, but this was a brief moment when he couldn't control the flow of tears that flooded his eyes and wetted his cheeks.

> The stars are with the voyager
> Wherever he may sail;
> The moon is constant to her time;
> The sun will never fail;
> But follow, follow round the world,
> The green earth and the sea;
> So love is with the lover's heart,
> Wherever he may be.

Realm of the Beast

> Wherever he may be, the stars
> Must daily lose their light;
> The moon will veil her in the shade;
> The sun will set at night.
> The sun may set, but constant love
> Will shine when he's away;
> So that dull night is never night,
> And day is brighter day.

He didn't remember where it came from. He didn't know the author and didn't even recall that the first line of the poem is its title. I told him the author is a romantic poet named Thomas Hood. That didn't mean anything to him. It was the words Sarah spoke that did. He would never hear them again.

75

United States
Boston

"Hello, May I speak to Anna, please," said Mr. O'Driscoll.

"Who's calling, may I ask?" said Anna's mother.

"Martin O'Driscoll, Father Ted O'Driscoll's father."

"Oh, yes, Mr. O'Driscoll. This is Anna's mother. I'll hand the phone to Anna."

"Thank you."

"Mr. O'Driscoll, how nice of you to call. I want to thank you for the flowers you wired to me when I was in the hospital in Rome."

"Oh, my God, Anna, that's the very least I could do when I heard about what happened to you and your friend. I'm so sorry that she died from her injuries, and I can only express my gratitude that you survived such a horrible car crash. I kept in touch with Ted almost daily to be informed about your condition. I couldn't believe what I heard when Ted told me that it wasn't an accident at all, but a deliberate attempt to kill you."

Remaining composed not wanting to be reminded of that horrid event, Anna said, "Well, thank you. I knew that you would be in contact with your son. He was right at the hospital every day that I was recovering, and was there when my mother arrived in Rome. He was very gracious to her and did all he could to help her while we were there.

I'm just thankful that my injuries were not life-threatening, and that I could walk out of that hospital after a short while."

Oh, Jeannette, Jeannette. I'll never forget you. Why were you taken away?

"Anna, I'd be a fool if I didn't apologize to you because it was at my urging to help Ted that you accomplished all that you did for him and me, and then were the one to suffer so much because of it. This will weigh on my conscience for a long time. I'm so sorry to have gotten you involved. I guess I infringed on your friendship with Ted which I should not have done. I feel badly that I acted out of selfishness."

"No! That's nonsense. I could have refused. I could have said that my commitments at work were too demanding at the time and I just couldn't possibly help you. But I didn't. I wanted to be of help to Ted and see justice for the men that Ted was going out on a limb for. Besides, it's all over now. I'm doing well and will be back to work soon."

"I'm glad to hear you say that. But I will always feel as though I overstepped. Ted has told me, Anna, that there was an identification of the man or men who ran you off the road. The Rome police captain, Lorenzo is the name, I believe, has an ID from cameras near the crash scene, or is it near the scene where the stolen car was found. Anyway, that's great news. I hope they can get these guys to trial soon and nail their asses with either the death penalty or life without parole. The fact is I don't even know if Italy has the death penalty."

"Yes, that's right, sir. The police know who the two men are, and are working on having the men in Mexico deported for prosecution. You can be sure that I will be fine and more than ready to go to Rome for a trial, and hope to see them hanged for what they did not so much to me, but to my friend Jeannette Libramont."

"From what I have heard Jeannette was a wonderful person. And what a twist of fate for her. I was told that some strings were pulled for her to be in Rome with you as a translator. I guess that as believers we have to see it as God's will be done even if it brings sorrow to those left behind. I mean…"

What the hell do I mean! Was that something stupid to say! What a complete jerk I am!

Anna understood where he was coming from and what he meant to say even if the words came out somewhat awkward. "You're right. If I hadn't asked in the first place, she never would have taken time off from the bank and gone with me. That's something that will weigh on my conscience forever. Jeannette was a super person and will be missed every day. I'm sorry I asked her to accompany me, but I thought it was an opportunity and a fantastic experience for us both."

Trying to express himself better, Mr. O'Driscoll said, "I hate to be so callous as to say it was to be. But God works in mysterious ways, and these are supposed to make a difference in all our lives. Lessons or something, they say."

"I want to thank you again for calling, Mr. O'Driscoll. Say hello to Ted for me if you speak to him soon. He called to see how I was doing a couple of days ago. That's the last we talked. I have a physical therapist coming to the house in an hour, so I'd like to get ready for my appointment." Anna was being polite, but truly desired to end the conversation.

"One more thing, Anna, and don't you dare say no. I am sending you a check for all that you did. I know it could never be enough to compensate for what you have endured, but I want you to know how I truly appreciate you."

"That is not necessary, Mr. O'Driscoll. I received my regular salary from the firm for the weeks I was gone."

"I know. This is something I want to do for you."

No amount could be enough for what's she's done, but wait until she sees the size of the check. It's the only thing I can do for her, and me.

"It's just a gesture of the admiration and respect I have for you. Also, when you get a week off, I want you and your parents to spend a few days on Boston's north shore with Mrs. O'Driscoll and me. I'll make the reservations at the Inn at Castle Hill for all of us. I know you will enjoy being there for a little "r and r."

76

United States Georgia

"I've been waiting for you to tell me what all happened in Rome, Ted," said Father Edmund. "From your call I got the feeling that there was a lot more that happened than Father Alfredo getting blitzed by the General Council."

"You better believe it. I was reluctant to say too much over the phone, however, I can tell you that things are far more critical than you'd ever think," said Ted. "I told you about the "accident" that wasn't an accident, but rather an attempted murder. Well, the police investigation led to an arrest of an Italian man involved in the drug trade. What the police did not want me to reveal was that Marco was in the car that drove Anna and Jeannette over the cliff. I was to pretend I didn't know anything so Marco wouldn't get suspicious when we met here on the school campus."

"If you feel you can't tell me something because it has to do with the police investigation, then don't break a confidence. I don't want you to do that," said Edmund, but he was really eager to hear the whole story.

"No, it's not really something I'm to keep in confidence, but rather some information that the police don't want me to react to. I know I can tell you without it going any further, and besides Marco has already left. Marco was in Rome, remember? When the police looked at the films of cameras located in the hotel and on a building across from the car that was abandoned after the crash, Marco was identified as one of the men who tried to kill Jeannette and Anna. He was with the Italian guy that Captain Lorenzo of the Rome police knew as an inveterate drug trafficker."

"That's incredible," said Edmund. "Marco was supposed to be in Rome attending a FD symposium. In fact, wasn't he slated as a speaker? I'm not sure about that, but I think John Largent mentioned it to me."

"Speaking of John. What was the reaction at the school when John and Dick found out that Marco took off?"

"Their fair-haired boy. They couldn't believe it. You know how connected they are to the Movement. Two guys who are converts to Catholicism and were completely immersed in Familia Dei. God, they couldn't be more devout. They were stunned that Marco left the school high and dry, and they tried to restrain themselves, but couldn't help using a few vulgarisms to express their feelings. Can't blame them. After all they're running a school and had to explain to students and parents that a long respected member of the faculty had become a fugitive. When so many were questioning them and wanting to know where Mr. Montoya was, they felt they were on the spot. I'm sure that privately when they discussed a replacement, they used some expletives to describe Marco. I heard Dick say that he hopes Marco gets what he deserves and they fry his ass. They phoned the head of the Order here in Atlanta and contacted Father Daly at his office in Connecticut, but I never heard what the Order said to them."

What might they say? Marco was their fair-haired boy wasn't he?

"That's tough for them, but I think after the mortification wears off, they'll get things back to normal. And to think that their biggest worry until all this exploded was having to release a teacher for having said "hell" two or three times in front of the students. Pales by comparison, doesn't it?"

Wonder what ever happened to him? He was one of the best teachers the school ever hired. Probably went to a community college where he made a name for himself.

"Yeah! And then there's the reaction that Marco's mother-in-law had when everything burst wide open. Bad enough that Sarah and he split. They thought that was the end of the world and nothing could get worse. What a shocker! Then to think their son-in-law was wanted, and ran, a fugitive from the law."

"Well, getting back to your question, Edmund, about Marco being slated to speak at the symposium. "No, Edmund. There was no event planned by the Familia Dei Movement. It was all a ploy set up by Father Alfredo. In hind sight, we should have checked on it through the Order."

And I'm the one who's supposed to be on top of these things for FD. Was I asleep!

"Yeah! But you had a lot on your mind at that time going to testify and all. I should have been more alert to things, especially when you blew up about Marco not being at the school. We thought he was visiting his sick mother down in Colombia and then found out he was heading to Rome."

"The police captain notified me of Marco's implication in the crime, and since he had flown back to Atlanta, I was asked to act like I didn't know anything so as not to tip their hand. I imagine that the police have contacted authorities here and in Mexico and will have a plan to have him extradited to Italy. Do you see what else is involved here, or rather, who else is involved, Edmund?"

"I don't believe it! You mean Father Alfredo!"

Geeze, not just a pedophile but an accomplice to murder.

"That's right. He set it all in motion. I think he planned to have Anna killed before she went before the Commission to present the evidence against him. It didn't happen, so the murder was to avenge the prosecution of him before the Cardinals."

"Incredible, Ted."

"Yeah. And then the police started adding things up when they saw that Marco was part of the murder. I can say murder because the crash did take Jeannette's life, poor innocent girl that she was. The connection to the Italian, Giuseppe Vilardo, gave them a piece they wouldn't have suspected, the drug cartel and Father Alfredo. That's how Interpol got involved. The Italian police know that Interpol has a wider jurisdiction when it comes to international drug trafficking."

"Where do things go from here, Ted?" asked Father Edmund in a befuddled tone.

"I'm not sure. I can only guess that Marco and Alfredo will be spending some time in Rome, and it's going to be one unpleasant experience for both."

"I'll bet you will have to go there for proceedings, too, Ted. You identified Marco that night in the hotel café, and the camera there verified his presence. I wonder if he was collaborating with Vilardo at that time."

"Oh, absolutely, Edmund. What other purpose might he have had in dealing with Vilardo just hours before a murder and both of them caught on camera together. Absolute collusion on their parts. They did more than simply have a couple of drinks at the hotel bar."

"Have you spoken to Sarah at all since Marco took off?" asked Edmund. "I heard later that he told her everything, and she was distraught beyond belief."

She is such a magnificent young woman. Too bad it has ended like this for her.

"No, I haven't. You can't think she'd be otherwise," said Ted. "Her entire life was turned upside down. The whole family is destroyed. The bastard didn't appreciate all that he had, especially what a fine wife and mother Sarah is. He'll pay the price for what he is when the police arrest him in Mexico and yank him away to stand trial."

"Sarah's better off. She never could have lived with him after all this. I talked to her mother Jennifer the other day after classes, and she's happy her daughter and grandchildren are safe and away from Marco. I'm surprised Bill didn't take a gun to Marco's head after he heard what Marco did to his daughter," Edmund said.

"Don't be surprised if he doesn't still try. I mean he'd never do anything like that, but if angry and determined enough, he's a powerful figure who undoubtedly knows someone who knows someone that would go after Marco."

"That'll never happen. He's too good a man to seek that kind of vengeance."

"Yeah, I know," said Ted with seeming resignation.

"So, what happens next?" Ted.

"I'm not sure I know," Edmund. "I can only guess until I know for sure that Marco and Alfredo are apprehended."

My mind's too cluttered to venture any guess that could be a certainty.

77

United States
Hartford, Connecticut

"Anna, give me the names again of those men the Italian police have identified, and also all the details that you can remember about anything relating to the murder," said Dr. Ralston. "I have every intention of using what influence, political and otherwise, I have to see to it that those criminals go on trial as soon as possible, and that they are hung out to dry with expediency."

Dr. Thomas Ralston became a very wealthy man. He had a PhD in physics from the University of Pennsylvania which paved the way for his gaining various positions in industry all of which were quite lucrative. Much of his fortune was made from the selling of property he inherited from his family in northern Connecticut, and his funds from successful investments in start-up companies. Having been an entrepreneur he was the type individual who enjoyed reaching out to smart people with ideas for good businesses and then investing in them. The patents he himself held numbered thirty-five.

He sold a lot of property, but he also retained a vast amount of acreage. He raised his family on the original family farmland in Stafford Springs, a small town environment he loved. Most of his work and dealings are from his office in Hartford which is a convenient location for conducting business. Dr. Ralston is a well-respected man and is an associate or an acquaintance of several important people nationally. One would say that he is of a select and elite social membership. There are the corporate magnates, senators, governors, many scientists, and others who are of the moneyed class. Though Ralston is not a Harvard or Yale or Princeton man, he is Ivy League and that's what is important for the relationships he was able to develop through the years.

"Dad, when we all left Rome, the police captain said that his department and Interpol will take control of everything, and that there's nothing to concern ourselves about. They know what they are doing, and I'm confident that they'll make the arrests and bring the men to trial."

"We're so far away. I'm not that positive they'll work at this case diligently enough," said Dr. Ralston with definite pessimism.

Contradicting her father, Anna said, "I'm not worried. I believe that the captain will do as he says, and you shouldn't worry either. Mom was there. Ask her what her assessment of their honesty is."

Asserting his self-importance, Ralston responded to his daughter, "No. I don't have to do that. I've got the connections that I can go to, if or when, I feel they're dragging their feet. I'm staying on top of this every single day, and I'll be placing calls to the Rome police routinely until they tell me what I want to hear. That'll make me happy."

"Dad, I'll be staying in close touch with Father Ted in Georgia. He'll let me know the progress being made. Being in the Order he has the contacts at the seminary and university in Rome where fellow Missionaries will know right to the minute what's happening, and will inform him."

"Has he told you whether or not that s.o.b. from the school, Marco, has been placed under arrest?" her father asked.

"No. He hasn't, but he has said that Marco fled to Mexico and is with Father Alfredo who is in the equivalent of house arrest. So, he can't go anywhere."

"Well, if the Italian captain is truthful, we can expect that both those guys will be arrested and taken to Rome. This is what I want to hear, so that we can make plans to be there for the trial. That's the time I'm waiting for, Anna."

"I know that, Dad. It's all going to work out for the best. You'll see."
That's what my mind and heart is telling me. That's what I pray for.

78

Mexico
Coalcojana

Standing erect with his lips tightened, Marco faced his father for one of the first times as an equal and not a cartel subordinate. He found the words that he could express with austerity and almost a fierceness.

"Truly amazing isn't it, how things unfold. Like the saying goes: "Oh, what a tangled web we weave, when first we practice to deceive," said Marco to Father Alfredo. "There have been new things I've recently become aware of, Padre. You know my mother, Consuela Montoya, passed away a very short time ago. When I visited her before her death being very hopeful she would recover, she said that she had something to tell me which she has held within her for a lifetime. She never got to tell me. She did regain her strength and vitality, but only for a little while. Also, I left abruptly to do your bidding in Rome, so my mother told me nothing. If I hadn't been in such great haste, I would have heard her words."

I wish I had been there to make it easier for her to tell me everything.

Stunned by Marco's directness, Father Alfredo said, "Yes, I knew your mother was ill for a period of time until she died a few weeks ago. I knew your mother had her other sons and your sister with her when she passed on through the gates of heaven to be with our Lord."

"But, Father, my mother had written a letter to me which I received from my brothers. It was surprising and shocking what I learned from her as she wrote lying on her bed and waiting to close her eyes for the last time. Do you know what it was she had to tell me, Father Alfredo?

I know it is something you have known your entire life, and especially since you have known me. Do you remember my uncle whom you recruited from my mother's village many years ago? I know you do remember, Father. You left my grandparents with only a girl to work the land and care for the animals and harvest crops. And you also left their young daughter pregnant with a child. You must remember that, Father!"

God knows there are other girls you got pregnant. I know that's true.

Disturbed by Marco's tone, Alfredo interjected, "What are you saying, Marco. Of course I can recall boys from Mexico and South America and Ireland that came to the seminary in Coalcojana, but I do not know so many years later all of the families and their children and names. How could I?"

Why was I cursed to behave the way nature made me and not adhere to my vows? I do have many regrets. My conscience has bothered me. Who would believe me?

"There must be some that you remember from carrying memories that would never leave your brain. They are memories of things that you have done. Those women from Mexico with children and the woman from Switzerland with a child who have told the Cardinals that you are the father of their children remember you. They say you supported them financially through all these years. You remember them, don't you? Then you must remember that young girl of the family in El Ritero, too. That girl was my mother, Alfredo. Now do you understand why I must know if you remember her? She was my mother, and she told me who my biological father is. I didn't know that Fernando Montoya was not my father. I didn't know that you were my father until reading it in my mother's letter."

"That's impossible, Marco. I can't believe what you are saying." He turned as though he intended to walk away, but knew leaving was cowardly.

"Why, Father? Why is it impossible? When three women have come forward and paternity can be proved for their children. Should I have to prove it, too? It can easily be done, if you agree to it, you fucking asshole." Marco shouted.

"Marco, I never knew. This is astounding to me."

"Will others come forward that you will either deny or accept, my father?"

"No, believe me, Marco." It appeared that Alfredo had no memory or wanted no memory to recall certain events from his past.

"What am I to think at this time? That without knowing this I have been so close to you for all the years as a member of your Familia Dei organization and a member of the cartel. That I have been witness to killings and committed crimes for you when you told me to do it or it was for the organization. That you have been giving orders to your own son to commit crime. This is what my life with you has been. I know I would never have gotten so involved with you if I had been told when I was young, or even after my father Fernando was killed."

"I can say that I am sorry, Marco, but that does not have any meaning to you, and I understand how it can't. Truly I am sorry that I did not know," said Father Alfredo sounding sorrowful and remorseful, but who could really know.

Alfredo sat in silence and brought back that memory of long ago by recalling the day in Tipperary when seeing how Father Edmund's mother had become worn over years of struggle, he wondered how another young, pretty girl in Colombia wore her years after so long a time. Now that he was an old man, he also wondered what Marco's mother looked like before her death, but preferred the image of her as a young virgin to remain in his memory. Without ever expressing sincere regret for transgressions to Marco, he arrogantly walked away from him. Marco was more incensed by Alfredo's actions than by his refusal to acknowledge another illegitimate son. It was more hope for acknowledgement than the realization that it would actually come from Alfredo that bolstered Marco to enter this conversation about paternity. Upon Alfredo's walking away from him, Marco's disgust and resignation were evident. No tears, only fire in his eyes and a very deep ache in his heart.

79

Italy
Rome

"We have used all the influence we had to get the Mexican government to send Father Alfredo and Marco Montoya to Rome where they would be apprehended and taken in custody to stand trial for murder," said Captain Lorenzo. "Interpol has been ineffective in their attempts to sway the Mexicans as has the American FBI. Our president, in fact, spoke directly to the Director, Mr. Marconi, in Washington when she went to the United States for a meeting of several EU representatives with President Rush. The director told her that his intervention will help us to get Alfredo and Marco out of Mexico. We were told not to enter Mexico and arrest any citizen. We offered more than one quid pro quo, but to no avail. Our ally in this endeavor was Colonel Renaldo Segoyas, but all of his efforts have been shunned. He was the only source of influence we had to see the success of the operation, but when he stood firm, other military officers on-the-take affirmed their superiority and had the Colonel shot dead in his home. The best intelligence identified that it was corrupt military, not the cartel that killed Segoyas.

"Being thwarted like this, our thought was to conduct a clandestine cloak and dagger type operation much like the Israelis did in Argentina to capture Adolph Eichmann. This did not set well with our friends at Interpol, and I'm sure the Americans had opposed the plan, too, even though it was one American citizen who was the target of an attempted murder when another woman of American and Luxembourg citizenship was murdered. We had to figure out another way.

"The fucking Mexicans were adamant about our not entering their country and the chief reason was quite obvious. A multitude of people were paid sums of money to protect Father Alfredo. These people ranged from the local police to higher government representatives. The bribes that Alfredo paid out over the years for unlimited protection included his being shielded from arrest, extradition, and prosecution. The Missionaries of the Holy Church and the Hombres en Negro cartel were totally safeguarded by the men in power, and even though the authorities knew Father Alfredo had been convicted of being a pedophile by the Cardinals of the General Council, and that he was being accused of conspiring in a plot to murder, they had no intention of shipping him to Italy to stand trial. Father Alfredo is a very powerful man in his country," said Captain Lorenzo with resignation.

Cardinal Salvacco listened and was as disappointed with the disapprobation of the Mexican authorities as was the captain. He responded, "Captain, do you recall the original method I mentioned to get Alfredo back to Italy? I said that I would send for Father Alfredo and have no concern that he will not return. Even though you have apprised me of your being flatly rejected by the Mexicans, I can assure you that I can positively get Father Alfredo to Italy by issuing one major threat: a censuring of the Missionaries that will stun the entire religious community, and confiscation of the Order's world-wide facilities and its accounts which total between six-hundred million and one-billion dollars. This will strike him heavily, and is sufficient leverage to have him on a plane hours after I speak to him. He will fight this threat more fiercely than put up a fight to the charge of attempted murder. I know him that well. I will inform him that Marco Montoya is to accompany him." The Cardinal spoke with complete resolve.

Hearing the cardinal's words the captain responded with a broad smile and said, "Yes, Your Excellency, that should work well. I only wonder whether the Mexican officials have already spoken to either Father Alfredo or Montoya, and they know they are suspects in a crime investigation by the Italian police. This could be a problem."

"I think I can deal with that by telling Alfredo that his trip here is to be held in the strictest confidence. After all, he has already been sentenced by the General Council and is to be held in house arrest in Rome. He is aware of the influence I have and the Holy Father has with the Roman authorities, so I will assure him of his being isolated from everyone during the time he is here. I can tell him to fly to Milan and we will have a car and driver waiting to take them to the Vatican. He has done this many times before when he wanted to remain incognito in Rome. A diversion of sorts."

Now I contemplate the reasons for his wanting to be incognito. I hate to think that he has been guilty of many things, but rationally I'd be ignorant to think otherwise.

"I can hope that this will work, Cardinal. You will keep me informed please, and let me know dates and times so that I can intercept the car when Father Alfredo and Mr. Montoya arrive in Milan. I'll want to take them into custody immediately, so that we can get the proceedings started. You do realize that I will be naming you on the list of witnesses. At the moment we only have limited evidence. Forensics has some DNA of Giuseppe Vilardo, but none of Montoya. We have the video tape which places Montoya in the car, but we don't have a strong link between him and Alfredo in terms of the murder."

I'm working on that to be sure. By the time we're ready for an arrest I'll have all that I need.

" I know the work you're devoting to this case, Captain, and I know that you will have more than sufficient evidence to connect all the dots to see these criminals put behind bars. I know my obligation to provide the help I can give you as a witness," the Cardinal said.

Dominus vobiscum, my son.

80

Luxembourg
Esch-sur-Alzette

256 Echternach Strasse
Esch, Luxembourg

Captain Fabrezzio Lorenzo
Rome Carabinieri
Precinct 25
Via Vittorio Vespucci 124B
Rome, Italy

Captain Lorenzo:

    I write to you on behalf of my murdered daughter and her heart-broken parents. Jeannette Libramont died a young vibrant woman taken from her youth far too soon and too shamefully. We mourn her loss each day and feel less a mother and father because she was our only child. One who has not suffered such a loss cannot fully comprehend the sense of emptiness that we feel. I know that you sympathize with us and know the immense holes we have in our hearts. Your profession immerses you in the tragedies that families painfully experience. We acknowledge the difficulty of your everyday work as it must involve so much emotional stress. As a human being it is not possible to be insensitive to the misery brought to families by criminals who take loved ones from them.

Realm of the Beast

You see far too often the evil that exists in a society we all wish was civilized. The needless taking of a human being's life through murder is the most immoral act that anyone can conceive of. Again, I say, you know this so well in your line of work each day, and we know it must weigh heavily upon you. We thank you for the compassion you have shown us.

We express our gratitude for the work of you and your officers in tracking the murderers of our daughter, and we thank you for the efforts you expend every day trying to solve each case you work on. It is frustrating to be sure when confronted with a crime where no clear evidence leads to an arrest. But you persevere and you let elements of a case disturb you until you locate all the pieces and solve the mystery. You are the example of the true professional who solves the crime to bring justice forward, but also to bring closure to people like my wife and me when a loved one has been taken away by a hard-hearted criminal who places no value on human life.

It is our wish to be in Rome and attend the proceedings against Jeannette's killers. We will appreciate and be indebted to you if you oblige us to be present. We can stay in Rome for the duration of the trial as we want to be in the courtroom each day with your permission. Though I travel a great deal mainly to America, I can adjust my schedule to be in Rome at that time. My wife's brother, Cardinal Joseph Lorentzweiler, is in Luxembourg, but will be at the Vatican at the time of the trial whenever it comes up. He, also, will be in attendance when the case is brought to court.

If there is any kind of information that your prosecutor will need about Jeannette, please have him contact us at the above address.

Thanking you again for your fast investigation of our daughter's murder.

Wir sind dir dankbar. Aufweidersehen.

M&M Josef Libramont

81

United States
Boston

"Ted, I got a call from Anna Ralston's father yesterday," said Martin O'Driscoll. "I knew the name Dr. Thomas Ralston immediately and was very curious why he would be calling me. Of course, his daughter and my son are the connection that we have, but I'd never expect to hear from him unless it had to do with the two of you."

"Yeah, Dad. Dr. Ralston is quite a famous scientist. I don't think I ever mentioned it at the time that he guest lectured a couple of times at Yale when Anna and I were there. I remember she got a real kick when he surprised her with a visit on campus to speak. He is quite a noteworthy scientist, and has acquired a small fortune with his inventions, or maybe it's a large fortune."

Those were some parties Christy and I attended at the Ralston mansion. Incredible estate; incredible money.

"Well, anyway, Ted. I wanted to talk to you about how upset he is over the attempt of those scoundrels to kill Anna, and the bringing of them to justice. He launched into a lengthy diatribe of Montoya and Alfredo. Listen to the proposal he made to me. Because of your involvement in this case, he wants me to join him in a venture to make sure the priest in Mexico and that criminal at your school, Montoya, get to Italy. Anna spoke to Captain Lorenzo, and he said they were hitting a brick wall with the Mexican government. It seems their contact, a colonel, got blown away. He told her of a new plan they anticipate putting into play. The

Cardinal in Rome thinks he has the fool-proof method to get them to Italy, but Lorenzo has some doubts. So, Dr. Ralston has come up with an idea of hiring a bounty hunter. He thinks we can get Spenser Austin, the guy who goes by the name "Cat" to stalk and get these guys. Ralston says that Cat has gone to Mexico before to apprehend a fugitive and has been successful. I don't mind shelling out the cash for the guy, but the way the Mexican government and the cartels deal with outsiders is not something I want to feel responsible for if something goes wrong. I wanted to bounce this off of you and get your thoughts. I feel it's too zany."

"Man, that's something I'd never have thought of. I know from conversations with Anna that her father is incensed with the thought of getting her would-be killers in custody. How does Dr. Ralston think it will work?" Other than that question, I have no thoughts."

Except has he completely flipped out!

"Well, he's the intellect, and Austin's the pro. They'll have to figure it out, not me."

"Gosh, Dad. To be truthful, I'd be one to scrap the idea and leave it all in the hands of Captain Lorenzo back in Rome. He a professional, too, and it should be the police who figure it out. I'd put my trust in Cardinal Salvacco to get Alfredo to Rome if it were up to me. It seems he's put the mechanism in place for a sound operation."

"You're probably right, Son. It does seem kind of a desperate move to hire a bounty hunter, but from the tone of Ralston's voice, he does appear desperate. I'll get back to him and tell him I've given it sufficient thought to oppose the idea. Too reckless. Austin would never be able to penetrate the cartel wall that protects those guys. Not in a hundred years."

"Okay, is that all you wanted to ask me?"

Yes, banish the thought of anything bordering on recklessness of that kind.

"What's happened with Montoya's family? You mentioned that the wife left the snake."

"She and the kids did leave, and I've heard they are living out of town, at least for the time being. I was never too close to Marco's family. Only saw them in the chapel from the altar in the mornings before classes. As a matter of fact, I was never informed about his mother's death until after it occurred, and he got the letter from her which must be the reason he left here in such haste. I don't know how it leaked out that Father Alfredo is Marco's father, but the scuttlebutt is that he told Mr. Gonzales and one other man who is an associate of Gonzales. That's funny, but that relationship was difficult to see. Besides the Familia Dei connection, Marco and Gonzales seemed real secretive, especially at times when they traveled to the other schools. So, my hunch is that one of these guys let the cat out of the bag regarding Marco's paternity."

He had to confront Alfredo, but what a terrible way to learn who your father is. A letter from your dying mother. What Marco must have felt is unfathomable.

"I only met those people once or twice, Ted, and never had a warm feeling about them. Seemed to be shady characters. Listen! I'll let you go. I know you've got things to do. I'll stay in touch though. You call me anytime, especially if you hear anything. And I'll get back to Ralston."

"Okay, Dad. Perhaps, Dr. Ralston or Anna will be calling soon."

"I have already spoken to Anna, Son. I gave her a call soon after she got back from Rome. I wanted to extend my appreciation for her work, and tell her how apologetic I feel for all that she's suffered. We had a very pleasant conversation, Ted. I told her I planned to make reservations at the Inn at Castle Hill for a long weekend she and her parents will enjoy with your mother and me. But, of course, that will be when she feels up to it." Nothing was said about the check.

"Great! That's a super gesture, Dad. I know the Ralstons will love going to the north shore. It'll definitely be a happy occasion, and will allow Anna to get her mind off any hurt she feels even if just for a weekend.

"Goodbye, Dad. Tell Mom I love her. I'll give her a call in a few days."

82

United States
Washington D.C.

Drew Dempsey had the reputation in Washington of being a stellar attorney. Many of the politicians knew him well, and sought his advice on all types of legal matters even though his specialty was dealing with international affairs. This, however, was a principal reason why he was consulted frequently by politicians. As a young lawyer he proved himself exceptional when he was with Covington and Crutcher. Later he held a prominent position with the Justice Department's Office of Legal Counsel. Before forming his own firm, he helped shape a legal network that developed new generations of lawyers for leadership positions in government and the judiciary. He knew the ins and outs of treaty law, law of the sea, and humanitarian law which at one time during the tenure of any given senator were the sources of invaluable information the senator needed to appear intelligent in committee. Besides the European Court of Human Rights, Dempsey had expertise with the workings of the Andean Community of Nations Jus gentium and jus inter gentes were the focus of experts, and congressmen did not have the time to devote to this study being so engaged in the minutia of the day as was their wont. So, they turned to Mr. Drew Dempsey when he could give them the knowledge to appear erudite on critical issues.

Needless to say, Drew Dempsey, Esq. was owed many favors by powerful men who had idled away in the halls of Congress for far too many terms. But, Dempsey was not the type to call in favors, as he seldom, if ever, needed them. If there was such a thing as a truly honest lawyer, Drew Dempsey was the paradigm. His work brought him enough money that he did not have to look beyond that for a comfortable life. His partners likewise derived satisfaction, and a healthy livelihood, from the work they did to reject any sort of situation that appeared remotely tainted. This was the attitude and disposition that was thrust upon the battery of lawyers in the firm. This reputation was a major factor that enticed Anna Ralston to join Dempsey, Rodriguez, and Schmidt. Another was that the Honorable Bernard T.J. Schmidt had attended the University of Pennsylvania and was a classmate of Dr. Ralston, Anna's father. Mr. Schmidt had been a judge in the U.S. Court of Appeals for the Fifth Circuit for several years before retiring and becoming a partner in the firm. His relationship with Dr. Ralston was well established over the course of the many years since college and through their careers. They had never become Saturday night poker players or Sunday afternoon football watchers together, but they had followed each other's careers, attended each other's weddings and knew each other's children by name. They regularly spoke and discussed major issues that were of significant concern to each, sometimes seeking wisdom, or just a humble and honest opinion.

Anna was well respected in the firm and proved herself to be more than competent, so it wasn't that she was to be guided by the Honorable Bernard Schmidt and taught how to make it in the profession when she signed the employment contract in Mr. Dempsey's office. She had the benefit of sage advice when she sought it. Otherwise she handled her cases independently with the team standing strong and committed behind her.

After Anna convalesced at her parents' home and returned to work, she was as eager as on her first day to enter the everyday fray again. Everyone was happy to see her return to work and was extremely gratified that her injuries, though severe, did not leave her impaired in any way. When fellow attorneys approached her, they were most candid when offering to be of any assistance when she gave an indication it was needed. A more sincere group of decent folks she had never known before. She was completely happy in this work environment.

Anna knew that she would be required to go to Rome to testify when the two culprits from Mexico were ultimately put on trial, and the partners knew that as well. Just when that date might be no one yet knew.

Anna had received periodic calls from another conscientious and sincere person in Rome from the time she left Italy. Captain Lorenzo of the Rome carabinieri called on occasion to inquire after her health and recuperation, and to keep her apprised of his ongoing pursuit of Father Alfredo and Marco Montoya.

Dr. Ralston had never mentioned to Anna his phone call to Martin O'Driscoll, and naturally, he never told her about his brainstorm to involve a private eye/bounty hunter to go to Mexico and attempt to extract her would-be killers, and somehow fly or float them to Italy. Anna would have thought her father somewhat demented if he had discussed this idea with her. By this time Ralston had gotten a response from O'Driscoll and dropped the notion of a bounty hunter. What else Anna did not know was that her father called his long-time friend and former classmate the Honorable Bernard T. J. Schmidt. Being the man of science he was, his conversation with Schmidt was direct and to the point. The assassins who attempted to end his daughter's life, and who killed her good friend were to be taken from Mexico to Italy to go on trial, and the Mexican government might prohibit such a move by an outside authority. What can be done? What influence can be asserted? Who can be contacted in our government to possibly assist in prompting the Mexicans to hasten extradition?

83

Italy
Rome

"Cardinal, I will speak to Miss Ralston," said Captain Lorenzo. "You know that she and her family are quite dismayed that the Mexican government will not relinquish the priest and Montoya. I have been in contact with her and have stated that we are doing everything we can do to hasten their arrests and bring them here as alleged murderers. I will tell her that you will be able to secure their release and deportation, and I know this will be good news to her."

Great news for the poor young woman. Come to Rome and face the men who attempted to kill you. Have a nice holiday in the courtroom giving testimony. I feel for the poor girl.

Cardinal Salvacco said, "By all means, Captain, give her my best wishes for a fast recovery, and also my assurances that soon she will be here to testify in court as the victim of a crime against her life. I know you well enough, Captain, that the police have sufficient evidence for a successful conviction of these men. I can be certain of that?"

With a smile of assent on his face the Captain replied, "Of course, Your Excellency. My men and I have more than enough to connect Montoya to Vilardo and to the accident and to Father Alfredo. If we had not seen the video, we would never have linked the priest to Vilardo and the Italian cartel. It worked out beautifully that we get them for murder and for drug trafficking. They'll be sent away for a long, long time. I'll try to get the priest in Iles d'Arda Prison in the Tyrrhenian Sea where he can see the towers of the Order's university from the prison yard. It will be good for the holy man to reflect on all that he cannot be a part of in the places he built in the name of God. And he can pray that his days there are short. He is not a young man, and I don't believe he'll have too many years to beg for forgiveness."

"You are too harsh in your words, Captain. I believe that he must stay in prison for the crimes, but I also believe that for his sins he will be forgiven by the Almighty when he repents. For a man who was ordained in the Catholic Church to be guilty of such heinous deeds against a fellow human being is incomprehensible to me and to any person who has respect for life. Father Alfredo has been a disgrace to all believers in the sanctity and dignity of life. There are thousands of good men who have taken the vows that could never contemplate the type of life that Alfredo has lived. A child abuser, a murderer, a drug user and drug trafficker are unimaginable to a rational man who professes the word of God."

"Yes, Cardinal Salvacco," said the Captain. "For most men who have never studied theology as deeply as you in the Church do, they wince at the thought of unjustifiably taking another's life. I have spoken to army men who were bothered for all of their lives after fighting in battle where they had to kill in order to live. It is the diabolically evil individual who is not tormented by killing. I have seen many of these men and women, and I do feel they should not be a burden on society, but should be sent to their early graves to stand before God for judgment and be punished for all eternity. If this is not Christian, I apologize to you, but unlike me, you have not seen the victims' blood that flows into the gutter from a shooting or stabbing or fatal bludgeoning by the hand of sanguinary killers. Seeing this too often has made me feel the way that I do, I am sorry to say."

As a young boy that's what I wanted to do. Seeing Dad in his uniform I was always impressed and awaited the day I'd be a peace officer and serve my city. But there are many upsetting scenes one has to encounter in this work serving the good of society.

"I realize where you are coming from, Captain. You are a good man whom I admire. Not everyone could do your work; most men would be affected by your experiences in the same way. I continue to pray for you and I continue to pray for the murderer that he can turn his life around and be more like you."

"Thank you, Cardinal. I appreciate that. One other concern I have is Ms. Ralston's safety. When I contact her I will warn her that she must be wary at all times of the danger she may still face. My experience has proved to me time and again that one does not trust men involved in the narco business. I know they would want to exact revenge."

"That is wise, Captain. Let your instincts guide you. Put her on guard to be extremely vigilant. I don't want to imagine what ruthless and despicable men might do in an act of revenge."

The Captain's thought was *We'll do everything to keep her safe. Of that you can be assured, my good Cardinal. Precautions and many extra precautions will be in place.*

84

United States
Connecticut
Washington, D.C.

Mr. Schmidt was surprised to see that his old friend whom he hadn't seen in a while called his office and left an urgent message. He set aside some work he was preparing for litigation and picked up the phone as soon as he could. After some friendly chit-chat, Schmidt said, "Thomas, those are three good questions that you ask, and I sense your frustration. I'm not one given to impetuosity of thought. Being first and foremost a judge and a lawyer I need time to respond with a legal rejoinder as your questions involve international relations with Mexico. And that isn't easy to do at the moment because for one thing I'm caught up in a load of work that Drew has strewn on my desk. I'm aware of the situation your daughter is embroiled in with the law authorities in Italy. I do feel for the poor girl. Her consternation is evident on her lovely face as I see her moving about the office every day. I've had some dialogue with her, but nothing reaching significant depths that would require my involvement. She has been looked out for, so to speak, by Mr. Dempsey who, from what I can tell, has done a marvelous job in directing her. She has placed a good deal of confidence in his direction, and also in the Italian police captain she has conversed with.

"Off hand, I can say that I have a direct line to our ambassador in Mexico who may be able to intervene on our behalf and make some progress with government officials. I should think that this route may be favorable for expedience sake. I cannot be that reliable to say that he can be effective in persuading any officials that are beholden to the cartels. They know to which side of the bread their butter is spread, and will place diplomatic relations at the edge of their plate. They are hard-ass creatures that I've had to deal with from time to time, and when it comes to money or friendship with our country, I'm afraid you know how the wind will blow. I've found many of them to be impervious to decency at times when it pays them greater dividends to be venal and corrupt. I know, Thomas, I'm not sounding optimistic at all, but reality is reality, especially in countries where criminals reward criminals."

All Dr. Ralston could do was listen as his long-time friend soured him on any hope that there was anyone to influence. He had money, lots of it, so why shouldn't he attempt to pay for influence to get some action from those who wielded the power? Well, that could be tried, but again Mr. Schmidt was not too encouraging. Why? Whatever the sum Ralston could negotiate, it wouldn't be enough. A one-time payoff for their help was just that, one time. They wouldn't turn their backs on a cartel that offered a continual flow of U.S. dollars. They were all in it for the long haul, and that meant years of graft and corruption. Father Alfredo was a force who will be forever protected as long as Mexican officials' palms are greased, and they know the kind of business he does in North America and Europe. Lucrative isn't even a strong enough word to describe it.

Dr. Ralston was frustrated because the league in which he felt he could be a player was not recruiting. They might lead him on and then swindle him of his money without aiding him in his quest. He would be querulous, but it would get him nowhere except killed if he was arbitrating in the wrong location. He knew he had to accept Mr. Schmidt's assessment, and hope along with Anna that Cardinal Salvacco's plan would work. He had no other choice at this point.

85

Italy
Iles d'Arda

Marco was continuing to have pangs of conscience. He was depressed, remorseful and disheartened. Depressed over losing his family, remorseful for the murder and type of life he had been leading, disheartened over his mother's death, and the realization, which finally sunk in, that Father Alfredo was his biological father. He couldn't have suffered worse torment if he had been subject to torture at the hands of a hostile cartel capo. He lacked total spirit feeling this low and about to face the inevitable, and said he didn't care about anything that could happen to him at this point. If he left Mexico and stood trial in Rome and was convicted, he could endure the punishment he would receive. If he was acquitted, he wasn't sure about anything. Where will he go? Mexico or Colombia.

Upon hearing this, I was in a state of disbelief because I found it hard to accept that a seasoned criminal would not have more than ample fight in him to resist arrest and possible deportation and what was to follow that. He indicated that he desired leaving for Italy with Father Alfredo and facing the consequences. He was, however, relieved when Alfredo told him of Cardinal Salvacco's conversation bidding him to come to Europe, and offering assurances that he and Marco will be secluded and safe from the police. It appeared from what Marco understood that the Cardinal was more concerned about confiscating the Missionaries' properties and wealth than he was about Father Alfredo's and his involvement in a murder. In fact, Marco felt the Cardinal was guaranteeing their safety by stating that he will send Alfredo and him to South America, presumably Venezuela, on a chartered jet where they can enjoy immunity from deportation to any place where authorities might return them to Italy.

Marco told me of some of the conversations he had with Father Alfredo during these days and weeks that they were in Coalcojana behind the gates of the seminary where Alfredo was confined as his habitat for prayer and punishment.

Alfredo, he informed me, was happier to have more liberty to control aspects of the cartel and leave the burden of being Director General of a religious order of priests placed on the shoulders of men who were his subordinates, but also quite efficacious in handling affairs. His position which was anonymous was ideal. He controlled most of the trafficking; he was hidden completely behind his collar when in public and traveling and behind the walls and gardens of the sem when he was performing his limited duties as a religious man and teacher. Wealthy Mexicans and government personnel in high echelon positions eager to accept bribes knew Alfredo, of course, as fund raiser for the Order and as the paymaster of bribes, but never were cognizant of the real power he had in the cartel. His name was never known to DEA as a leader of any organization except the Order he founded. Unlike the leaking of capos' names of super cartels in Colombia, Father Alfredo's anonymity was secure outside Mexico. It was only now in Rome that the local police headed by an astute and assertive Captain Lorenzo knew about Alfredo's international drug involvement, and was making preparations to bring him down.

It was easy to understand how Marco could have mixed emotions about the ordeal facing him. I wasn't sympathetic, however, because I knew he had been doing the devil's work for so long, not being so sure if I meant Father Alfredo's or Satan's, but probably both. Also, there was something that he had promised to tell me, something he hadn't even alluded to during the entire time I had been recording his life story. When I had broached this issue in my conversations with him, he skirted any intention he may have had to tell me anything. He merely asserted that he wasn't prepared to say anything yet. It's something which vexed me because I felt I was entitled to know why he had contacted me through my office to first meet with him, and then acquiesce to hear and write the story he felt compelled to tell. This wasn't the first time I wondered if I was just being used as the instrument to get his story out.

Alone, I wondered what the circumstance was, or who was connected to me that provided the reason why he selected me to come to a prison in Italy and ultimately get to know him fairly well. There was no one in his background that remotely could have formed a connection between him and me, so I was left a bit baffled at what I might learn from him. At this time I suppose I was more curious than annoyed that he hadn't revealed anything, but I knew we had a longer trip to take through his life before coming to an end, and the discovery would then be unveiled. I could be patient and hold the anticipation of a future revelation in the back of my mind until he was prepared to discuss it. Until then my work is to listen, record, and write, as I silently let my own private thoughts ruminate through my mind. I could wait. I didn't want this mystery to interfere with my task at hand which I knew was a book I would easily put together and send off to my agent when I got back to America. My work here could prove to be a very lucrative deal. Agents and publishers always seem to gravitate toward biographies that include material from the seedy side of life. Send them something pure and wholesome and most reject it as not being saleable to a broad audience. I knew I was working on a real money-maker. But also, I felt deep in my bones that Marco had been involved in my brother's death, and the truth was eventually going to be told.

86

Italy
Rome

"Cardinal, when do you propose to send for Father Alfredo and Montoya?"

"Everything will be underway presently, Captain. I've learned that Marco Montoya is in Mexico, but you probably already know that if you have spoken to Father Ted O'Driscoll in America. I've conversed with Father Alfredo, and have all but guaranteed his safe arrival in Italy where he will be transported to my office here at the Vatican. I know I am repeating myself as we discussed some of these specifics before, but no need to worry. Also, I don't think I mentioned it to you, but I told Alfredo that a chartered plane will take him and Montoya to Seminaria del Fontanara in Spain and then to South America."

"Yes, we did discuss some of the procedures, and yes, I did speak to the priest in Georgia. Your mentioning a private plane for their departure from Rome is a sterling idea, Cardinal. Father Alfredo will feel he can negotiate with you over the property and money of the Order, and then will be free to leave. Won't he be surprised when he sees the police intercepting them after they arrive in Milan! There will be no negotiating anything for him."

It was easy for Cardinal Salvacco to see that the captain was anxious to apprehend the suspects and get proceedings started for an ultimate trial. And he understood.

"I think the plan is viable. He hasn't questioned me about anything that leads me to believe he is suspicious of any plot against him, anything Machiavellian," said the Cardinal auspiciously.

"My only thought," said Lorenzo, "is that he questions ahead of time your authority to dissolve his Order and confiscate what they have built including their enormous wealth."

"Captain, I've made it perfectly clear, in fact, the General Council which condemned his pedophiliac actions made it perfectly clear to him that I represent the Curia and have every authority to be as lenient or harsh as I care to be. He is aware of my stoic position regarding his case and his situation. He'll question nothing. He can only be open to the invitation I extended him to talk, and then be free to leave afterwards."

"I wish, Cardinal, that you had been a member of my force. Perhaps, if you ever decide to leave the Vatican and begin a second career." He said this jokingly, but on another level, he actually meant it.

"Oh, yes, Captain, there are times, especially when I have to become involved in cases like Father Alfredo's, that my preference in a different line of work enters my mind.. But police work, I don't know. I don't think I would like to constantly see the criminal element that you are keeping society safe from. I think it would be depressing and disgusting and wear on me after a short time. This is not my option for a second vocation."

"Well, it is that, depressing. I've been at it for many years now, and certain things don't affect me anymore the way they used to. But the times I see the innocent victims of crimes who should never have been dead, I feel deeply emotional. For those who are responsible for those innocent victims, I relish bringing them to justice, and I smile when they get the punishments they deserve. My poor wife knows me so well, She knows when I don't talk much that I have investigated a crime where an innocent has suffered, and when she sees me come home smiling, she knows I feel good about a bad guy being punished for his crime."

"You have a tough job, Captain, that's why I pray for you and others doing your kind of work." The Cardinal sounded sympathetic and very sincere.

"I will be smiling when we get Father Alfredo and his accomplice back to Rome where judge and jury will do everything to see them punished. The Council's banishing Alfredo for his crime against all those seminarians will be nothing to the years of isolation from society that he will endure. True, he will have many years to pray before he dies in prison if he stays healthy. If he and Marco have people outside that they love, and can never see, they will have years and years to repent for the sins of their lives."

"Yes, Captain Lorenzo, and I want you to remember them in a prayer at mass on Sundays regardless of your satisfaction that they are to reap their just desserts. None of us are without some sin, you know. I don't know of many even here in the Curia who would cast the first stone."

"I know. I completely agree with that, Excellency."

Does he think I attend mass? But Father Alfredo the criminal is as ugly as a platypus, and I don't pray for ugly platypuses.

▲ ▲ ▲

By all standards, especially priestly ones, Cardinal Salvacco was the epitome of the devoted servant of God and the Church. He was ordained at twenty-five and proved himself a scholar while studying in the major seminary. His superiors saw the brilliance of his mind and sent him forward to attain a doctorate in theology and later, a J.D. in law. But aside from the astute mind he possessed a loving heart for all mankind, and when he performed parish and missionary work for his church, he reached out in a special way that others hoped to emulate. His sincerity and goodness were noticed during his early years as priest and pastor, so it came as no surprise when he was designated to become a solid choice as the Cardinal of Bologna.

No one would be stunned by his words with Captain Lorenzo as they knew the Cardinal to be a just and forgiving man. Father Alfredo's guilt was completely repugnant to Cardinal Salvacco, and he felt Alfredo deserved the harshest of punishment, but he also wanted the captain to know that all sinners are to be forgiven by God and man. He believed in reconciliation.

87

Italy
Rome

AR@DRSfirm.Org

Dear Ms. Ralston, I have been in constant communication with Cardinal Salvacco regarding the possible date on which Father Alfredo Legados and Marco Montoya will leave Mexico for Italy. The Cardinal has been extremely persuasive in convincing Father Alfredo that he has no choice but to come to Rome. I can explain the ins and outs of the Cardinal's arguments after you arrive here and get settled to await the trial. I needn't remind you that all of this is to be kept secret. If your father or both parents will be accompanying you to Rome, please simply inform them that your cooperation with my department is required, and your participation in any proceedings is mandatory in a capital crime. They aren't to be given any specifics of the matter as we do not want anything to leak out that the priest and Montoya might become aware of. As a lawyer I know you understand my precautions. I realize that the investigation has taken several weeks and may have appeared too lengthy, but it took time to be certain we had enough evidence to implicate those who made an attempt on your life.

    I shall be contacting Father O'Driscoll informing him of the above. He is a crucial witness in the case, as you know. I owe much gratitude for all his assistance as he was the single person who pointed us in the right direction that included our apprehension of Giuseppe Vilardo whom we had previously only been able to arrest on more minor charges over the years of his criminal career. This is a major contributing factor as we have tied him to the link of imported drugs from Mexico. That scoundrel has eluded us on the big stuff, but finally we got him on something where we can put him away for a long time. He won't be making tons of euros any more while keeping addicts in the gutter.

The parents of Jeannette Libramont and I have already spoken and a formal request for their presence has been sent through the post. They sounded to be relieved that the moment has finally arrived when justice will be sought for the horrible death of their daughter. I sensed the frustration they have felt as the days have worn on, but now they can be satisfied that the killers will be tried and faced with proper punishment. The ordeal for them is yet to come as they sit in the courtroom and listen to the testimony, however, the end result will bring closure even though Jeannette cannot be brought back into their lives.

I have no doubt that our prosecutor will be successful in trying the case with the evidence we have against the criminal defendants. Be assured that we will not be hasty to disregard or overlook any item, however small and seemingly insignificant, that will jeopardize our successful prosecution.

Extend my best regards to your parents. I am aware of the turmoil that they have been through since the beginning of all of this. They have been a great support for you as has been your firm. I am thankful that the people you work with in the U.S. are as intent upon seeing your good friend's murderers brought to justice as we are. You are fortunate that you have received the help given by them to see you through the past weeks.

I shall be eager to see you in Rome, and I shall provide transportation each day from your hotel to the courthouse. I feel the need to provide you with ample security during your stay as I do not want to dismiss the reality that someone connected to the defendants may want to harm you. You will have twenty-four hour security which means that a plain-clothed officer will be assigned. Please don't view this as an encumbrance, but a safeguard. Thank you for your patience and cooperation.

    Captain Fabrezzio Lorenzo

88

United States
Georgia

mvtodriscoll@mindspring.org

Dad, greetings. I received word from the police Captain in Rome that he is close to apprehending Father Alfredo and Marco Montoya. It should only be a matter of days from what he is saying. I hope the plan comes off without a hitch, so the police can proceed and finalize these entire proceedings. I feel for the Captain as it has to be a messy proposition when you are in one country and the criminals you're pursuing are in another. He told me that things could have gone faster and smoother, too, I guess, if the Mexicans had been cooperative, but I don't have to tell you how all that works in Mexico. I'm just informing you and Mom so that you know the day is coming when I will be flying to Rome, so you will not be wondering where I am if you try to contact me at school. I'll be calling you a couple of days before I leave as a reminder.

I've got to say that I hope everything goes free of obstacles or interruption. You don't know what kind of stuff has been going on since Alfredo got convicted by the General Council in Rome. It has been such an embarrassment to all of us in the Order. You should see the memorandums and notices that have come from the newly appointed Director General. The mortification that we have all suffered because of Alfredo has been penetrating to the core. Even though everyone knows it was one bad apple and the rest of us are guiltless, it's the sense of shame that we all have to bear. The writings that have come down have hit on every possible thing you can imagine. I'll try to remember to send you a copy of the lengthy correspondence we got about Father Alfredo's plagiarized writings. It's a difficult struggle knowing that in the sem and in the congregations all the materials, book length and periodical articles, which he foisted on us, were not his at all. Incredible! Incredible that no one before this had studied the writings to recognize it as another man's body of work. Father Iraenaus who is the Order's keeper of archives and an outstanding scholar wrote the piece about the plagiarism. I'll dig it out and forward it. I will ask you not to share it with anyone. I think it was intended just for members of the Order though there was a similar correspondence that went public. I think Father Iraenaus mollified the content somewhat in the public version though the heart of the matter was not obscured in any way. Perhaps, you have seen it already. I'll send off what we were given for you to read.

I should add here that I heard from Anna recently. She's been worried and concerned about the police getting Alfredo and Marco to Rome and the time she'll have to be there. She said she was worried about me as I'm a major player in the case. I told her she has nothing to be concerned about; the police in Rome are great and will be protective of both of us. I remember a couple of incidents when I was studying in Rome before ordination. One that I'll mention was where the police investigated a robbery of two paintings at the Vatican Museum. They are thorough, I can tell you that. They questioned anyone who appeared on the cameras for the ten months before the robbery. All of us were told to report to the police station for questioning, but they could tell fairly quickly if someone was involved. The rest were politely told they could leave with the understanding that the police were just doing their job, and certainly wouldn't we all want to see those invaluable paintings restored to their proper places on the walls of the Raphael Loggia. As professionals they know how to handle all types of situations that involve keeping people and property safe. They are good. I have no worry about safety.

Anyway, Dad, things are fine. Classes are great. Students are cooperative and eager to learn. Oh, yeah! With a little more than a nudge from time to time.

Tell Mom I said hello. I e-mailed her last week and reported in. Make sure she doesn't worry her head off about my heading to Rome when I get the call. Everything's going to work out fine. I'm convinced of that. Right now I'm more worried about Father Edmund who doesn't seem to be himself lately. It appears things are bothering him, but he doesn't open up with me like when we were younger and in the seminary. I'm thinking he's very concerned about my testifying in Rome. I've asked him if there's any problem with his family back in Ireland, but he says no. Anyway, Dad, remember him in your prayers. When this whole thing is over, he and the rest of us can get back to normal. But at the moment I'm quite concerned about matters that seem to be bothering him where he's not being his old self.

Love, Ted

89

Italy
Rome

"Captain Lorenzo, please. This is Cardinal Salvacco at the Vatican. I need to speak to him immediately. I believe he is expecting my call." A sense of urgency was obvious.

"This is Lieutenant Giancarlo, Cardinal. Yes, the captain told me that a call from you was imminent. He's in the outer office. I'll get him right now."

"Thank you, Lieutenant."

"Cardinal, this is Lorenzo. Have they landed yet?"

"No, not yet. I had gotten word last evening, 10:30 pm Mexican time that they would be leaving Mexico City on flight 1109 this morning. They should land at 5:00 this afternoon. They believe I have a car and driver greeting them when they check through customs. What do you intend to do? Intercept them at the airport, or wait until they are on the E-35 from Civata Castellana? I ask because I think for appearance sake it would look much better if you apprehended them where our car will not be seen by the citizens of Rome. Our vehicles are recognizable. This should be kept quiet until you have them in custody."

Holding the phone in one hand while placing his holster and revolver on his desk, Lorenzo shook his head affirmatively and said, "I agree, Cardinal. I don't want the public to become aware of anything newsworthy until we have had a chance to talk to them. You know they will be contacting either you or the Missionaries about a lawyer once the charges are read to them."

"Yes. I know that. If Alfredo contacts me later, I'll let him know that it will be wise for him to call his Order. We are not providing counsel to him. It will be up to the Director of the Missionaries to answer his plea for help. I know they will offer legal services to one of their own. They rejected the conclusions of the Commission when Father Alfredo was found guilty, and they regarded his punishment as too severe, so they will defend him and Marco now and have one or more of their attorneys available."

"I hope the Director asks him to spell out the charges. Murder and drug trafficking might be sufficient to alarm the good Director to carefully consider whether to help or leave them to shift for themselves."

It takes all kinds. There's a lawyer waiting who'd defend a monkey if it brought notoriety and a pile of money.

"I don't think that will happen, Captain. As long as both the accused are attached to the Order, the Director has little choice but to think them innocent, and do all that he can to keep the name of the Order clean, but he and the hierarchy of the Order will be sweating profusely through the whole ordeal. No one likes bad publicity, Sir."

"Also, with the threat you made to sanction the Order and seek proprietorship of their holdings, they will want to hire the best battery of attorneys in Europe to defend their colleagues, hope to win the case, and safeguard their property from Papal confiscation."

"I don't think we will pursue that, but we can let them worry to death about the possibility of it happening. The last I spoke to the Holy Father he indicated that it would be a mistake to strip the Missionaries of their accumulated wealth in light of the good work the Order does throughout the world with their schools and universities. He's also very agitated that it might discontinue the flow of funds into the foundations that the Order controls from the hundreds of affluent people in Mexico, Spain and the U.S. I proposed the argument that the influx of money may already have slowed, or even halted in view of Father Alfredo's past life being exposed and his designation as a pedophile."

"Yes Cardinal, after all there are hundreds of other charities and foundations around the globe that church-going Catholics can contribute to.

Perhaps, this is an opportunity for some of them to solicit money for their worthy causes."

"I'm sure the Pope has thought of that, too, my friend."

Returning to the main point of their dialogue, Cardinal Salvacco then said, "Captain, I have given instructions to my secretary who is at the airport to notify me as soon as the arrival board signals that flight 1109 from Mexico City is within minutes of landing. This is just so I'll know when they get here, and that I can inform His Holiness. I know you will have officers stationed there as well. It's all in your hands now, Captain. Good luck. You have waited patiently for this moment, and have done everything to make it happen. All of Rome is proud of you and the Force. Proud, too, of your perseverance and adroit detective work that brings these two criminals to justice," said Cardinal Salvacco graciously.

"Thank you, Your Excellency, but I can't take credit for all the help I got from others. The young priest from America who spotted Marco in Rome, the surveillance cameras, and you who were invaluable in determining how to get them back to Rome were of great help to me. Still, it should never have happened that a young woman was killed."

"You are correct. It never should have happened. But I have to believe that Ms. Libramont is looking down on us from heaven, and with the guidance of God is somehow leading us to take action to seek justice for her."

"I appreciate the call, and as always, the conversation with you, Your Excellency. We all pray that things work out, and we can return to a little peace for a while. Good bye."

"Goodbye, Captain Lorenzo."

The good Cardinal held his phone in his hand and sat staring at the top of his brightly polished mahogany desk. He sat thinking for a time very much vexed that long before this time the Vatican did not fully accept the importance of Terre des Hommes International, an organization that promotes child protection and welfare. If that had been the case, he would not be confronting the woes before him, and Father Alfredo might be a good priest whose psychological troubles had been stamped out with adequate professional counseling. Cardinal Salvacco reflected on what new rules and laws must come into being to provide for new situations which could occur. He sat deep in thought for quite a while.

90

Mexico
Over the sea to Milan

Marco spoke about his feelings, and how different they were from Father Alfredo's as they left Coalcojana for the air terminal in Mexico City and during the long flight across the Atlantic. Marco expressed regret for the fact that he was connected to the murder of the woman from Luxembourg who happened by chance to be the interpreter for Anna Ralston. He said he would have had different emotions if it were Anna who was killed going over the cliff-side because he said he saw her as the enemy, the one going to take the case of the abused seminarians to the Commission in order to condemn his mentor. Father Alfredo became a bit philosophical with him when he heard Marco say this. He made the point that a killing is a killing regardless of conditions. He used several examples to prove his point, one of which was killing an enemy in war versus the accidental killing by running a man down with your car. The taking of a life is the taking of a life for which a man must feel guilt. Later, he tried explaining the "double effect" concept to Marco by saying that it was obvious that if a person was to save himself by killing another, even an infant or a group of infants who were in the way of his escape, he shouldn't feel any sense of guilt, but probably would. He would feel more a sense of sadness and uneasiness, but not real compunction. Alfredo said that the man need not feel any guilt at all because it was a matter of self-preservation, but by being human most people likely would feel guilt and harbor it for all their lives..

▲ ▲ ▲

Listening intently to what he was saying were his feelings and Father Alfredo's feelings regarding the matter of killing, I interjected my views of the "double effect."

I uttered my opinion at this point and told Marco what I thought about remorse and guilt. It didn't seem to interest him. This was another instance where Marco was talking to a reporter and not being interested in a thoughtful discussion. I understood, and obligingly kept my mouth shut to accommodate his blind eye and deaf ear.

▲ ▲ ▲

In his conversation with Father Alfredo he said he became aware of the basic differences between them. In terms of the murder and guilt question he saw that Alfredo being a priest saw killing as killing while he saw it in varying degrees. He felt some compunction for the death of Jeannette, but would have been thrilled if she had survived and Anna had perished in the car crash. I thought to myself: how could he have half a heart, compassion for one person's life being lost, and none whatsoever for another's lost life.

Another meaningful difference was in terms of his versus Father Alfredo's view of the illegal drug trade. In the simplest description, he believed the money derived from sales was the means to provide a life of luxury, and like any business if there was a strong demand for the product, the bottom line was the profit that gave him that life. He could not distinguish between this product and another. It was merely, if there are customers for a product and they buy it, I will supply it and make money. Alfredo saw drug trafficking as supplying a product, but not to gain the same end. As he was a tremendous fund raiser in legal arenas, such as churches and community groups, he saw the money coming from illegal drugs as additional capital to use for the wonderful purposes of his Order. Schools, universities in Mexico, Italy, Spain and the United States built and operated for the good of mankind. He wasn't to blame if the bottom feeders of society chose to spend their or someone else's money by whatever means they acquired it on living in ecstasy if only for an hour or so. They were satisfied with the product they purchased, and he was satisfied with the price they paid for it. Simply business. He saw it no differently than Marco in this sense, but felt that his altruistic view was noble. "Noblesse oblige" he would say. It was a business and he only saw the benefits of it to himself being impervious to the harmful or fatal effects it had on the customers.

Murder was a necessity of the trade. Alfredo was forever separated from it so there was no closeness to a death or a hanging corpse in the street that would haunt his sleep at night. So he could say his masses on Sunday mornings without seeing faces other than that of Jesus on the crucifix above the altar and those of the other religious icons that adorned the church. Marco began as a halcone and saw blood flow in the gutter when there was no other way to preserve oneself. He was too familiar with murder from the stories that his father and uncle told although their experiences in the cartel were short-lived. To Marco the man shot in the street was very different from the girl killed in a car crash.

▲ ▲ ▲

I found it quite interesting to hear all this as he related it, and wondered how other criminal minds regarded killings, whether there were categories or gradations, or just how they compartmentalized murder. I suspect the criminal psychiatrist is the professional who engages in this conversation with felons convicted of murdering, and tries to derive some answers to their way of reasoning. There are numerous books that detail the warped thinking and illogical conclusions that serial killers seem to feel are justifications for their heinous acts. It was my thought at this time wondering if someday a criminologist would include Marco's views alongside those of the notorious murderers the world has known.

91

United States
Washington, D.C.

"I'll drive you to Ronald Reagan as soon as you're ready, Anna," said Drew. "I'll be at your place in thirty minutes. I've thought of a few things I'd like to go over with you that might be critical when you testify in Rome."

A half hour later, Anna answered the doorbell. "Come in Drew," said Anna. "I'll only be another minute."

"Anna, I have reviewed several cases in the past weeks during my leisure time at home of situations the firm has been involved in overseas, and I think there may be some invaluable tips we might apply to the court proceedings you're going to face soon. Some of those lawyers that represented Hahm Salehd who was that Hamas thug that instigated the attack on the embassy in Beirut and was convicted of the murders of two marine guards and two diplomats were the best that I've ever witnessed. We picked up some valuable pointers from them, I can tell you.

"We don't exactly know who the defense attorneys are that will represent Montoya and Legados, but my gut feeling is that their defense will have at least two from the Order and someone from a big firm in Rome. The Order has the money to defend them by hiring the best they can get in Italy, maybe even somewhere else in Europe. My guess is that it will be someone quite experienced from Rosetti, D'Agostino, Carabezzi, and Carlossi. I know they have defended murderers before that they've gotten off because of technicalities. I know of one case they had where jury tampering and bribery were thought to be a part of their success, but it could never be proved. Aside from that, they are very sharp and know how to handle themselves before a jury. I know the prosecutors are sharp litigators and will have you well prepared to take the stand."

After their conversation in the car on the way to Reagan International, Anna felt a little more comfortable knowing that her boss had taken the time to apprise her of certain key points that she as a lawyer should keep in the back of her mind. She was appreciative and was glad she had the support of her colleagues which made her more confident. She was determined and strong and did not fear any opposing battery of lawyers in Rome as a force majeure when she was to be called to testify.

▲ ▲ ▲

Anna met up with her parents who had flown to Washington from Hartford to accompany their daughter to Italy knowing that she would feel far less stress and anxiety during the time in Rome if they were by her side. The family talked about the case but tried to free their minds often with small talk as they flew across the ocean. They were a solid New England family who were good people, and although extremely wealthy, were very charitable to others. The family foundation had been established years ago and had contributed millions of dollars to various types of research, mainly medical.

Dr. Ralston had always thought his daughter would follow in his footsteps, but when she said she had become intrigued with the workings of the law and wanted to go in that direction, he was nothing but encouraging. He was very proud of her academic and professional career. However, while sitting between his wife Susan and Anna, he couldn't help but think that if Anna did not engage in the practice of law, she would not be flying to Rome to testify in a murder trial where a very good friend lost her life. But he did realize that time and place were also critical elements that determined events in one's life as did one's profession, so he couldn't blame her legal profession as the cause of this situation. He did have it in the back of his mind that if Anna had never met Teddy O'Driscoll in Madrid on a pleasant sunny day that she and he and Susan would not be on a plane scheduled to land in Rome in a few hours.

Dr. Thomas Ralston was a practical man and a scientist so the workings of his mind centered on the present and the "what is," and he was ready to deal with that. His intelligence would be applied to guide his daughter in any way possible to ensure that she had the best counsel to emerge from this state of affairs as unscathed and whole as when she was a young girl riding her horse as she galloped over the pasture land of their expansive acreage in Stafford Springs. Safeguarding his daughter was paramount in his mind always.

Susan Ralston had met her husband several years after college. She was hired by him at one of his companies as a researcher, and was a diligent employee who demonstrated greater perspicacity than most people he had ever employed. It had taken two years before Tom had actually taken real notice of her. He decided, after having looked at her beautiful legs under her desk across from his office, day after day, and having seen the results of her work, that he was interested in a very intelligent and beautiful lady. From that day romance bloomed and they were married eight months later.

What was going through Susan's mind during that six hour flight were thoughts of keeping calm and placid, not allowing anything negative or counterproductive to arise in her or Anna's minds. Susan had practiced yoga for several years and knew how to put the mind and body in a safe place to avoid bothersome forces that always seemed to be present. Her techniques, she imparted to Anna over time, and was now using every ounce of her ability to convey peace and tranquility to Anna for the duration of the flight, so her relaxed state would prevail. Though confined to tight quarters in the plane, some breathing exercises and occasional struts to the rear of the plane smiling at friendly faces along the aisle seemed to help. Whatever could take Anna's mind to another place and succeed in shortening the ride across the Atlantic was welcome as a physical and mental process to produce a favorable result.

92

United States
Boston

In response to Father Ted's telling his parents that they didn't really have to fly to Rome as they had plenty to do at home in Boston, his mother sent off an e-mail.

TedOD@crestbrook.edu

Teddy, we're coming!
    Your father says there's no sense in our meeting somewhere and flying to Rome together, and he's quite right about that. Although I'd like to be able to talk to you for the length of time it takes to get to Rome, it isn't practical, so we can book out of Boston and meet you at our hotel in Rome. Besides, now that I know Father Edmund is going with you, you'll have his companionship to enjoy on the trip over.
    I never wanted to mention it before, Ted, but there is something that's bothered me for a time. I suppose now is as good a time as any to bring it up and at least you can hear what has concerned me and disturbed me.
    Anna Ralston is a beautiful girl and I know you have been corresponding these past months on the common issue at hand, but is there any other common interest you two have? I know you'll think I'm crazy, but a mother's instincts aren't completely wrong all

the time. And neither are they correct all the time. But mine have told me that at least on Anna's part there's a love interest. Please tell me I'm all wet, if not off base in thinking something is going on. I've sensed that she's had a thing for you since the years at Yale. I never said anything, but I spoke to her once long ago when you and Christy Reiman were going together. She was not laconic, or concerned with measuring her words, when expressing herself about you. I knew then just from the sounds of things, she had eyes on you. If you had not been so serious about Christy, she would have made a play towards you. I guess she assumed you and Christy had married until she accidentally bumped into you in Madrid. She told your father that night at dinner at the Ritz in an aside that she was very surprised that you were engaged in your studies at the seminary, and would later be in Rome for further study before being ordained. Ted, I wouldn't even be mentioning this if I didn't believe she has the hots for you, and I mean the hots. Something re-igniting from the college days. I have seen the glances she has given you, and have seen how she hung on every word you uttered. I truly sensed there was something there. It was more than obvious. When I told your father later that evening what my feelings were, he didn't know whether to agree with me or not. I don't think he saw it quite like I did. I just wonder if her mother made any such observations when you were in Rome especially at the hospital.

I know how devout you are and how dedicated to your ministry you have been since becoming ordained in the Order of the Missionaries of the Holy Church, and I know better than to believe that you would ever give up your sacred vows, but I do have to hear it from you, your own spoken words, that you have no feelings for Anna other than as a friend whom you are helping through a difficult time in her life. I also need to hear that you are happy in the sacred profession you have chosen. Your happiness is the most important thing that your father and I care about.

Love, Mom

Realm of the Beast

JOD@mindspring.com

Mom, are you out of your cotton-picking head? I can't begin to believe that you could think there is any romantic interest between Anna and me. Truly, I can't speak for her, but I can tell you without hesitation that I have none for her. I do have other feelings for her as you are well aware, but for you to even suppose that there is anything else blows me away. I guess I saw things across the table at El Restauranti Goya a different way. Naturally, I noticed her interest in what I was saying, mainly because Anna was somewhat shocked that I was going to become a priest, and she was honestly interested in what I was saying about the sem, the courses I was taking, and what the remainder of my studies was going to be. I can't fathom how you would have seen the interaction at the table any other way. I'm grateful to have such a terrific mom whose only concern is to look out for her son, but I can't believe you'd think me so vulnerable. I had opportunities to become involved with Anna, I suppose, when I was with Christy, and might have found Anna more compatible, and looked at her as a possible life partner down the road. But I didn't. She's a wonderful woman that I respect and admire, and whom I believe will make a wonderful wife and mother some day when she meets the right man. I'm happy that you need to know that I am happy. Well, I am, Mom. I love the life I have chosen, or that has chosen me. It's more fulfilling than I could ever have imagined. I have devoted my life to God to pray for and to help people get to heaven and enjoy eternal life in paradise. It is my mission to do all I can to help my fellow man lead good lives. This is what I live each day for.

    I hope this puts to rest any misconceived notions you may have. I am totally committed to my calling, and will do anything I can to be of help to others, including Anna, which is why I am going to Rome. You have to remember, Mom, that I'm the one who started this whole thing by Edmund and my bringing the seminarian abuse case to the General Director in Madrid. And Dad suggested calling Anna Ralston and having Jeannette Libramont contact her uncle in Luxembourg. So, that's the story as it stands.

You are wonderful and I know you will always have my best interests at heart. I can't express how great the feeling is to know that, Mom. You and Dad have been rock-solid supports for me since I was a kid, and I couldn't begin to tell you how I have appreciated the stalwart parents I have been blessed with.

Love, Ted

I did notice how attractive Anna is when I saw her in front of the hotel in Madrid. I wonder now if Mom noticed or read into my...Did I project something at St. Nicholas Hospital in front of Mrs. Ralston?

93

United States
Atlanta

"I'm glad John drove us to the airport so we didn't have to leave a car in long term parking. It would cost a small fortune, especially since we don't know how long we'll be gone," said Father Ted O'Driscoll.

"Yes," said Father Edmund, Ted's long-time friend and confidant. "Usually I like getting away for a while for a carefree vacation, but this little excursion isn't the fun type trip I'd prefer like when I'm able to go with parents and students out West skiing."

"I'm glad you came along with me. I need the moral support, Edmund."

"With school out now the timing was right for me to go with you. Besides, Ted, I feel that I was a part of all this with you from the beginning when we decided that we had to do the right thing and take the information we had to the director at Fontanara. It's amazing, though, how everything has played out over the past years. First, we approach the head of the Order when we're still seminarians and try to get him to listen to us. Then much later, after eight guys come forward to tell their stories which verify our accusations, Father Alfredo is brought before the General Council of the Curia and found guilty. I figured that was the end of it."

"Yeah. Who could have foretold that the next thing would be a murder that implicated Alfredo?"

"Not only him, but Marco Montoya, too. The guy handling discipline and teaching religious classes in the middle school. The son-in-law of one of the founders of Crestbrook. The bastard!" Edmund said in a hushed voice.

"It's hard to figure, Edmund. I get headaches just thinking about it all."

"It's not over yet. We're just leaving Hartsfield-Jackson and have several headache days before us. You're the guy who has suffered through this while I've just been on the sidelines," said Edmund.

"I got a letter from my mother a few days ago which really shattered me for a while," Father Ted quietly mentioned. "She asked me if I had romantic feelings for Anna Ralston, if there were mutual feelings of love. I couldn't believe what she was asking. Man, someone tries to help us out and my mother thinks she sees sparks flying between Anna and me."

"Oh, my God, Ted! You're joking aren't you? Anna Ralston and you?"

Actually, I can understand it. Anna is a beautiful young woman that any guy would love to get to know. Ted did have an early acquaintance with her in college. But Ted's strong in his commitment to the Church.

"Yes! All because of that night in Madrid when I asked Anna to have dinner with my parents and me. Mom saw something in Anna's eyes, and heard something in her voice."

"Oh, God! That's funny, Ted. It really is. It' so funny, I'd die laughing if I believed it, my friend."

"Ha, ha, you're funny, Edmund. Let's change the subject."

"You brought it up, I didn't."

"Edmund, I'd like to have a pleasant flight. There are many topics, secular or theological, we can talk about on a five hour flight. I only mentioned that because it was on my mind, now it's off of it."

After this ordeal in Rome life will be back to normal. I can readjust to my placement and fulfill my mission, and any thought of the good and bad of this situation will fly out of my mind. I hope.

"Did I tell you, Ted, that when I called ahead to notify the Order in Rome that I'd be staying at the university, Father Maurice Ryan told me that some members of the Curia were considering taking over some of the Missionaries' assets? He said it's going to be a very interesting battle that's being led by Cardinal Salvacco. Have you heard anything?"

"Yes, I've heard that rumor.

I wish I was able to tell you all that I know, my good friend.

"I think it's just to shake things up among the higher-ups in the Order so that not too many of them side with Father Alfredo when he goes on trial. I think it was the Cardinal's way of gaining some leverage to get Alfredo and Marco to Italy. You know, Salvacco has a very strong dislike for Father Alfredo; he always has. He wants to see justice done, of course. But he wants to see Father Alfredo's ass in jail. After the abuse scandal Cardinal Salvacco felt that the Order was badly tarnished and he personally feels that Alfredo has betrayed every devout Catholic on the planet. I know I feel that way, and I'm positive ninety-nine percent of the Missionaries and Catholics around the world do too. It is a disgrace and the Cardinal wants to see the Roman court put Alfredo and Marco behind bars for a long, long time."

"I agree with the Cardinal, Ted. If the police can bring their case against them with enough evidence and witnesses, I'm sure the Cardinal will get his wish. As I said to you once before, you're a key witness in bringing down Marco. The police have the tough job of convincing the jury that Father Alfredo engineered the plot."

"I think they have enough through the drug connection with Giuseppe Vilardo. Would you ever have thought that Father Alfredo was a drug lord? You talk about a scandal. This is the scandal of the century. It could bring down the entire Catholic Church."

"I don't believe that, Ted. It's a veritable scandal without doubt, but I have faith that the Church can, and will, withstand the assault that will come out of the trial. I have faith that the people will see this for what it is and condemn it wholeheartedly, but they know that the greatest force in existence is goodness, and that's what we steadfastly stand upon and symbolize. The Church has withstood many instances of corruption through centuries, over 2000 years, and prevails because true goodness and virtue prevail."

"I know, Edmund. The Church, like society in general, has confronted example after example of attack and has remained concrete hard in its teachings and beliefs, never rocked by those who bring disgrace and embarrassment and attempt devastation."

Libra nos a malo. "Cardinal Salvacco will prove the strength and enduring intransigence of the Church by seeing Alfredo convicted. The Cardinal is as stoic and impassive as the great martyrs who firmly stood their ground in the face of opposing and massive and deadly forces."

"I'm tired, and I'm closing my eyes to get a bit of rest for the next few hours, Edmund." Ted was elated that Edmund didn't seem to have anything bothering him. In fact, he appeared totally serene. Ted wished his mind was equally calm as he attempted to turn all thoughts off.

"Me, too. It's been a long day, my friend," whispered Edmund as he tried to get more comfortable in his seat and turned to close his eyes even though his mind was not entirely ready to shut down.

In the name of the Father and of the Son....

94

United States
Georgia

During this time of upheaval the drug operation was continuing. Marco and Alfredo had left everything in the hands of Mr. Gonzales who was going between Georgia and Coalcojana and Juarez. Their Colombian supplier was more than a bit nervous with the kingpins of the Hombres en Negro not conducting business, but shipments were still flowing and distribution points were safely getting the drugs to market. That is, until a slip-up occurred where the DEA made a discovery that CNN reported as a major bust at a port of entry. Several kilos concealed in some kind of machine parts had been sniffed out, and the discovery yielded marijuana valued at eighty million U.S. dollars. Marco regarded this as a major setback that never should have happened. He forwarded the usual encrypted e-mails to Mr. Gonzales to get word to his lugartenientes to stay far under the radar for a while. Of course, the Colombians were shouting that it wasn't at their end that the fault be placed. They were out too much money, and demanded that someone pay for the blunder. Marco argued that it was a freaky event; no one should have been able to detect anything hidden in the shipment. Some goddamned dogs just got too close to the goods. Who would have thought that the dogs' sniffers could detect drugs so cleverly embedded in tightly welded machine parts? They must have been some kind of super breed with noses that could poke through iron.

Meanwhile, Father Alfredo and Marco, still in Mexico behind the walls in Coalcojana, were plotting their defense in preparing to go to

Rome. Marco said he did not want to make it seem that he and Alfredo were fleeing Mexico and escaping any culpability associated with the cartel's loss. He contemplated traveling to Medellin to smooth things over, but had more than serious reservations from doing so, one of which was that he might get killed if they thought he was lying. He decided not to take the chance of risking his life, but to try to assuage his supplier with argument from a distance where he felt secure. The tried and trusted relationship between Colombia and the Mexican cartel was what he relied on. With the input, mainly assurances, from Father Alfredo, and Marco's explanations rather than excuses, their lives and futures were secure, at least until another debacle should occur where the feds uncovered a cache that would cost the cartel millions.

Marco told me that his relationship with Mr. Gonzales and his other cohorts in the Metro Atlanta area was stable, and that he could rely on them to continue distribution to the East and Mid-west until he could get back and take full control. He was confident that he would not be arrested in Italy, but would be questioned only, and there was not any evidence to tie him to any murder or attempted murder. It turned out that, although the Mexican authorities would not extradite him and Father Alfredo when Interpol and Rome police sought their deportation, the Mexicans never said anything about murder charges against Marco. Listening to his story, he was thinking at the time that he would be defending Father Alfredo and providing him with a strong alibi that would free him of any participation in the murder of Jeannette Libramont. He thought the diversion of the flight to Milan and the limo ride to Rome was a great scheme of Cardinal Salvacco to keep him and Father Alfredo out of sight and safe from anyone connecting them to a story or picture in *El Espresso*.

Though his ties with Mr. Gonzales were strong, after all, he made Mr. G. a very wealthy man, he had some apprehension that the Colombians might solicit Gonzales to eliminate him, and if need be, Alfredo too. This didn't pry on his mind, but having the mind of a seasoned criminal, he had to always alert himself to the what ifs. After the big loss suffered recently,

Marco said he thought that if his life was in real jeopardy, a hit would be put on him before he and Father Alfredo left for Italy. He had to have eyes in the back of his head for a while because he knew that even behind the walls of Coalcojana he wasn't completely safe from a quick and ignoble death. He always said he most feared what he called the scimitar death.

Marco had given me several examples where he knew egregious killings had taken place. Besides the regular shootouts that were frequent occurrences in Juarez or along the Juarez-El Paso border, there were the murders that were carried out quickly, quietly, and secretly. He mentioned the recent discovery of twenty bodies slain and buried near the dunes of Cuidad Juarez. He apparently was knowledgeable of the facts behind this from the detailed description of the mass burial site near Mexico's northern border, and from the manner in which eight of the twenty men were tortured before having their bodies perforated by bullets.

Any accounts of cartel massacres that I could recall from reading through the Associated Press or Reuters, or that I read in lengthy articles from the New York Times were stories familiar to Marco. The insider always seems to have knowledge of what killings have been carried out, and which are about to be carried out that would help produce a real story for a reporter. From what I learned from him over the span of time I listened to his experiences, I could write two documentaries. I know he could not have had any physical involvement with any of the known events because of his occupation in Georgia which kept him tied to a desk, but through the network, he was fully aware of the Mexican cartels' activities. From what I understood unless having bad information, at certain times Mr. Gonzales accrued more fly miles, and was much closer to the ground forces than Marco who was blanketed from the dark shadowy figures who caused mayhem on the streets. This was the shielding he and a top dog like Father Alfredo expected and enjoyed as the brains behind the machine. But Marco had strong doubts about Gonzales being one who could carry out a death plot. He knew Viktor well, and knew him as a man to avoid violence. But Marco thought that he was never absolutely certain what Gonzales was all about.

95

Italy
Milan
Rome

I recorded Marco's description of the flight to Milan:
The plane was right on time as it landed on the runway of Milano Malpensa International Airport. The flight had been smooth and the conversation between Father Alfredo and Marco was congenial and pleasant as though they had no care in the world, which seemed to reflect the false belief in their complete innocence. They were a father and son. There was no obvious evidence of any cause for alarm in the deportment of either man, or on their facial expression. Besides the usual length of time during a cross-Atlantic flight that would be devoted to rest and sleep, the men spoke of the situation that Father Alfredo was about to face. They had a special time together to discuss many things in their past lives as well as a philosophical discussion on killing. Alfredo was contrite about many things as they pertained to his son. Also, Alfredo spent a good portion of the flight in prayer. To an observer fraught with the fear of flying, or experiencing terrorist activity, one would have gotten the impression Alfredo was a man consumed with fright and intent upon saving his soul. His rosary was noticeable on his lap.

From the insight I gleaned into the man from everything Marco had revealed about him, I felt that I could understand Father Alfredo fairly well. There was never a moment when I felt he was an innocent man, or felt that anyone could condone any of his actions, after all, he was a pedophile and a criminal. No one can accept him as anything but a criminal. But I began to see into the sociopathic mind of the man to comprehend the motivation that directed, or rather misguided, his life from a young person born in innocence to a narcissistic aggressively antisocial psychopath.

Marco regarded Alfredo as a mentor and an astute pedagogue. He told me that he had read all of Father's writings that were intended to encourage and promote the profession of faith in the ordinary person, but especially the members of Familia Dei. He wrote to direct the lives of people in the faith, but was a corrupt man doing it, I explained to Marco. He didn't see it that way at all. One of those things, I told him, where he was so close to the trees he was not able to see the forest. No impression was made.

When Marco began to quote chapter and verse of sections of The Salvation of my Life, I insisted that he further his study of the veracity and authenticity of the instruction offered in that work. When I began this association with Marco, I knew I would research all information I was to record. That included the writings of Father Alfredo. In terms of Marco's undying belief in the thoughts expressed by Alfredo in The Salvation of my Life, I found a report in *El Mundo* that positively refuted the authenticity of his book. The paper had discovered the true source of the material that Alfredo had plagiarized.

When I confronted Marco with this he said that, regardless of the source, the words were worthy of repetition by Father Alfredo, and were invaluable in imparting the message to members of Familia Dei. I agreed that he may be correct that the words do bear repeating to a world uncommitted to religious practice, as well as to an organization of faithful adherents to the Church, but that doesn't negate the fact that the instructive message had been stolen from a profound work by a noted philosophical scholar. Again, my words fell on deaf ears, as the expression goes.

The seat belt light flashed overhead, the landing gear was heard descending from the body of the plane, and the stewardesses paraded down the aisle to check that belts were secure. Marco said he braced in his upright seat waiting to land. When the plane landed on the tarmac and rolled toward the terminal, there was only darkness visible through the small window with the reflection of Marco mirrored in it. The plane came to a halt and the passengers readied to retrieve their baggage from the overhead compartments and alight the airbus. Marco said it took extra time for him and Alfredo to walk from their seats which were close to the rear of the plane as it was at full capacity. His experience was that with a struggling economy for the past number of years, fewer flights with every seat occupied were not uncommon, but the norm. He said they walked from the gate down the distance to the escalators to the tram and finally to the baggage claim. It was at this point they were greeted by several men wearing badges of the Rome police force on their belts and with revolvers not entirely concealed. Taken by complete surprise, Father Alfredo inquired after the presence of Cardinal Salvacco's driver. He had been informed that the Cardinal would have a car waiting to take the arrivals to the Vatican from Milan.

Immediately, Marco recognized Captain Lorenzo and heaved a heavy sigh. He told me he was dumbfounded, perhaps not as much as Father Alfredo, but enough to know that all was not well in the land of the Caesars that night. He said his heart ached terribly, not because he felt he was trapped, but because he had been unwary, and that was a mistake that no one in his position should ever be guilty of. Training from the early years by men who would endure and never be taken alive was instinctive, and yet he succumbed to allowing his instincts to fail.

96

**Italy
Milan
Rome**

"Bonjiorno! Welcome to Italy, Father," said Captain Lorenzo.

"Where is the Vatican driver who has been sent to take us to my Order's university?" asked Father Alfredo apparently surprised and curious and wondering where the Vatican's car might be. He had been greeted in the past with a car parked close to baggage where a young cleric sent to drive gathered Father's luggage and rolled it directly to the waiting car.

"No, Father, I'm afraid that plan has been altered. You may be staying at the Missionaries' university for a time while in Rome, but at present you are my guest and Mr. Montoya also. There are a couple of matters we need to address before you go on your way."

He's obviously too stunned to be angry and annoyed at the moment.

"I don't understand what the meaning of this is. If there is some reason you have to delay us, then, I must ask that you contact the Vatican announcing our arrival, and contact the Director General of my Order so that a lawyer will be summoned." Alfredo's manner hinted at astonishment and discomfort. Uneasy, he continued to banter with the captain.

"Why would you think that a lawyer should be called, Father Alfredo? Is there something I should know about?"

Okay. It didn't take too long for him to catch on. He's starting to put two and two together. He'll be perspiring profusely in minutes. The son of a bitch deserves to sweat.

"It would seem to me that you must have some reason for meeting Mr. Montoya and me at the airport. To my knowledge we did not request a police escort, Sir."

What the hell is Salvacco doing? He's behind this for sure. He's one of the very few who always kept his distance

"I am honored to offer the auto escort services of the Department to you, Father. I will enjoy the pleasure of your company for a while. If you have gathered all your luggage, gentlemen, shall we depart?"

When the surprise and shock wore off, indignity took hold of Father Alfredo who bellowed, "This is an outrage! I won't be treated as a criminal! If I am not under arrest I refuse to be put into your police car. This is bullshit!"

"No one said anything about your being a criminal, Father, but with anyone who may be suspected as one, it is my duty to allow you to prove otherwise. Right this way, Father Alfredo. And I'm sorry but you have no other transportation available for the long ride to Rome."

▲ ▲ ▲

Marco stated that the police took him and Alfredo to unmarked cars so that no one would recognize them as police vehicles, and they were driven to Rome. The Vatican's vehicle was parked nearby only that Cardinal Salvacco's driver could observe the event at the airport and then report back to the Cardinal. The police secured their suspects' luggage and took it by another car to the Order's residence where Father Alfredo and Marco thought they were going without interruption. The officers had parked the vehicles in an inconspicuous area of the airport where the police could leave the terminal without being noticed, and anyone being escorted by them could remain anonymous to a bystander who might be nearby.

Realm of the Beast

Marco said he was as stunned by the police reception as much as Alfredo was, but through the unexpected and fear, he remained quiet. He said there was silence as they were driven away, and there was silence all during the long ride to the police station at Via Vittorio Vespucci 124B. He sensed how Father Alfredo must be fuming as the cars made their way along the highway. When they got to the station, the two men were separated and each taken to separate rooms that they observed were interrogation areas of the precinct. The rooms were stark with two chairs and a table and a one-way mirror on the wall just like one sees in the movies. This was a new experience for each of the men, but in the back of each one's mind was the realization of why he was there. Marco said that there were times long before this night that he pictured himself in a situation like this, and he always told himself how he would react. He would never say a word, or divulge any information that might incriminate himself while all the time appearing sincere and willing to comply agreeably with the proceedings. Marco was not a stupid person who would falter or become fatigued with the process and cave in to any questioning. He had great presence of mind to control his feelings and what he might say. His instincts told him that the interrogation practices of the Rome carabinieri were quite different from what he would undergo in the U.S.

▲ ▲ ▲

Later, in the sanctity and quiet of the Missionaries' quarters during his conversation with Father Alfredo, Marco asked the priest how it went with his interrogators. Father Alfredo told him he was shown more respect, in part, because of his collar and the fact that the police were Catholics, who in their heart of hearts did not want to believe that Alfredo, a priest, could be suspected of murder. Marco didn't receive the same level of respect. He was guilty. They knew that as they had him on tape with Giuseppe Vilardo getting out of the car that ran a young woman off a cliff to her death. Why should he be shown any high degree of respect?

But then, he knew the police weren't stupid either. They strategized that by being decent and civil to him they hoped they could urge him to implicate Father Alfredo. They would strive to get something from him if merely implicit.

▲ ▲ ▲

The questioning of the priest was terminated after approximately two hours, Marco said. His own interrogation lasted for four hours with the Captain's hope of a confession but one which never came. Undaunted, Captain Lorenzo determined that another day will yield favorable results, and besides, these two men weren't going anywhere. Though he doubted surveillance would be necessary, he decided to have Marco watched for a while until he called him back for further questioning. Alfredo certainly wasn't going to be shielded by the Vatican. Of that he could be sure. The Order, upon threat of its properties being taken away, would do nothing to shelter Father Alfredo from legal proceedings. Some comfort or consolation they might give to their founder in terms of legal assistance, but nothing in addition that might be viewed as using influence or circumventing the law.

Both were worried a great deal about what might be the outcome of the questioning. After leaving the precinct and while sequestered at the Order's guest house, Father Alfredo and Marco had time to think of corroborating narratives designed to appease the police, but Marco obviously had the most to lose if the worse was to happen, being accused of Jeannette's murder. There wasn't any question in Marco's mind that Alfredo, his own father, would throw him to the wolves to save his own hide and preserve the legacy of his own esteemed Order of priests. Marco knew that Alfredo was adroit enough to convince him, his own son that it was the noble thing for him to do: self-sacrifice for the good of the Missionaries. Allah, be praised. He thought of that expression not in a defamatory way, but rather, thinking of the many who truly believed their sacrifice or self-immolation was meaningful. Would he feel that way, a martyr, if he indeed did self-destruct at the bidding of his own father?

97

Italy
Rome

Marco had said that after Ramon Munoz was killed, Carlos de Rigga took full control of the cartel, and the relationship between his group and the Hombre en Negros in Mexico couldn't have been more harmonious. Carlos was supplying and Alfredo and Marco were distributing. It was Alfredo's connections in Italy that were attributable to the success of allocating drugs through southern Europe, thereby creating a bottom line that was extraordinary. The capos were satisfied with the network Father Alfredo had developed. Until the recent incident at the U.S. border when the loss to Carlos was in the millions, and extensive heat was being felt due to the pressure the American DEA and the Colombian government were putting on his operation, Carlos was a happy little man. Now that both Father Alfredo and Marco were in Italy, Carlos didn't have all the facts, but did have some unfounded suspicions.

de Rigga called Gonzales to Medellin. This stunned Mr. G. because he was under the impression that his cover was perfect and his existence unknown to the Colombians. Not knowing what might come about, he froze. If it was one thing he didn't want, it was any idea that he was connected to Marco's U.S. distribution system. He had a business profession and was respected in the community. How did de Rigga know anything about him he wondered? Someone had fingered him as one of the Hombres en Negro, so he had no choice to make. He flew to Medellin offering some excuse to his wife which she accepted. Before leaving, he had told her to take their son and go to their place in Mexico. Though she didn't particularly care for the inconvenience of leaving Georgia, she knew that good shopping at the Rinaldo de Questa Mall awaited her. She gave no resistance to going as she knew from her husband's disposition it was a critical matter.

The best information that Marco had received told him that the meeting between de Rigga and Gonzales was abrupt. Carlos had already drawn some conclusions which he said were based on information from some of Father Alfredo's men in Coalcojana. One disloyal lugarteniente for whatever reason, most likely he felt he got short changed on a payout, planted the notion that perhaps Father Alfredo had manipulated some drug sales, and was it possible he and Marco have channeled the money through the Order to Rome? Being as paranoid as these type individuals are who head a drug empire, Carlos put a plan together and needed a man most trusted and revered by Alfredo and Marco and that man was Viktor Gonzales.

Marco had no idea who could have been the turncoat that betrayed him and Alfredo. He felt that all the members of the cartel were treated decently and shared in the profits of the trade to where each man went home with a respectable sum of dirty money. All men were asked to volunteer for assignments that were particularly dangerous, and no one was ever singled out to complete a job because he was regarded as too soft. There was no reason for a traitor to emerge from the ranks unless there was promise of something big by Carlos, and it would have to be very big.

When I asked Marco if one of his men could be guilty of betrayal because Father Alfredo made demands or promises he didn't keep, Marco said that was absurd. Alfredo was not feared as much as he was revered, almost idolized, by the cartel which in any other criminal organization is an anomaly. Because of his station in the Order, Alfredo was put on a pedestal, as Marco said, like one of the patron saints, but he didn't like to use that imagery. Marco was crestfallen to imagine that anyone in the organization would have that kind of hatred in his heart to betray a brother. "May his soul be damned for all eternity," Marco shouted vehemently. Loyalty was key and loyalty was expected.

And there the lion's ruddy eyes
Shall flow with tears of gold.
              (Wm. Blake)

98

Colombia
Medellin

"Mr. Gonzales, first, tell me what you know about the way Alfredo handles the money," said de Rigga.

"I don't have any information about that. You can believe me." Gonzales was scared.

"I hope so. I think I do. But, I need your help. You are a close ally of Montoya and I know your position in his distribution system, and I know, also, that you thought your involvement was perfectly camouflaged. I know of your residence in Mexico and that your wife and son spend some time there. Your boy is in school in Georgia, but many vacation days your family is in Mexico." Carlos de Rigga was getting right to the point and didn't waste words. Gonzales knew that and cursed him under his breath.

"That's right, Carlos. What are you after? I know you're going to be direct. I got that feeling when I walked into this room, and I've never met you until this day."

"I like it when someone is specific and asks me immediately what it is that I want from him. I'll tell you what I'm after, my friend."

"Please do."

"You are going to do a job for me that I can't ask any other lugarteniente or halcone to do. You are going to Rome and you are going to kill Father Alfredo in a clandestine way. See. I can be specific and get right to the point too, Viktor. Is that specific enough, my friend?"

"What! You're insane! I can't do that! I've never killed anyone!"

"Mr. Gonzales, did you think you could be a member of a drug cartel and not be expected to kill at some point in time? Your time is now!"

"Impossible! How could you think I could do it and get away, or don't you care if I get away?" The chill that came over him paralyzed him, and he knew that any pleading with Carlos was superfluous. He stood frozen to the spot.

"I certainly do care, and you will get out of Italy without a worry that the police will ever discover you. My plans for such things do not fail, and I take care of my faithful. You became obsessed by money, Gonzales, like all of us in this business, and as you were loyal to your capo, you will be loyal to me, your new capo."

"This is something I cannot do, and will not do," said Gonzales. His immediate past was casting an ominous shadow over him.

Carlos replied in his meanest stentorian voice, "No! This is something you can do, and will do, Gonzales, you dumb fuck. I don't mean to sound like the villain in a James Bond film, Sir, but remember that your wife's and son's future as well as your own will depend on your cooperation. Listen to me now, Asshole. You are the only man who can get close to Alfredo to pull a trigger, and you will do it."

"Why? Why do you want him dead?" asked Gonzales too frightened to react to Carlos's language. "He's been a partner for all these years and has made you rich beyond belief."

"A partner, yes, he has been. But there are others who can take his place. Amigo, any business or industry that looks forward to prosperity must implement foundational change periodically. You ask why. Do you know why he and Montoya are in Rome? I have heard that one of the Cardinals has called Alfredo there to discuss the taking of his Order's assets because of his conviction as a pedophile from long ago, and the disgrace of having had relations with three women who bore him children. That is not the reason he was called to Rome."

"What else could there be?" Viktor asked in blind ignorance.

With obvious paranoia, Carlos answered, "The police want to question him about the drug trade. They know of his contacts in Italy. I do not want Alfredo to bring down my operation. When pressed he will cave in because the police have enough evidence to put him in prison for a very long time. Do you think, Gonzales, that I have only relied on what Father Alfredo tells me? Over the years I have not been so stupid as to only get my information from one source, Alfredo. Many times I may not know something immediately, but I find out later. Do you think I have not bought off halcones and lugartenientes to keep me aware of activity in Mexico and North America? We in Medellin are the suppliers and shippers, but we know what happens beyond Colombia. The unfortunate discovery of our shipment by the dogs was not expected, and there is no blame put on the Hombres en Negro for it, but when there is sufficient cause to believe the capo has siphoned off a lot of money, the suspicion is that he has done it before many times. I have no alternative; I take action."

You're scared shitless, Gonzales, but you value your life, don't you?

▲ ▲ ▲

Carlos de Rigga was a man who knew no mercy and showed no mercy. He was raised in the cartel and rose to the highest level chiefly because of his ruthlessness. His extreme hatred was incited by the high number of deaths when drug gangs fought each other for turf, and the paramilitary took on a get-tough strategy to eliminate drug flow. There wasn't any part of society that he hesitated launching violent attacks on. Whoever positioned himself between Carlos's objectives and the destruction of them was in extreme peril for as long as he may live, and de Rigga guaranteed that the living wouldn't be very long. His legacy was well phrased in the expression he used: live by the gun; I kill with the gun. He ruled his turf with extreme violence. This is what made him successful and kept him alive. He believed in Al Capone's expression that speaking nice and carrying a gun got you further that just speaking nice.

99

Italy
Rome

"Edmund, I'm going out for a while just to walk around the city. Want to come along?"

"No, Ted, I'm staying here. I'm waiting for a call from my brother. You know the time difference between Ireland and here, so I'll hang in so I don't miss the call."

You don't know how this is a conversation I'm dreading. And may regret for a long time.

"Okay, I'll see you in chapel before dinner tonight. If my mom or dad rings, just say I'm out and I'll get back with them later on."

"Sure, I'll do that. Hey, wait a minute. Here's the phone now. Hello!"

A very pleasant voice said, "Hi, is this Father Edmund? This is Anna. Would Father Ted happen to be in?"

"Yes, he's right here just about to leave our room, Anna. Ted, it's for you. It's Anna."

Ted acted surprised. "Hi, Anna, when did you get in?" he asked cordially.

"Not long ago. I met my parents at the airport and we took a cab to the hotel. I knew you were flying in from Atlanta, and I just thought I'd call to see if you got here."

"Yeah, around 3:00. Edmund and I got settled, took a few minutes to see some of our Order, and spoke to the Director for about 30 minutes. I was just leaving to get some refreshing Roman air in my lungs. Would you like to meet?"

"I think I could do that. Mom and Dad are here and wanted to go to the Pallazo Doria Pamphily near Via D Gatta while they had a chance. So, I'm free, I guess." She sounded eager.

"Good! I'm about three blocks from your hotel. Let's meet at the Pantheon Via D Seminario near Piazza della Rotundo in twenty minutes."

"See you then," Anna said enthusiastically, but not absolutely positive she knew the way to the Piazza. She'd hope to see an officer and get quick directions.

"I'll be dressed in black. You won't be able to miss me, Anna," Ted said with a low laugh thinking he was being funny. He said goodbye and hung up. He then said goodbye to Father Edmund who seemed to not want to meet Ted's glance, but he mumbled a soft "Anna, huh? Yeah! See you later, Ted."

Ted left and a few minutes later he met Anna at the Piazza. They hugged.

"Hello, there. Wow! That's a smart outfit you're wearing, Anna. Great for this time of year in Rome. And very colorful."

"Oh, you like it?" Anna responded with a broad smile and sparkling eyes. " I thought the color was just perfect for me when I tried it on in Bloomingdales last week. I wanted to change up the old wardrobe knowing I would be here for who-knows-how-long. You guys don't have to worry about that sort of thing, do you?" She giggled when she uttered this question.

"What do you mean? You think we wear a black suit all the time. I've got some colorful classy looking sweaters in my closet. You'd be surprised."

Maybe not. She must remember some of my college wardrobe. Colorful to be sure. Seems I always wore a loud sweater.

"No, I don't think I would. I remember how you dressed when we were at Yale. You were about the preppiest guy in your dorm; I remember those sweaters, Father. That sounded strange."

"What do you mean?"

"Well, I was thinking and talking back to our college days and would have said "Ted."

"Oh, yeah! I see what you mean," answered Ted. "Anyway, glad you're here. Let's walk." Within a few minutes they found a secluded place to sit that afforded them privacy to talk away from the passel of travelers and tourists and residents that glided along the avenues.

"I know you must have given a lot of thought to testifying, right, Anna?" said Father Ted sounding quite serious.

"Yes, absolutely. And you, too, I'm sure."

"It's one of the things that you can't get off your mind, no matter how hard you try."

"Yes, I know." Then thinking about something else, perhaps inappropriately, Anna said, "And there's more than one thing I can't get off my mind."

"Such as?" Ted asked looking a bit puzzled.

Becoming somewhat taciturn, "No! Not now," she said. "I wouldn't want to talk about it at this time. Maybe I'll have the nerve to discuss it later on, or maybe never."

Probably never. I know I don't have the guts. Hopefully, it's because I do have some brains.

Caught in the moment and not recalling his e-mail to his mother, Ted said, "It's always better to get things in the open, Anna. Not only saves a lot of time, but usually clarifies and irons things out for the better. There are multiple examples of that."

"Oh, I'm not so certain about this, Ted."

I walked right into this like an absolute idiot. I can't let that happen again. Why did I open my mouth? Just plain dumb.

100

Italy
Rome

"Hey, Shamus, good to hear from you, brother," Father Edmund said with joy and excitement at hearing his brother's voice. " How's Mum doing? Everything alright?"

"Yeah, Edmund, Mum's doing fine. Just has the same complaints she had ten years ago. You know some things never change. Except when she hears your voice or gets a note from you. Those are what make her day."

You always were the favorite son though you left home early, but you're the priest in the family. Oh, well!

"Yeah, but since you married Ellen and had the kids, you know Mum became a changed woman. She felt she had lost me, but knew what she gained after you and Ellen tied the knot. I wish I could have been home to officiate at the last christening. I'm sorry I couldn't get away."

Changing the subject and being curious about why his brother wanted him to call, Shamus asked, "So, what's going on that you're in Rome, Edmund?"

"I came over with Father Ted, Shamus, because he's to testify in a trial, and school has let out, so the Order thought I could lend moral support to my friend and colleague."

"Great! I hope that gives you a little time to do some exploring around the eternal city. You've got to take advantage of the opportunity, you know."

"Yes, I'll get around a bit before I return to Atlanta. Some of my classmates in the Order are positioned at places here. I'll renew the old acquaintances, and see how they've changed. I always think everyone gets older but me."

That's so much bull. I feel quite old.

"Well, I know you didn't leave the message for me to call you to simply chit chat. What's really happening in your life?"

"Father Alfredo has been summoned by Cardinal Salvacco to defend himself against charges brought by the Rome police, and Marco Montoya has been charged too."

"What are they accused of doing, Edmund?"

"Murder!"

"You've got to be kidding me!" Shamus shrieked in disbelief. "Holy crap! Murder! Who?"

"No. I'm not kidding by any means. They are charged in the death of the woman who was the translator for the attorney who represented the abused seminarians. You do remember? Jeannette Libramont."

"Of course, I remember. Holy shit, Man. What's going to happen?"

"I don't know, but the prosecutor here in Rome is bringing the case against them. Marco and Alfredo were already questioned by the police when they arrived in Rome. It's a long story that the world won't believe. Father Alfredo set up Marco to run a car off the road, and it just so happened that the car was being driven by the woman who opposed Father Alfredo. See the connection? To top it off, an accomplice in the car driven by Marco is a cartel guy in Italy who's connected to a Mexican cartel headed by none other than Father Alfredo. See the picture?"

"Good Mary, Mother of Mercy, I don't believe it."

Oh, please tell me you're not implicated in anything, my Brother.

"Believe it, Brother. That's the story. And Ted's more than involved, so he has to testify."

"Do you think you could get me in the courtroom, Edmund, if I come to Rome? I'd love to see how all this plays out. It's incredible. I'd sacrifice a week of work for this."

"No. Stay home and go to work. It might be quite a while before this case is closed."

"Mum will be shocked out of her shorts when I tell her this story. She still says a prayer and lights a candle at mass on Sunday for Father Alfredo for taking you to the sem and allowing you to answer the calling. She's thankful that you've enjoyed a good life in the service of the Lord."

"Shamus, that brings me to something else I want to say to you." After a long moment of quiet hesitation, Father Edmund said, "I'm thinking of leaving............................

Shamus, did you hear what I said? Say something dammit."

"I think I heard what you said, but I can't believe I heard what you said. You mean the Church?"

"You heard me. I'm serious."

"What the hell is going on over there?"

Oh, God! He must be involved in something very bad.

"I can't tell you too much right now; I'll be able to speak more freely to you when I get back to Crestbrook. Just don't say a word to any one, especially Mum, and including Ellen. I'm mixed up about a lot of things, but I've given substantial thought to what I might have to do."

"Edmund, I can't believe I'm hearing all of this. Don't blow me off like this saying you'll talk to me later. Don't be surreptitious with me. Are you a part of Alfredo's problems with the law?"

"NO! Look. I'm so disillusioned with everything that's happened. I've prayed and prayed and prayed, saying don't let me feel this way. Get these devilish thoughts out of my head. When I say I've been tormented, Shamus, you don't know the half of it. Since the Father Alfredo scandal my world's been turned upside down. And the worst part is I can't talk to anyone about this. Oh, there have been times when a bunch of us entered conversation where the topic of the right choice in life has come up, but it was only talk, just that. None of us actually meant we'd leave the Order. But, now, I'm contemplating it seriously, and I don't like the thought of it at all. I'm churning inside day and night."

"Listen to me, Edmund. Please listen! Maybe you should just take a leave of absence for a while. Come back home and clear your head. Be around family where you won't be so close to your friends in the Order. I don't know what else to say. Maybe you should try to talk to Ted. He's your closest friend. If anyone understands you and what you're experiencing, it's Ted. He can help. I know he can, Edmund." Shamus sounded frantic.

"I'm afraid to even mention it to him."

"Have you even thought about what you might do if you left?"

"No, Shamus, I haven't got that far yet. I'm battling with the decision. If only the scandal and this bs that is going on now with questions of Alfredo's drug activity. It's a mess. I'm a mess, and I can't stand it. Every day is a tribulation, and destructive."

"Edmund, you have to keep a level head about all of this. My advice is simply wait until this crap in Rome is finished and you go back to Georgia. Then, take time with Father Ted and figure it all out. I know you can work this out with good counsel and much prayer. Ted will know exactly how to help you. I know you'll be okay and do what's right in the eyes of the Lord. Please promise me you'll handle it this way."

I can't bring myself to tell him he sounds suicidal. I just can't.

Edmund never before heard such urgency in his brother's voice.

"I promise, Shamus. But remember, don't speak of this conversation to anyone, please!"

"I promise, Edmund," Shamus said shaking his head in bewilderment.

When Edmund hung up the telephone, he wondered if he had spoken too prematurely to anyone, especially his brother, about leaving the priesthood. He knew Shamus was the type person who'd keep everything bottled up inside and worry himself sick. With his head in his hands, Edmund sat in a forlorn state, and began to sob. He had never come near the brink of anything resembling disaster in his life, but now his mind and his feelings were taking him to the very edge of an unknown region, and he had no idea how he might cope.

101

Italy
Rome

"Lieutenant, bring Montoya back in," said Captain Lorenzo leaning forward on the desk in front of him.

"Yes, Sir. I'm on my way," said Lieutenant Giancarlo.

Montoya knew his stay away from the police station and further interrogation wouldn't last very long. He hadn't given the police very much information when he was questioned only a short time ago upon his arrival in Rome. He had time to think and knew how he needed to respond to further questioning because he knew the tact they would use to come after him.

"Good day, Mr. Montoya," said Captain Lorenzo after Giancarlo led him from a holding room and ushered him into a chair in the Captain's office. Both officers stayed in the room, the Captain behind his desk and the Lieutenant seated near the door. The lieutenant had the occasion of leading the interrogation earlier, and now it would be the Captain's turn to use his approach. Lorenzo felt it might be a little premature, but he was going to try to pry a confession out of Marco. He was a clever investigator who had years of experience dealing with interrogations, and felt assured he could mold Marco to his satisfaction.

"Marco, do you know who Jeannette Libramont is? Have you ever heard the name before?"

With the stubborn thought of resistance in his mind, but no fool-proof plan to be evasive, Marco said, "I don't know her and I have never known anyone by that name. I first heard it when I was questioned the day before yesterday."

"Do you know a woman named Anna Ralston?"

"No!"

"Have you ever heard the name before?"

"Not until the day before yesterday."

"Marco, where were you during the second week of March of last year?"

"How do I know?"

"You should know quite easily. You have a position in a school and you know the days and months the school is in session. You know the days and weeks that the school is not in session. Isn't that correct, Mr. Montoya?"

In a guarded tone Marco answered, "Putting it in those terms, yes. I am very familiar with the number of days I am in school, and I know the vacation schedule for students and teachers."

"So then, that helps you recall where you were last March, doesn't it?"

"Yes!" shaking his head affirmatively.

"Where were you?" Lorenzo asked in a firm and direct manner.

"The school schedule would show that the holiday break was at that time."

"Fill me in on some details of your whereabouts during that time."

"My brothers had notified me that my mother was very sick. I went to Colombia to see her because they said she was close to death. My family joined me there to see my mother."

Captain Lorenzo already knew much of this information through a conversation with Father Ted.

"Did you go directly from Atlanta, Georgia to Colombia when you visited your ailing mother?"

"Yes, I mean, No. I went to Mexico City first."

"Why did you go there? Did you see Father Alfredo?"

"Yes, I saw him to confer about things."

This son of a bitch already has the answers he wants to hear from me.

"Did you remain in Colombia very long after you left Mexico?"

"No! In grave disappointment to my wife, I left." The unhappy memory of that occasion and the following confrontation with Sarah was noticeable on Marco's face.

"Where did you go, Mr. Montoya?"

"To Rome."

"To Rome," the Captain repeated. "For what purpose did you come here?"

"Business," Marco replied.

"What business. You are a teacher, or have some administrative post at the school, don't you?"

"Yes, I do, but I am a director in an organization that I'm sure you are familiar with, Captain."

"Oh, yes, Mr. Montoya. Familia Dei. Isn't that right?"

"Yes, that's right." Is that so surprising to you?"

"What was the nature of that business?"

"I was here upon the request of the Missionaries of the Holy Church to take part in an event that was scheduled."

"Did you take part in the event? How long did it last? Where did you stay while you were here?" Lorenzo asked without taking a breath between questions.

"I did speak at the event where I laid out plans for a program that I was directing for Familia Dei members in Georgia, and at two other Missionaries' schools in the United States. If I remember correctly, the meetings lasted two days. While in Rome I was the guest of the Order and stayed at the Order's university in the city for a day."

"Where else did you stay?"

"Nowhere." Marco was showing some signs of feeling quite warm under this line of questioning.

"Who requested your presence and participation at the event?"

"Father Alfredo Legados."

"Was he here in Rome at that time?"

"Yes!"

"Was he with you at that time?"

Realm of the Beast

"What do you mean by with me? With me at the event? With me at quarters at the university?"

"Both," Mr. Montoya.

"Yes! To all of my own questions. He participated at the event and he also stayed at the guest priest's quarters. He is a priest in the Order of the Missionaries of the Holy Church, you know. And you also know why he was primarily in Rome."

"Yes, Mr. Montoya, the world remembers why Father Alfredo was in Rome at that time, doesn't it?"

"Would you like a drink of water? A cigarette, if you smoke?"

"Water. Yes, please. I don't smoke. I don't think anyone in Familia Dei smokes."

"Lieutenant, kindly bring a bottle of Avian to Mr. Montoya. And one for me as well. It's a bit warm in this room."

As warm as it is for him, this guy is staying a bit cool. I hope I can get him. He demonstrates a persistent sense of savoir faire, and that pisses me off.

"Marco, from what I understand you have been a faithful follower of Familia Dei and that is one main reason that you are so respected by the Order and have attained a certain level of status in the religious organization. Isn't that fact?"

"Yes, I suppose that is a fact."

"Who has been your mentor through the years and brought you to that respected status?"

"I have known Father Alfredo for a long time, Captain, and I thank him for the guidance he has given me through the years."

Where's he headed now?

"So, your close association with Father Alfredo has brought you to great involvement in matters of the Order."

"Yes!"

"Has the good Father requested many favors from you in the past during your close association with him, Mr. Montoya?"

Grilling him and he stubbornly defends that satyr.

"He has asked for my participation for the good of the Order at different times. I don't know that I was doing any favors. I am indebted to Father for the immense help he has given to me and to others in the Familia Dei community in Mexico, Spain, and the United States," said Marco.

"Yes, I know you are indebted to him for many reasons. Could one of those reasons be that he needed your help when he was confronted by the General Council of the Curia who brought charges of child abuse against him?"

"How do you mean that, Captain? Father Alfredo was quite capable of defending himself against those allegations, and he had the help of his Order's lawyers. He didn't need my help."

"You may have helped him in another way, not as part of his defense team."

You think you're freaking clever, Captain.

"I have no idea what you're talking about!" Marco was fearful that Captain Lorenzo was closing in. He felt he had kept his cool all through the questioning and didn't want to believe that things were caving in but he was aware his nervousness was discernible.

"After your presentation at the Familia Dei event last March, did you remain in your quarters at the university?" Captain Lorenzo asked.

"For most of the time I was not at the podium or in the audience, I congregated with other members or with the priests of the Order."

"Most of the time? What about the rest of the time?"

"Yes! I went into the city either alone or with someone."

"Can you account for your time in the city, My Montoya?"

"What are you getting at, Captain?" Marco was perspiring, but remaining calm.

Speaking loudly and showing anger, Lorenzo said, "What I'm getting at, Sir, is that you, upon the command of Father Alfredo, and an accomplice stole a car in Rome, and at the precise time that two women, Anna Ralston and Jeannette Libramont, had left their hotel to go to a café, you ran them off a road. One of those women was killed. One of those women was prosecuting the abuse case against Father Alfredo. Does this clear your memory, Mr. Montoya?"

"That's absurd, Captain. How do you contrive a story like that in your little mind to build such a superficial case?"

With this remark, the Captain sensed that Marco was feeling the heat of being on the hot seat, and the seat just got a lot hotter for him. Marco sensed the enjoyment that Captain Lorenzo was getting from this interview and felt himself getting very agitated with the questioning. The Captain was aware that Marco was not giving him all he wanted, so he decided to stop at this point knowing it was premature to expect a confession. Lorenzo was satisfied that he had cornered Marco and he sensed Marco's realization that the interrogation with his line of questioning wasn't a one-time occasion. He wanted Marco to sweat for a while knowing he was a principal suspect in the murder of Anna Ralston. Sitting for a moment in quiet reflection, the captain knew for certain that this young man would end up being the fall guy because for many years that was his role in a life-long play directed by a manipulative and malevolent Father Alfredo. Now he anticipated hauling Father Alfredo in next for grilling.

102

Italy
Iles d'Arda

Marco was nervous. He had been interrogated twice now and had handled himself as well as he figured he could, but the anticipation that anything could go wrong, even the slightest little mistake that either he made or Father Alfredo made, and would be serious enough to lead to dire consequences, bothered him. He was somewhat complacent to believe that he and his father had rehearsed their past actions well enough to escape worrying about a grand jury indictment, and didn't want to think that he could weaken and eventually crack under pressure.

I said to Marco that the various studies by criminologists have proven through their statistics that there are not accused criminals that don't submit to harsh questioning over time. Even people who aren't guilty of a crime have yielded under severe pressure and confessed. There have been famous cases where false confessions have sent innocent people to prison for years who eventually were released because DNA that was hidden ultimately emerged and led to a retrial. I reminded Marco that police and prosecutors from anywhere in the world have the same motivation when it comes to solving a crime. Their intent to have someone convicted for the crime is paramount, and doesn't always signal that truth has prevailed, or will prevail. He hoped what I said was factual in a small number of cases. Having been a reporter for many years and having been witness to miscarriages of justice, I disagreed that the number was small.

I made attempts to humanize Marco after I had gotten to understand him. Periodically, Marco appeared to demonstrate a penitential attitude. Perhaps knowing deep within the confines of his soul that he was reproachable, and would be compelled to make restitution, he would forestall any attempt to further transgress the law. If things were going adversely, why would he make them worse?

I didn't recognize that change as being the same man who previously pronounced himself to be a tempered and vulcanized bad guy with a malleable heart. This description had to be formed in part from a couple of sources: his having had a highly religious involvement and his having a family. Marco was never hesitant to give his impressions of people and of situations in which he was a part. He revered the clergy that surrounded him at Crestbrook and in the Order in general. There were a few assholes he consented, just as there were in the membership of the Familia Dei, but he said he was chastened by the goodness he saw in others and in the beneficent work they did. He could have been so different a man had he never continued in the cartel, the service of sin, but then the other side of him would never have emerged. He was strictly a dichotomy who ineluctably had to self-destruct. Hardly virtuous, but hardly a truly crystallized criminal. So often I was bothered by the mixed emotions I felt about him.

103

Italy
Rome

"Father Alfredo, I'm afraid I can't offer you better accommodations during this inquiry," said Captain Lorenzo sarcastically. "These will have to do for a while, but things won't be too disagreeable, I can promise you. That is, of course, dependent upon how agreeable you are."

Without showing any consternation, the priest said, "I am at your service, Captain, to be my usual cooperative and charming self."

You'll learn what invective means before this interview is over.

"That is how I have always known you, Father Alfredo. And how are my friends at the Vatican, Father?"

In the exchange of repartee, Alfredo said, "That depends on who you mean, Captain. You see, some of them have not been friendly to me in the recent past, so I'm forgetful about who is friendly and who is not."

Now that Salvacco has turned most of the prelates against me.

"Then we'll just say that whoever knows that I do the work of the Lord and the work of the people will be friendly to me, and as I am well, I pray they are, too."

"We all pray for goodness and justice. Don't we, Captain?"

"That is reassuring, Father." Then returning to serious business, he said, "Now, our reason for being here. I won't belabor the matter which I know you will appreciate. I am aware of the Curia's findings as regards the case that was brought against you. That is none of my concern as the case was never brought to a criminal court where perhaps we may have become involved

This damn ass tries to present a panache to seem like an innocent.

Desiring to stand his ground in argument, Alfredo said, "I can say to you, Captain, that of the crime I was accused, I am not guilty."

"I'm sorry, but the General-Council saw things differently through the evidence that was presented by the American lawyer, Ms. Ralston. She is at the center of my questioning, Father Alfredo, as I'm sure you are aware. Did you meet Marco Montoya in Mexico prior to your coming to Rome last March?"

"I have met with Mr. Montoya several times, March included, as he is an officer of my universal religious organization Familia Dei."

"I know what he is. So, you did meet him. Where? And why?" said the Captain hastily and with some agitation.

"I'm certain it was at the seminary in Coalcojana. I met him to discuss upcoming conventions at our Order's schools in regions of North America."

"Is that all you discussed? I know your having to go to Rome for the hearing must have been the most important thing on your mind at that time."

"Of course, that was on my mind, but other than to deny those charges against me to my Order, and to the members of Familia Dei, I would not be talking of it to anyone including Mr. Montoya."

"Father, I remind you that the truth is of great importance. I remind you, also, that we have done investigative work through the American FBI and Interpol. There may be incriminating evidence that was gathered which can be used against you."

Again attempting to proclaim his innocence, Father Alfredo said, "Captain, there is nothing that I need to conceal. For whatever reasons you have for questioning me, I am innocent on all accounts." Another attempt to palliate his atrocious and vile behavior.

"How did you come to know Ms. Ralston?"

"When she appeared in the court with the testimonies of men who said I wronged them many years ago."

"Do you know Father James McGlynn in New York? Do you know his bishop?"

"Yes, I know both of them, not personally."

"Did you ever speak to Father McGlynn by telephone or correspond by e-mail before you were on trial in Rome."

"Yes! What bearing does that have on anything?" Alfredo said with a sneer on his face.

"Father, I have a copy of an e-mail sent by Father McGlynn to you in which he mentions the name Anna Ralston, and tells you she has been asked to take the testimonies of eight men who attended your seminary when they were young boys."

For years you were a contaminant in sacred vestments.

"I don't recall the woman's name from having seen it in a letter."

"Father, do you know who Jeannette Libramont was? She was killed in a car that was forced over a road way here in Rome. Do you recall hearing about that 'accident'?"

"Yes, I do! Why? Do you think I ran them off the road?"

"Why did you say "them", Father?"

"I read it in the paper at the time that there were two women in the vehicle."

This yokel thinks he's clever and going to trap me. Fool.

"Father Alfredo, I am going to prove that you orchestrated the incident with the intention of having Ms. Ralston killed. I'm going to show that your motive was simple revenge, that you originally intended to have her killed before she brought the case to the Commission."

Remaining quite calm in view of the allegation, Father Alfredo said, "That is preposterous, Captain. You have no proof of any such allegations."

"I can also prove that you had the perfect instrument for committing the crime—Marco Montoya."

"Ludicrous, Captain."

"Why did you ask Mr. Montoya to go to Rome with you?" asked Lorenzo feeling he was tightening his grip on Alfredo.

"I didn't; he went to visit his mother, and flew to Rome from Colombia."

"Why was he in Rome, and I don't want to hear that it was Familia Dei business?"

You evasive son of a bitch!

"I don't know. He was subpoenaed by my lawyer to be a character witness, I believe."

"Father Alfredo, Mr. Montoya was never in the room with you and the General-Council. He was never seen by and never spoke to any member of the Council. He never was called to testify. Did you and Montoya confer at the quarters of the Missionaries where you stayed in Rome?" asked Captain Lorenzo.

"Yes! We discussed the false charges. And that is all we discussed."

"Father, how well do you know Giuseppe Vilardo?"

"I never heard of him."

"He says he knows you. We have him in custody. Shall I call him in so you can see if you recognize the man?"

"No! That's not necessary."

"Father Alfredo, I think you had better start telling me about your connection to the Clan dei Casamonica where Mr. Giuseppe Vilardo has a life time membership."

"I don't know Vilardo, and I don't know anyone connected with a cartel," insisted Alfredo with a steely gaze focused on the captain.

Standing over him and speaking in hand movements as well as words, the Captain sought the crucial moment of the interview when he peered down at Father Alfredo and said, "Father, Mr. Vilardo is in custody and he has been cooperative. I'm prepared to bring you down and expose to the world the corrupt life you have lived in organized crime. You have had the most perfect cover imaginable, but it's all over, Sir"

"Incredulous! You can prove nothing to make me appear guilty of any crime!" Father Alfredo bellowed.

"I've given you much to ponder, Father Alfredo. I will end here. Oh, you should know that Mr. Montoya is sequestered, shall we say. You will no longer have communication with him. You've spoken to him for the last time. You will see him only in court when the prosecutor brings the case. You are dismissed. I'd suggest you think seriously about a strong defense with the lawyers whom you have already retained. Lieutenant, escort Father Alfredo to the door, please. His less comfortable accommodations await him on the third floor."

"You bastard!" Alfredo said as he stood to be cuffed and led from the room.

I guarantee you will feel repercussions from this!

104

United States
Georgia

Marco told me the story of the meeting between Viktor Gonzales and Carlos de Rigga. Gonzales left Medellin a changed man whose change was for the worse. He was terrified, and didn't have any idea what to do, except follow Carlos' order, or see his family shot to death and have his own head severed from his shoulders. Carlos wasn't joking about what he wanted done, and Viktor clearly understood that. When given instructions he would fly to Rome and comply with de Rigga's command to eliminate Father Alfredo. What he went through emotionally for the next couple of weeks was wrenching, and how he explained the extreme agitation to his wife was that work wasn't going too well. Business was slow and he had challenges to face and hurdles to overcome. He told her the strain was intense, and would get worse when he would have to do some unexpected traveling to check on operations at other locations. She was used to him being away periodically when he would go with Marco to the other Order's schools for what she thought were conventions. His position at Hartwell also required him to travel at times.

He spoke Spanish and knew some Portuguese, so in business he was responsible as a liaison with the South American countries and parts of Europe. This, he told her so there would be no questions when he had to fly out of Atlanta for several days at a time. Naturally, his secretary would make all travel arrangements, so his wife would not ask to see plane tickets or even memos regarding his business. Gonzales had a cover story for his company to throw off any questions from his boss when he was gone. He would be reached if need be by his cell phone. There was a contrived situation where he said he had promised his family a European vacation because he had several days coming. In this way no one would call the house to check if the family was gone. With his wife at their place in Mexico, no one would call the house in Georgia. There was no reason for suspicion; Viktor could be convincing, and he deserved a vacation for a couple of weeks. He was a great administrator and had the respect of his co-workers.

As the time got closer, Viktor Gonzales desperately tried to bolster himself for the plan he would have to carry out. Carlos placed his occasional calls on his non traceable cell phone to Gonzales in order to strengthen his backbone, and give the assurances that all would go well, and promised that, after he succeeded there would not only be substantial reward for his work, but he could count on taking over as capo of the Hombres en Negro. He could retire from Hartwell and Smith and live a satisfying life in Mexico. Besides, isn't that what his beautiful wife and his kids would prefer? The wife should be more comfortable there, he thought, where she didn't have to pretend to like the gringo neighborhood where they lived.

And Viktor would not have to pretend to attend conferences with Familia Dei which were decoys for getting to spots to distribute the drugs to American streets and addicts.

There was no way to be positive that Gonzales would not crack and go to the police, but the fear that a drug lord can put into one's being was sufficient to keep Viktor loyal. Knowing how the cartel worked, Gonzales figured that Carlos would always have a backup plan. If Viktor chickened out, there would be a man lurking in the shadows who would pull the trigger of his Glock two times, once to kill Alfredo, and the second time to eliminate Viktor Gonzales. And then, someone would go after the family and make it seem like an accident. Some Mexican authorities who were beholden to the cartel would never allow a thorough investigation of a house fire. The cause of the fire was always electrical and the bodies were burnt to an unrecognizable state.

Viktor Gonzales would carry out the plan that was given to him. He would fall in line like all the others, and he would be compensated. But there were no 100% guarantees and Viktor knew this. The prisons were full of men where a tiny slip up fingered them, and they were sent to a nasty place for the rest of their lives.

The day arrived, Gonzales said goodbye to his wife and kissed her. The kids had left for school. Okay, she would see him in a couple of weeks. He had to go to Bolivia and then he'd be heading to Italy.

Viktor really lied about Bolivia. After he saw to his responsibilities at the office, he picked up his one-way ticket to Rome and left for Hartsfield-Jackson. Not knowing exactly how long he would be gone, he couldn't be concerned about paying top dollar for a ticket back to Atlanta.

It was one of the longest flights Viktor Gonzales ever took. The thoughts, the regrets, the recrimination were crushing his soul as he peered into the sky from his window seat, and wondered how his life had brought him to this dangerous time and place.

105

Italy
Rome

Viktor Gonzales landed in Rome and checked into his hotel, the Margutta at Via Laurina 34 at Piazza di Spagna. He went to the bus depot where he would use the key that had been left at the hotel for him with a note telling him what locker to open. He destroyed the note, took the key and opened number 777. Lucky number 7, he thought. Great omen! Viktor removed the small package and placed it in his attaché case which he carried, and then he went back to the hotel knowing that his package contained a deadly weapon which was something he was not used to handling. Back at the hotel he shook with fear as he opened his case and removed the soft cotton scarf that concealed the pistol. His white face stare and open mouth were visible signs of his internal turmoil. Could he go through with it was his only thought. He thought of soldiers in combat who had to kill in order to live. Now, he had to kill in order to keep his family and himself alive. He sat straight up against the pillows on the bed and gazed into the mirror on the wall above the desk next to the mounted TV. He felt weak and sick to his stomach.

It would have been just as easy, Gonzales thought, for Carlos de Rigga to contact someone in Rome to do his dirty work, and then escape into the landscape, or leave the country and not be found. Why me? was the gnawing question he kept asking himself. "That lousy prick in Medellin" reverberated in his mind.

Even with the help of Lunesta in his toiletry bag there was no way Viktor would get a good night's rest.

106

Italy
Rome

Physical and psychological changes were noticeable in Father Alfredo. Marco said that he was aware that his father was showing distinct differences in his being. Cracks had formed in the exterior and interior of the man. This was difficult for Alfredo to comprehend as he had always demonstrated a rugged façade regardless of how dire circumstances had become. There were many times when stoicism had to be the single characteristic of his demeanor to prove to others that he was totally in control and dictated what the outcome of events would be. But now...

Alfredo had not been a man who could relax; he was not one who had leisure activities to rely on to bring peace and tranquility and contentment. He did not paint or sculpt or ride horses. He had no recreational pursuits that could take him away in mind and body from the everyday operations of his Order and his cartel. Actively engaged in either religious or evil functions, this dichotomy, this irony dictated his life.

Now, however, Father Alfredo sensed the changes that had gradually been forming because of his recent fight to maintain his innocence, but that resulted in loss. He had not been a person accustomed to defeat, but defeated he was. He wondered how he would have the strength to fight this new battle, for physically and mentally he was much older and less fit without the heart to sustain a lengthy courtroom onslaught. The contention would be too much to endure unlike the past battles which he regarded as crusades. Marco emphasized to me that this was a new time in which Alfredo found himself, and he hated to think of himself as vulnerable. Interesting, I thought, as I saw Marco's position quite similar to his father's.

Just how hard Alfredo would be willing or able to fight, he didn't know. Inwardly, he felt he would capitulate before he would embark upon a defense, regardless of how well represented he was to maintain a prolonged and stressful ordeal witnessed by a global audience of accusers and antagonists. He knew he was weakened to a great extent, and his adversaries were bolstered by an incredulous adrenaline rush to see him to his death. The forces levied against him were enormous in the witnesses that could literally hang him if, in fact, they have the testimony of his former underworld colleagues that they say they have. Alfredo wobbled in faint-like fashion at the thought of a once obsequious cadre of trusted men banding to crucify him for the less harsh sentences they would serve.

Father Alfredo was at a low point which became much lower. After being formally arrested, Marco and his father were separated, of course, and confined to different cells, but in the way that prisoners have of secretly communicating, they were able to exchange their thoughts, although irregularly. Marco knew his father's new disposition and said he gave considerable worry to what may ultimately happen to him before the trial. There was some respite felt by Father Alfredo when he was released during the period the authorities were constructing their case against him. Marco, on the other hand was never released due to the body of evidence the police had to keep him in custody.

While staying at his Order's compound, Father Alfredo was free to exercise his mind and body wherever his legs or the local transit system took him. He walked quite frequently to merely get some air, as he put it, and he occasionally took a bus or the train to any nearby town to free his mind of the encumbering thoughts of his future. He relished these occasions which gave him opportunity to ruminate upon the good things that he remembered, especially from his youth before the days of untoward and ungodly activities, but he remained a pariah within the confines of the Order he created long ago.

107

Italy
Rome

Jeannette Libramont's parents and Anna Ralston and her parents and Father Ted O'Driscoll had arrived in Rome within days of each other. Anna had met Ted and talked for a time while her parents had gone to an art museum. Josef and Antoinette Libramont had lost a daughter at the hands of a murderer, and had a difficult time trying to put aside their emotions and enjoy any aspect of the city. At earlier times they could submit to traveling about for sightseeing as visitors do, and for sitting at a sidewalk café having a coffee and a pastry, but not today. There were days previous that they would go to the coliseum and mingle with tourists enjoying light conversation. The Gladiator Restaurant across the boulevard would offer respite through a relaxing atmosphere with a bottle of Chianti accompanying Mediterranean gourmet. Their prior experiences had been shared with Jeannette who was the center of their universe. And that universe was no more. They did not anticipate anything but more hardship and a dismantling of any good emotion they could still feel knowing that the trial would drain them of all feeling—except hatred for their Jeannette's premature death. They didn't require nor expect sympathy from anyone, but hoped for a quick trial and sentencing, and perhaps, execution of two convicted murderers. Their lives had been in abeyance since Jeannette's interment in her town of Esch near the Alzette River in Luxembourg. What rejoicing could they ever expect in life after this monumental devastation they suffered?

Anna was the only person who might be able to one day bring more than a modicum of glee into the Libramonts' lives. She vowed that she would always remain in close touch with them and be there to see Josef when he came to Washington on business. The Ralstons invited the Libramonts to come to their home in Connecticut at any time. They were always welcome as friends and family for they shared a bond that was forever intact.

Although an accomplished writer, Josef did ask Anna if she would help him gather and write some remarks that he would offer the court after the trial when he might be asked if he and Jeannette's mother had any words to address the defendants. Josef said that he and his wife would not remain in Rome for the trial of Giuseppe Vilardo, but would follow it through communications with the prosecutor's office. They were only intending to be present daily at Father Alfredo's and Marco Montoya's trials for however long those might be. Anna said she would be honored to offer some thoughts to Josef that would be appropriate to express the incomprehensible anguish that was caused by two heartless men. Josef and Antoinette's gratitude was shown by tears streaming down their cheeks.

▲ ▲ ▲

Marco, although labeled heartless by the Libramonts, did not see himself fitting the description. He knew he didn't need a lengthy expensive trial to prove him guilty of a heinous crime. He wasn't heartless, so it wasn't that adjective which led him to murder, but greed and a desire to one day live an opulent lifestyle. In dialogue I discovered that Marco could have achieved a respectable level of wealth by pursuing it through the natural talents he had. He had entrepreneurial instincts from an early age, and if properly nurtured he would not have had to become another farmer, but a successful and prominent businessman. His choice to follow his father, Ferdinand, the only father that he really knew and loved as a boy and a man, and his uncle, Benito, to Medellin ultimately nurtured his tragic flaw and ultimately his demise as a free man.

108

Italy
Rome

Trying to sound honest and forthright, Viktor Gonzales left the following message on a machine at their house in Mexico. Hearing it, his wife would believe he was on company business, and of course, she had no idea who Grimaldi was nor did she have a number by which to reach her husband.

Masking his voice so as not to sound hollow, he spoke in his first language, Spanish. "Hello, Dear, I'm in Rome now. I got settled into the hotel last night. Had a brief meeting this morning with Rocco Grimaldi, VP of sales for Southern Europe. His schedule wouldn't allow me much time, so I'm meeting him for dinner tonight and will see him tomorrow in the office. He insisted that I stay at his pallazo while I'm here instead of at the hotel for the purpose of accomplishing more in a short time. I've gotten a car so I'll follow him to his place tonight. He's a congenial man and I know I can reflect the company's issues that we have with poor sales during this last quarter. But I won't bore you with any of that stuff. Say hello to the kids for me. Enjoy the few days we're apart. See you as soon as I can.. I'll let you know definitely when I'll be leaving Rome.

I love you, Darling,   Viktor.

If she was ever the suspecting wife, the ending of his call might signal some contemplation as he never called her "Darling" even in the excitement and pulsation of their lovemaking.

▲ ▲ ▲

After he left this message he called the prosecutor's office to inquire of the progress of the State vs. Marco Montoya asking specifically about the date the trial was set for. The bureaucrat in the office asked him his identity and he smoothly and confidently passed himself off as a reporter for a newspaper outside Rome. She was gullible enough not to question him further and thought he was inquiring so as to set his court schedule for trials he would be reporting on. The secretary gave him the information he needed to carry out the plan provided by de Rigga and his Italian associates. Naturally, some leeway was given Gonzales because Carlos couldn't possibly know every move that the Italian authorities or Father Alfredo would make.

Viktor Gonzales was to follow Father Alfredo and keep surveillance of his every move until the absolute perfect time to kill him. It had to be done in some lonely spot where no one was around to witness the shooting following the method used by la cosa nostra. It could be days before the unknowing victim was in a location where he could be eliminated with the single witness being the wind blowing through the trees. It was not expected that Father Alfredo would visit any shadowy corners of the city, so presumably, he would be shot at late evening or night on an open but vacant street, but definitely when darkness was descending. It would be a place of concealment where Gonzales might be able to hide or crouch low behind a barrier after his victim goes down.

Father Alfredo walked openly through parts of Rome close to the seminary and not far from the Vatican. Occasionally, if someone besides Viktor Gonzales were to observe the man in black sauntering along Via Della Lungara he would notice that the priest stopped at points along his way seemingly to reflect on an item of interest whether a young woman strolling along or a small boat sailing the Tevere. He was never in a rush and never appeared to have a definite destination. Because of this, Gonzales had to be extra cautious following him. At any moment Alfredo may turn around and reverse his direction and notice a person whom he had seen several blocks before, and perhaps wonder. Being familiar with Father Alfredo's past, Gonzales knew that he was a suspicious man often confronting and questioning anyone he might feel was in his way, or was competing with him or violating his space. Gonzales pictured himself a Native American tracking a white man, a scene that was familiar in American westerns that he loved to watch. So, he was careful not to be too close, after all, the man in no rush was not going anywhere. Gonzales told himself repeatedly that he was out of place in the capacity of a would-be killer. He actually prayed that this predicament was not real. He knew he should be home, not in Rome, doing things he always did as a father and as a husband.

After an hour and ten minutes Father Alfredo began his walk back to his quarters observing other people strolling along or window shopping along the avenue. He admired the architecture of old buildings which was what he routinely did when visiting Rome and having free time. Alfredo had often thought he would have liked to study architecture if he had the opportunity.

The hour was getting late and darkness would be falling in a location too little isolated from public scrutiny. This was not to be the time. Viktor could live another night and day an innocent man.

ID # 109

Italy
Rome

During the trial Marco said that there was someone he missed seeing in the courtroom. He wondered what could have happened to Father Edmund. He knew he had come to Rome because he spoke to the priest a couple of times, and Edmund had been gracious to offer counseling to Marco when he felt he needed someone who would listen and do whatever he could to salve any open wounds. Edmund knew the inner tumult Marco must be experiencing and encouraged him not to be timorous in speaking to an old acquaintance and fellow teacher. He sincerely wanted to help.

But that was several days past. Edmund seemed to have disappeared. He did. His zeal for the priesthood first diminished, and later dissolved. After he had spoken to his brother and laid it on him that he was discontent, disheartened, and depressed, and said he would seriously take Shamus's advice and talk to Father Ted, he believed it himself. He earnestly wanted to do that, but evidently had reached such a low plateau that he decided to walk away without saying goodbye. He flew back to Georgia. The airline confirmed that. And he removed the few items that were sacred to him from his apartment one of which was the picture of Mum and his brother and himself each raising a pint in front of Paddy's Pub before he left for Mexico. That seemed a hundred years ago, he thought. But why? He had great experiences after ordination where his assignment had taken him. He loved the people he met, the children he taught and counselled, the camaraderie of his fellow Order priests, the many community families that had been so welcoming. He almost wished that it had been a woman that he had become involved with and the attraction was so magnetic that he lacked the courage and strength to resist. But that wasn't the case. That might have been understandable to those who knew him. He was a good looking young man who would have appeal to a female that let her heart go out to him. People could possibly accept that, and forgive him.

He had simply lost the desire to be in God's service. His despondence seemed attributable to the disillusionment he felt. There were the Alfredo business and other things he witnessed inside a rectory that he told Marco he did not want to talk about. I suspect that homosexuality may have been a small part, as well as the drinking problem that some men had. He spoke once, Marco recalled, of one who had a strong gambling addiction. Having known almost all of the clergy through the Familia Dei movement, Marco was convinced that the problems Edmund saw with people were not those of the younger priests. He perhaps felt that he did not want to fall into the same vices that ensnared others after many years and old age setting in. Who knows? Who can judge?

When Marco related all of this to me, I couldn't help think of my own background. Raised Catholic and having gone to all parochial schools, I was a student of clergymen and knew some who left the priesthood for whatever personal reasons, but most often the allurement of a woman. In fact, I myself had an uncle who was ordained and remained faithful to his vows for ten years before he made the heart wrenching decision to leave and follow a woman to a distant town where no one knew them. He married her and lived a long life as a good man and a loving husband and father. It was better in the eyes of God that he was a good man rather than a hypocritical priest.

Edmund simply packed up and went away. What resources he had only he knew. I surmise he had sufficient funds to take him to any destination he chose.

He left a note for his faithful friend Father Ted O'Driscoll. It simply read:

> *"Ted, I'm sorry. This is not the way I ever would have intended my life to go. I don't know if you will completely understand, but it is what I have to do. I don't love God less, but I know I cannot remain and be the best priest that I truly desire to be. I will always love you and be grateful for your friendship and for your efforts to counsel me. Thank you for all your prayers. You will be in my prayers daily. Please, try to bring some comfort to my mother. Only you can explain this to her. Edmund"*

Ted was saddened. He had lost a best friend. And worse, he knew how Mary Kelley would suffer upon hearing that her younger son, who from his early years in elementary school, only thought of becoming a priest, and was enthralled when given the opportunity to enter the seminary at Coalcojana and study to enter the Missionaries of the Holy Church. Ted could sense the anguish of a mother brought to distraction and grave mental distress when she would be told that Edmund decided to leave the priesthood. Ted prayed that Mary Kelley would not try to lose herself in a whiskey bottle.

110

Italy
Rome

Captain Lorenzo had no fear that Father Alfredo would be a flight risk being allowed to walk freely about the by-ways and avenues of Rome. He was free for the time being until the mountain of evidence against him was assessed by the prosecutors who would bring him to trial. Meantime, Marco's trial was under way, and Father Alfredo attended sessions and kept abreast of all proceedings. With the charges against Marco, Alfredo was ultimately to be called to the witness stand to testify unless, of course, Alfredo was arrested beforehand as a co-conspirator. The prosecutor's strategy was to have Marco implicate Father Alfredo as the mastermind behind the plot to kill Anna Ralston. When questioned, Giuseppe Vilardo squealed loud enough to let the world know that Father Alfredo ran the cartel called Hombres en Negro in Mexico and had drugs sent to Europe. What proof was there? The police were exhaustively working on that. Vilardo sang to the cops because he knew his conviction of murdering Jeannette Libramont was imminent, so he had nothing more to lose.

Marco knew he was finished. His lawyers provided by the Order would never succeed in getting him off. In court Marco looked sullenly at his father who wondered if his son will tell all that he knew and hang him, or if he would adhere to the code of the cartel and not implicate a capo. Father Alfredo would never be one to take a bullet, or be a fall guy, even for his son, and Marco knew this.

Marco said that the trial went quickly. Realistically, He didn't have a prayer, or a hope to be acquitted with his face on film from two cameras and the testimony of Father Ted O'Driscoll who took the stand and identified Marco as being in the hotel café. It really wasn't much of a trial by most standards; the prosecutor didn't have trouble in making his case and proving his arguments. It was what might be seen as an open and shut case. In fact, it seemed at times the jury seemed to be half listening as a verdict was already certain in their minds. The tapes were powerful evidence for them. However, many thoughts buzzed through Marco's head as he sat at the defense table thinking about a miracle, and looking to at least one juror who might be able to convince himself or herself that there was reasonable doubt. Even he didn't consider that there could be reasonable doubt from what he was hearing in the courtroom, and seeing in the mannerisms of the jurors. There was nothing evident in any of their facial expressions to indicate to the defense that their case was predictably favorable. In the court the lawyer Carlozzi himself was reluctant to gaze in the direction of the jury and attempt to read anything into their facial expression or posture. He occupied himself with the papers and notes that were spread on the table in front of him, and seemed uninterested in making eye contact with anyone in the court. In fact, Carlozzi never spoke to the media on the courthouse steps either before or after sessions. The prosecutors, however, took full advantage of that venue to be heard. They eagerly responded to reporters' questions while staring directly into the camera lenses of local and world-wide television networks.

O World! O life! O time!
On whose last steps I climb,
Trembling at that where
I had stood before;

(P. B. Shelley)

III

Italy
Rome

On the fourth day of Marco's trial, Alfredo sat and listened to witnesses, discomfited by being the target of the glaring eyes of Anna and her father and Josef Libramont. At one point, Josef became so incensed that he wanted to lunge at Father Alfredo because he knew Alfredo had set the plan in motion which took his Jeannette's life. Antoinette restrained him from budging from his seat and tried to calm him with whispered and tender words. They were something to the effect that the court would hold the priest accountable. He responded to his wife's plea and to her sense that justice would see Alfredo convicted and punished.

Emotion that Josef felt transferred itself to Father Alfredo, but in the form of guilt; it registered on his face and his nervousness was noticeable. Alfredo got up and left the courtroom. He walked outside, aware that it was late afternoon, and decided to walk toward the river. The massive fortress of Castel Sant'Angelo was visible across the water. This time he wasn't looking at things that might have caught his eye as they did on previous walks. He seemed to be dazed.

Viktor Gonzales was following as he had done on other occasions when Father Alfredo ventured out, and he, too, sensed that Alfredo was different. As daylight was turning to dusk, Viktor, also, seemed in a daze. He was in a perpetual daze since he had been given his assignment by Carlos, but not so out of it that any compunction left him. He was petrified about killing Father Alfredo, as anyone unaccustomed to killing even a small animal on a hunt might be. What it would be like to pull the trigger of a powerful weapon and see the bullet strike your unknowing victim. You would wince if you shot a squirrel and saw it jump and then fall, or shot a deer and saw it run a short distance, blood dripping, and fall uncontrollably to its death. You approach the animal and its eyes might stare up into yours, and you think it was just a harmless animal, a part of nature.

But Viktor couldn't think that way right now. He had to dismiss thoughts of that kind. Chase them from his brain. He was trying to maintain a steady pace to match the thoughts flowing through his mind.

Father Alfredo got closer to the river as the darkness settled and the street became less inhabited. Gonzales got closer to Alfredo. He knew. This is the time. Alfredo will not reverse his direction and begin his trek back to his lodgings in the center of the city. Viktor became quite tense, the perspiration beading on his brow, his throat dry and unable to swallow. He'd thought so long about this. Finally, he would know the feeling, not just of killing a living being, but of being a killer, something he'd have to live with and be haunted by for the rest of his life. The river was dark and flowing rather swiftly. He passed by the Palazzo del Commendatori and the smaller church of Sante Maria in Traspontina and some historical buildings. It was relatively silent in this spot, only traffic heard, but that was in the distance. Gonzales was aware of the silence surrounding him, but was conscious of the drumming in his brain that was deafening. He had to keep his senses and keep his mind on his surreptitious task. An explosion was imminent.

Father Alfredo thought about his son Marco as he walked. A bandeau of moonlight following him. His illegitimate son whose existence he hadn't even known about for more than half his life. His son that was complicit in all the evil he was responsible for; his son being tried for a murder that his own father planned and commanded him to carry out; his son who could realistically go to his death or spend the remainder of his life in prison; his son who was raised ood parents in Colombia, but had the misfortune to become a f an evil empire ruled by his true father. His father! He choked on the two words.

The bane that came to my son. What father? What am I? He asked himself. I have been only a beast in the eyes of God and men. And all for what? My realm. My vicious world that was the realm I ruled and roamed. Forlorn, he cried, something he had never done. No tears had ever clouded his eyes before even during those times tormenting young seminarians at Coalcojana; no feelings like these had he even experienced before. As he walked he looked at the river and sobbed. He had come to realize how much he had been his own enemy. The verses entrered his mind:

> *The enemy pursues me,*
> *he crushes me to the ground,*
> *he makes me dwell in the darkness like those long dead.*
> *So my spirit grows faint within me;*
> *My heart within me is dismayed.*

Viktor was close enough to see that Father Alfredo was distraught, but could not read his mind to know the reason or reasons why the priest appeared emotional. He stood knowing his presence was not known to the priest; he was a distance away but closing that distance so that when he felt the perfect second was upon him, he would ease out the revolver, take quick but careful aim, and shoot. The throbbing temples, the shaking knees, and the lump forming in his throat signaled Viktor that an event, life changing event, would occur simultaneously with another event that would also change a life. His would go on, the other would end.

Only once was Viktor Gonzales distracted. He had put himself into a trance-like state ready for the kill when two people came strolling near to where he felt he was secluded, but still able to see Father Alfredo a short distance away. One of the two shouted to the priest without knowing in the darkness that he was a priest: "Don't jump from the bridge, pisano!" Gonzales heard the admonition and stifled a brief chuckle. Little did they know that their pisano was going to be dead from a gunshot.

Father Alfredo heard the remark that the Italian shouted in his direction, snickered, and silently expressed how prophetic that guy is.

Viktor Gonzales got past the irony of the situation and relaxed a moment. He glided quietly from the barrier he hid behind and took short steps in the direction of the bridge crossing the river. He thought that Father Alfredo was extending his walk to get more exercise by crossing over to the east side of the river, so he quickened his pace, the gun swaying at his side, his nerves going crazy. He was watching Alfredo's dark silhouette crossing the bridge. One more time to think about it. Why not just go home, and… He walked on not completing the thought. Alfredo was at the top of the bridge, and then stopped. A pair of ebony eyes glanced down and stared momentarily at the glistening water and slowly gliding current. He seemed mesmerized. *How can I live any longer? I've come this far to hate myself as I never believed I would. My conscience disturbs me day and night. Opportunities only proved to be the Devil's incentives, and I stupidly and insanely grasped them. What right do I have to feel forlorn? I betrayed humanity by sins of the flesh and I betrayed the Church. Principles, philosophy, vows, all that I believed. I only deserve Hell. Ironically, that's the Heavenly reward I truly deserve. If self-destruction is opposed to the teachings and beliefs as my entire life has been, then my punishment for eternity is to be guaranteed. For the suffering I have caused by my hand, let my suffering be a thousand times worse in devouring flames and all the punishments Dante imagined.*

Viktor's moment. He raised the gun, pointed it at Alfredo, ready to fire. Father Alfredo leaped from the bridge, and in seconds was swept by the current into the darkness beyond sight.

112

Italy
Rome

Marco told me that his lawyer, Henri Carlozzi, advised him that it was not in his best interests to take the stand, and he knew this was generally sound legal advice, but when the news reached him that the body found in the Tiber River was that of Father Alfredo, he decided to allow himself the chance to be heard. When he was given the news by Captain Lorenzo that Alfredo was dead, he broke down and wept for several minutes. He said that he finally controlled his emotions and then looked at Lorenzo and said, "The river swallowed his body that he willingly surrendered to it when he knew his life was not to be spared in a criminal court in Rome. The river keeps secrets from times before the reign of the Caesars, and there are secrets that Alfredo has drowned with him which the world will never know. If the current had taken him southward to a watery grave in the sea, his corpse would have decomposed as a bloated mass, or it would have been consumed by some creature of the deep. Feeding on the carcass would kill anything that devoured it from the poison that was the man. But his body washed up." And then he took several more minutes, presumably to reflect on the aspects of their lives that they shared, the times before Marco knew his true parentage, and the few times after.

Before entering the court and being asked by Judge Giuseppe Rosario if it was his choice to take the stand, Marco sat, sad and angry, at the defense table. Carlozzi whispered a few things to him. All present in the room saw him nod his head affirmatively, and then, he told me, he rose and slowly walked to the witness chair beside the judge's elevated platform. His attorney asked him the leading question that they had agreed to in the whispering they shared before the session, and which Marco was fully prepared to respond to. This was his opportunity to make his peace with himself, to ask for forgiveness from God, Jeannette Libramont and her parents, Anna Ralston and her parents, and anyone else not present whom he had harmed in any manner during his life. He knew he had already been found guilty in the minds and hearts of the jury, but he needed this opportunity to cleanse himself and speak true to the world.

With humility and in a soft voice he said, "Judge Rosario, you ask me if I am guilty of killing Jeannette Libramont by intentionally running the car in which she was riding with her friend off the road. She sustained injuries because of it and was in critical condition and never awoke from a coma. She was pronounced dead the next day. That is a crime I am guilty of."

He told me that he was not going to mention the driver of the car he was in because Vilardo was being tried separately. So some truth was withheld.

"I am sorry and ashamed for the crime I committed. I am sorry for what my life has been. I beg your indulgence to hear my story because in it you will hear me admit to other events of which I am as guilty as the one I just confessed to. I will begin with the most startling admission, one that will not be as shocking to you as it was to me when I first learned it: Father Alfredo Legatos is my biological father."

When the court heard that revelation, he said, there was an audible moan-type sound, and then a hush that lasted until he continued his narrative.

"Yes. That's true. I never learned that until my mother wrote to me on her deathbed. She felt I had to know because I was engaged in unlawful activity with Father Alfredo for many years. I can't express the emotion I felt when I read her letter. But, I was determined not to be crazed by the discovery. My father was a criminal. The General Council at the Vatican brought punishment to him for the crimes he committed against seminarians. He was also guilty of wanting Ms. Ralston killed, and he instructed me to carry out the murder. Fortunately, she did not die in the crash, but unfortunately, Ms. Libramont did. Captain Lorenzo told me and my father's attorneys yesterday that the police had sufficient evidence to convict my father. If he did not suicide, he and I would be spending the rest of our days in confinement.

"Many of you have never heard of Hombres en Negro, a cartel in Mexico. Men in black refers to Father Alfredo and some others who right now are scattering to save themselves.

"My father was a capo who controlled a portion of the drug flow to many places including Italy. His connections through his Order were widespread, and he operated safely and without fear of apprehension. I don't have to say more about this as I know you are familiar with aspects of the drug world from news reports the media has been reporting since my trial began, and the world was informed that Father Alfredo had been arrested."

▲ ▲ ▲

It was with extreme emotion that Marco unfolded his story. Later I heard from Captain Lorenzo and Cardinal Salvacco how Marco suffered through the narration of his criminal life. There were mixed emotions experienced by many in the courtroom who had become familiar with the defendant during the proceedings, and the judge, too, seemed overwhelmed at times. He had never heard an accused man take the stand to admit guilt, and confess to things that would put him away for two life terms. A few of the spectators who were present seemed to feel some compassion for the man, perhaps, due to the honest revelations that were so stunning. But all in the court felt abhorrence for what they heard.

▲ ▲ ▲

In describing his activities Marco was direct and graphic.

"I've been involved in battles between drug groups because that's part of the business. If I killed, it was not the same as deliberately seeking someone out to annihilate. Never did I engage in capturing an adversary and applying torture, and then beheading him and tossing his body in a river or to the dogs. Mutilations were not part of any hostilities with our rivals. My father and uncle were killed as soldiers in a gun battle in Colombia. That's how we saw ourselves. Soldiers defending our piece of the trade."

▲ ▲ ▲

The judge abruptly intervened and asked Marco to leave the stand. He was now going to allow the court to recess. Marco said that Judge Rosario felt the jury, as well as others in the court as observers, needed time to get out of their seats. Each jury member required time to personally reflect on what was heard at this point. Judge Rosario apprised everyone that what Marco admitted to was not testimony relevant to the case, and it was not material that he expected the court to hear. He asked Marco and Mr. Carlozzi how long his statement might run. Marco said he laughed at this thinking that the judge didn't need to hear more, as he and the twelve jurors had enough to convict and sentence him. Marco told the judge that he was satisfied he told most of his story, and that he had expressed his sorrow, and hoped that the victims and their families would forgive him. He also said that he wanted to give the jury and the observers in the courtroom an understanding of his participation in Familia Dei and what that movement in the Church was about. He felt this was necessary for two reasons, the first being that many people never heard of the Church laity organization, and the second being that the judge and jury might take his work in Familia Dei into consideration when imposing the sentence on him. He hoped for some modicum of leniency. The judge said he understood and would put Marco back on the stand to complete his story.

As Marco continued, it was as difficult then, as the first time he sat to face the court and look at the many people staring at him, some seeing him as a monster of evil, a devil, while some others seemed to show slight sympathy for him as he read their faces. It was all over in a brief few minutes.

He did ask for whatever leniency the court thought permissible by law, and then heard the judge ask if there was anyone present who wanted to address the bench and speak directly to the defendant. Marco said he held his breath as the blood rushed to his head and his heart pounded fiercely. He knew he had to show some composure both for himself, and for the person who would step forward and nervously speak while displaying indescribable emotion. If one thing was going to certainly work against him, it would be a parent on the stand falling to pieces begging the jury to commiserate with him as they listened to him extol the life of his daughter and cry over the loss he suffers.

The first of two who stepped to the microphone was Josef Libramont who by nature was a diffident man, but knew his time to be heard was now. Marco was so sorrowfully moved by the man's words that he said everything he heard sunk in at the time and affected him deeply, but became a blur to him days later when he was still wiping tears from his eyes.

The second speaker was Father Ted O'Driscoll. He spoke to Marco with fastidious preciseness through a series of questions, each beginning with the word "Why." He presented a litany of questions that only required Marco to think of the past, and the hurt he caused. His questions also were designed to encourage or prompt thoughts in all those present in the court. Though not his primary intention, he knew the deeper they weighed his words, the greater would be their sympathy for the victims. This was vital.

Marco said that it wasn't necessary for me to record the specifics mentioned by the two men; those would remain with him in the privacy of his mind. He felt that I knew enough about him to be able to conjecture what Josef Libramont and Father Ted brought to the minds and hearts of their listeners. There were no truths spoken by them that Marco could obviate or deny.

113

Italy
Iles d'Arda

Later, Marco was able to tell me that he had regrets that an innocent woman had died as a result of his carrying out the orders of Father Alfredo. At the time of the incident, however, he was so hardened to what his motivations were that he never cared about whose life was to be sacrificed. But now he felt differently about it, and showed remorse, not that it would be enough to possibly spare his life or shorten his sentence to be served. I had no attitude one way or the other toward him at the beginning of our relationship, but I did come to have some empathy for him as I got to know him. He ultimately did admit guilt, and the public could feel good about it, but I kept thinking about his wife and children. I suppose that we all have given thought to the family of the accused or condemned person of a heinous crime. We know the guilty deserve the punishment, but the family doesn't. Marco seemed to acquire a conscience as he sat and told me the unfortunate events in his life, and how his realization of having prostituted his life left him despondent.

From having observed Jeannette's parents in the courtroom, seeing the look of agony on their faces as they listened to testimony, and sat reflecting on the presence of the defendant and the thoughts that might be in his mind, Marco was glad that no member of his own family was present. He looked askance at Mr. Libramont at intervals, and tried to determine what thoughts were in his mind. He saw Josef as a successful businessman and a good person who contributed to his community. What he saw most vividly was the man as a good and caring father who loved his daughter, and was now missing her like Marco was going to miss his own children after the verdict was read, and he was sent to spend the rest of his life in a distant penitentiary far from his home. Marco was not a particularly eloquent person, but when he expressed these thoughts to me, it was plain to see that he was sincere. If I could be judgmental, I felt from what I was learning he had changed during the course of the trial and became softer and truer to himself. He even acknowledged that he transitioned to a sincere penitent. Was this common in men, or do most yell loudly to proclaim their innocence, I wondered.

With great remorse Marco said to me, "You know, if I could begin all over again, my desire to leave my home in El Ritero is the same because I would never have survived as a rancher or farmer. I would have left, but I might never have joined the cartel with Ramon Munoz. After being with the priests, I mean the good ones like Father Edmund and Father Ted, I might have joined the Order. I don't know if it would have been possible, but Father Alfredo did come to our village to talk to boys who felt they had a vocation. I would be one of those who would go to the seminary. If I had known the good things that I have seen done by the priests and by the true Familia Dei members, my life may have been a good one."

I had a strong feeling long ago that he would tell me this. I said, "Marco, I am sorry for you and what you were. I am sorry for all those you hurt. They were innocent people who did not harm you. For reasons that were not just, you damaged many people, and for this you cannot be exonerated by them. However, you may be forgiven by God. You have years left where you can possibly do things that can be beneficial, not that they will make up for the evil you have done, but to bring some meaning into your life."

"Yes," he said, "especially, when I see in my mind's eye those sad eyes and heavy hearts of those parents in the courtroom. That haunts me always. When I see the sadness and feel the hurt of my family in my mind and heart, that haunts me as well. This will not be the only time that I say to you that I pray for forgiveness, and ask for solace in my life."

114

Italy Rome
Iles d'Arda

After sentencing which took place quickly, Marco was destined to spend the remainder of his life in prison. Sentencing brought closure, and Marco was taken from the court for processing into the penal system where he would become a life-time resident.

Later, after being processed, Marco was astonished that a visitor had requested to see him. Before leaving Rome Viktor Gonzales, former friend and cohort, had spoken to Captain Lorenzo to acquire the specifics and protocol about visiting an inmate who had recently been sentenced to life. The Captain heard Viktor's story about stalking Father Alfredo, but Gonzales was careful not to give any indication that he was intending to murder Alfredo. Also, he would never mention that he was connected to a cartel where he was a close associate of Marco Montoya. He led the Captain to believe that he was an old friend and member of Familia Dei, and said he would appreciate the chance to pray with Marco. Lorenzo still having Marco under his jurisdiction felt the man was sincere and said he would allow a short conversation between them before the transfer to Iles d' Arda Penitentiary.

"Marco," Viktor said, "I stood there squeezing the trigger when Alfredo jumped. I couldn't believe what was happening. It was so swift that I dropped to my knees. I did that out of total shock, and as I think about it, I did it selfishly, thinking to myself that he saved me. His last deed on earth was a good and noble one which liberated me from the misery I have felt for days and weeks. A feeling of calm suddenly enveloped me. He prevented me from becoming a killer, a murderer. The life I was intending to take from him, he gave to me. I ran not to try to save him; I might have been able to do that. But I ran from the bridge to save myself."

Gonzales continued to tell Marco of de Rigga's orders and threats. Marco was astounded that Carlos had planned such treachery.

Some of Viktor's words stung irritably as Marco heard them because Gonzales, who owed so much to Alfredo, did not know that he was talking about Marco's own biological father. Marco told me that Gonzales may have tempered his words if he had known, but after the remarks Marco made to his victims in court, he understood that God had spared Gonzales to live another day without blood on his hands.

"What have you told the police?" Marco asked.

"Nothing. Believe me, there were times I wanted to tell them everything that they could use in their case against you. I thought that after I shot Alfredo I figured that if anything went wrong, the cops here would give me a break for having strengthened their evidence to convict you. Who knows if it would have worked for me, or not, but I did consider talking if I was arrested."

"Well, without any shit from you, they had enough evidence, but as you probably read in the paper, I went to the stand and told them everything. I want to be free too. Free from the guilt; I'll never be free from the crime as long as I live."

▲ ▲ ▲

Knowing he was able to leave Rome immediately, Viktor Gonzales couldn't get to the airport fast enough to purchase a one-way ticket to Atlanta. While on the plane, his mind poured over the last few days, and he prayed for forgiveness over what he might have done, what he would have become, if events had turned out differently. He laughed inwardly as he pictured himself running from the Ponte Santa'Angelo and throwing the Glock as far as he could into the river, then wiping his right hand vigorously on his pants as he ran, as if to cleanse himself of poison that had been seeping through his pores. Gonzales had placed a call to his wife before leaving Rome, and he told her how much he loved her and missed her, and said he didn't mind if she spent too much money shopping while he was gone. He knew that even if she had returned to Georgia there was no need for her to pick him up at the airport. Besides it might be very late when he got in. He knew he'd be greeted by someone else. They'd be waiting for him.

Gonzales thought of what he would tell Carlos when he returned, and knew he would be greeted at Hartsfield-Jackson by someone wearing a black suit holding a sign imprinted with his name. Dragging his single carry-on behind him, he followed the man whose eyes were hiding behind dark sunglasses from the baggage carrousel to the black limo where a lugarteniente of Carlos de Rigga sat in the front passenger seat. When he would be questioned, Viktor knew he would be telling the truth: He saw Father Alfredo die. That's all Carlos wanted to hear. He simply wanted to know that Alfredo was finished, and Viktor could verify that Alfredo was no longer alive.

Viktor realized it would be a very unpleasant ride home, and he couldn't feel comfortable sitting in the back of the limo between two burly halcones who had their orders from Carlos. He tried to distant his mind from his situation, but his discomfort was multiplied by the thoughts that centered on Marco and the nightmarish days of his "Roman holiday" and the scene of Father Alfredo tucking something between the rails of the bridge and then leaping over the wall into the river.

The slower than usual hour and a half ride up the I 85 to North Georgia couldn't go quickly enough as he checked off the familiar landmarks through the side window along the route from the airport, through Midtown, past the Perimeter, through Gwinnett to some unknown place in the area of Banks County. It was a rendezvous point that provided a strip where Carlos's plane could land and take-off in secrecy.

115

Italy
Iles d'Arda

Marco finally thought the time was right to tell me why he had selected me to hear, and then tell his story. The long awaited moment had arrived at last.

The entire story of this man's life was completed as far as I could tell except for one significant item to be put in place. I sat looking Marco in the eye, and said, "Tell me the reason, Marco, that you called me to write your story."

He gave me an inscrutable look, and didn't hesitate to tell me how he had come to know my brother Joe, and how he had him killed. My manner abruptly changed, and noticing the transition he could sense anger and he continued with a troubled expression in his eyes, one that only matched my own as I breathed deeply and waited to hear words I knew would be frightening.

Marco related to me that Joe got too close to finding out things about the cartel. The capos knew that an investigative reporter was doing a lot of snooping, and asking too many questions. He said the cartel tried to let him go along and follow the story, but when it was clear he was getting too close to the heart of matters, he was making things uncomfortable with the articles he was writing. The order had to be given. Too many specifics and too few superficialities were being described. Marco was first asked, he said, to speak to the reporter without revealing his identity, and to use persuasive measures to get him to back off thinking intimidation would get results. But when Joe attempted to delve into the mysterious world of education, politics, and religion mixed with the narco business, the end had come. Politicians on the take and the dots being connected to Father Alfredo were finding their way into print. Marco said Alfredo was responsible for the mandate. Joe's final resting place was a mass grave where many skeletons were later unearthed along the Northern border of Mexico. He was interred after having been shot in the head.

Knowing what my emotions were upon hearing this, Marco apologized. He was truly sorry he said. What is that supposed to mean? I asked him. Within me, I could feel surging a feeling of revulsion for him. I was roused with an instinctive feeling of hate and outrage. If no guard was present I would have strangled him with the belt around my waist.

"You miserable fucking scum; you called me here, you bastard," I yelled as I jumped up and lunged for the swine. The guard who was a permanent fixture in the room and had observed the meetings between Marco and me was always within earshot of our conversations. He saw me leap forward toward Marco and immediately came up behind and threw his arms around me and tightly restrained me before we both fell to the floor. I grappled furiously to break away, but the guard's size and strength prevented that, and I was left subdued and hollering every vicious expletive I could bring to mind at Marco.

When I quieted down as I saw it was no use struggling, I was released and stood near the table hurriedly grabbing my notes and briefcase. I was the first to speak and my emotion took over. "You know what it's like, Marco, to lose someone you love when you learned that your father had been killed. But you knew your father's situation as to why and how he was killed, and that's the difference. Until now, I never knew the truth behind my brother's death. Do you know what it is when one day you hear that a loved one is gone forever? Just missing. Disappeared. There's no trace of what happened. No one can tell you where he went, or when he was last seen. Even the investigators working the case have no clue and can offer nothing. But a seasoned and reputable reporter like my brother, whom I revered and respected as a real professional and sought to emulate, goes out to do a story and is never seen again. And all you hear from the cops is that there was a car accident in Mexico and no bodies were recovered from the explosion that occurred. That's what happened! No one just falls off the planet and is never heard of again. I was infuriated and could do nothing about it. My family and I tried to get facts and information, but now I know you paid people off to hide everything and create a false story."

Hearing Marco recounting my brother's death, I thought back to my family's anguish, and tears filled my eyes again. The memory of anything dreadful is always with you. It was constantly with me.

"You took a lot away from me, you son of a bitch, without ever knowing who I was. Joe was not just my brother, but my best friend. Have you ever had a real friendship that lasted over twenty-five years of adult life? Then you have no idea what it means. You ended something that all the money in the cartel's coffers can't buy. It's like having a part of oneself sliced off that can never be regrown. We used to talk about things like two friends do when sitting down having a sandwich and cup of coffee. We did this throughout our careers until you ended it."

This was the venting that was long overdue, and I felt I owed it not only to myself, but to my family who suffered for years.

"We always hoped to continue our closeness as brothers long after retirement even if we were separated geographically in different parts of the world. In fact, I wrote a letter to him before he planned to retire and before you had him killed. I told him that retirement would be a terrific respite from the grueling mental work that drove him every day to go out into the world and find the most newsworthy story for public consumption. I told him that his new life could be spent anywhere; it didn't make any difference just as long as he maintained his smiling, laughing, joyful relationship with those he loved, but you took that all away, Marco.

"He would have loved talking on the phone periodically to his children, but you took that happiness away from him. He loved history, and we talked about how spectacular it would be to travel to see the greatness of the world's cities and the natural treasures of countries. You took all that away, Marco."

The words were becoming difficult to find as I struggled to keep from choking up. I cleared my throat and continued in a raspy voice all the time glaring at the bastard responsible for the misery that he caused.

"I told him, Marco, how great it would feel not to have routine dictate his life, that time is incidental, that walking to a park and breathing in the air and feeling good about himself are important things that many other men never experience. I told him about meeting people who are absolute strangers with whom he would pass five or fifty-five minutes in conversation because he would find them to be interesting people."

The asshole said nothing to me during my rant, but stood against the far wall away from the table where I stood, and not very distant from the guard who stood alert near the steel door and prepared to intervene again if my anger and instincts overcame my better judgment.

"Time goes by so rapidly. If the work-a-day world sees time fly by, retirement sees the days of the week slide into each other even quicker. But you took all this away from him, and you took him away from me."

I was talking and talking not even knowing if he was comprehending the surge of feelings I showed through all that I was saying. I stopped. I was exhausted. I sat and put my head down and sobbed. I felt empty.

Marco appeared contrite because he had reached a point in his life where reflection brought such great guilt. But to me I simply felt, so what? Except for the love he had for his wife and kids, Marco had been an absolute scoundrel his whole life. Spending the remainder of it in prison without ever walking the free earth again might give him time to truly repent. Forgiveness is supposed to be in one's heart, if he feels he's truly a Christian. I didn't have a sense of whether I was one or not at this point upon hearing what Marco just finished telling me. In a few minutes of conversation, I didn't realize how Marco had stripped me of a vital propriety that had been steeled within me my entire life, and a staunch principle that had always guided my personal life and my professional life. Unfortunately, now my attitude was Who cares? What really matters in life? Marco can live the remainder of his days in this hole of a prison, and then spend eternity in hell. I turned from being ambivalent toward him as he told me his story to feeling only hatred for him as I turned and walked from the prison for the last time.

116

United States Georgia

I had left the prison and Italy feeling like an empty man. While I initially sensed that I was destined to write a man's story to properly advance my standing in the world of journalism, and also for it to be a very rewarding experience, Marco's last sentences telling and describing my brother's death stifled any enthusiasm I could have taken away with me. I was saddened and felt depleted in spirit and knew I hated Marco more deeply. It was easy to walk from the prison and say that I could pray every day for Marco to suffer hell on earth.

I left Italy and came home to Atlanta. Thinking about all that I knew, I realized that there were certain pieces of the story I didn't have. One thing I knew I had to do.

The only follow up to Marco's story after he ended it was to seek out Father Ted O'Driscoll and ask a few questions the answers to which would bring everything I had heard to a satisfying conclusion. I needed to do this to fill in some of the blanks with information that Marco didn't have.

I drove from Peachtree City to the school after I placed a call to Father Ted in which I piqued his interest in knowing how I was part of a story which had become an integral part of his own life. When I met him in his office I identified myself and my purpose and explained my connection to him and significant other people in his life, and I asked Father what it was like after the police led Marco from the courtroom. He understood that I needed to know this in order to create a final chapter to Marco's life. Also,

I had a strong desire to meet the man whom I regarded as a hero for instigating the attack that brought down Father Alfredo, though Father Ted didn't see himself as any type of hero. His humility prevented that.

In a soft voice and with devout reflection on what he was to tell me, Father Ted began:

"Anna and her parents, the Libramonts, and I hugged and kissed each other and were overjoyed, not because we saw a man sentenced to spend the rest of his life in prison, but because justice had been served. Nothing could bring Jeannette back to earth, but her parents could feel solace for their loss. My parents had left a day before the trial ended which was when my testimony was finished. They were going to take the train to Monte Carlo and relax at a quiet and quaint place in Vilafranche for a while, now that all the trauma was over.

"The rest of us went back to our hotels and later met at Da Lucia, a popular trattoria, for dinner. All of us had called and made our plane reservations earlier, and intended to leave the next day. It was a tremendous occasion just being with the wonderful people I had come to know, perhaps the single best thing that emerged from the tragedy that brought us together."

Father looked at me with the saddest countenance and said, "The only answer that I don't have, and this haunts me because I may never have it is where my friend Edmund Kelley is. Internally, I feel I must find him. I pray he's safe and has found peace, but I'll never truly know peace until I see him again. I received information that the Order gave him some help after he submitted his letter of intent to leave. I think he may be teaching religion and Spanish in a parochial school somewhere in the West. Edmund's background and his credentials and altruistic nature would be positives toward his securing a teaching position.

"I received word that Josef Libramont retired. He and his wife enjoy a private life in their family home in Esch. Both are busily involved in charitable work in their community. And believe it or not, they are working with a service agency to take a foster child which they say will bring some joy and laughter into their home."

I asked Father if he knew anything more about Marco's family. How they were getting along. He said that the Internal Revenue and Justice Department had closed in on the secret off-shore accounts forcing compliance with FBAR. Sarah surrendered a portfolio of materials belonging to her former husband that he had kept hidden for a long time. The Missionaries of the Holy Church give a substantial monthly allowance to her and the children. They also continue to give money to support Father Alfredo's illegitimate families. Sarah is continuing under a doctor's care, but somehow has retained the necessary strength to carry on as she struggles to get past her excruciating pain and undeserved depressed emotional state.

When I brought up the name Viktor Gonzales, Father didn't know what his actual involvement was in the entire saga of Marco and Father Alfredo. I filled him in with all that I knew which is that Viktor was cleared by the Italian carabinieri so he was able to return to the United States. My follow-up on him revealed that his cooperation with U.S. authorities against the cartel gave him immunity from criminal prosecution, and that he is in the witness protection program. A source said he could be living in or near New Zealand. He has appeared to vanish.

Father Ted said, "Father Alfredo's body was interred at the Missionaries of the Holy Church Cemetery in Rome. He was shamefully buried under an unmarked headstone with only a number engraved to identify the location. The Director General of the Order has had Alfredo's name stricken from all places of honor within the Order where previously he had been recognized and held in esteem."

I asked about Anna.

Father Ted replied in a rambling way, "Anna is a respected attorney still practicing in Washington. She is in constant touch with the Libramonts. She is delighted at their intention to have a child come into their lives because she knows the goodness in their hearts must be shared. Anna's parents are still in Stafford Springs. Anna dates occasionally and says she has felt an attraction to one or two of the professional men she has seen, but."

Realm of the Beast

When Father ended his sentence with "but," I read into it that Anna was still carrying a memory in her mind. She's been unable to develop interest in men she meets because there is another man against whom she measures them.

I'm certain that was all Father Ted had to tell me, but as I sat listening to him, he went in a direction that I least expected. He appeared to have drifted to some far off area in his mind when he resumed speaking.

"I reminded Anna of that first evening in Rome when we met at Piazza Della Rotundo and talked that she said, 'And there's more than one thing I can't get off my mind.' She didn't feel the time was right to talk about it. I said that I believe things can only be ironed out when they are talked about. She wasn't so sure, so I guess what was unsaid will forever be unsaid. I believe it's better to leave it that way."

The priest went over to his desk and picked up a box nicely wrapped in red paper with a ribbon on it. It seemed to me that it might have been in his possession for a while where he looked at it and thought about it, waiting for a right moment to open it. Sensing the strain he was experiencing, and feeling a bit awkward, I said, "Well, Father, thank you. I know you're busy with Church business, so I'll be on my way. Thank you for all you have given, not just to me over the past hour, but to those you helped so nobly in the name of God."

Listening to me, but looking at the box with no expression of excitement or anticipation, he said, "Wait for just a minute longer, please! This gift box is from Anna. I'll open it now. It's as good a time as any. I've just been staring at it for a time since I received it." He removed the ribbon and bow and set it aside, and then removed the wrapping carefully as if he were folding back the pure white dress of an infant about to be christened, and slowly he took the white cover off the box. A glint of light from the bright rays coming through the casement danced in his eyes.

Inside was a very colorful and preppy-looking sweater and nestled on top of it an old partially wrinkled four by six photograph of himself standing on the step of his frat house at Yale with Christy and Anna. He stared at the photo for a couple of seconds in remembrance and placed the palm of his hand on the sweater almost as if he were blessing it. A broad smile lightened his face and his eyes misted as he simply said, "She's incredible! And sometimes can make things either very sensible and fascinating or very suspicious and difficult."

Author's Note

Realm of the Beast is a novel, a work of fiction. Names of characters and places or locale and incidents and events portrayed emerged from the author's imagination. All have been used fictitiously. Resemblance to actual persons, living or dead is due to the complete invention of story between the lines of known truths and accepted facts. Any familiarity to real life elements is purely coincidental.

Prolific documentation is in evidence proving that a foreign born priest who established an Order and an organization of Catholic laity was accused and punished for the crime of having abused boys in his seminary. Some references used for background to create a fictitious character were The National Catholic Reporter, April 6, 2010, an article by Jason Berry; "The Hartford Courant", May 11, 2012, article by Erald Renner and Jason Berry; Wikipedia article on the priest whose contents included biography, history, notes, references, and external links. I'm certain there is nothing in the literature to suggest he ran a cartel which was solely my invention to create a fictitious villain from imagination.

Fathers Ted and Edmund were brought to my imagination from my memory of two wonderful priests (different names) whom I had known in the past. They were, in fact, teachers and religious counselors who were phenomenal models for their students and for the laity for whom they ministered. My intention in portraying both Father Ted and Anna Ralston as I did was to show the strength of character and devotion to the Church that was Ted's underpinning, and simultaneously to show some vulnerability as a human capable of a weak moment. Father Edmund was merely Ted's contrast, not to depict frailty, but to give an understanding to psychological perplexities that cause one to need time to reflect on the path one takes in life. I know that the imaginary Cardinal Salvacco like the present day Pope Francis I would readily comprehend Edmund's state of mind. In leaving the priesthood Edmund may become a superior man by living an exemplary life. In this respect many including clergy could admire him, and some persons could even aspire to emulate the life he now lives if he is truly a happy man.

Most of the place names were made up. For example, Coalcojana and Tulavatio del Rio are not Mexican cities and do not exist. Isles de Arda is not an Italian penitentiary. Del Fontanara is neither a seminary nor the location of one. Other place names in Rome do exist, the vias, hotels, bridge. El Restorante Goya is a real restaurant, but I've never researched its bill of fare and don't know if the gazpacho is truly the best in Madrid.

Documentation on the notoriety of Colombian and Mexican cartels is abundant. Articles referenced included "Drug Cartel" and "Medellin Cartel" from Wikipedia and a Worldcrunch Newsletter translation detailing a story from Die Welt on the cartels' use of submarines. Several reports and articles from the New York Times, Wall Street Journal, and the Atlanta Journal and Constitution were read, and some of their content was blended into the storyline.

I'm a former English teacher and have never worked as a reporter for any newspaper. Nor have I ever interviewed any man in a prison.

Made in the USA
Charleston, SC
30 September 2015